A Watch in the Night

BOOK I
Give Your Angels Charge

ROSEANNA LEE

A Watch in the Night

This book is a work of fiction. Names of characters, places and incidents are products of both the author's imagination and based on certain historical facts. Any resemblance to actual persons, living or dead, business establishments, events or locales are entirely coincidental.

Copyright 2019
ISBN: 978-1-945190-79-7

FV-2
Cover Design and Layout: Isaac Rivera
www.isaacsifontes.com

This book, or parts thereof, may not be reproduced without permission. The scanning, uploading and distribution of the book via the Internet or via any other means, including storage in any form of informational or retrieval system without the express written consent of the author, except for newspaper, magazine or other reviewer who wish to quote brief passages in connection with a review, is illegal and punishable by law. Your support of the author's rights is encouraged and appreciated.

First Edition: December, 2019

www.IntellectPublishing.com

Roseanna Lee

For Alex, Dancy and Adelynn
who allow me to see the world through the eyes of a child

A Watch in the Night

Roseanna Lee

Arise, cry out in the night, as the watches of the night begin; pour out your heart like water in the presence of the Lord.
Lamentations 2:19

A Watch in the Night

PROLOGUE

And like a mighty oak, they grew strong among the trees of the forest!

It was snowing in Florida on the night that Millie and Mango were born. A thick sheet of white tumbled from the sky and settled, drop upon fluffy drop, until it formed a glimmering white blanket inches deep on the ground. Doc Adams took that as a good sign. Doc had spent over fifty years bringing people into this world and then seeing them out, and he knew that God gave signs to those willing to see. Snow was a good sign; it meant these babies would be special.

Millie and Mango were born in Tate's Hell, a desolate swampland, lying on the outskirts of Trinity, a small coastal town in the Florida Panhandle. A few—a very few—of the town's more fortunate inhabitants worked for the city or the state where the hours were regular and the paychecks certain.

But the majority of Trinity's residents depended upon the plentitude of the gulf waters and the abundance of the surrounding forests for their survival. These people earned a living by fishing, shrimping, harvesting oysters or cutting timber.

For them, the hours were long, the physical labor demanding and the pay uncertain. Because most people worked outside, the weather was always a favorite topic of conversation.

Lily Whatley, the mother of Millie and Mango, was the only child of Ephram and Bessie Whatley. The Whatley clan had lived for generations in Tate's Hell, Trinity's version of the wrong side of the tracks.

Little was known about the Whatley family, other than the fact that years back Ephram had distinguished himself in Trinity by surviving an encounter with a moving freight train. He had passed out drunk on the tracks early one Saturday morning, as the story was told.

Fortunately for Ephram, he was lying vertical on the tracks, and as the train hurled along, only inches above his body, Ephram remained inert. Had it not been for the account of the train's engineer, the episode may well have gone unnoted.

"I weren't the least bit surprised that it was Ephram Whatley and that he's alive," Sheriff Tate said, later, as he recounted the incident to some of the townspeople in Harry's Tavern, the local watering hole. "Them Whatleys always could drink, and Ephram, he ain't no different. I weren't the least bit surprised when the engineer called in a body on the tracks, and I went on over there to find Ephram Whatley passed out drunk. Hell, he'd still be sleepin' if I hadn't made 'im get on up and go home."

Shortly after surviving the incident with the freight train, Ephram was back in the local news. He was working at the timber mill when he caught his leg in a saw. Gangrene set in and Doc Adams had to amputate. Ephram suffered from diabetes, a condition greatly exacerbated by his fondness for the bottle. If not for the diabetes, the leg might have healed, or so Doc Adams had said.

Although the two events—the encounter with the freight train and the loss of the leg—were unrelated, the people in Trinity attributed divine intervention to the loss of the leg.

Trinity, for the most part, consisted of a God-fearing people, and the consensus of the town was that God had given Ephram a second chance by sparing him from a certain and horrible death on the train tracks. When Ephram failed to heed God's warning, the theory was that God smote him down by the loss of the leg.

But Ephram did not feel at all smote by the wrath of God. Quite to the contrary, Ephram regarded the loss of his leg as more of a blessing than a burden. The Whatley clan had always been known as a family with an outright disdain for hard work.

The missing limb allowed Ephram to qualify for a permanent disability check. Life didn't get any better than that for a Whatley. With his newfound wealth and freedom, Ephram devoted himself full-time to his favorite pastime, drinking.

Bessie shared her husband's fondness for the bottle. So, while the First Baptists clucked their tongues and warned their children of God's vengeance whenever Ephram hobbled by, Ephram and Bessie rejoiced in their good fortune.

Lily arrived late in Ephram and Bessie's marriage, a change-of-life baby. But she was just seventeen when she gave birth to her own children. While the birth of twins, particularly a boy and a girl, may have sparked a tad of interest, at least among the women, on an ordinary day in Trinity, it was anything but an ordinary day when Lily went into labor.

Because snow in the Florida Panhandle is so rare, most people in Trinity could expect to see snow maybe once, but certainly no more than twice, in a lifetime. Most of the town's inhabitants were born, raised and then died without ever traveling more than fifty miles from home.

Doc Adams was one of the oldest citizens in Trinity, and he could recall seeing snow only twice, the last time maybe fifteen or twenty years back when the snow had fallen in brief flurries without sticking to the ground.

On the day Millie and Mango arrived, all that anybody in Trinity could think of or talk about was the weather. The weather forecast on the local radio station predicted snow.

Naomi Ivey looked out of the window from her small cabin in Tate's Hell and marveled at the sight of snow on the giant oak tree in her front yard. Snow on moss—that was different.

Something seemed in the air; something more than snow.

A Watch in the Night

Give Your Angels Charge

First Watch

A Watch in the Night

CHAPTER ONE

Doc Adams was comfortably settled at home for the night when Bessie Whatley called. Dressed in his old flannel robe and slippers, he had eaten his supper and then planted himself in his recliner by the fire. The weather was bitter cold out, and the wind was blowing hard enough to rattle his windows. Closing his eyes, he relaxed and listened contentedly to the familiar sound of his wife puttering around in their kitchen as she cleaned the supper dishes.

"Damnation," Doc snapped, as he heard the ring, knowing that a call at this hour could only mean trouble. The closest hospital to Trinity was over fifty miles away. In an emergency, Doc was Trinity's only medical resource. People called him at all hours with emergencies, some of them real, some of them imagined.

If Doc's office was closed and he deemed the call to be a bona fide emergency, and not one that could be handled by telephone, he saw patients at his home. And when patients couldn't come to Doc, he went to them.

Doc grumbled, complained and threatened to retire daily, but he had accepted the demands of his profession long ago, and despite his daily tirades, he loved his work. Everyone in Trinity knew as long as Doc was able to work, he wouldn't retire.

"Mildred, get the phone," Doc hollered to his wife. Mildred was listening to the Reverend Samuel Spears' Inspirational Hour on the radio as she cleaned. When the call came from Bessie Whatley, she was humming along with the gospel music, oblivious to the ringing of the phone or Doc's shouting.

"Damnation," Doc mumbled again, using a word frowned upon by his wife. Mildred, a devout member of the First Baptist Church of Trinity, stood firmly against sin of any kind. She found cursing to be particularly offensive.

"Damnation," Doc bellowed, as he hoisted his two-hundred-and-fifty-pound frame up from the comfort of his recliner and lurched towards the only telephone in the house. It was mounted on the wall in the hallway leading to the kitchen.

"Hello," he barked into the receiver.

"Is that you, Doc?" Doc detected a slight slur in the woman's voice. Doc was no stranger to drunks.

"That's who you called now ain't it?" Doc retorted. When there was a long pause on the line, Doc immediately regretted that he had been so abrupt with the caller. Drunks needed doctoring, too.

"You got Doc Adams," he said, more gently this time. "What can I do for you?"

"This here's Bessie Whatley from up in Tate's Hell."

"What's your trouble, Bessie?"

"My girl Lily is 'bout to have her baby."

"Lily is having a baby! I didn't even know that she was pregnant. She hasn't been in to see me."

"I been meanin' to bring her in, but Ephram, he don't drive much no more."

"Never mind about that. How far apart are her pains?"

"I don't rightly know, Doc. All I know is that the pain is comin' on her strong. She needs help."

"Alright, Bessie, calm down. I'll be there as quickly as I can."

"You gotta hurry. Please, Doc."

"I will. But it's blowing hard out, and the radio is calling for snow."

Doc hung up the phone and shouted to his wife. "Damnation, Mildred. Turn down that confounded radio."

Mildred shot him a warning look before lowering the volume as Doc entered into the kitchen.

"That was Bessie Whatley on the phone. I need to go out to her place in Tate's Hell. Her daughter's baby has done gone and picked the worst night of the year to come into this world."

"I didn't even hear the phone ring," Mildred answered. Doc briefly considered remarking upon the volume of the radio, but he changed his mind. It wasn't his wife's fault that he had to go out in this bad weather.

Doc left the kitchen, and when he returned, he had changed his clothes and filled his medical bag. Mildred stood leaning over the sink screwing the lid on a thermos of hot coffee.

"You be careful tonight," Mildred said, handing him the thermos. "We don't need any trouble, especially not right here at Christmas."

"I'll be fine," he replied, giving her a peck on the forehead.

Before the door closed behind him, Mildred was back at her chores. Doc heard the last strands of the Reverend Samuel Spears leading the First Baptist Choir in singing a spirited rendition of *God Rest Ye Merry Gentlemen*. He stepped off of the porch and set out for his old Ford station wagon.

Doc swung the station wagon onto the road as the first flurries began to fall. They swirled in the beams of the headlights. Doc gripped the steering wheel and drove carefully through the outskirts of Trinity.

He noticed that children were still outside. Snow was such an unusual event that some parents had stretched the bedtime rules and allowed their children to stay outdoors and play. The children waved to Doc as he passed by them. Everybody in Trinity knew and loved Doc Adams.

Christmas lights and a tinsel "Merry Christmas" banner swayed in the breeze over Main Street. Doc recalled the time several years back when the former mayor, Buck Sellers, ordered new Christmas decorations.

When the shipment arrived, it included a tinsel banner with a "Merry Xmas" greeting. City workers strung the new banner and blinking lights on the Friday after Thanksgiving, the annual day designated for decorating the town. The banner had not been up for more than an hour when the uproar occurred—of all the gall the Baptists said—the mayor had taken the "Christ" out of Christmas.

Mayor Sellers had immediately gone on the defensive; he blamed the mail order company. *They* had sent the wrong banner; it wasn't his mistake, he explained. There simply had not been enough time for him to re-order and meet the decorating deadline. It was for just one season.

The new banner was down and the old banner was up before noon. But Trinity's citizens were not so easily appeased. He had put the banner up in the first place, and that was "pert near blasphemy" or so the First Baptists said. Mayor Sellers was ousted the next election.

As Doc drove along Main Street, he could see the First Baptist Church of Trinity looming ahead. It was a large, red-brick monstrosity with four white columns on the front and a rolling green lawn, now turned brown by winter. It filled almost one whole city block.

This church was one of only two churches in Trinity. The other church was the Shady Grove Baptist Church housed in a small wooden building on the edge of town. The church on Main Street was for the whites and the one on the outskirts of town was for the blacks.

In Trinity you were either a Baptist or a heathen. There was no middle ground. This was a point on which both the whites and the blacks agreed, although they chose to live out that belief in separate establishments.

Each year the First Baptist members assembled a nativity scene on the church's front lawn. Doc could see the glow of this nativity scene ahead. An outsider to Trinity might remark that the nativity scene itself was a rather pitiful sight.

It displayed years of wear and tear. The donkey's ears were missing, the work of young pranksters a number of years back. A wise man had been lost in a church fire. Faded paint peeled off of the entire holy ensemble. But the First Baptist flock remained undaunted; the nativity scene proudly adorned their front lawn, assembled the first Sunday after Thanksgiving by the women's auxiliary, year after year.

Doc turned onto County Road 27, and the lights became sparse, except for an occasional glow from far off of the road. The snow changed from an occasional flurry to a steady stream of white. Doc had to strain even harder to stay on the road.

Through the cloud of white, he saw a light set back off to the left of the highway, the Bass homestead. This landmark helped Doc to get his bearings. He knew the turn-off to the Whatley home could not be far ahead.

Doc glanced away from the road and up at the lights of the Bass home. He remembered the night that the homestead had gone up in flames with the Bass baby trapped inside.

Dewey Bass, the baby's father, returned from his child's funeral and went to bed. He never got back up. One week later he died.

When recounting the story, people attributed Dewey's death to a broken heart. Doc had failed to find any medical evidence to the contrary. "Smoke got the baby and grief got Dewey," folks said.

Now Mrs. Bass lived alone in the trailer home bought with the insurance money from the fire. It was her lights that Doc could see. Five years had passed since the fire, but Mrs. Bass still kept Dewey's boots by the door. People in Trinity said that it might have been better if all of the Bass family had died that night. It simply hadn't been God's will.

Doc passed into the first stretch of land known as Tate's Hell. It was a desolate mixture of swampland and pinewood flats. Only the staunchest of Trinity's citizens even considered homesteading this far out. There were no lights to guide the way, and Doc crept slowly along until he spotted the Whatley Road, a two-rut dirt lane.

The road resembled a washboard, and Doc's Ford rattled and shook as he inched along. This road was an eerie sight on any night, but even more so tonight with the snow obstructing Doc's view.

Ancient oak trees, with massive limbs shrouded in moss, lined both sides of the road. The moss hung low, swaying ominously in the beams of Doc's headlights. When a branch scratched against the side of Doc's car, he jumped and then instinctively locked the car's doors.

He hunched lower over the steering wheel, his face screwed up into a tight ball, as he struggled to see the road. The fork in the road up ahead was a welcome sight for Doc. The right prong of the fork led to the Whatley homestead, the left to the Ivey's small cabin. Doc veered the Ford to the right.

The Whatleys and the Iveys were the only residents of this part of Tate's Hell. Doc knew both families well. The Whatleys—Ephram and Bessie—were two of Tate's Hell's worst drunks, which said a lot, because Tate's Hell was infamous for more than its share of hard-core drunks.

The Iveys—Washington and Naomi—on the other hand, were a hard-working black couple. Doc recalled sadly that Washington had died last spring leaving his widow and a grown daughter living alone.

In Trinity whites and blacks didn't often mingle. Change was slow in coming to this isolated little fishing village. As Trinity's only doctor, Doc tended to the needs of the people. He didn't dwell on color. Doc reckoned people were people, some were good and some were bad, and by Doc's way of thinking, that was a matter of the heart and not the color of the skin.

Doc pulled into a clearing and came to a stop near the Whatley's front door. The light from the car's headlights showed beer cans, threadbare tires and a lawn chair covered with rust and missing most of its webbing, all scattered in various places around the yard.

Three dogs with ribs protruding through mangy fur ran out to meet him. Barking and growling, they formed a semi-circle around the car door.

"Go on now, get out of here," Doc shouted, pushing at the dogs with his foot as he struggled to get out of the car. The dogs backed away, baying suspiciously before slinking into a hole under the porch.

The Whatley's front porch was constructed of wooden planks, and it sagged in the middle. Doc thought it looked dangerously close to collapsing, and mindful of his weight, he approached the structure with some trepidation.

The steps were made from cement blocks stacked one on top of the other. A bare light bulb, with a string hanging down to pull it off and on, dimly lit the porch.

Doc tested one of the wooden posts, which supported the porch's rusty tin roof, and finding it sufficiently intact, he used it to steady himself as he climbed the wobbly cement steps.

A screen door, with most of the screen pushed out, hung precariously attached to two of the door's four hinges. Doc opened it and knocked at the wooden door just beyond.

Nobody answered so he shouted, "Bessie, it's Doc Adams." When he still did not receive any response, Doc turned the doorknob. The door swung open, and he stuck his head inside.

A blast of heat and kerosene fumes hit Doc in the face, causing him to pull back his head and suck in his breath. "I'm too old to keep doing this," he grumbled aloud, thinking about his son, Walter Jr., whom he had sent to medical school at Duke

University. Doc and his wife had hoped their son would return to Trinity and take up his practice, but much to their disappointment, he had not.

While at Duke, Walter Jr. met and later wed Leona Hartsfield. Leona's father was a urologist with a thriving practice in an upscale section of Raleigh. His practice had bought the family a fine home in the suburbs and a coveted membership to one of Raleigh's exclusive country clubs.

Leona wore the pants in Walter Jr.'s family, and her plans did not include being married to a country doctor. When Walter Jr. completed his medical training, he joined his father-in-law's practice, and Leona joined the Junior League. Doc and his wife didn't hold out much hope for Walter Jr.'s return to Trinity.

Doc shook thoughts of his son out of his head. He took a long drag of fresh air and stepped inside the door. The inside of the Whatley home fared no better than the outside.

The smell of kerosene hung thick in the air, and the walls were yellowed and covered with its filmy residue. The front room, a living room of sorts, housed an orange, crushed-velvet sofa and a matching chair, both soiled and worn shiny and threadbare in spots.

A single spring, partially concealed by a pillow with the plea to *Bless This House,* protruded through the seat of the chair. The sofa and chair sat strategically perched close to a kerosene heater.

Doc stared at the heater. It was a curious conglomeration of pipes and metal, and he was surprised that it had the ability to warm the room as it did. The room was so hot that a line of sweat popped out on Doc's forehead.

The heater consisted of a metal boiler with a thick copper pipe protruding out of its back side. This pipe joined to a metal joist that connected to a pipe leading down and out of the wooden floor to what Doc guessed was a storage tank outside.

A second pipe, wider than the other pipe and made out of thin aluminum, ran out of the top of the heater and up through the roof. Doc surmised that this pipe was to vent the fumes, although based upon the odor in the room, this system was not working up to par.

A cast iron pot, half-filled with water, sat on the top of the heater next to the vent pipe. Even with this make-shift humidifier the air was dry, and it burned Doc's nostrils.

A single cord attached to a bare bulb dropped down from the ceiling in the center of the room, the same set-up as the light on the porch. This bare bulb shed a pale circle of light around the room.

Doc felt a draft and noticed a brick fireplace to his left behind the sofa. The bed of the fireplace was sealed off by several sheets of plywood nailed together and then propped over the hearth, held in place by several cement blocks pushed up against the wood. The plywood warped out at the sides, and the cold air from the outside ran down the chimney and escaped into the room.

Doc called out Bessie's name again, but still he received no answer. The house was silent, and this made Doc uneasy. He walked cautiously towards the back of the house, past the red-hot heater, calling Bessie's name as he went. To his right was an open door, and Doc stopped to look into a small bedroom.

The room was furnished with a chest of drawers and a rusty wrought iron bed. The chest of drawers sat in one corner, its drawers pulled open with clothes spilling out onto the floor. The bed filled the remainder of the room.

A lamp on the chest of drawers cast enough light for Doc to make out a person lying crosswise on the bed. Doc stepped inside and looked more closely at the figure on the bed. He smelled whiskey and was not surprised to discover that it was Ephram Whatley lying passed out drunk with his clothes still on.

A Watch in the Night

Doc left Ephram as he had found him and continued on into the kitchen. It was empty. Attached to the kitchen was a tar paper addition, which comprised the back of the house. Doc followed the hallway, which connected this area to the remainder of the house.

He passed a tiny room that appeared to be a crude attempt to add an indoor bathroom to the shack, and then he stopped at the entrance to a small bedroom, not much bigger than a closet. Doc guessed this room had been added when Lily was born.

The kerosene heater was the only source of heat for the entire house, and whatever small amount of heat that managed to penetrate this far back was lost to the cracks and crevices in the tar paper. Doc stood in the doorway to the small bedroom, and a shiver ran up his spine, caused partially by the lack of heat but mostly by what he saw.

He shook his head and pulled his coat up tighter around his bulky frame. Doc was no stranger to death, but that didn't make what he saw any easier. Lily Whatley lay on a single, twin bed covered with gray, dingy sheets; sheets now soaked in blood. Her eyes stared vacantly upwards.

Doc pushed on into the room, and leaning over the body, he tenderly closed Lily's eyes and pushed the hair back from her forehead. He looked around for something to cover her body, settling on a blanket tacked across the window to guard against the cold.

One firm tug and the blanket dropped into his arms. Doc snapped the blanket open letting it float down to drape Lily's body. Feeling tired and saddened, he lowered himself onto the corner of the bed and slowly surveyed the room.

A crate turned on its side served as a make-shift night table at the head of the bed. A green lamp molded into the shape of Bambi, cracked and chipped with no shade, sat perched on the top of the crate. Several magazines were neatly stacked into a pile on the crate next to the lamp.

Doc picked up one of the magazines and absent-mindedly thumbed through its pages. Teenage girls with flowing blonde curls and glossy red lips smiled up at him from the pages of *Seventeen*. He closed the magazine and wearily gazed down at Lily.

The sound of a slamming door caused him to look up, where he saw Bessie Whatley emerge from the hallway and clutch at the doorframe for support as she stared down at Doc and her dead daughter.

"I did the best I could, Doc," Bessie said, sighing, after a few seconds of silence passed between them. Her voice was flat and dejected.

"I'm sure you did," Doc replied, placing both hands on the edge of the bed to push himself up onto his feet.

"She just weren't able to hang on." Doc stood next to the bed and let Bessie talk. "I'd been meanin' to bring her on in to see you. But Ephram, he don't get 'round much no more, and I never learnt to drive. Ephram's cousin, Fred, usually takes us where we gotta go, but Fred never could find the time to carry Lily on into your office."

Bessie paused, pressing her hand against her forehead as if she were trying to force memories back inside. "I didn't figger on it bein' so close to her time. She started gettin' pains a little after dark. That's when I called you."

Bessie swayed in the doorway, and Doc took the two steps needed to cross the room. Firmly grasping Bessie by the arm, he helped her over to the edge of the bed.

"Sit, Bessie," he said, gently. It really didn't matter how it had happened, Doc thought. Lily Whatley was dead.

"Where's the baby?" Doc asked.

"Babies, Doc. Lily had two babies. I believe she coulda hung on if there had been just one baby. But by the time that second baby come along, the fight was just drained outta her. She died."

A Watch in the Night

It wasn't the fight that drained out of her, it was her blood, Doc wanted to say. Lily had hemorrhaged to death. But what was the point of saying that, Doc thought. What was done was done.

Instead, he asked, "What did you do with the babies, Bessie?"

"I took 'em next door. I wrapped 'em up in a blanket and took 'em over to the Ivey place. Then I come back here to sit with Lily 'til you got here. I ain't in no shape to tend two babies."

Doc perked up at Bessie's last comment. "Are the babies alive?" he asked incredulously.

"When I left 'em at the Ivey house, they was." Bessie answered. "They's mighty weak and scrawny, but they's still breathin'."

"How do I get to the Ivey house from here?" Doc asked, hurriedly stooping to retrieve his medical bag that he had placed on the floor beside Lily's bed.

"Head on out the back door and go down the path a short piece. You'll run smack dab into it."

"Wait here," Doc instructed Bessie. "I'll go check on the babies."

The path to the Ivey house was a short one. Snow continued to fall, and in the dark, even with the flashlight that Doc had retrieved from his bag, it was slow going. Doc pulled his coat up tightly around him, fighting off the cold. Naomi Ivey opened her door at the first rap of Doc's knuckles.

"Doc, thank Jesus that you're here," Naomi blurted out.

"I've come to check on the babies," Doc said, stomping the snow off of his boots.

"Come on in. They're over on the couch in that bundle next to Karen. We was tryin' to keep 'em warm by the fire."

Naomi's daughter, Karen, smiled up at Doc. "We're sure glad to see you," she said.

Doc looked across the room at a large fireplace, which filled most of the wall opposite the door. Behind a metal screen placed in front of the hearth he saw a roaring fire, its flames licking high up the sides of the chimney.

A metal bin, sitting on one side of the hearth, was stacked neatly full of logs. A poker and small shovel sat poised in a holder next to the bin. The fire flooded the room with heat and light, and Doc was happy to step inside out of the cold.

Naomi trailed behind Doc as he crossed the room to the babies. Karen rose from the sofa to give Doc her seat.

"Let's have a look," he said. Naomi had cleaned the babies and wrapped them together in a single cotton blanket. Doc unfolded the corners of the blanket and looked down at the infants.

The girl, who was much smaller than the boy, was thin and long. She had pale, translucent skin with a tuft of blonde fuzz on her head. The boy was shorter, and more filled out, with a skin tone much darker than that of his sister. He had a crown of curly black hair.

Doc carefully examined the babies. He listened to their hearts and lungs, counted their fingers and toes, and stretched their arms and legs.

Naomi and Karen stood hovering anxiously over him, watching his every move. When he had finished, Doc sat back, and looking up at Naomi and Karen, he pronounced the babies, as far as he could tell, to be healthy.

"Twins?" Doc said, with a curious smile. "I haven't seen a set of girl and boy twins for years around here. If this don't beat all," he added, shaking his head. Naomi and Karen nodded their agreement with Doc. *This did beat all!*

Doc folded the blanket back around the babies and reluctantly stood up. He was tired, and he would have liked to rest for a short while in the comfort of the Ivey's living room. But there was still work to be done.

A Watch in the Night

Backing up to the fire, he extended his hands behind him to catch the warmth of the flames. His eyes traveled about the room. The Ivey home was neat and clean. Its wooden floor was swept and scrubbed spotless, with hand-braided rugs scattered about.

The sofa, where he had just been sitting, ran lengthwise the room and was positioned in front of the fireplace. A rocking chair sat on one end of the sofa angled in to face the fire.

A wooden table separated the sofa and the rocker. The opposite end of the sofa was anchored by a big wooden easy chair with hand-stitched cushions tied to its back and seat. A matching ottoman sat in front of the easy chair with needlework piled carefully in its center.

Doc recognized the voice of the Reverend Samuel Spears from the Inspirational Hour, and his eyes followed the sound to a small table in the corner of the room. A lamp, the light from its bulb softened by a red-fringed shade, sat in the middle of the table. Under the lamp a radio played softly. Next to the radio was a large, black *Bible* with a red, satin marker jutting out from between its pages.

As he turned to warm his frontside, Doc stared into the peacefulness of the fire and pondered the situation. After a few moments, he turned back to face Naomi and Karen, who stood rooted to their spots next to the couch waiting for Doc to tell them what to do.

"Could ya'll help out a little longer?" Doc inquired. "Bessie is not in any shape to look after these babies, not after losing Lily, and I don't want to take them with me. Not in my old Ford on a night when only God knows what this weather is gonna do."

Naomi gasped. "Lily's gone?"

"Oh, I'm so sorry," Doc said, seeing the pain flush across Naomi's face. "I thought you knew."

Naomi sank down onto the sofa next to the whimpering babies. "Bessie didn't tell us that Lily had passed on," she said.

Karen cast a worried look over at her mother, recalling the ordeal of her own brother's death. She sat down next to her mother and took her hand.

"We can watch over these babies a spell longer," Naomi said looking up at Doc, the rim of her eyes barely containing a sudden rush of tears.

"Are you certain?" Doc asked.

"Of course, I'm certain," Naomi said, shaking off the shock of Lily's death. "Bessie is a neighbor in need; we can help."

"In that case, I've got a packet of dried milk and a bottle in my bag," Doc said. "I always carry milk with me when I'm called out to deliver a baby. Sometimes a new mother can't nurse," he added. "Naomi, you haven't forgotten how to feed a baby, have you?"

"I don't reckon tendin' to a baby is somethin' a mother ever forgets, Doc," she answered.

"Then I'll get on back and look after them folks next door. I'll call Sheriff Tate and have him send some help out," Doc said. "It shouldn't take long. He told me earlier that all of the deputies would be working tonight—due to the bad weather, and all.

"Sheriff Tate can see to it that the babies get taken to the hospital in Cartersville. You can hang on for an hour or so, can't you Naomi?"

"We can manage," Naomi assured Doc. "You go on and see 'bout Bessie."

"Thank you," Doc said. He shuffled through his medical bag and pulled out a small container of dried milk and two small bottles.

"Luck's with us," he said. "I've got not one, but two bottles. This dried milk should do you until I can get some help out here. But the babies need to be fed right away."

"I'll see to it," Naomi replied.

Naomi walked Doc to the door and watched him as he trudged back up the path. She noticed that his shoulders stooped and his steps were slow. He's feeling the pangs of old age, same as me, Naomi thought, before turning her attention back to Karen and the babies.

CHAPTER TWO

Karen closed the door behind Doc and gave her mother a bewildered look.

"Karen, don't look so scared; it'll be just fine," Naomi said. "Didn't I do a good job with you and your brother?"

"But, Mama, that was a long time ago."

"That don't matter none," Naomi answered. "Now we need to feed these babies. I'll make the bottles. You sit here in the rocker with 'em." The babies were beginning to fret.

Karen sat down in the rocker, and Naomi placed the whimpering bundle in her lap. "Rock 'em a little. I won't take long."

As Naomi went about the business of preparing the bottles in the kitchen, she heard the whimpering from the living room escalate into a full-scale wail. She smiled to herself as she remembered how afraid and uncertain she had been on her first night with Nathan, her firstborn.

Naomi wrapped the bottles in a clean dishcloth and puttered back into the living room. At her age, getting in too much of a hurry wasn't an option. She smiled again, when she saw Karen frantically rocking back and forth, the bundle now clutched to her chest.

"It's alright, Karen. They just hungry; that's all. The only way they got to tell you that is for them to howl."

"Well, it's very unsettling," Karen said, her voice full of desperation.

"It's a good thing that Doc come prepared," Naomi replied calmly, as she placed the bottles on the end table next to the couch. "We gonna need both these bottles, and we gonna need another blanket. I'll be right back."

"Mama, really," Karen said, casting an anxious look up at her mother before Naomi turned and left the room again.

Naomi returned carrying a second cotton blanket. "Give me one baby," she said, bending down and plucking the red-faced, screaming boy from Karen's lap.

"There, there, little fella, it's gonna be alright," Naomi crooned, as she lowered herself down on the couch and arranged the thrashing bundle into the crook of her arm. She picked up one of the bottles with her free hand and splashed a few drops of milk from it onto her wrist. Satisfied that the milk was warm, but not too hot, she passed the bottle to Karen.

"Put the nipple in the baby's mouth," Naomi said. "She knows to suck."

Karen did as she was told, and a welcome hush fell over the room. It was several moments before Karen broke the silence.

"Mama, I can't believe this is happenin' to us," she said. "It weren't more than an hour ago that we's sittin' here mindin' our own business, and now here we sit both of us feedin' a baby. And a white baby at that."

Naomi chuckled at her daughter's observation. "There's one thing that's for certain in this old world," Naomi mused, pausing to reposition the baby in her arms, "life is full of surprises. Old age teaches you that! You never know what God's got in store for you. Now, place the baby on your shoulder and softly pat her back 'til you hear a burp. Otherwise, we sure nuff gonna hear some hollerin'."

After the babies were fed, Karen and Naomi laid them on the sofa in front of the fire, tucking the blankets in around them.

"What now?" Karen asked.

"We wait," Naomi answered, picking up her needlework from the ottoman where she had laid it when Bessie came knocking at the door. "They oughta sleep for a while now that they're fed."

Naomi's knitting needles started to clack as she went back to working on a sweater. The fire occasionally gave a loud pop, and the rocker creaked as Karen rocked back and forth listening to the music which drifted over from the radio. Now that the babies were quiet, Karen had managed to calm herself somewhat.

Naomi worked along in silence until she noticed that she no longer heard the rocker. Glancing up, she saw Karen slumped down in the rocking chair, her head cocked to one side and propped against the back of the chair. Naomi looked down at the babies beside her. All were sleeping.

She wrapped the string of yarn around her knitting needles, and leaning forward, she placed the needles and the half-finished sweater next to the ball of yarn, which sat nestled in a basket on the ottoman.

Rubbing the stiffness out of her fingers, Naomi rose from the sofa. As she stood stretching her back, the Reverend Spears concluded his Inspirational Hour with a short but fervent prayer. Looking up at the clock, Naomi wondered why help had not arrived. It had been a couple of hours since Doc had left.

"That 'bout wraps it up folks," the radio announcer droned in a nasal twang from the corner of the room. "Join us tomorrow morning at 6:00 a.m. sharp for the weather report, followed by Juney Davis with *The Market Basket*. Until then, sleep tight and don't let the bedbugs bite."

The radio started to emit static, and Naomi limped across the room, her joints stiff from sitting, to turn it off. She turned the dial and then paused, pulling aside the curtains to look out of the window.

The snow had stopped. Dropping the curtain, she crossed the room to the hall closet, where she retrieved her flashlight and her coat. She pulled on her coat before slipping quietly out of the front door.

A white blanket covered the ground under a sky brilliant with stars. Naomi paused briefly and stared out across the clearing that she and her husband had claimed from the surrounding woods.

Poking the flashlight under her arm, Naomi used both of her hands to grasp the porch rail as she maneuvered herself carefully down the steps. There could be ice; she didn't want to risk a fall.

As she padded across her front yard, the crisp night air caught in her throat before coming out in small white puffs that hung briefly in the air in front of her before dissipating into the night.

Stopping, she stooped down and scooped up a handful of snow. It shimmered in the palm of her hand. She touched her tongue to its coldness before she let it sift through her fingers. She watched as it floated softly back to the ground. It had been over twenty years since she had seen snow.

Naomi would have liked to linger and savor the tranquility that enveloped the night like mist over water. But she was on a mission, so she pressed on until she stood in front of the door of a small wooden shed.

The shed sat on the edge of her yard next to the woods. This had been her husband's workshop, and she had not been out to it since the day that she found him inside, slumped over his workbench, dead from a heart attack.

Tears welled up in her eyes, and she swiped the back of her hand across her face to clear her vision. Naomi was a strong woman; but losing Washington had hit her hard. The prospect of entering his workshop flooded her with memories.

Washington and Naomi married on her twenty-first birthday, and they had been husband and wife for forty-four years when he died.

In all of those years, Naomi had spent only one night away from him. The year their son, Nathan, had been killed in Vietnam, Washington had gone to Cartersville to meet the hearse carrying Nathan's body back home.

When the hearse arrived in the middle of the night, Washington was there to claim his boy. He drove back to Trinity behind the hearse. That trip was the only time that Washington ever left the county.

Now both Naomi's son and her husband were gone, and her tears rolled unimpeded across the creases on her cheeks. There ain't no tellin' the road that God's laid out for you, Naomi thought, as she watched her falling tears make tiny dots in the snow. I guess that others done suffered through troubles far worse than mine. But old age and loneliness sure walk hand in hand, and the end of life is filled with lots of sorrow.

Naomi plucked a hankie from the pocket of her skirt and used it to dab at her eyes and then blow her nose. She reared up her head like a frisky colt and mentally chided herself. There was precious little time to waste on memories.

Two newborns were asleep in her house with no mama to see them through the world. God's give me the job of startin' 'em on that journey, Naomi thought, and my mind needs to be on what lays up ahead, not behind.

Naomi pushed back her shoulders and taking a deep, cleansing breath, she opened the door to her husband's shed.

The shop was exactly as Washington had left it. His tools hung in a precise formation along the wall according to size; the pieces of wood were sorted—pine, oak, cedar, and cypress—all stacked carefully into cords in a corner; the sawdust was swept up neatly into a pile.

Naomi picked up a block of wood from the workbench. It felt smooth as she rubbed her calloused fingers slowly over the grain. She lifted the wood up to her nose and inhaled the sweet fragrance of cedar.

A Watch in the Night

Washington always loved his wood, Naomi thought, fondly. "My mammy said that I cut my teeth on her broom handle," she had heard him say on countless occasions. "And as soon as I was old enough to stop gnawin' on wood, I went to whittlin', carvin' and choppin' on it. If idle hands is the devil's workshop, like the preacher man likes to say, then I 'spect this here wood has done saved my mortal soul."

Washington would always add this last line, with a devilish grin creeping across his face, before he threw back his head to laugh. When Washington announced to Naomi on the eve of their wedding day that he had taken a job as a logger with the Hillman Lumber Company, she wasn't surprised. It seemed like the natural thing for him to do.

After they were married, each morning he left home an hour before dawn so he could be in the woods by sunrise. And that's where he stayed until sun-down.

As the years passed and his strength diminished, Washington went from sawing the trees to marking the ones to be cut by the younger men. On his sixty-fifth birthday, he retired from the Hillman Lumber Company with a small pension.

When they were newly-weds, Naomi and Washington lived in a boarding house in the "colored quarters" of Trinity, a conglomeration of dilapidated shacks and washed-out, dirt roads on the edge of town down in the river bottom. From the window of their small, second-story room, she had waved good-bye to him each morning.

"I ain't no city man, and the quarters ain't no place to go raisin' up a family," he would say to her as they laid side-by-side at night in a narrow, single bed, listening to the noise of too many people crowded into too few rooms.

Early on in their marriage, Washington proved to Naomi that he was a man of his word. On their first anniversary, he surprised her with the deed to a five-acre tract of land in Tate's

Hell. Washington had bought the land from the Hillman Lumber Company.

Roy Hillman, the owner of the Hillman Lumber Company, charged Washington twice what the land was worth, but Washington didn't mind because Mr. Hillman agreed to let him pay for the land by holding the money back from his check each week. The First National Bank of Trinity wasn't in the business of loaning money to blacks back then; so, Washington was content to pay the extra money in exchange for the credit.

Shortly after buying the land, Washington struck a deal with Nate Marshall, a white man who operated a sawmill out by the county line. Washington agreed to work for Mr. Marshall at his sawmill on Sundays in exchange for the lumber Washington needed to build a house.

When Naomi heard about this arrangement, she immediately objected to it. This was one of the few times in her marriage that she saw fit to cross her husband.

"Now, I know that *The Good Book* says that a wife is 'pose to follow her husband's lead, but I don't believe that holds true, if he's done set them on the path to hell," she had huffed defiantly.

"A man ain't 'pose to work on the Lord's day. That's one of the Lord's commandments. You know that, the same as me, Washington Ivey," she declared with finality, stomping her foot and crossing her arms.

"Now, woman, you listen to me," he shot back at her, rearing his six-foot, three-inch frame up tall and proud until he looked like one of those mighty oaks that he loved so much out on their five-acre tract.

"I ain't got but one day off from the Lumber Company, and I don't reckon that the Lord is gonna fault a man who just aims to build his family a home. It ain't work, Naomi—I do it for love, not money."

A Watch in the Night

Eventually, they reached a compromise. Naomi agreed that Washington could work on Sundays if he would stop long enough to attend services at the Shady Grove Baptist Church.

They spent another year at the boarding house while Washington worked out the lumber, and Naomi prayed ceaselessly that God would forgive Washington this transgression.

On their second anniversary, Washington escorted Naomi out to their land and proudly pointed to the lumber that he had earned by working at the sawmill.

He had hauled the lumber out to the land and stacked it under a majestic oak, the exact spot where he planned to build their home. Washington quit the mill the next Sunday, and he started to use his Sundays to construct their home. They moved in when their little cabin consisted of only one room.

After they moved in, Washington continued to build onto the house until it had a living room, a kitchen, two bedrooms and an indoor bathroom.

Together, he and Naomi etched a yard out of the forest, cutting some of the smaller trees and planting the cleared ground with grass and flowers and shrubs.

They fenced and plowed a plot for a garden, which they planted and tended faithfully every spring and fall. The only thing missing from their marriage was children. Year after year, Naomi failed to conceive.

"Do you think we was too willful building our house on Sunday?" she once asked Washington on one of the rare occasions when they discussed the subject of their barren marriage.

"Nonsense, woman," Washington snapped back.

"Now do I gotta go quoting *The Good Book* to you? God will bless us with a child when he sees fit, and not a second 'fore then. Sarah was close to eighty years old so I think that you got a few good years left," he said, with a wink. "So, stop all your worryin'; 'cause like *The Good Book* says, worryin' ain't gonna change a thing."

And he was right. On their tenth anniversary, it was Naomi's turn to surprise Washington by announcing that she was pregnant with their first child.

"See there, woman, you done worried yourself sick over nothin'. I knew God weren't gonna waste no good mama like you," he said, squeezing her so tightly that she had to beg him to release her so that she could catch her breath.

When Karen was born seven years later, Washington built a room onto the house for her. As time went on, he added a tire swing to the big oak out front and hung a wooden bench swing, suspended by chains, on the end of the porch. There wasn't a year that went by that Washington didn't do something to improve their home.

When Washington retired, he planned to keep himself busy and earn spare money by selling his handmade wares to the townspeople. But he had died shortly after his retirement. All that was left of that dream were the pieces that he had so painstakingly crafted and then left behind.

Naomi went to the storage area at the back of the shed and pulled back a tarpaulin. Her flashlight ran up and down the length of the shelves.

She stopped, only for a moment, letting the light pause on a shelf of wooden toys that Washington had carved for his children. Washington reclaimed these toys as the children outgrew them. He polished out the nicks, dings, bite marks, and scratches until they were as good as new.

"One day our grandbabies gonna play with these same pieces of wood," he said, when Naomi discovered what he was doing.

"You go on and laugh woman," he said good-naturedly to her. "But one day when these fingers are old and stiff and can't make no more toys, you gonna be glad them grandbabies got somethin' to take their minds off their cryin'. You mark my word on that woman."

Her eyes followed the light as it traveled from one piece to the next—a rocking horse, a set of wooden farm animals, a dollhouse, building blocks and wooden rattles. All had memories attached.

Naomi's light skipped to the next shelf. A large box sat on the top pushed back against the wall. She didn't need to lift the lid to know what was inside.

This box had been with them as long as the children. Inside were handmade Christmas ornaments. Washington started making the ornaments the year that Nathan was born.

Each Christmas, he carved and painted a special ornament for Nathan and then Karen, when she came along. His plan had been to give the ornaments to the children to take with them when they left home to start families of their own.

But Nathan had died and Karen still lived at home. This was the first Christmas since Washington's death. Neither Naomi nor Karen had mentioned a tree. Naomi turned her eyes away from the box and looked down at the floor.

Her light found what she had come looking for. On the bottom shelf were two wooden cradles—cradles that Washington had built for his son and daughter.

When Naomi suggested to Washington that she could use Nathan's cradle for the new baby, he wouldn't hear of that. A new baby should have a new cradle.

Naomi remembered the night Karen was born. "A good wife, a son and now a baby girl," Washington said, when Naomi gave him the baby to place in her cradle. "My cup sure nuff runneth over."

Naomi carried the cradles inside, one at a time, and placed them by the fire. She hung up her coat and went to work; she polished the cradles with a cotton cloth until they glowed.

When this job was done, she went to the chest in Nathan's room and opened the top drawer. Inside, carefully pressed and folded were stacks of baby clothes; all handmade by Naomi.

She had saved these clothes for the same reason that Washington had saved the toys. She had hoped that her grandchildren would someday wear them.

Naomi selected a gown and diaper for each baby and returned to the room where Karen and the babies were still sleeping. She took a throw from the couch and gently tucked it around Karen's shoulders before turning her attention to the babies.

She lifted the girl from the cotton blanket and dressed her in a diaper and a gown. The gown, once white, was now yellowed, although the tiny embroidered pink flowers on the collar still held their original color.

The baby started to cry, rousing Karen from her sleep. Karen sat straight up in the chair when she saw the cradles and her mother holding the squirming baby.

"Mama, what on earth are you doin'?" Karen asked.

"I might as well make these babies comfortable while we wait." Naomi said this as her fingers fidgeted with the tiny buttons on the gown.

"Now, Mama, you know good and well that you ought not to have toted them cradles in from that shed alone," Karen scolded her mother. "You got a bad back. I coulda helped."

"I don't know no such thing. There ain't nothin' wrong with my back but a little old age," Naomi said defensively.

"And you was sleepin'. I didn't have no heart to wake you. Fetchin' the cradles just made the time go by," Naomi said, her voice softening as she smiled up at her daughter.

Karen glanced at the clock on the wall. "I thought we'd get some help by now," she said.

"I 'spect with the bad weather, we've got us a bit of a wait."

A Watch in the Night

As Naomi talked, she placed the baby back in the cradle, which had Karen's name carved in its side.

"Let me help you," Karen said, rising from the chair. She paused to tenderly stroke the small of her mother's back.

"The babies need feedin' again," Naomi said, patting Karen's hand on her back. "You dress this little fella, and I'll see to the bottles."

By the time Naomi returned with the bottles, Karen had the boy dressed. She rocked him in her lap, while rocking the girl's cradle with her foot. Both babies were crying.

"You're gettin' the hang of things," Naomi said with a grin.

"Sit down, Mama, and I'll give you this little guy to feed. I'll feed the girl. We don't need you to get down in your back from liftin'."

"I do declare that you take after me, not your daddy, when it comes to worryin'; my back's fine," Naomi said, lowering herself down on the sofa.

Karen passed her mother the squirming boy and then lifted the girl out of the cradle. This time Karen tested the warmth of the milk on her own wrist. "I guess I am gettin' the hang of this, after all," she said.

When both babies were fed and laid back in their cradles, Karen looked over at her mother.

"What now, Mama?" she asked, again.

"We just wait some more," Naomi answered with a shrug. "The babies won't need feedin' again for a while, and by that time, maybe help will be here. Why don't you go and lay down in your room. I'll rest here."

"Mama," Karen started to protest, "you're just as tired out as me."

"Karen, please don't fuss with me. We don't know when help will get here, and we both need to rest. I'm just takin' the first watch, that's all."

Karen knew that it was pointless to argue with her Mama. "Alright, I'll try to sleep," she said, "but, do you promise to wake me up in a couple of hours if help ain't here and let me sit with the babies?"

"I promise. Now go." Karen stopped and kissed her mother before leaving Naomi alone with the babies.

CHAPTER THREE

The room was silent except for the crackling of the fire and the ticking of a clock. Naomi sat back in the rocker and stared down at the cradles. The girl looks like Lily she thought, sighing. Naomi closed her eyes, and as she slowly rocked, her mind drifted to thoughts of Lily.

Lily was born the year that Nathan left for Vietnam and Karen started to middle school. Naomi worked as a housekeeper for the Brodies, an elderly man and his wife who had moved to the Plantation, an island community situated thirty minutes north of Trinity. She had taken this job the year that Karen had started to school.

Lily's birth came as a surprise to everyone, including her parents, Ephram and Bessie, who had been married for over twenty years without conceiving any children.

Most people, or at least those who bothered to give the matter any consideration, had long ago decided that the Whatleys were doomed to have a childless marriage.

Matters of life and death were in God's hands, of course. When it came to children, God either sent them to you, or He didn't. And God had not blessed the Whatley union with offspring. It was as simple as that. Most of those who knew of the Whatleys and their drinking habits agreed that God knew what He was doing.

Bessie conceived Lily shortly after she turned forty-five, a change-of-life baby she later told Naomi. A few people adopted the view that Bessie's pregnancy was a blessing. Most took it as a sign that sometimes even God is asleep at the wheel.

Most of what people knew about the Whatleys was based on rumor. Like rumors generally, some are true, others not.

When Washington and Naomi built their home, Ephram and Bessie had already lived in the Whatley homestead as husband and wife for about five years. Washington learned that fact at the lumber company where he and Ephram both worked at the time.

According to lumberyard gossip, Ephram took over the Whatley homestead when his father died. Little was known about Ephram's mother other than the fact that she was considerably younger than Ephram's father and that she came from Westberry, a town forty miles west of the Trinity County line.

Old man Whatley had left town for a couple of days and then returned home with a young bride in tow. Rumor was there had been some kind of trouble in Westberry involving Ephram's mother, but nobody knew for sure.

In those days it was hard to come by reliable information from a town forty miles away. It just stood to reason that *something* must have happened to cause a pretty young woman to wed an old codger like Whatley. The Whatley clan never commanded a dab of respect in Trinity.

Ephram was the only fruit of that union. Ephram's mother died suddenly and at a young age from unknown causes. Her death raised an eyebrow or two, and some even suggested that Ephram's father had a hand in her passing.

But dying young was not unusual for people living in Tate's Hell. Life in Tate's Hell was hard for everyone, but even more so for Ephram's mother, a young girl who had not been brought up there. Her death certificate said "natural causes" and that about summed it up as far as the town was concerned.

Unfortunately, Mrs. Whatley died when Ephram was still a young boy leaving him in his father's sole care. "The fruit don't fall far from the tree," people in Trinity were fond of saying, and in Ephram's case this adage proved to be true.

He acquired his father's fondness for the bottle at an early age, an affinity which contributed to his decision to live at home into adulthood. He said he was "looking out for the old man" but everybody knew that he stayed on for the free room and board, which included liquor.

Shortly after his father died, Ephram married Bessie and brought her to live in the house. Without his father's monthly social security check, for the first time in his life Ephram was forced to go to work.

When sober, and often when not, he worked for the Hillman Lumber Company. That is, he worked until fortune smiled upon him by way of an accident at work which cost him a leg but gained him a permanent disability check. This check marked the end of Ephram's productive days.

Naomi's dislike for Ephram took root when he attempted to thwart the Iveys' purchase of their five-acre lot next door. When Ephram learned that Washington and Naomi intended to buy the adjacent land, he raised a ruckus, ranting and raving to whomever he could find to listen that it wasn't right for the timber company to sell that land to "niggers."

Fortunately for the Iveys, Ephram's campaign against their purchase ran into two problems. Ephram ranted and raved in the local juke joints where nobody cared who bought the land next to him unless he was buying them enough liquor to keep them interested.

Ephram was always short on money, and thus, short on friends who wanted to hear his troubles. And the Hillman Lumber Company pumped a considerable amount of money into the local economy; most people agreed that the Hillmans could do whatever they pleased so long as the money continued to flow.

Bessie and Naomi never became friends, but they were pleasant enough to one another on the few occasions when their paths crossed. The closest store was eight miles away in Trinity, and so occasionally one of the women would venture to the back door of the other to borrow some ingredient for cooking or to deliver a piece of mail the mailman had placed in the wrong box. It was on one of those occasions that Naomi discovered Bessie's pregnancy.

It was a Sunday morning when Bessie knocked on Naomi's kitchen door to ask if Naomi had any spare milk. Ephram was a stickler about his coffee Bessie explained to Naomi; he would only drink it with milk and sugar. She had milk in the refrigerator, but the milk had curdled.

Ephram would be waking up at any time, and she did not want to tell him that he couldn't have milk with his coffee. He was sure to throw one of his fits.

"I got some milk," Naomi said to her. "Step on inside, and I'll pour you some up in a jar."

Bessie rarely visited the Ivey home, but she stepped gingerly inside the back door. As she did, a breeze blew through the kitchen window, wrapping the folds of her thin skirt tightly against her body. When Naomi turned to hand Bessie the jar of milk, she couldn't help noticing the protrusion below Bessie's skirt.

Bessie saw Naomi's look of astonishment and blushed. "After all these years, me and Ephram are gonna have us a baby. Who woulda thought *that* would happen?" Bessie said by way of explanation.

"Who indeed," was all that Naomi could think of to say in response.

Several months later, Naomi returned home from work one evening and saw Doc Adams' car parked under the oak in the Whatleys' front yard. Later that evening, Naomi mustered up her courage and paid the Whatleys a visit. When Naomi knocked at the back door, it was Ephram who opened the door, scowling to see that it was Naomi.

"I come to see if everythin's alright," Naomi managed to say. This was her first face-to-face encounter with Ephram, and she was extremely uncomfortable. She was, after all, one of the "niggers" he had tried to keep out of Tate's Hell.

Ephram didn't speak to Naomi but instead stared at her contemptuously.

"I seen Doc Adams' car. I thought ya'll might need some help," Naomi muttered.

Ephram still didn't answer. Glowering down at Naomi, he pulled back the door so he could use all of his strength to sling it shut. The door would have slammed in Naomi's face if Doc hadn't intervened by grabbing Ephram's arm before he could thrust the door forward.

"Let her pass," Doc ordered Ephram, "so she can come see the baby." Ephram glared over at Doc while continuing to push as hard as he could against the door.

Naomi watched helplessly as Doc and Ephram became locked in a showdown. Doc had challenged Ephram's authority right in his own home, a bold move, Naomi thought, even if he was a doctor. You didn't do *that* in Tate' Hell.

"I didn't mean to be no bother," Naomi stammered, backing away.

"You're no bother at all," Doc replied calmly to Naomi, while tightening his grip on Ephram's arm as Ephram pushed harder on the door.

Naomi stood rooted to the ground wishing for all of the world that she had used the good sense to stay home and mind her own business.

Finally, it was Ephram who broke and released his grip on the door. Doc gave Ephram's arm an extra hard squeeze for good measure before slinging it down to Ephram's side.

Freed from Doc's grasp, Ephram went slinking back to the front of the house, clearly defeated. "Damn bothersome bitch," he said loud enough for Doc and Naomi to hear before making his turn into the kitchen.

"Coming over is very neighborly of you," Doc said pleasantly, turning his full attention towards Naomi. He was not ruffled in the least by his run-in with Ephram although Naomi had found it to be very unnerving. "And you can put your mind at ease. Bessie had a girl. Both mama and baby are fine."

"That's real good," Naomi answered, as she tried weakly to return Doc's smile. "But I reckon that I ought to be gettin' on back home now," she added, backing away. "My husband's due in. Tell Bessie to call on me if she needs anythin'."

"I'll do that," Doc said.

Bessie never called on Naomi.

Lily was born in the fall, but Naomi didn't see her until the spring of the following year. She often wondered how Bessie was faring with the baby, but it wasn't her place to interfere. Naomi and Washington were planting their spring garden the first time she met Lily.

Bent over their hoes hard at work, neither Washington nor Naomi saw Bessie and the baby as they approached. Both were startled by the sound of her voice.

"I thought ya'll might wanna see my baby girl," Bessie said shyly. Washington straightened up and smiled at her, wiping sweat from his forehead with a rag he kept stuffed in his back pocket. "Sure we'd like to see your baby," he said.

Bessie pulled back the blanket and held Lily up so Naomi and Washington could look. Lily was strikingly beautiful with skin so pale that it appeared translucent.

The wind blew Lily's fine, wispy strands of blonde hair, causing them to stand up on her head. Naomi caught a glimpse of sparkling blue eyes before the baby buried her head into her mother's shoulder. This was Lily's first encounter with anyone other than Bessie and Ephram, and she shied away from the strangers.

A Watch in the Night

"She's beautiful," Naomi said, smiling over at Bessie. "What did you name her?

"Lily. I named her Lily," Bessie replied.

"Now that's a pretty name," Washington said. "And she's a pretty baby. I don't reckon I've ever saw one that's prettier, 'cept maybe my own girl," Washington added, laughing. Bessie timidly smiled back at them.

"I better get back inside," she said. "I just thought ya'll might wanna see her." Bessie turned and walked back to her house.

After that first encounter, Naomi saw Bessie with Lily more often, usually in the evening, about dark, walking her around the yard and sometimes down the dirt road towards the main highway. On several of these occasions, Naomi tried to strike up a conversation with Bessie, but Bessie didn't seem interested, and Naomi didn't press her.

From the little that she saw, it seemed to Naomi that Lily had changed Bessie. Bessie didn't appear to be drinking. She kept the baby neat and clean, and Lily seemed happy. Naomi even noticed changes in Bessie's appearance. Her dress was pressed, and she kept her hair swept back from her face, secured with two tortoise shell combs.

Lily was still a toddler when Naomi stopped at the Whatley house late one afternoon to warn Bessie that she had seen a wild dog on the dirt road and to suggest that Bessie not walk the baby until Washington got home and removed the dog.

Naomi rapped lightly on the door, and Bessie opened it with Lily straddled over one hip. Bessie didn't invite Naomi inside, but instead thanked her at the door for the warning. This was before the Whatleys had added the tarpaper addition to their house, and Naomi could see clearly over Bessie's shoulder into the kitchen.

Naomi was pleased to see that the room was cleaner than the night she had come over when Lily was born. It was neat and orderly instead of cluttered. On the walk home, Naomi thought to herself that maybe the Lord had seen fit to send Bessie this baby to give her a reason to put her life in order.

The year that Lily started school, Naomi would see Bessie and Lily as she left for work each morning. They were waiting at the end of the road for the school bus, which transported the children from Tate's Hell to the elementary school in Trinity.

Naomi waved to them as she passed, and they always waved back. Both mother and daughter were clean and properly dressed, which Naomi took as a good sign. But appearances can be deceiving, and it was not until later in the year that Naomi discovered life in the Whatley household had taken a turn for the worse.

Maybe it was having Lily away at school that caused Bessie to fall back into her old ways. Perhaps, Bessie missed her child's company or no longer felt as needed. Or, maybe, it was more than the usual amount of chaos living with Ephram. Naomi couldn't be sure of what exactly had happened to trigger Bessie's relapse. More than likely it was a combination of many things, but for whatever reason, Naomi learned that Bessie had gone back to the bottle.

When the weather permitted, Ephram liked to drink on his front porch. He was a loud, rambunctious drunk. During the spring, summer and fall months, Naomi and Washington were often distressed to hear bits of Ephram's hollering and cussing even though the Iveys' yard was a good quarter of a mile through the woods from the Whatley place.

More than once, Washington said to Naomi that he had a mind to call in Sheriff Tate. But blacks didn't call the law on whites, and the sheriff only wanted to be called to Tate's Hell for matters of life or death. A man's drinking in his own home, even if he did disturb his neighbors, didn't warrant a visit from the sheriff.

A Watch in the Night

Ephram usually passed out before supper time so the nights were quiet. The Ivey family learned to tolerate the outbursts from next door until Ephram's stupor set in.

It was on one of these early evenings, when Ephram was drinking and carrying on, that Lily first came to the Ivey home. Naomi was standing at the sink peeling potatoes when she heard a faint knock at the bottom of her back door. She looked up, and there stood little tow-headed Lily.

"Hello there," Naomi said gently, as she wiped her hands on her apron and crossed the kitchen. "Won't you come on in?" Naomi asked, holding the screen door open for Lily to enter.

"No ma'am, I can't," Lily said without looking up.

"Well, is there somethin' that I can do for you?" Naomi asked.

The child shook her head from side to side. As Naomi kneeled down next to Lily, she could see that tears were streaming down Lily's cheeks. Naomi gently raised Lily's chin with her fingers so that she could look into Lily's eyes.

"What's troublin' you child?" Naomi asked soothingly. "You can tell me. Are you hurt?"

"No ma'am, I ain't hurt," Lily said, tears gushing from her eyes. "It's my mama. She won't wake up. I shook her, but she won't wake up."

Lily buried her head in Naomi's breasts sobbing. "It's gonna be alright, child," Naomi whispered into Lily's ear. "I'll go see 'bout your mama."

Naomi lifted the sobbing child and carried her across the room where she sat down with her at the kitchen table. Naomi cradled Lily in her arms and rocked her until Lily's crying became little sniffles.

Karen, who had heard the commotion from her room in the back of the house, was startled to see her mother holding the little girl from next door when she walked into the kitchen.

At the sight of Karen, Lily tightened her grip around Naomi's neck. Naomi motioned for Karen to stop in the doorway.

"Lily, this here is my girl, Karen," Naomi said to the child in a voice not much louder than a whisper. "Would you stay with her while I go see 'bout your mama?" Lily nodded her head that she would.

Before she was halfway down the path to the Whatley house, Naomi could hear Ephram on the front porch cussing the dogs. His words were slurred, and Naomi knew that he was probably too drunk to get out of his chair.

She slipped into the Whatley house through the back door, undetected by Ephram. By this time, Ephram had added the tarpaper addition.

Once inside she stopped, letting her gaze travel down the short hallway to the kitchen. It was a mess. Dirty dishes sat piled everywhere—on the counter, on the table and forming a pyramid over the sink. Open cans littered the stove, and garbage spilled out of a paper sack onto the floor.

Naomi started her search for Bessie in the back of the house. She didn't dare call out Bessie's name for fear that Ephram would hear. She hadn't seen him since the night that Lily was born and wanted to avoid another encounter at all costs.

Fortunately, Naomi didn't have to go far. Bessie was lying on the floor next to a bed in a small room, which was part of the tarpaper addition.

Rushing in, Naomi knelt beside Bessie. The smell of alcohol saturated the small room. Naomi shook Bessie, and her eyes fluttered, opened halfway and then closed again. Bessie was out cold, and Naomi knew about all she could do was to let Bessie sleep it off.

Bessie was small and frail. Naomi guessed that she couldn't have weighed one hundred pounds soaking wet as she lifted Bessie by the shoulders and pulled her up onto the bed.

A Watch in the Night

Naomi removed Bessie's shoes and pulled a dingy sheet up around her shoulders. "Go on sleep now," Naomi said. She didn't feel contempt for Bessie, only pity.

The thought of Bessie's suffering weighed on Naomi's heart and slowed her steps on the walk home. And what kind of life was this for a child?

"Your mama's alright, child," Naomi said to Lily as she entered the kitchen door. "She's feelin' a mite sick, that's all. I put her to bed. She'll be just fine in the morning. Meanwhile, you can stay here and eat supper with us." Naomi couldn't let the child go back home. "You can help me cook while Karen finishes up her lessons."

"Homework," Karen said to her mother. "It's called homework, Mama, not lessons. You're so old-fashioned."

"Don't sass me, girl," Naomi said to Karen teasingly, before turning her attention back to Lily.

"Lily, you get up here," Naomi said as she pulled a chair up next to the sink. "You can wash these here potatoes and hand 'em over for me to peel." Naomi wanted to keep her distracted.

Lily hesitated. She wanted to stay. That was obvious. But Naomi could tell by the way that her eyes darted from Karen to the door that she was afraid to be away from home.

Naomi picked Lily up and stood her in the chair she had pulled up to the sink. "It's alright, baby. You can stay here. Your daddy won't mind none." Naomi wasn't really sure about that last statement, but what else could she do.

"We're havin' my husband's favorite meal tonight—fried chicken and mashed potatoes," Naomi said, tweaking Lily's nose. Lily smiled. "But if we don't get started here real quick like, Karen's daddy will come home for the first time in over twenty years, and his supper won't be waitin' on the table for him.

Over the coming years, Lily spent many nights at the Ivey home. The pattern was always the same. She would knock on the Ivey door, saying that her mother was sick. Naomi would walk over to the Whatley house and find Bessie and Ephram drunk. Lily would then stay with the Iveys until the next morning.

The Ivey family enjoyed having Lily in their home as much as she enjoyed being there. She was a bright and energetic child. After several visits, Washington built Lily a small bed, which he placed in the corner of Karen's room.

The nights when Lily slept over, Washington would rise a little earlier than usual and carry her, usually half asleep, back home. The back door of the Whatley home was never locked. Washington placed Lily in her bed with instructions for her to stay there until Bessie got up.

Neither Bessie nor Ephram ever confronted the Iveys regarding Lily's visits. When the arrangement first started, Naomi and Washington feared there might be trouble from the Whatleys. They agreed that it would be best to discuss the visits with Bessie, but the opportunity to have that discussion never occurred.

Naomi and Washington believed that the Whatleys surely must be aware of the visits; but that the Whatleys simply didn't care what happened to Lily when they were drinking. The Iveys' love and concern for Lily soon outweighed their fear of the Whatleys. The visits continued once or twice a week for years and then stopped abruptly.

When the visits stopped, the Iveys grew concerned for Lily.

Eventually, Naomi went to the Whatley home to satisfy herself that Lily was alright. She picked an early evening to visit, hoping that Bessie and Ephram would be passed out. They were. She found Lily alone in the kitchen.

Lily smiled when she looked up and saw Naomi standing at her door. The look in Lily's eyes told Naomi that Lily missed the Ivey family as much as they missed her.

A Watch in the Night

"I'd like to be coming over," Lily said, "but my mama is sick most every night. I can't leave her alone at night anymore."

"We was just worried 'bout you, Lily," Naomi said. "We miss you. We don't mean to interfere."

"And I miss you, too," Lily said. "But I got to stay here now. My mama needs me." Lily put her arms around Naomi's neck and hugged her tightly.

"I understand, child," Naomi whispered into her ear. "But you can call on us day or night if you need help."

Lily released Naomi and looked her in the eyes. "I will. I promise." Tears welled up in both Lily and Naomi's eyes.

After that night, the Iveys only saw Lily in passing. But when they did see her, Washington and Naomi observed that she was growing into a beautiful young girl.

The willowy, tow-headed child had grown tall, with a body that remained thin, but taunt and strong. Her blonde hair was long and thick and usually pulled away from her face in a single braid, a style that Karen had taught her. Her skin was clear and pale, and her brilliant blue eyes sparkled in the light even from a distance.

When school was in session, Naomi looked forward to seeing Lily each morning at the bus stop. As Naomi passed by on her way to work, she and Lily exchanged a wave and a smile.

Then one year school started, but Naomi didn't see Lily waiting for the bus. When Naomi mentioned this to Washington over supper one evening, he told her that he had seen Lily coming out of Harry's Tavern the past week while he was over on River Street buying fish.

"I was meanin' to tell you that I saw Lily, but it slipped my mind. Judgin' by the way that she was dressed, in jeans and a Harry's T-shirt, I figgered she musta taken to waitin' tables there."

Harry's Tavern, a local bar and restaurant frequented by the logging crews and the fishermen on their way home from work, had an unsavory reputation with the God-fearing population of Trinity. Naomi's eyebrows shot up at the mention of Lily working there.

"I hate to hear *that*," Naomi said with a sigh. "Harry's Tavern ain't no place for Lily. I reckon that explains why she ain't been at the bus stop. I 'pose she's done up and quit school. I hoped that she'd be able to do better than her mama and her daddy."

"I hoped the same thing myself," Washington said. "But you know that a child is like a garden. You got to tend to a garden if you want it to grow into somethin' good. Nobody tended to Lily, and she can't be blamed if she didn't grow like we think she oughta."

"I ain't judgin' her," Naomi said. "I'd just hoped that she could do better."

"And I understand why you'd be troubled," Washington said, "but we done all that we could for Lily. Life's got to take its course now. So, stop frettin' over Lily and finish up your supper. Speakin' of gardens, we still got enough daylight left to hoe ours."

Six months later Washington was coming home from work when he saw Trey Hillman's truck headed back into the Whatley place. Trey was the only son of Roy Hillman, the owner of the Hillman Lumber Company. The Hillmans were the richest and, consequently, the most powerful family in town.

Washington was certain that it was Trey he saw. He recognized Trey's fancy truck. But he didn't think too much, at the time, about seeing Hillman out in Tate's Hell.

The dirt lane, which led up to the Whatley place, continued on past the Whatley house and circled behind the Ivey house. The lane ended in a clearing behind the Ivey property.

Years ago, the road had been used by logging crews. The clearing was the beginning of a two-hundred-acre plot of planted slash pines, all owned by the Hillman Lumber Company. The lumber company cut the clearing and then moved on. Washington never inquired why they had left; he was just glad to have them gone.

The road back to the clearing had grown over with weeds when the logging crews stopped coming, but it remained passable for someone who had a four-wheel-drive vehicle and knew the lay-out of the road.

Washington hoped that seeing young Hillman didn't mean that the lumber company was considering cutting the pines. He never mentioned seeing Hillman to Naomi. No need to worry her.

The window over the Ivey kitchen sink faced the clearing. Naomi couldn't actually see the clearing from her window because trees and brush obstructed her view, although she knew the clearing was there. She and Washington considered asking Mr. Hillman if it could be plowed for a garden. But it was so filled with roots and scrub brush, they abandoned the idea.

One winter's evening, as Naomi stood washing dishes at her kitchen sink, she was startled to see a light moving through the woods towards the clearing. She blinked her eyes several times to be certain that she wasn't imagining the light before she called out to Washington to come have a look.

"What's all this fuss 'bout, old woman?" Washington asked, stepping into the kitchen.

"I saw lights back in the direction of the clearin', but they seem to have disappeared now," she answered.

"Are you sure 'bout that, Naomi?" Washington asked. "That road ain't been used for years. I don't 'spect nobody would go back there this time of night. Are you sure you saw lights?" he asked again.

"I'm as sure as these old tired eyes can be," she replied.

"I don't feel good 'bout this," Washington said in a strained voice. "Maybe I oughta walk on back there and see if I can tell what's goin' on."

"It's probably nothin'," Naomi quickly said. She didn't want Washington going back to the clearing alone at night. She regretted having mentioned the lights.

"You're likely right; it's no more than the addled mind of an old woman," he said with a wink. "But, on the other hand, I won't be able to lay down and rest if I don't get to the bottom of this. I'll take the dog and my gun with me."

Washington took down his gun, which hung on two pegs by the back door. He was out the back door before Naomi could say anymore. Naomi followed him outside, continuing to protest his going.

"If you ain't back here in fifteen minutes old man, I'm gonna call Sheriff Tate. Do you hear me? I'll call Sheriff Tate if you don't come right back."

"Don't you go doin' nothin' foolish like callin' the sheriff. You go back inside and lock the doors. I won't be gone long. Old Duke will look out for me," Washington said, before he whistled for the dog and was gone.

Washington wasn't back in fifteen minutes, but Naomi didn't call Sheriff Tate. Instead, she paced the floor, wringing her hands and stopping every few seconds to stare out of the kitchen window. When she saw the light from Washington's flashlight cutting through the trees, she rushed to the back porch. "Thank you, Lord," she said aloud. First Duke emerged from the darkness and then Washington, following closely behind.

"Get back inside where it's warm," Washington admonished her. "Everythin's alright. There ain't nothin' to worry 'bout."

Naomi didn't budge from her spot on the porch. "What did you find out?" she demanded to know. Washington wrapped his arm around her shoulders and pulled her with him back into the warmth of their kitchen.

"I do declare, woman, you do the worryin' for this whole family. I told you that everythin's alright; ain't that enough for you."

A Watch in the Night

"Of course, it ain't enough," Naomi said, exasperated. "I know you saw somethin', and I won't give you no peace 'til you tell me what you saw."

Washington pulled off his jacket and sat down at the kitchen table. Naomi poured him a cup of coffee and pulled up a chair across from him.

"It's not good, Naomi. The lights you seen was Trey Hillman's headlights goin' back into the clearin'."

"What on earth would Trey Hillman be doin' back there this time of night?"

"I wondered the same thing myself, so I slipped up close to Hillman's truck."

"You what? Washington, you coulda been shot."

"I wasn't shot so hush up if you want me to tell you what I saw."

"Go on," Naomi said.

"I saw two people sittin' in that truck, and one of them was a woman. I don't think lookin' at timber brung young Hillman out our way."

"Washington, this don't make a bit of sense. Why would Hillman bring a woman all the way out here?"

Suddenly, Naomi clutched Washington's arm. "Oh good Lord, I hope this ain't what I'm thinkin'. Don't that Hillman boy have a wife? Was Lily in that truck?"

"I couldn't make out for sure who the woman was with Hillman. And I got to admit that the same thought crossed my mind. But we ought not to go rushin' to judgment."

Washington looked Naomi in the eyes, and his voice took on a more somber tone. "We don't know for certain who was back there with Hillman. But this much I do know. It won't do no good for us to go stickin' our noses into this, even if it's Lily. Lily's a growed up girl. We can't go mindin' her business. We're better off to just keep this to ourselves."

Naomi shook her head that she understood. She had a troubled look on her face.

Washington took her hand and pulled her up from the chair. "Come on, honey. Let's go to bed. I'm sure that the Hillman boy don't mean us no harm. We both got to work tomorrow. We won't be no good at work if we miss sleep over this."

Naomi could tell by Washington's tone of voice that the subject was closed. Besides, he was right. This wasn't their business.

The remainder of that winter it wasn't unusual for Naomi to look up from her dishpan and see lights inching back towards the clearing. A couple of times she mentioned the lights to Washington, but he always cut her off.

"It's none of our business," he would say to her sternly. "Ain't no good gonna come from black folks gettin' mixed up in other folk's business—'specially when that business is 'bout white folks. The richest, most powerful white folks in town at that. Leave it be, woman."

So, Naomi stopped mentioning the lights to Washington. Still, she couldn't help but fret when she saw those lights snaking through the woods.

Winter turned to spring. The days became longer, and Naomi was out of the kitchen before dark. She put the lights out of her mind. Then one evening she and Washington met Hillman on the road into their house.

They were coming in late from a church supper. Hillman was going in the opposite direction towards the main road. They met just before the road forked. The road was narrow. The trucks were only inches apart when they passed.

"Keep your eyes straight ahead," Washington cautioned Naomi. As the trucks inched slowly past one another, Naomi briefly cut her eyes towards the other truck.

A Watch in the Night

She could clearly see Trey Hillman's face, but he never looked their way. Both he and Washington kept their eyes straight ahead. Neither acknowledged the presence of the other.

Shortly after that night, Washington died. Any concerns Naomi had about Trey and Lily were forgotten as she grieved her loss.

As Naomi sat by her fire looking at the cradles, she pondered what she knew to be the truth about the babies. Then Washington's words of caution rolled through her mind. "It don't pay for black folks to be messin' in nobody's business 'specially when that business concerns the richest white folks in town."

It's a shame, a crying shame, she thought, as she pushed the rocker to and fro.

"It's a shame, alright," Washington's voice said in her head. "But it ain't your business."

CHAPTER FOUR

About an hour before daybreak, Naomi fed the babies the last of the milk. She picked up the phone, but the lines were still out. Staring down at the empty bottles, she realized that she had no choice but to go into town for help. She would try and find Doc Adams, but if that failed, she would go to the sheriff's office.

The thought of going into the sheriff's office made her nervous. Black people in Trinity rarely found law enforcement officers to be particularly friendly. She put on her best Sunday dress and shoes to boost her confidence. Still feeling unsure, she added a hat.

Naomi smoothed her dress and adjusted her hat, taking one final look in the mirror before going in to wake Karen.

"Come on, Karen, you need to wake up," Naomi said, as she gently shook her daughter's shoulders.

"What?" Karen asked groggily.

"Doc never made it back last night. And he didn't send help."

Karen bolted upright in the bed. "Help never came?"

"Nope. And we can't wait no longer. Them babies gotta be fed. I'll have to go into town, and I'll need for you to look after the babies while I'm gone."

Karen rolled out of the bed and quickly pulled on a robe, following her mother into the living room. While Naomi gathered up her purse and coat, Karen stared terrified at the cradles.

"The babies oughta be fine 'til I can get back," Naomi said, seeing the fear in Karen's face. "I fed 'em the last of the milk 'bout an hour ago. They oughta sleep for a while. When they wake up, there ain't much you can do but rock 'em. I'll hurry."

Karen heard the strain in her mother's voice and saw the tired droop in her shoulders. "Mama, maybe I should go and you stay," she said.

"No," Naomi said firmly. "I'm dressed and ready. And I've got to drive your daddy's old truck. I can't be sure what shape the roads are in. I don't think our car would make it to the main road. You ain't ever drove that truck much. It's best if I go."

Karen didn't like the thought of her mother venturing off in her daddy's old truck any more than she liked the thought of being left alone with two newborn babies. But she knew that her mother was right. They didn't have much of a choice.

The sun was starting to come up when Naomi and Karen stepped outside onto the front porch. More snow had fallen during the night. An icy wind whipped the snow around and filled the air with the smell of the smoke, which billowed out from their chimney. Karen stood mesmerized. This was only the second time that she had seen snow.

"The snow is so beautiful," Karen said.

"Yes, it is," Naomi replied. "I wish we had us some time to enjoy it together. But we don't."

Karen gave her mother a quick hug and helped her down the steps.

"You be careful, Mama, you hear," she called after Naomi, as Naomi plowed through the snow towards the truck, praying that it would crank.

Naomi climbed inside the truck and turned the key, which she always left in the ignition. The engine whined but didn't quite turn over. She pumped the gas pedal several times and tried again. This time the engine fired, sputtered and then chugged rhythmically. Relieved, Naomi revved the motor and then wheeled the truck out of the yard and down the lane. The ruts of the lane were concealed by the snow, but she knew the way.

Naomi had made it halfway down the lane to the main road when she spotted a patrol car up ahead. As she got closer, she realized that the car was pulled off onto the side of the road. Her first thought was that help had arrived after all. Then she saw Doc Adams' Ford wagon in the ditch and knew there must be trouble.

Gingerly braking the truck, she eased up beside the patrol car. Sheriff Tate stepped up next to the truck and motioned for Naomi to roll down her window. She pumped the hand-crank until the window was three-quarters down.

"Good mornin' to you, Ma'am," Sheriff Tate said, as he bent over and peered into the window.

"Mornin' Sheriff," Naomi replied politely.

"You're Washington Ivey's wife, ain't you?" the sheriff asked. "Ya'll live back up by the Whatley place, right?"

"Yes sir. That's right. I'm Naomi Ivey. But Washington, my husband, he passed last spring." A blast of cold air and the close proximity of Sheriff Tate caused Naomi's voice to tremble.

"Oh yeah. I remember now," the sheriff responded. "I sure did hate to hear 'bout that. He was a good man. Kept to hisself and worked hard."

That was about the best eulogy a black man could get from the white community in this town, Naomi thought, as she avoided looking the sheriff directly in the eyes.

Naomi peeked up at the sheriff, and she immediately noticed that his smile had faded and that he had leaned in closer. She shuddered.

"We got trouble here, Ma'am," he said. "I got a call from Mildred Adams tellin' me that Doc never made it home last night. That he had gone out to the Whatley place to deliver a baby. So, I come lookin' for him. Found his car over there in the ditch. Looks like he hit a deer.

"He musta tried to walk back to the Whatley house. But he didn't make it. I found him layin' in the road, not more than five minutes ago."

Once he started talking, the sheriff's words poured out like water from a broken faucet. Naomi tried to interject, but she found it impossible to slip even a word into the exchange.

And then as quickly as he had started talking, the sheriff stopped and stood up to leave. Naomi thrust her head partially out the window. "Sheriff, I need to tell you somethin'," she hurriedly said, before he got away.

"Later," he replied curtly. "Right now it's freezin', and I got to see 'bout gettin' Doc's body back into town." The squawk of the patrol car radio interrupted the sheriff.

"I'll be out to the Whatley place later, and I'll stop by your place."

"But, Sheriff," Naomi stuttered. It was too late. Sheriff Tate had turned and was walking swiftly in the direction of the noise from the radio.

"We'll talk later," he called over his shoulder.

"Now what?" she muttered to herself, clutching the steering wheel, uncertain of what to do. Her mind raced. She could go on into town to get some milk for the babies. The sheriff did say that he would stop out later. Lily was gone. There weren't nothin' the sheriff could do 'bout that. The babies would be alright 'til later.

The sound of a honking horn brought Naomi out of her thoughts. When she looked up, Sheriff Tate was impatiently waving her to come on through.

She pressed the accelerator. As her truck passed slowly by Sheriff Tate's car, she knew that she ought to stop right then and there and make the sheriff listen to her. Fear made her hesitate, and the opportunity to act was lost. The patrol car started to crawl forward, and Naomi knew that she had missed her chance.

Glancing into her rearview mirror, Naomi caught a glimpse of Doc's body lying in the snow before she turned her attention back to the road ahead.

Naomi was almost to Trinity when she saw the Shady Grove Baptist Church up ahead. A plan quickly formed in her mind. The Reverend Samuel Taylor had been the minister at the Shady Grove Baptist Church for the past fifteen years. Naomi knew him well. The reverend would be able to help.

The sun glared on the snow as Naomi squinted, trying desperately to locate the turnoff to the parsonage. When she recognized the two fir trees, which stood guard on either side of the reverend's driveway, she stomped the brakes and wrenched the steering wheel hard to the left to make the turn.

The truck swerved, rocked, and, after several harrowing seconds, skidded to a stop in what would be Reverend Taylor's gardenia patch in the spring. Sweat beaded up on Naomi's forehead in spite of the cold. She dropped her head on the steering wheel and didn't look up until she heard the truck door open.

"Naomi, is that you? Are you alright?" Reverend Taylor asked.

"Uh huh," she answered, raising her head up slightly and giving him a weary look.

"What in the world is going on?" he asked. "I was looking at the snow through our front window with my children when we saw your truck come careening into our yard. For a moment, I thought you might end up in our living room."

"I need help," Naomi managed to say. "We had trouble at our place last night. Lily Whatley died leavin' me and Karen to take care of her two newborn babies."

Once Naomi found her voice, the words tumbled out of her mouth so rapidly that Reverend Taylor could scarcely understand a word that she was saying.

A Watch in the Night

"Slow down," he commanded her. "You need to come on in out of the cold, and let Abigail take a look at you. We can talk inside." He steadied Naomi by holding her arm and helped her to dismount out of the truck.

"You kids go get your mama," Reverend Taylor said to the four children who stood behind him gawking at the truck.

"Hurry," he said, shooing them along.

Reverend Taylor held Naomi firmly by the arm as he led her towards the house. The reverend's wife, Abigail, met them at the door.

"What's going on?" she asked, holding the door open for her husband and Naomi. The four children lurked behind their mother, trying to sneak a peek around her skirt.

"I'm not sure," Samuel said, as he led Naomi to a chair in front of the fire. Abigail followed.

"Now, what's the trouble?" he asked, when he had Naomi seated in the chair.

Naomi took a deep breath and started to tell Samuel and Abigail all that had happened, beginning with Bessie's knock at the door and ending with her encounter with Sheriff Tate.

Neither interrupted her, but they exchanged a distraught look at the news of the death of Doc Adams. Doc Adams was a friend to whites and blacks alike, and he would be sorely missed. When she finished, Naomi leaned back in the chair.

"That's some story," Reverend Taylor said, looking over at his wife to gauge her reaction. Abigail sat shaking her head.

"Put your mind at ease," he added. "We can help."

When Naomi heard these words, she slumped forward and put her head in her hands. "Thank you, Jesus," she whispered.

"We have everything that you need for the babies here," Samuel said. "Give us a little time to pull ourselves together, and we'll go with you out to Tate's Hell. In the meanwhile, you should rest and maybe pray for Karen." Reverend Taylor made this last remark with a smile.

The Taylors operated like a well-oiled machine when responding to emergencies. Like good shepherds, they tended to the needs of their flock. Their home was stocked with an assortment of emergency items that could rival any Red Cross shelter.

Abigail, as the only black midwife in Trinity, was frequently called to deliver babies. She kept a bag packed with all the items that a newborn might need.

She retrieved this bag and sat it by the front door before beckoning for her children. The children followed Abigail's instructions without protest or delay. The Taylor troop knew the drill.

Samuel smiled at Abigail as she came into the room. He was proud of his wife, and he had always thought that if she had been given the opportunity that she could have become a fine doctor.

He placed the receiver of the telephone back in its cradle.

"The phones are working, again. Miss Summers has agreed to watch the children," he said.

Samuel roused Naomi, who sat dozing by the fire. "We're ready to go," he said. "If it's agreeable with you, I'll drive the truck, and you and Abigail can follow behind in our car."

Within an hour of her arrival, Naomi was back on the road. Abigail and Naomi followed Samuel, who quickly adapted to the eccentricities of driving Washington's truck.

The sun shone brightly, and the road was wet and glistening from the melting snow. Already patches of brown could be seen on the sides of the road.

About a mile before the turnoff onto Route 27, they passed Sheriff Tate in his patrol car with the wagon from the Davis Funeral Parlor and a wrecker from Johnny's Amoco following behind him. Samuel nodded to the sheriff as they passed, but everyone kept moving.

The Davis Funeral Parlor had been the only funeral home in Trinity for as far back as anyone could remember. It was a family-owned business and had passed through several generations of Davis family members.

Its wagon doubled as an ambulance and a hearse. Because Trinity lacked sufficient resources to fund a full-scale rescue squad, the county contracted with the Davis Funeral Parlor to provide limited emergency services. Several Davis drivers had been marginally trained in emergency medical care, and the wagon was equipped with a stretcher, a portable oxygen tank, bandages and a removable siren.

When a medical emergency occurred, Doc often called for the wagon either to pick up the body or to transport anyone who needed to be hospitalized to the hospital in Cartersville.

For a funeral, the wagon was transformed into a hearse—the stretcher was draped with a black cloth, the oxygen tank, siren and bandages were removed, and its black exterior was polished to a high sheen.

The wrecker from Johnny's Amoco trailed the Davis wagon on the drive into Trinity. The front of Doc's Ford hung from the wrecker's wench as its back wheels rolled along the pavement. Doc's Ford was covered with mud and displayed a badly smashed front, right fender.

Naomi and Abigail bounced along behind the truck in the Taylor's station wagon as they cautiously traversed the dirt lane. The ruts were muddy and slick, and both Samuel and Abigail had to take care not to slide off into the ditch. Naomi fidgeted in her seat eager to get back to Karen and the babies.

When the Taylor's car rolled to a stop in her front yard, Naomi was out of the car and rushing towards her front door before Abigail could turn off the engine. The Taylors followed closely on her heels. All three could hear the sound of crying babies as soon as they stepped onto the porch.

Naomi flung open the door, and Abigail and Samuel almost collided with her as they all hurried inside. Karen sat frantically rocking a baby in her arms. The other baby was in a cradle, which she rocked with her foot. She gave them a frazzled look.

"Thank you, Jesus!" she exclaimed, looking straight up as if she were turning her eyes towards heaven.

"They must be starvin' by now," Abigail said. "Karen, give your mama the baby in your arms. You can help me with the bottles. Samuel, pick up the baby in the cradle."

Samuel scooped up the baby from the cradle and started to pace about the room bouncing the baby in his arms. Karen gladly passed the other baby to her mother, who plopped down in the rocker.

Samuel paced and Naomi rocked. When Naomi started to croon softly, Samuel joined in. But only milk was going to appease the hungry babies.

Neither Samuel nor Naomi was a stranger to a crying baby, but the constant cacophony of the wailing duo was sufficient to rattle the steadiest of nerves.

They stared at the kitchen door as if this act of staring would hasten the return of Abigail and Karen. Both Samuel and Naomi were on their last nerve, when Abigail and Karen bounded through the kitchen door, each carrying a bottle.

Abigail handed one bottle to her husband before turning to Naomi. "We'll feed the babies," she said, raising her voice to a near yell to be heard over the squalling babies. Naomi passed the baby up to Abigail.

As soon as the babies started to suck peacefulness descended over the room. All that could be heard was the faint sucking noises made by the babies, the ticking clock, and the creak of the rocker.

Karen went outside to get a breath of fresh air. Her nerves were shot. When she returned, she carried an armload of wood, which she dropped into the bin on the hearth. She stoked the fire, while Naomi went into the kitchen to put on a pot of fresh coffee.

A Watch in the Night

When Naomi returned, the fire was blazing and Karen was collapsed into the easy chair. Samuel and Abigail sat next to one another on the couch intent on feeding the babies.

Naomi slumped into the rocker and allowed herself to feel the weariness that she had thus far managed to keep at bay.

Samuel was the first to speak. He removed the bottle from the girl's still puckered lips, laid her across his shoulder, and gently patted her back.

"I think we need a plan," he said. Abigail raised the boy to her shoulder and started to pat his back. He gave an audible burp. After a few more pats, his sister did the same. Samuel and Abigail lowered the babies to their laps and plugged their puckered lips with the nipples before either baby had an opportunity to emit even the tiniest of whimpers.

Samuel cleared his throat "I suppose we should assess the situation," he said like a general addressing his troops before a battle.

When nobody answered, he continued. "We are four black adults in Tate's Hell charged with the care of two white newborn babies. There's snow on the ground, the telephones are out, and the babies' mother and the only doctor for fifty miles around are both dead.

"As far as we know, the grandparents are next door, but chances are they're passed out drunk. Sheriff Tate has promised to come out, but we have no way of knowing when that'll be. We've got plenty of food and clothes for the babies, a good warm fire and God on our side. Now, that's the facts folks, as I see them, unless, of course, somebody has something else to add."

Nobody had anything to add.

"Oh, and for the record, this is the most bizarre situation that I've found myself involved in during all of my fifteen years in the ministry."

The group sat staring at Samuel. Then Naomi started to laugh. The laughter started as a chuckle, but it quickly developed into a full-fledged, down-in-the-belly, I-don't-know-what--else-to-do laugh.

First, Samuel joined in, then Karen and finally Abigail. The four sat and laughed until sheets of tears streamed down their faces. The babies, who had both finished feeding, started to cry, which made the four adults laugh even harder.

"Oh my Lord, I do wish that my Washington coulda lived to see this sight," Naomi choked out. She slapped her knees and wiped her eyes on the tail of her apron.

When everyone finally simmered down, Samuel tried again.

"I suppose that we need to check on the folks next door," he said, rising to place his baby back in the cradle.

"They could need help, and I don't think that we can wait on Sheriff Tate to make his appearance. Sheriff Tate is an elected official, and right or wrong, he's goin' to see to the needs of the Adams' family before he wastes any time on people from Tate's Hell."

They all nodded, indicating that Samuel had hit the nail on the head with that last observation.

"Naomi, you know the Whatleys best, so perhaps, you should go with me next door," Samuel said. "Abigail and Karen can hold down the fort here. I don't think that we can make much of a plan until we assess the entire situation, including what's going on next door."

Bessie woke up before daybreak lying on the couch. She knew something was wrong, but she couldn't remember what.

She tried to lift her head, but the slightest movement sent a searing pain pulsing through her temples. A wave of nausea erupted deep within her gut, which she barely managed to contain by dropping her head back on the pillow stuffed under her head. The room was too hot; she was washed down in sweat.

A Watch in the Night

As her eyes floated around the room, she was surprised to discover all three of the dogs curled up into a ball sleeping by the door. The dogs were never allowed inside.

"Lily," she called softly before passing back out.

The sun shone brightly through the living room window when Bessie woke up again. Clover, Ephram's favorite dog, stood by the sofa licking her face.

The pain in her head and the sickness in her stomach remained. Her throat was parched, and her mouth felt as if it were filled with cotton. She licked her dry, cracked lips and tried to sit up. Her foot struck an empty whiskey bottle, causing it to spin across the room.

Something was wrong, bad wrong. But she couldn't remember what. She massaged her temples, trying to think. All that came to her mind were fragmented thoughts of Lily—Lily as a little girl hopping off the bus; Lily as a teenager her hair pulled back in a braid; Lily lying in a pool of blood.

Frightened, Bessie sat up and struggled to rise to her feet. She had to find Lily.

She tried to focus. The only sound that she heard was Ephram's snoring in the next room, a noise that grated on her already raw nerves. Gripping the arm of the couch, she steadied herself. She tried to call out to Lily, but she couldn't get her voice to rise above a whisper.

The throbbing in her head grew worse. Releasing her grip on the couch, she pressed her temples with the palms of her hand. Her stomach gurgled and bile pushed at her throat before she was able to choke it back down. Steadying herself again, she took a tentative step towards the kitchen.

Ephram would be up soon, she thought. He would want coffee. That was Lily's job. Lily should be up making coffee. Lily must be at work. Then she remembered that Lily hadn't gone to work for months.

Bessie decided that she would make the coffee. Then she would find Lily. She shuffled slowly into the kitchen. Resting against the counter, she caught her breath before filling the percolator with water. Her hands shook as she filled the basket with coffee, and some of the ground coffee spilled onto the counter.

Lily liked to keep things clean, Bessie thought. So, she picked up the dishcloth and made a half-hearted swipe at the spilled coffee. Dropping the cloth, she leaned over the sink. The nausea was back.

Bessie remained hunched over the sink until the sickness passed. The coffee started to perk; its aroma filled the small room.

The smell of the coffee made her feel better. Everything would be alright. She would find Lily, and everything would be just fine. Bracing herself on the backs of the chairs and then the wall, Bessie staggered the short distance to Lily's room.

Lily's blood had seeped through the blanket Doc had used to cover her, forming a dark red circle.

Bessie saw this stain and her knees buckled. She clutched at the door, but she couldn't hold on. She fainted.

Naomi knocked at the Whatley's back door. There was no answer. She called out Bessie's name. Still no answer. She turned the doorknob. The door was not locked. Naomi glanced over at Samuel, who motioned for her to step aside. She did.

Samuel took the lead and cautiously opened the door. He stuck his head inside. A woman was lying sprawled out on the floor in the hallway.

"It's Bessie," Naomi said from over his shoulder.

Samuel took two long strides and dropped to his knees beside Bessie, putting his fingers to her neck to feel for a pulse.

A Watch in the Night

"Get me a cold, wet cloth," he instructed Naomi, who stood hovering over them. "I think she fainted."

Naomi dashed into to the kitchen and grabbed the dishcloth that Bessie had used to wipe up the spilled coffee. She rinsed it quickly, wrung it dry, and then hurried back to where Samuel squatted next to Bessie, holding her head in the crook of his arm.

Naomi passed Samuel the dishrag and watched anxiously as he rubbed Bessie's forehead and face with the cold cloth. Bessie's eyelids fluttered several times, but she didn't open her eyes.

"Bessie, Bessie Whatley," Samuel said, lightly tapping the side of Bessie's face with the palm of his hand. "Can you hear me? Speak to me if you can."

Bessie didn't speak, but she opened her eyes. Naomi leaned in thinking that Bessie might respond to a familiar face. Bessie's eyes slowly came into focus.

"Naomi, is that you?" she croaked, trying to sit up.

"It's me," Naomi said.

Samuel lifted Bessie up into a sitting position. With Naomi's help, he was able to get her onto her feet, although she swayed and clung to his arm for support.

"Let's go into the kitchen," Naomi said, glancing inside the doorway at Lily's body lying on the bed. Samuel followed Naomi's eyes, saw the blood-stained sheet, and took Naomi's cue.

Samuel pulled Bessie in close to him, which shielded her eyes from the doorway. He walked her into the kitchen and lowered her into a chair that Naomi had pulled out from its spot at the head of the kitchen table.

Naomi smelled the coffee and then spied the percolator. Hurriedly, she searched the cabinets for a cup.

"This should help," Naomi said, as she placed a cup of steaming coffee on the table in front of Bessie. Bessie reached for the cup and tried to take a sip of the coffee.

Bessie's hands shook, and the coffee sloshed onto the front of her dress, which was already covered with a large stain. Naomi pulled up a chair next to Bessie and helped her to guide the cup to her lips.

With Naomi's help Bessie managed to get down several swallows of coffee before she motioned to Naomi to stop. Placing the cup on the table, Naomi turned to face Samuel, who had pulled up a chair on the side of the table opposite Naomi.

"Bessie, this here is the Reverend Samuel Taylor," Naomi said, nodding her head in Samuel's direction. "We've come to help."

Bessie looked up at Naomi and then over at Samuel, but she didn't speak.

"Do you remember last night, Bessie?" Naomi continued. Bessie dropped her eyes and stared intently into the cup of coffee. There was a long pause. Bessie's lower lip quivered.

"Not really," she finally said, without looking up. "When I woke up this mornin', I knew somethin' was wrong, bad wrong. I just weren't sure what."

Tears pooled in the corners of Bessie's eyes and then spilled over, rolling down her cheeks onto her soiled dress. Naomi pushed her chair up next to Bessie's chair and pulled her head down onto her chest.

"I never 'spected to find my Lily gone; I never 'spected *that,*" she sobbed into Naomi's breasts. Naomi rocked Bessie in her arms and let her cry. Samuel went to the sink and freshened up the cloth that he held in his hand with ice-cold water from the tap.

Bessie's sobs slowed down, and Samuel passed Naomi the wet cloth. Naomi pulled away from Bessie and used the wet cloth to stroke Bessie's forehead and cheeks.

"Bessie, do you remember the babies?" Naomi asked. When Bessie didn't answer, Naomi continued. "Lily had twins, a girl and a boy. You left 'em at my house last night. Do you remember that?"

"Not really," Bessie replied, keeping her head low on her chest.

Bessie squirmed in her seat and then rolled her swollen, bloodshot eyes up to look at Naomi. "I got to have me somethin' to steady my nerves. Would you reach up to that top shelf and hand me down that bottle," she said to Naomi. Bessie pointed a gnarled finger with a long, curved-under nail towards a cabinet over the sink. "Would you do that for me? Please Naomi," she begged.

Naomi and Samuel exchanged a troubled look. There was a lot to be done, and Bessie needed to be sober. But they could see Bessie's hands trembling and her head shaking. Her voice was pitiful and desperate.

Samuel made the decision. Standing, he opened the cabinet and retrieved a bottle of whiskey. He poured a splash into Bessie's coffee. Using both of her hands to guide the cup to her mouth, Bessie quickly drained the spiked coffee and set the cup back down in front of her. Samuel poured it half-full of straight whiskey.

"Bessie, where's Ephram? Naomi asked. Bessie sipped from the cup without answering.

"I'll look for him," Samuel said "You stay with her."

Samuel found Ephram sprawled across his bed. His eyes were open, but he didn't respond to Samuel's coming into the room. Samuel stationed himself at the foot of the bed.

"Mr. Whatley, I'm Reverend Taylor," Samuel said. "You've had some trouble come down on your house in the night, and I'm here to help. You need to get on up and out of this bed and come into the kitchen where we can talk."

Ephram didn't move. "Lily shoulda brung me my coffee by now," he said. "I swear that gal ain't good for nothin' these days."

"Lily won't be bringing the coffee," Samuel said. Ephram looked up at Samuel. His eyes were glazed and unfocused.

Samuel realized that he would have to force Ephram to move. Moving to the side of the bed, he took Ephram's arm and tried to pull him up. Ephram didn't help, but he didn't resist either.

The odor of urine, sweat and stale whiskey permeated upwards from the bed, and Samuel felt the muscles in his stomach tighten. He held his breath and managed to pull Ephram up onto his good leg, but Ephram wobbled and swayed.

Samuel spotted the crutch which rested against the head of the bed. Wrapping one arm around Ephram to steady him, he grasped the crutch with his other hand.

With the aid of the crutch, Samuel and Ephram managed a few steps towards the door before Ephram's strength and motivation failed him. He collapsed against Samuel, and the crutch went clattering to the floor.

Samuel fought to regain his balance, and hoisting Ephram over his shoulder, he plunged headlong towards the back of the house.

Samuel registered the shocked look on Naomi's face as he staggered past her and through the kitchen. He knew that if he stopped to explain that he would lose his forward momentum.

Pushing on, Samuel navigated the turn into the bathroom. He leaned against the wall to catch his breath before dumping Ephram into the shower stall. Ephram slid down the wall and plopped into a sitting position with his back against the wall of the shower. His head lolled to one side.

Ephram let out a blood-curdling howl when Samuel turned on the faucet, and the ice-cold water hit his face. Ephram struggled to climb out of the shower, but he was too weak.

After several seconds, Samuel turned the water off, and, with considerable effort, he managed to strip off Ephram's soggy clothes. A quick search of the room uncovered a bar of soap that

A Watch in the Night

Samuel used to lather up Ephram's body. Satisfied, Samuel left Ephram sitting in the shower covered with the soap. A good soak will do him good, Samuel thought.

"What in the world is going on?' Naomi asked when Samuel made another pass through the kitchen.

"Mr. Whatley decided that he needed to take a shower before he was fit to receive guests," Samuel said. "And he has opted to put on some fresh clothes."

Samuel returned to Ephram's bedroom and surveyed the situation. The room looked as if it had been hit by a tornado. Rummaging through the chest of drawers, Samuel was delighted to find what appeared to a clean pair of overalls and a flannel shirt.

When Samuel returned to the bathroom, Ephram was sitting complacently in the shower stall. Samuel gave him a second blast of cold water to rinse off the soap. This caused Ephram's head to spring forward, and he released a string of profanities as he clawed at the shower wall, trying to pull himself up the wall.

"Simmer down, and I'll turn off the water," Samuel said. Ephram quietened down, but his face remained contorted with rage.

Samuel used one arm to lift Ephram up and out of the shower; dropping the clothes he held in his other hand at Ephram's feet. Before leaving, Samuel laid Ephram's crutch across the top of the toilet bowl.

"Get dressed and come on into the kitchen," Samuel said. Ephram didn't protest. Ordinarily, he would have refused to follow orders given by anyone in his own house, especially somebody he didn't even know. But these weren't ordinary circumstances. The cold shower and a raging hangover had him subdued. He did as he was told.

When Ephram hobbled into the kitchen, Samuel pulled out the chair next to Bessie and ordered him to sit. He sat and Naomi passed him a cup of coffee. Ephram looked first at Bessie and then over at Samuel and Naomi, who now stood side by side next to the stove.

"Would some goddamn body tell me what the hell's goin' on here," he growled.

"I would thank you not to take the name of the Lord in vain in my presence," Samuel said tersely. "As for what's going on, last night your daughter died giving birth to twins."

Bessie stared down at the table sipping her whiskey. Neither she nor Ephram spoke.

"Sheriff Tate should be here soon," Samuel added.

While the news of his daughter's death left Ephram mute, the mention of Sheriff Tate's impending visit got an immediate response from him.

As a younger man, Ephram had on several occasions, found himself on the wrong side of the law. The last time this happened he had been sentenced to thirty days in the county jail. After that experience, Ephram made it a point to steer clear of the law.

"I don't want the goddamn sheriff out here," Ephram snarled. "Who the hell went and called the law?"

"It really doesn't matter what you do or do not want," Samuel replied. "The sheriff is coming. And that, sir, is that!"

Ephram hunkered down lower in his chair. He mumbled some obscenity under his breath before taking a loud slurp from his coffee cup.

"There's work to be done before the sheriff arrives," Samuel said, ignoring Ephram's last comment. "He'll send the Davis wagon out for Lily's body, I'm sure. So, we probably need to get together some clothes for her burial. And, more importantly, we need to decide what to do about the babies?"

Bessie and Ephram sat silently their eyes focused on the table. Naomi saw a tear plop into Bessie's cup. She took pity on her.

"Samuel, I think this has all been too much for Bessie and Ephram. They suffered the loss of their only child. Don't you think that it might be better if they laid back down to rest. I can get Lily's things ready. The babies will be alright for now."

"Perhaps, you're right," Samuel replied, also taking pity on the pathetic pair. "Wait here with them, Naomi."

Samuel returned to the bedroom. He stripped the sheets, flipped the mattress and cracked a window to let in some fresh air. He quickly passed back through the kitchen, gathered up the dirty clothes in the bathroom and deposited both clothes and sheets into a garbage can sitting on the back porch.

When he returned to the kitchen, Naomi stared at him stupefied.

"I tidied up a bit," he said, shrugging his shoulders.

"Alright by me," Naomi replied.

When Samuel attempted to help Ephram to his feet, Ephram shoved him away.

"Leave me be," he snarled up at Samuel. Samuel stepped back and away from Ephram, who used both of his hands to push up from the table.

Ephram swayed precariously. When he regained his balance, he poked the bottle of whiskey under his arm, gathered up his crutch and tottered off back to the front bedroom, muttering under his breath.

Naomi helped Bessie back to the sofa. "You rest up 'til the sheriff gets here," Naomi said. "And don't you worry none 'bout Lily's babies. I'll look after them."

CHAPTER FIVE

Sheriff Tate knew that he was getting too old for his job. He had been elected Sheriff of Trinity County more than forty years ago after serving for two years as a deputy sheriff under Frank Jakes. A rattlesnake killed Sheriff Jakes while he was out working in his garden. The snake struck him on his neck as he stooped to pick his tomatoes. Sheriff Jakes never had a prayer. When his wife found him, he was already dead; his head swollen twice its normal size.

The day after Frank Jakes' funeral the governor appointed Jonas Tate to serve out the remainder of Sheriff Jakes' term. He was just twenty-four years old and the only deputy in Trinity County at the time.

Some in Trinity said that he was too young for the job, but Sheriff Tate proved himself to be the right choice. For the next forty years, nobody ever ran against him in the election for sheriff. People in Trinity didn't like change.

Generally speaking, Sheriff Tate enjoyed his work. But during the past few years, he had suffered a plethora of health problems, and he had promised his wife that he would retire at the end of his current term. The Tates owned a small cabin out on the river. Their plan was to sell the house in town and live on the river.

He was not at all prepared for the shock of finding his dear and old friend Doc Adams dead on the side of the road. Over the years, the sheriff had come to view Doc as he viewed himself—as invincible. The sight of Doc Adams lying dead in the snow brought Sheriff Tate's health problems screeching to the forefront of his mind. At last count he had high blood pressure, gout and phlebitis in his leg.

On the drive into town, with Doc's body and car in tow, the sheriff contemplated his own mortality. It was a dismal picture. If Doc could up and drop dead, so could he. The sheriff decided that it was time to quit. Whatever time that he had left, it would be spent on the river with his wife, not on the roads of Trinity County.

As Sheriff Tate and his procession entered the outskirts of Trinity, people stood and stared. The sheriff knew that it wouldn't take long for people to put two and two together and figure out that Doc was gone.

They were sure to recognize Doc's car dangling from the wrecker. And then there was the wagon trailing behind. The phone would be ringing off of the hook at the Davis Funeral Parlor. He wanted to tell Mildred himself before she heard the news elsewhere.

The sheriff stayed with Mildred until she called Walter Jr. and her sister arrived. As he drove back into town, he remembered his encounter with Washington Ivey's widow that morning. She had been worked up over something.

He needed to go back out to Tate's Hell and speak with the Whatleys so that he could make an official report on Doc's death. Might as well go now and put the whole damn mess behind him. He could swing by the Ivey woman's place and see what was up with her. Kill two birds with one stone.

Sheriff Tate fumed as he drove back out to Tate' Hell. Damn bunch in Tate's Hell bred like rats. The town had lost its only doctor, and a good man at that, because Doc had gone out to deliver another brat in Tate's Hell.

Of course, that hard-headed old geezer Doc wouldn't listen to a damn thing he had to say. Hadn't he told him time and time again that it wasn't safe to go out alone like that at night. But Doc wouldn't listen. Now he was dead.

Sheriff Tate could feel his blood pressure rising. He would give that Whatley bunch a piece of his mind. It wouldn't bring Doc back. But cussing out the Whatleys would make him feel a whole helluva sight better, and right about now, he needed to feel better.

When the sheriff stopped the patrol car under the oak tree in the Whatley's front yard, he was surprised to see that Ivey woman and the Reverend Taylor headed towards the Whatleys' back door. Reverend Taylor was carrying a large cast iron pot. He got out of the car and called out to the pair. They stopped and waited for him in the yard.

"Mrs. Ivey, Reverend Taylor," Sheriff Tate said, nodding to them as he came close enough to speak.

"Sheriff," Samuel said, nodding back.

"What brings you out to Tate's Hell on such a cold day, Reverend?" Sheriff Tate asked Samuel.

"God's work does not depend on location or weather, sir," Samuel responded. "Mrs. Ivey came seeking my help this morning, and if rendering aid to others requires me to be in Tate's Hell on a cold day, then so be it."

"So, what's going on out here?" the sheriff asked, annoyed by the reverend's remark. He wasn't in the mood to banter with the reverend. He planned to cut right to the chase.

"It's cold out here. And we've got people inside who need feeding. I wouldn't want the stew that I'm carrying in this heavy pot to get cold. If it's all the same to you, Sheriff, I would prefer to answer your questions inside."

"Suits me," Sheriff Tate said. "Lead the way."

Samuel gave a perfunctory knock at the back door, but he didn't wait for a response before going in. He went straight into the kitchen and placed the pot on the stove. Naomi stayed as close as she could to Samuel; the sheriff made her nervous. Sheriff Tate brought up the rear.

A Watch in the Night

"Wait here," Samuel said to Sheriff Tate, "we'll get the Whatleys."

"Sure thing," he said and plopped down into a chair.

Bessie, who was lying on the couch, struggled to sit up when she saw Naomi and Samuel.

"Naomi, you help Bessie into the kitchen, and I'll bring Mr. Whatley," Samuel said.

In less than five minutes the group sat assembled around the kitchen table. Ephram made certain that he sat as far away from the sheriff as possible.

Naomi served the stew to Ephram and Bessie. Ephram attacked his food with all of the gentility of a hog at the trough while sneaking an occasional peek at the sheriff.

Bessie picked at her stew, pushing it around in the bowl with her spoon while she eyed the cabinet over the sink. As they ate, Samuel told the sheriff all that had happened.

"That 'bout explains it all," the sheriff said when Samuel finished. "Doc musta been headed back into town for help when he wrecked. His heart musta give out on him when he tried to walk back here."

The sheriff stood up. "I reckon we need to straighten out the mess we got here," he said. His voice hardened, and he looked sternly at Ephram. Ephram stared at the table afraid to look up.

"First, I'll get the Davis wagon to pick up the girl's body," Sheriff Tate said. Bessie winced at the mention of Lily's body but did not look up or speak.

"I don't suppose ya'll got nothin' saved up for an emergency." The sheriff directed this last comment to Ephram. Ephram slithered down lower in his seat and said. "Naw sir," we ain't got no money."

"I didn't think so," the sheriff said. "The First Baptists keep a fund for charity cases. I'll ask them to help out." Bessie shifted uncomfortably in her chair when she heard Lily referred to as a charity case.

"Ya'll gonna have to pay them back a little each month from your check," the sheriff said harshly, his eyes still fixed on Ephram. "If you don't pay, I'll come back out here to personally collect. It ain't right for God-fearing folks to bury your dead while ya'll waste your money on liquor. Your girl can have a spot in the city cemetery. It has a section for indigents."

Bessie looked up at him confused. "Indigent means for poor folks; the plot won't cost you nothin'."

"That just leaves us with the problem of what to do with the babies," he added. Bessie's face took on such a pitiful expression the sheriff's heart softened a bit towards her, but not Ephram. "Bessie, I don't 'spect you up to takin' on two babies."

"Do ya'll got any kin who can help you with the babies? If not, I reckon, the Davis wagon can take them over to the hospital. The welfare workers can take it from there."

"I got family over in Westberry that might help," Bessie answered hesitantly. "But I ain't spoke to them lately. I'd have to get in touch with 'em."

"What 'bout the father?" the sheriff asked.

When Ephram heard this question, his eyes flew up, and he shot Bessie a warning glance.

"We don't know nothin' 'bout the father," Ephram growled, his eyes fixed squarely on Bessie. "Lily went to work at Harry's Tavern. Next thing we knowed, she come up pregnant and quit. She never told us who the daddy was. And nobody never come 'round here to see 'bout her. Let the welfare people take them babies. Me and Bessie can't be bothered up with 'em."

The sheriff's angry eyes bore down on Ephram, who quickly looked away. The sheriff considered giving Ephram a piece of his mind. He considered knocking the sniveling, no-count bastard off of his chair. That's what he deserved for dropping his mess on somebody else to clean up.

A Watch in the Night

But Sheriff Tate reined himself in. His blood pressure was through the roof. And he didn't want to risk having a stroke. Lashing out at Ephram wouldn't change a thing.

"I'll let the welfare people take 'em," the sheriff said.

Bessie turned on Ephram, furious that he had been talking down Lily and her in the next room—dead. Anger gave Bessie the courage to speak up.

"I won't hear of them babies goin' to the welfare people," she said emphatically. Before Ephram could respond, she turned her eyes away from him and focused on the sheriff.

"It ain't right to give Lily's babies to the welfare people to be brung up by strangers," she said to the sheriff. "I know that I ain't able to raise 'em up myself, but I want them babies to go to blood kin, *not strangers.*"

Bessie's outburst stunned everyone. Naomi had already decided that the Whatleys were tempting fate when they didn't speak up properly as soon as the sheriff asked them a question. But this time Bessie had clearly crossed over the line.

She ought to be more mindful that she's from Tate's Hell, Naomi thought, which barely—just barely—raised her up a smidgen above the coloreds. A colored would never act out like this to the sheriff. The room was silent as everyone waited for the sheriff's reaction.

When the sheriff spoke, Naomi thought she might fall over. There wasn't a bit of heat in his voice when he answered Bessie, not a bit.

"Bessie, you've done gone and got yourself all worked up," he said. "I'm tellin' you right now to take holt of yourself and simmer down." This was all that the sheriff said to Bessie as a reprimand. But it was enough to signal the group that he had taken the situation back under control. Nobody else dared speak.

"We can decide who *keeps* the babies later," he added. "Our problem is caring for the babies now. You said this yourself, Bessie; you ain't up to the job. I don't see no way 'round sendin' 'em to the hospital. You can thrash out with the welfare people later who *gets* 'em."

The sheriff's voice was calm, not raging as Naomi expected. Heartened by the sheriff's kind demeanor, Naomi surprised even herself by speaking up.

"Sheriff," she said tentatively.

"Yes, Mrs. Ivey," he said, shifting his focus to her. "If you got somethin' to say, let's hear it."

There was a tremor in Naomi's voice, but she forced herself to speak. "If I wouldn't be out of line, I got somethin' to say 'bout the babies."

"Go right ahead, Mrs. Ivey," he said. "Judgin' from the story I just heard, I'd say that you've earned yourself the right to speak out."

"You think it'd be best to send the babies on over to the hospital," Naomi said. "And as the sheriff, you surely know best," she quickly added. She wanted to be certain that she gave the sheriff the proper amount of respect. Naomi had limited experience in dealing with white folks; and none in dealing with the law. She didn't want to overstep her bounds.

The sheriff sat listening, so Naomi continued. "I been 'round a good number of babies in my time, and them babies of Lily's look fine to me."

"Doc checked 'em over good. He said they's alright, just small, that's all. I can help Bessie out 'til she can talk to her kin. A couple of days ought not to matter. We could keep 'em here."

Samuel realized how important this was to Naomi. So, he tried to come to her rescue.

"I have to agree with Mrs. Ivey," he said. Samuel had considerable experience in dealing with white people, including those in authority, like the sheriff. When black folks got tangled up with the law, he was often called to "work things out." He spoke with confidence, not so easily intimidated as Naomi.

"My wife Abigail has been a midwife for years. Granted, she's not a doctor, but she said the same as Doc Adams. We can help by checking in on them."

The sheriff didn't stop him, so Samuel continued to plead his case. "We *are* pressing down on Christmas. I know the babies are too young to understand this, but it doesn't seem right to take them away from their own family, not at Christmas. God meant for families to stay together."

The room fell silent. Sheriff Tate appeared to the others to be pondering what they had said.

Finally, he spoke. "I don't know of no law that requires me to take 'em into the hospital 'less they in some kinda danger. And that don't appear to be the case here."

Bessie, Naomi and Samuel took heart from this comment and their faces brightened. Ephram sat sullen. Again, there was a long silence.

The sheriff directed his next remark to Bessie. "I got to call the welfare office 'bout the babies. That's the law. But maybe they can send somebody out here to check on 'em. I'm gonna agree to let you keep the babies here 'cause these folks are willin' to help you. But it's up to you to work out with the welfare people who keeps the babies."

"Thank you, Sheriff," Bessie said.

"Now, I want somebody to take me over to have a look at those babies," the sheriff said. "I got to make out an official report on Lily's death. Before I do, I wanta see the babies."

"We can walk with you over to the Ivey house," Samuel said, stepping up next to Naomi.

"Naomi," Bessie whispered. The spunk was clearly gone out of her. "I'd like to see the babies."

"If the sheriff doesn't object, we can all go over," Samuel said. Samuel did not want to usurp the sheriff's authority any more than he already had.

"I ain't got no problem with that," Sheriff Tate said, "but's let's get goin'." He was tired and hungry and ready to wrap this matter up.

"I ain't goin'," Ephram grumbled. "I don't see why ya'll makin' such a fuss 'bout them babies. It's me and Bessie that's gonna need help. Lily left us in a helluva mess."

"Let's go," the sheriff said, resisting once again the urge to drop down full force upon Ephram.

As everybody else filed out of the kitchen, Ephram stood up and reached for the bottle of whiskey he knew was in the cabinet.

Samuel led the way. Sheriff Tate followed closely on his heels. Halfway there, he stepped up beside Samuel to strike up a conversation. "Tate's Hell is a hard life; there's no denying that," the sheriff remarked.

"Life is what you make of it, Tate's Hell, or otherwise," Samuel replied.

The sheriff wasn't sure how to respond. He decided to forget about conversation and dropped back behind the reverend.

Naomi and Bessie walked slowly, a number of paces behind the sheriff. Bessie was weak, so Naomi helped her along. The reality of Lily's death was beginning to set in fast and hard with Bessie. When Bessie stumbled, Naomi gripped her arm to prevent a fall.

"I don't know how I'll get by without Lily," Bessie said.

"It will be hard, but you'll manage," Naomi replied. "I thought when I lost my boy that I couldn't live no more. But I did. God sets you on a hard path; then he shows you the way to travel it."

Bessie leaned into Naomi. "You'll find your way," Naomi said, squeezing Bessie's arm, although she wasn't at all sure this was true at the moment.

Abigail met them on the front porch. She had been watching out the front window for their return. Samuel placed his arm

A Watch in the Night

around his wife's shoulders. "Sheriff Tate and Mrs. Whatley have come to see the babies," he said.

"This is my wife, Abigail," Samuel said, turning to the sheriff and Bessie.

"Pleased to meet ya," the sheriff said politely. Bessie said nothing.

"Pleased to meet you, too," Abigail replied. "Try to be quiet as you come in. The babies are sleeping in the cradles."

As they entered the Ivey's front room, the group fanned out around the cradles. Sheriff Tate nodded at Karen, who sat in the rocker, but nobody attempted introductions.

"They're sure tiny," Sheriff Tate said softly. "Of course, I don't know much 'bout babies. Me and Mrs. Tate never had us no children. It come as a hard blow to my wife, but for my part, I reckon that you don't ever miss what you don't ever have."

"They're really not that small, considering they're twins," Abigail said.

"I ain't seen many twins," the sheriff said. "I don't recollect ever seein' a pair that had a girl and a boy."

As the sheriff spoke, Bessie inched closer to the cradles. Samuel and Abigail stepped aside to let her through. When Samuel saw that Bessie was trembling, he took her arm. "Mrs. Whatley," he whispered, "you sit in the rocker next to the cradles."

Bessie didn't sit. She stood staring down at her grandchildren. When she tried to kneel beside the cradles, Samuel tightened his grip on her arm and eased her down.

Bessie balanced herself by holding onto the girl's cradle with one hand. With her other hand, she reached out with calloused fingers to touch the soft skin of the baby's face.

"Oh Lily," she whispered in a voice too faint for anyone but Samuel to hear. He had knelt beside her to brace her up.

Abigail went into the kitchen, and when she returned, she had a bottle in each hand. She put her hand on Bessie's shoulder and leaned over to whisper into her ear. "Mrs. Whatley, it's time for the babies to eat. Would you like to help me feed them?"

Bessie didn't answer. She stared into the face of her granddaughter. Bessie's mind had peeled away the last seventeen years, and she was looking at Lily. She was back in that one perfect moment in her life when she had first looked into the face of her own child and hope had flickered faintly in her heart before it was snuffed out by the harsh reality of her life with Ephram in Tate's Hell.

Samuel reached out to touch Abigail on the shoulder, and she gave him a troubled look as they knelt one on either side of Bessie.

Emotion charged the room like an electrical current dancing around at the end of a loose, live wire. It touched one then another as they stood watching Bessie and the babies.

Sheriff Tate felt the tension. He had seen about everything, or so he thought, in his forty years as sheriff. He had witnessed more human suffering and misery than he liked to recall. He had learned to harden his heart and distance his feelings. That, he had found, was the only way to survive in his line of work.

But his own memories pressed in on him, until he felt like a trapped swimmer being pulled under by a current too powerful to fight.

He remembered his own mother who had died when he was a boy. The scent of her bath soap filled his nostrils, and the sweetness of her voice rang clearly in his ears. He realized in horror that he was experiencing a feeling that he thought he had buried in his mother's coffin. Sheriff Tate experienced the urge to cry.

Samuel broke the spell. "Help me, Abigail," he said. Together they lifted Bessie to her feet and then lowered her into the rocker.

A Watch in the Night

"Mrs. Whatley, would you like to help me feed the babies?" Abigail asked again. Bessie answered with an almost imperceptible nod of her head.

Samuel placed the baby girl into her arms. The baby squirmed and started to cry. Abigail placed the nipple into the baby's mouth and folded Bessie's fingers around the bottle.

The sheriff bolted towards the door. The cold air stung his face, mercifully bringing him back to his senses. The sun was gone and the temperature had fallen. He couldn't believe his eyes. The snow was back, swirling to the ground in gentle flurries. He heard the door open and close and looked over to see Samuel standing next to him.

"Well, I'll be damned," Sheriff Tate said. "It's snowin' again." He chuckled. "Even at my age, life still has a few surprises."

"Sheriff, I sincerely hope that you're not damned," Samuel said, also laughing. "And you're right. Life, at any age, is full of surprises. God works in mysterious ways. Sometimes, even I'm amazed at the road he places before us."

"Life can take some strange twists, if that's what you mean to say, Reverend," the sheriff said.

"But the mystery of life is the beauty of life for those brave enough to follow God's path," Samuel added, with a gleam in his eye. Both men stared at the falling snow.

"And God is at work here tonight," Samuel said, looking through the window at the cradles by the fire. "I don't pretend to know God's plan. But I believe that we have all witnessed one of God's miracles here this day."

"I don't know nothin' 'bout no miracle," the sheriff snorted. "But it has been one helluva day."

"Praise the Lord," Naomi said. The men had not seen her and Abigail join them on the porch.

"Praise the Lord, indeed," Abigail added.

"You can save that praise the Lord business for church on Sunday," the sheriff retorted. Religion always made him uneasy, and it was starting to sound like a revival out here to him.

"We got business to take care of," he barked. "Let's get to it. I'll send the Davis wagon out for the girl's body. Somebody needs to be there to meet them. Mrs. Whatley ain't up to it and that son-of-a-bitch Ephram is sure to be drunker than Cooter Brown by now.

"There's no need for cursing, Sheriff," Samuel said politely.

"Yeah right," the sheriff muttered.

"I'll see to Bessie," Naomi said.

"I'm gonna call the welfare people soon as I get back to town," the sheriff added. "But they only get over this way on ever other Tuesday. That means they probably won't be here 'til after Christmas. Can you folks hold out that long?"

"We can," Naomi said.

"Alright then, it's settled," the sheriff said.

"Only one thing left," the reverend added.

"What's that?" the sheriff said. He had assumed that everything was wrapped up. What could they possibly drop on him now?

"Relax, Sheriff, all I need is a small favor."

Sheriff Tate eyebrows shot up suspiciously.

"Would you mind dropping my wife at home?" Samuel asked. "We have five little ones, and in less than six hours it will be Christmas Eve. Mrs. Summers, our babysitter, reaches her high-water mark with five kids in just a few hours. My guess is that she's praying for relief by now."

Sheriff Tate's face softened. "No problem," he said, relieved that Samuel hadn't sprung some new crisis on him.

"But I want to get goin'," he added.

"I'm ready," Abigail said.

Naomi and Samuel stood in the yard and watched as Abigail and Sheriff Tate pulled away.

"Naomi," Samuel said, when the car was out of sight.

"Yes, Reverend," she answered.

"The next time I see your truck come careening into my front yard, I'm liable to turn and run out the back door. I've handled a lot of emergencies, but this one tops them all. Yes, Ma'am, I got to say that this one is the topper."

"And the next time I hear a knock on my front door at night, I'm liable not to open the door," Naomi replied.

Samuel swung his arm around Naomi's shoulders and pulled her in close to him. Together, they laughed.

"We are soldiers in God's army," he said, "and tonight we are on the march."

Sheriff Tate and Abigail drove silently back into Trinity. Abigail thought about her children. The sheriff thought about Tate's Hell.

It didn't surprise him that young girl had died. It was a shame, but it was hard to survive in Tate's Hell. That was simply the reality of the place. Over the years, he had adopted the view that it was best to let Tate's Hell take care of itself.

In fact, he had often said that it didn't matter how much time or money you put into Tate's Hell, it was always going to stay the same. Most people agreed with him, although nobody had ever spent any time or money to put his theory to the test.

That is, except for a few of the First Baptists. They had made one run at saving Tate's Hell, but they had quickly gone down in ignoble defeat. Sheriff Tate smiled as he remembered that episode.

Years back, some of the more sanctimonious members of the First Baptist Church, upon hearing instructions from the pulpit that one must be in love and charity with one's neighbor, decided to extend the loving arms of the church and embrace some of their less fortunate brethren residing in Tate's Hell. A committee was duly formed, co-chaired by the Widow Sparks and the pastor's wife.

The Committee's first official act of charity was a vote to deliver Christmas food baskets to those poor, lost souls in Tate's Hell. The Baptists did everything by a vote—they were democratic to a fault. Feed the body, and the spirit will follow. This was the theory used to justify the food baskets.

The Committee with the help of a few of its parishioners spent an entire week preparing the baskets. The Widow Sparks stayed up late on several nights baking fruitcakes. The baskets were slated to be delivered the week before Christmas.

The Committee, which consisted of the pastor's wife, Widow Sparks and John Duly, the retired postmaster, all agreed to go along when making the deliveries. There was safety in numbers, particularly in Tate's Hell, or so they thought.

The first stops went fairly well, although later the pastor's wife reported that she found the response of the selected recipients disappointing.

One family refused the basket altogether, and those who did accept did not appear at all grateful. The pastor's wife, failing to comprehend that gratitude is not an emotion often experienced by those doomed to scratch out a living in the swamp, took their ingratitude as a personal affront. She became lukewarm on the project early on into the trip.

But the Widow Sparks and Mr. Duly remained undaunted. and the Committee pressed on. After delivering four of the ten baskets, Widow Sparks and Mr. Duly felt flush with success.

That's when the Widow Sparks spied a number of rather pitiful and ragged looking children playing in front of a rundown shack. That shack was the home of Wiley Grantham and his family.

In a spontaneous and magnanimous gesture, the Widow Sparks suggested they make an impromptu stop at the Grantham home. They, after all, had an extra basket.

A Watch in the Night

The pastor's wife emphatically opposed the stop. Sheriff Tate had reviewed and approved all of the recipients well in advance of the delivery date. He had sternly warned them not to make any unauthorized stops. There must have been a reason for *that* she was quick to point out.

But the Widow Sparks and Mr. Duly found themselves consumed by the spirit of the season. Enamored with their own unselfish efforts on behalf of the downtrodden, they disregarded the concerns of the pastor's wife.

With one swift vote, they threw all caution to the wind and turned the church van into the Wiley's dirt driveway. That's when things "went to hell in a handbasket," the pastor's wife later reported.

Mr. Duly was quickly elected to make the call at the Grantham's front door. His job originally was to drive the van while the ladies handed out the baskets. He didn't like the idea of deviating from their plan. But, then again, this was an unplanned stop. They had already deviated by stopping. Reluctantly, he agreed to take the basket to the door.

He had barely cleared the running board of the van when he was met with a blast from Wiley Grantham's shotgun. Dropping the basket, he dove headlong back into the driver's seat and jammed the van into reverse. The Committee was speeding back to Trinity before Wiley had an opportunity to reload.

The Committee immediately reported the incident to Sheriff Tate as an attempted murder. When the sheriff heard the details of their story, he assured Mr. Duly that if Wiley Grantham had intended to kill him, he wouldn't be alive to report the shooting.

Wiley Grantham was as good of a shot as there was to be found in Trinity County. Wiley had fed his family for years by hunting the swamps of Tate's Hell the sheriff explained to the Committee.

What the sheriff stopped short of telling them was that when Wiley wasn't hunting, he kept himself busy by making moonshine. That's why he didn't want visitors. While the First Baptists *officially* took a staunch stand against liquor, most folks, including some of the Baptists, were content to leave the moonshiners alone.

"I warned you to stick to the route I mapped out," Sheriff Tate said. "You didn't have no business goin' up to the Grantham house. A man is entitled to his privacy."

The sheriff didn't want to arrest Wiley, not right here at Christmas. But there was no appeasing the Committee, short of picking up Wiley.

Reluctantly, the sheriff went on out to Tate's Hell and picked up Wiley. Later that same day Wiley appeared before Judge Adler. The Judge, who was known to occasionally partake of a swig or two of Wiley's moonshine, begrudgingly sentenced Wiley to ten days in the county jail.

With Wiley in jail, most of the men living in Tate's Hell, and some living in Trinity, faced the holiday season without their usual supply of holiday cheer. They were forced to drink Harry's over-priced, water-downed whiskey, or not drink at all. Not drinking at all wasn't an option.

Damned meddling Baptists they groused while sipping their whiskey at Harry's. *Who the hell would want a scrawny turkey and a fruitcake over moonshine.* "For God's sake you could shoot a turkey any day of the week in Tate's Hell," one drinker was heard to say.

While some of the First Baptists may have felt that it wouldn't be Christmas without one of Mrs. Small's fruitcakes, those who faced Christmas amid the rigors of Tate's Hell found that the holiday season went a little smoother with the aid of Wiley's home brew. Mrs. Small's fruitcake wasn't even a close second.

The lights from the parsonage brought the sheriff out of his thoughts. He pulled into the Taylor's front yard. Four small heads sat perched in the window.

A Watch in the Night

"Can I see you inside, Mrs. Taylor?" he asked.

"That won't be necessary, Sheriff, but thanks for the ride," she said, opening her door.

The sheriff waited until she was safely inside before backing out of the driveway. Davis Funeral Parlor was on his way home. As much as he hated to, the sheriff thought that he ought to stop in on his way through town.

Sheriff Tate parked the car at the back door of the funeral parlor next to the wagon, its black paint glowing in the light. It had already been cleaned and polished since bringing in Doc's body. He walked through the back door and down the long hallway into the front room. He didn't see or hear anyone. The place made him shiver. It's cold as an icebox in here, he thought, buttoning up his coat.

"Anybody here," he called. There was no answer. He turned and walked towards the back where Davis had installed the embalming room.

"Anybody here," he called, louder this time.

James Davis stepped out of the embalming room. "Why, Sheriff, if you don't stop hollering like that, you're liable to wake up the dead," he said, smiling at the sheriff.

The whole Davis clan was a despicable lot as far as the sheriff was concerned. He particularly disliked James. His crude attempt at humor, especially at the expense of his old buddy, Doc Adams, who was lying stretched out on the embalming table, added to the sheriff's disdain for James.

Pulling an apron over his head as he walked, James approached the sheriff. Under the apron, he was dressed in his customary black suit, although his jacket was missing and the sleeves of his white shirt were rolled up to his elbows.

As he drew closer, the sheriff noticed that James' skin was flabby and white, and his lips were too red, as if he had smeared on some cheap lipstick. James had the look of a man who spent too much time indoors and not enough time on hard work to suit the sheriff.

James dropped his smile. He made a business out of reading people, and he saw that the sheriff wasn't in the mood for humor. Better to play it straight, although inside he felt like grinning.

He was delighted to have a visit from the sheriff. It could mean only one thing—more business. James was the front man for the Davis operation, and although it was a little too uncouth to admit to in public, he loved his work.

One of his many duties included guiding the recently bereaved through the treacherous straits of sending their dearly departed out of this world and into the next. James' angle was to hone in on the need for the family to pay the proper amount of respect to the deceased. And pay they did. The funeral business was a racket, and a good one at that.

Sheriff Tate had fallen victim to James' con, learning his lesson about funeral homes and funeral directors the hard way, when he had arranged a funeral for his father earlier in the year. This was the first time the sheriff had seen James since his father's funeral.

James had greeted him on that occasion dressed in what appeared to be the same black suit he had on today. He realized that he had never seen James outside of a funeral setting. He wondered if James slept in that black suit.

James always used the same *modus operandi*. After expressing his sincere condolences and exalting the virtues of the deceased, he ushered the mourners down a long hall to the casket showroom.

He walked slowly, with his head slightly bowed. There was a reason for the slow, long walk. He used this time to ferret out if the deceased had life insurance, how much and the identity of the named beneficiary. Even the poorest of people in Trinity usually carried life insurance. But just enough to pay for the cost of a funeral.

By the time James and the mourners reached the showroom, James invariably had a good feel for finances and the identity of the family member controlling the purse strings.

This allowed him to maneuver the bereaved to the right casket. The cheaper caskets sat at the entrance to the showroom. They were almost exclusively for show. He rarely actually sold one of these.

James hurried the family past these caskets as if he were embarrassed they were even in the showroom. As they passed, he assured the family that he wouldn't waste any of their time here. Those caskets were for others he said somberly; but certainly not appropriate for their dearly beloved. The phrase "dearly beloved" got a lot of work in his presentation.

James was so skillful and his delivery so smooth that usually the family members were too ashamed to even so much as cast a glance in the direction of the cheaper coffins. Their fear of bringing disgrace down upon the head of their *dearly beloved* kept them moving.

He always stopped in front of a casket priced on the high end of what he knew the family could afford. Once there, he let go, full force, with his standard sales' pitch.

The theme of his pitch never varied. A funeral was the family's *last chance* to express their love for the *dearly beloved*. What better expression of that love than to send the *dearly beloved* out of this world and into the next in style for all to see.

James hammered home the phrases *last chance* and *all to see* to seal the deal.

He was slick. It was as easy for him as taking candy from a baby. Before getting out of his clutches, the family had usually signed a contract purchasing a funeral far beyond what they could afford to pay.

For those who couldn't pay up front, the Davis Funeral Parlor offered the family a special accommodation—financing.

What James neglected to tell the family, but instead put into the small print on the back of the contract, was the fact that the Davis Funeral Home accommodated the family by charging them a down payment sufficient for the Davis family to make a handsome profit.

On the remaining sums, Davis charged them the highest rate of interest allowed by law. It often took the family years to pay the bill. No wonder that the Davis family was one of the richest families in town, running a distant second to the Hillmans.

James was good. So good that he was even capable of putting one over on someone as worldly as Sheriff Tate. At the time that he had signed the contract, Sheriff Tate knew that he was being pressured. Still, James somehow managed to get the better of him.

Weeks later, when he and Mrs. Tate had to dip into the family savings to pay the balance on the bill, Sheriff Tate knew that he had been right. James had conned him—the sheriff.

Sheriff Tate was much too proud to complain that he had been taken in by James. He was the sheriff, after all. He should have known better. But he had vowed to himself not to forgive or forget the con. A day of reckoning was coming. James just didn't know it yet.

"Whatever brings you here?" James asked, wiping his hand on a cloth tucked into his belt buckle before extending it towards the sheriff to shake as if they were long-lost friends. Short of being downright rude, Sheriff Tate couldn't see any way around taking James' outstretched palm. He gave it a quick pump.

The sheriff was immediately repulsed. James' hand was smooth and soft, and he had returned the sheriff's quick, but firm, grip with only a weak little squeeze.

James' fingers were damp and clammy, and the sheriff resisted the urge to wipe his own hand on his pants. Instead, he jammed his hands into his pockets rubbing them against the

A Watch in the Night

lining as he thought to himself that he didn't even know any women with hands as smooth and soft as James'.

Sheriff Tate wanted to be done with this business and to get out of this room and away from James as quickly as possible. He regretted that he had not simply telephoned and made a mental note not to make this mistake again.

"I'm here on business," the sheriff said. "Ephram and Bessie Whatley's daughter died last night. I want you to go on out and pick up the body."

Sheriff Tate couldn't help but notice the little smile that formed on James' lips before he got himself under control and molded his face back into his permanent expression of sympathy and grief. "Oh, I *am* sorry to hear that," he replied. "Do I know the Whatleys?"

"You probably don't know them, but I'm certain that you're still real sorry to hear about their loss," the sheriff said. "You'll be even more sorry to hear that the Whatleys live in Tate's Hell and don't got a pot to piss in. I'm going to ask the First Baptists to put up some money out of their charity fund to lay her away. You might as well know right up front that it won't be much. We can bury her in the county cemetery as an indigent."

"But, of course, we can handle the arrangements," James said without any change in his facial expression or tone of voice. "Always glad to help a neighbor in need."

"Yeah, right," the sheriff said.

"I've got to finish up with Doc Adams," James said. "I'm preparing him for the viewing myself. My guess is that the whole town will turn out. But never mind about that. One of the drivers can take the wagon out to pick up the Whatley girl's body."

"Fine," the sheriff said, turning to leave. But Davis was not finished yet. He blocked the sheriff's retreat.

"Isn't it a shame our losing Doc Adams," James crooned. "The telephone has been ringing off of the hook ever since the wagon brought him in.

"Some folks think that we're a newspaper instead of a funeral home. They started calling as soon as the wagon and the wrecker cleared town. I hear there will be an announcement about Doc's passing on the Reverend Samuel Spears' Inspirational Hour this evening."

Sheriff Tate didn't answer, but instead, he abruptly pushed past James to leave. As soon as the sheriff stepped outside of the door, James discarded his contrived look of sympathy and broke into a broad grin as he walked back over to the embalming room.

"Rude old bastard," he said to Doc Adams' body. "But that's alright. I made a good profit on his old man's funeral. And from the looks of him, I wouldn't be surprised if the wagon doesn't come bringing him in before long. I'll make another handsome profit there."

James hummed as he applied a smidgen of rouge to Doc Adams' cheeks for color. The visit by the sheriff had greatly enhanced his already jovial mood. Two funerals in one week. Business was booming. And he still had the usual holiday car wrecks, shootings and stabbings to look forward to.

Too damn bad that Whatley girl was a charity case, he thought. Can't make much on that. But Doc Adams, now that was another story. His funeral ought to be a real humdinger.

"Damn, I love my work," he said to Doc's body as he finished him up by plastering Doc's few strands of remaining hair down to his forehead with hairspray.

He was absolutely exuberant as he looked at his finished product. He put Doc's old black medical bag beside him. Perfect. Simply perfect.

CHAPTER SIX

The house was quiet when Naomi and Samuel went back inside. The babies were sleeping; one in Bessie's lap, the other on Karen's shoulder.

Naomi looked around thinking that too much had happened for just a single day to have passed.

Time, as it is apt to do in a crisis, had become all distorted. Life could change in one split second; she knew that. But even knowing this, it always came as a surprise when it did.

Less than twenty-four hours ago, she and Karen had been alone. Now they had the company of two newborns. She sat down on the end of the sofa to catch her breath. She was deep in her thoughts when she heard Samuel speak.

"Mrs. Whatley needs to rest," he said. "I'll walk her home, wait for the Davis wagon and then follow it back into town. If you can hold down the fort tonight, we'll be back tomorrow."

"We can manage," Naomi said. She braced herself on the arm of the couch and boosted herself up. Her joints ached, and her eyes felt heavy.

"I'll take the baby," she said to Bessie. "Reverend Taylor will take you home."

Naomi lifted the baby from Bessie's arms and laid her in the cradle. A sharp pain shot up Naomi's back. She walked Samuel and Bessie to the door where she heard the crunch of frost and ice under their feet as they started down the path.

Closing the door, she turned to Karen, who had placed the boy in his cradle. "I'll sleep on the sofa here by the babies," Naomi said.

"I won't hear of that," Karen replied. "Tonight, you sleep in your bed. I'll take the night watch."

"I won't argue," Naomi said. "I'm bone weary. But wake me up for the next feedin'."

As Naomi got ready for bed, she briefly saw headlights on the lane before they turned towards the Whatleys. The wagon had come for Lily. She still found it hard to believe that Lily was gone.

Karen was still awake when the clock chimed midnight. It was Christmas Eve. She thought about her father. He had so loved Christmas. The Hillman Lumber Company gave its employees Christmas Eve and Christmas day off. These were the only two days of the year that Washington could devote entirely to his family. He cherished that time.

Each Christmas Eve her father would get up before daylight and build a fire; then he would awaken his children. She and Nathan would scurry into the living room, wrapped in blankets, where they would dress by the warmth of the fire.

Tonight, she could almost hear her father's voice as she stared into the fire: "You youngens get up. The sun'll be up soon. Christmas don't just happen. We got to make it happen. Shake a leg."

As the sun came up over the horizon, she and her brother would be tromping along beside their father headed to the clearing in back of their house.

Washington carried a shotgun slung over his shoulder and pulled a sled loaded with an ax and ropes. Her father had a long stride and walked at a brisk pace. Every few steps, she and Nathan had to break into a slow trot to stay up with him.

Her father was at home outdoors. He had a name for all of the plants, trees and wildlife. They weren't scientific names that a person educated by books would use, but practical names passed down from one generation to the next.

A Watch in the Night

She and Nathan learned to love the outdoors as much as their father. She remembered how vividly Nathan's letters home had described the jungles of Vietnam, never mentioning the hardships of the war.

The trip to the clearing started on a path at the edge of the backyard. Enormous oaks, some of them over one hundred years old her father had said, bordered the path.

The massive, moss-covered limbs of the oaks intertwined high above the ground to form a canopy, which blocked most of the light on the path, even in the winter.

For her, this path was a dark, mysterious tunnel, and she had always moved closer to her father as they entered the path. But this was not true for Nathan. He had no fear of the woods. He had always skipped ahead of them calling back for them to hurry up.

After several hundred yards, the stand of oaks became less dense, yielding to tall, swaying pines, palmetto bushes and an occasional cabbage palm. Here the sunlight made the path bright and cheerful, and she would run ahead to catch her brother.

But they would go only as far as the swamp. Even the seemingly fearless Nathan was ten or eleven years old before he was brave enough to pass by the swamp without having his father close by.

She was a teenager before she felt safe enough to not hold her father's hand. The path circled the swamp for less than a quarter of a mile. But as a child she had viewed that quarter of a mile as a distance much greater.

Cypress trees grew out of the swamp, with thick, tangled roots that clutched at the bog below like the outstretched fingers of a giant hand.

The murky water shimmered in the sunlight under blooming lily pads and clumps of sawgrass reeds. During the winter months, ducks, red-beaked coots and other small water fowl, which had migrated south for the winter, languished on the water.

Raccoons, with black-banded heads that made them look like troops of small roving bandits, prowled the banks of the swamp looking for food. A sharp eye could occasionally spot an osprey or maybe even a bald eagle as it sat majestically guarding its nest wedged into the limbs of a dead tree.

She and Nathan knew that alligators, some ten to twelve feet in length, lived in the swamp submerged below the tranquil water. Their father had told them this.

And snakes, black bears, bobcats and panthers all lived here. He had told them that, too. But none of this frightened them so long as their father walked beside them.

Once they were past the swamp, she and Nathan bounded full speed ahead to the clearing. It was here that they would find their Christmas tree.

The clearing was a bright oasis surrounded by a sea of green and brown forest. The center of the clearing was filled with sage, ferns, palmettos, wax myrtles and pine saplings. These had quickly sprung up to reclaim the land after the timber was cut.

Evergreens—loblolly pines and juniper—bordered its edges. Each year, they chopped one of the evergreens for their Christmas tree.

The children selected the tree after much debate and bickering. If they couldn't agree, Washington made the call.

He chopped the tree with a few swift strokes from his ax, and together, they tied it on the sled to carry home. That evening the family trimmed the tree with their handmade ornaments.

She had never missed a year going with her father to find a tree. Even the year that Nathan died, they still made the sojourn.

It had been difficult for both she and her father, but they had never even considered not going. Time does not heal all wounds; her brother's death had taught her that lesson.

A Watch in the Night

But it does lessen the pain. As the years passed after her brother's death, her grief turned from a fierce, searing pain into a dull, relentless ache. It was a pain that she learned to accommodate, like a missing limb. Over time, she found joy, once again, in the Christmas tree ritual, even without Nathan.

Her mother never joined them on the search for the tree. It was her father's time to be with his children. But Naomi always greeted them on the porch when they returned, heaping praise on the tree before hustling them into the kitchen to heap pancakes and sausage on their plates.

After breakfast, her mother had to leave for work. Her mother had not always worked; she had stayed at home until Karen started the first grade.

But her mother only worked for a half day on Christmas Eve, and this was time that she and Nathan had exclusive rights to their father.

Before leaving for work, Naomi laid out her family's Sunday best. The Hillman Lumber Company hosted an annual Christmas party for its employees on Christmas Eve. Washington always took his family, although when Naomi started to work it was just him and his children.

They went because the unspoken word was that the party was mandatory. Otherwise, Washington would have spent the day at home. But, even so, they always managed to have a good time. Washington was prideful when it came to his family. He enjoyed a chance to show them off.

The entire town turned out, blacks and whites. It was one of the few occasions where blacks and whites mingled socially. Even those people who didn't work for the Hillmans were expected to attend.

While most people believed that the Hillmans were more conceited than magnanimous, and that the party was nothing more than an opportunity for them to flaunt their wealth, they still came. Nobody wanted to offend the Hillmans.

Besides, the food was free and although alcohol was not allowed (the party was held at the First Baptist recreation hall and the Baptists would not stand for alcohol on church property), any of the men who wanted a free drink could walk across the street to the Amoco parking lot where a bottle of Wiley Grantham's moonshine was passed around. That is, of course, except for that one year when Wiley spent the holidays in jail, thanks to the First Baptists.

The Ladies Home Auxiliary decorated the recreation hall for the party. The focal point of the decorations was a large Christmas tree placed in the center of the room.

The tree was wrapped with strand after strand of twinkling, colored lights and then all available space on the branches was draped with store-bought Christmas ornaments, the theory being that more is better, particularly where the Hillmans were picking up the tab.

Under the tree, the ladies placed small brown bags filled with an apple, an orange, several pieces of hard candy and a small toy. The bags were tied at the top with a red or green ribbon.

Karen had always thought that they were the best-looking family at the party. It was only after she grew older that she appreciated the effort her mother put into dressing them for the occasion.

Many nights, long after her children were in bed, her mother had stayed up by the fire hand-stitching her family a new suit of clothes for the party.

Naomi starched and ironed Washington's white shirt until it could stand up on its own. She polished their shoes until they glowed. Like her husband, Naomi was prideful when it came to her family.

"Nobody's gonna say my family looks second best," she would say as she admired her husband and children all decked out for the party. "Not so long as I draw a breath."

A Watch in the Night

But it wasn't the new clothes that made her proud. It was her father. He stood tall, straight, sturdy—as solid and majestic as the big oak that he so loved in their front yard.

The starched shirt stretched tautly across broad shoulders rippled with muscles strong and firm; the fabric bleached to a pure white set off his skin, which was smooth and the color of rich, dark mahogany.

When he smiled, which was often, his coal black eyes danced in the light. Karen was as prideful as her parents when she walked into the party holding her father's hand.

Mr. Hillman donned a Santa costume for the party, and with the help of his family, he distributed the bags to the children.

Bags with green ribbons were for the boys, and bags with red ribbons were for girls, although some years the ladies would miss the count, and a boy might find himself disappointed to open a bag with a plastic necklace or a girl might cringe to find marbles in her bag.

Santa's grand entrance into the recreation hall was the signal for everyone to take their places, and parents herded their children into a line in front of Santa's throne.

Mrs. Hillman and the Hillmans' daughter, Missy, who always wore matching holiday outfits ordered from a catalog, stationed themselves at the front of the line to the right of Santa's throne.

Before receiving a bag, the children had to shake Mrs. Hillman's hand and give their names. Mrs. Hillman then presented each child to Santa, who gave that child a bag.

Most of the children, including Karen and Nathan, felt fearful and intimidated by the Hillmans, even if Mr. Hillman was dressed like Santa and Mrs. Hillman was the keeper of the bags. The children agreed to participate only after some urgent prodding by their parents.

Karen was shy and refused to stand in the line at all unless Nathan stood next to her, and her father strategically positioned himself in the crowd where she could see his face at all times. She would have never had the courage to step forward and receive the bag without a reassuring wink from her father.

Karen remembered with revulsion Mrs. Hillman's handshake. She could almost feel her soft, plumb fingers with those long, red nails close about her own hand.

Mrs. Hillman grasped her hand lightly and then gave it a slight, almost imperceptible, little squeeze. As a child, she had wondered if this fleeting touch was brought on by Mrs. Hillman's fear of the dread *cooties* that Karen had heard so much about in school.

The Hillman's youngest child, Trey, dressed in a stiff white shirt, green velvet trousers and polished black boots stood at attention to the left of his father. She remembered him as looking more like a toy soldier than a boy. His job was to retrieve the bags from under the tree and pass them to his father.

Trey's face never cracked a smile, and his eyes constantly blinked with a nervous twitch as he picked up the bags and thrust them over on his father's command.

It was plain to see that Trey was uneasy in the presence of his father. And although she had admired those soft velvet trousers, and those shiny black boots that came all the way up to Trey's knees, she wouldn't have traded places with him for anything in the world.

Karen's eyes traveled around the room. On the mantle sat a framed photograph. It held a picture of her father with her and Nathan as small children. A photograph taken at the Christmas party, purchased with odd jobs—precious dollars—and then secretly stashed, retrieved months later as an anniversary surprise for her mother.

Her father's death had come as a crushing blow to Karen. It was as unexpected and devastating as a sudden hurricane blowing in from the Gulf.

A Watch in the Night

When he died, she felt as if she had lost her anchor in life, cut adrift to flap and flounder about in turbulent winds, unable to find her way back to the shore.

The sound of a child's whimper brought Karen out of her thoughts. The girl stirred in her cradle. Karen smiled down at her, giving the cradle a push before she went into the kitchen to warm the bottles.

If she could manage to feed them one at the time, get the girl fed and back to sleep before she roused her brother, then there would be no need to wake her mother.

Her mother needed the rest. Although Naomi waged a valiant battle against old age, Karen could see subtle changes in her mother, especially since her father's death.

He had been her anchor, too. Since her father's death, she noticed that her mother's steps were a little slower, her shoulders more stooped. Often, she discovered her mother, staring off into space, lost in her thoughts.

Even when Karen managed to fall asleep, she slept fitfully, listening for the slightest sound from the babies. She fed and changed them once in the wee morning hours. Then she was up with them again just before daybreak. This time as she fed the babies an idea formed in her mind.

The babies fell back asleep after eating. Karen, however, was fully awake so she quietly retrieved her coat and hat after deciding to follow through on her earlier idea.

As the first light of morning started to brighten the sky, she slipped out the back door and crossed the backyard pulling her father's sled, which she found by the woodpile.

This was an adventure. Karen had never gone to the clearing without her father. As far back as she could remember, he had warned his children to never go on the path alone. Warnings that were unnecessary for her. Until this morning, she had never felt even the slightest urge to go it alone.

As soon as she left the backyard and entered the path, fear started to nibble at her heart. She fought the urge to abandon her plan and turn back. But she didn't. She kept going. With each step, she became a little more confident, a little calmer. Excitement began to replace fear. She wanted to do this.

She stepped from beneath the oak canopy and her breath caught in her throat. A light film of snow covered the landscape.

Snow on palmetto bushes. It was a magnificent sight. It lifted her spirits and dispelled her fears. "Christmas don't just happen. You got to make it happen," her father's deep voice whispered in her ear.

Naomi sat up in bed and stared at the clock. She was shocked to see that it was seven o'clock in the morning. She couldn't remember the last time that she had slept so late.

Sunshine streamed in through the windows giving the room a warm and cheerful glow. Falling back on her pillow, she pulled the warm covers up around her, savoring a few more minutes in bed.

The babies! Wide awake now, she sprang out of bed, pulling on a robe as she rushed into the living room. All was quiet.

A fire burned hot and bright in the fireplace, and had it not been for the two cradles sitting next to the fire, she could have, perhaps, persuaded herself that yesterday had been a dream. She leaned over to look into the cradles. The babies were asleep.

Returning to her room, she quickly pulled on a dress and sweater and swept her hair back into a bun. She expected to find Karen in the kitchen, but she wasn't there.

Probably out getting more wood, Naomi thought. She would put on the coffee and go help her. Duke's raucous barking drew her to the window.

Naomi was shocked to see Karen emerge from the path, pulling Washington's sled behind her. It had a tree tied on its top.

A Watch in the Night

A broad grin erupted across her face as she went out to meet her daughter. Karen dragged the sled the last few feet to the porch, untied the tree and placed it upright on the ground.

It stood at least a full foot over her head. She carried it onto the porch and laid it at her mother's feet like a birddog dropping its kill.

"What in the world is goin' on girl?" Naomi asked.

"I don't know why you are actin' so surprised," Karen said, returning her mother's grin. "We always get our tree on Christmas Eve."

"You can't understand why I'm surprised," Naomi retorted, mocking Karen. "I wake up an hour later than usual to find two sleepin' white babies in my livin' room, and my own child done gone off trompin' through the woods, alone, to chop a Christmas tree. And me not even rememberin' that it's Christmas Eve."

"It's the babies' first Christmas. I just thought that we could try to make it a little special," Karen said.

"You got a heart of pure gold—just like your daddy," Naomi said. "Now come on in out of this cold. I don't know 'bout you, but I'm starved and so are two others."

The sound of the babies' cries floated through the kitchen and out onto the porch. "And here is one of the first rules of motherhood," Naomi added, "babies eat first."

Karen and Naomi fed the babies together and then sat down to have their own breakfast. A knock at the back door took them by surprise.

Naomi and Karen exchanged a puzzled look, before Naomi shrugged her shoulders and then went to open the door. There stood Bessie in a fresh dress with her hair brushed and pinned back with two combs.

"I hope it ain't too early to come callin'," she said, "but I couldn't wait no longer to see the babies."

"Of course, it ain't too early," Naomi answered, holding the door open and beckoning for Bessie to come inside. "We was havin' our breakfast. Why don't you join us?"

"No. I don't aim to be no bother," Bessie was quick to say. "I just wanted to check on the babies."

"Well, they're fine. We just fed 'em. They are in sleepin' by the fire. You're more than welcome to see 'em," Naomi said.

"Don't let me mess up your breakfast. I can wait," Bessie muttered, standing awkwardly by the door.

Naomi pulled out a chair for Bessie. "If you won't eat breakfast, at least have a cup of coffee."

"Thank you," Bessie said. She walked with some trepidation into the kitchen where she sat on the edge of the chair Naomi held out for her.

Karen poured the coffee and sat the cup in front of Bessie. Bessie's hand shook as she brought the cup to her mouth. "I'm still a little weak," she mumbled. "I didn't sleep much. I was up when they took Lily." Tears pooled in Bessie eyes and Naomi passed her a cloth.

"I can't hardly believe that she's gone," Bessie said. "I woke up this mornin' 'spectin' to hear her in the kitchen. Then I remembered that she's gone."

Naomi remembered that feeling well. That one brief moment of peace each morning before you realized that the one you loved so dearly was gone forever.

"It was a long time after Nathan died that he wasn't my first thought each mornin'," Naomi said. "But that will pass. God will show you the way." Naomi patted Bessie's hand as she spoke.

Karen wanted to change the subject. "It's Christmas Eve, Bessie," she said. "We've decided to celebrate. You could stay on and help us with the babies, if you're willin'."

"Christmas. That slipped my mind," Bessie said, a little more at ease. "I'll do what I can to help out with the babies. I'd like that."

Naomi spent the morning cooking. She had always found solace in the kitchen. To make a real Christmas dinner, she would need more groceries. But she didn't want to risk driving into Trinity. They would make do.

After lunch, Karen placed the tree in the same corner where it stood every year. The pungent fragrance of evergreen blended with the aroma of Naomi's cooking gave the women's spirits a lift.

Karen brought the ornaments in from the shed although she found it difficult to actually open the box. It was full of memories.

The snow stayed on the ground, and after a brief showing from the sun, the day turned overcast. The Taylors had left plenty of supplies for the babies. But still, Naomi expected a visit from them. Samuel had said they were coming, and Naomi knew him to be a man of his word.

The sound of a car engine startled Karen as she was bending over the woodpile gathering up logs. Looking up, she spotted the Taylor's station wagon coming up the drive.

She rushed inside, dropped the wood into the bin and called out to Naomi, who was in the kitchen, that they had company.

Naomi hurried out of the kitchen, drying her hands on the tail of her apron. Joining Karen on the front porch, they stood waving as the Taylor's wagon circled down the lane and into their yard. Reinforcements were a welcome sight.

When the car stopped, all four doors immediately popped open, and the entire Taylor clan tumbled out.

"Merry Christmas," Samuel called, before lifting the door to the back of the wagon and loading every Taylor child with a bag or a box. Abigail brought up the rear of the brigade, carrying the baby.

"For heaven's sake, what's goin' on here?" Naomi asked. The children, being unfamiliar with the territory, scurried behind their father.

"Naomi, why are you asking such a ridiculous question?" Samuel asked, giving his family a conspiratorial wink. "You know as well as the next that it's Christmas Eve.

"We decided with all of the excitement going on around here that you probably haven't had a chance to get ready for Christmas. So, we decided to pitch in and help.

"You've got to agree that it just wouldn't be right for the babies to miss out on celebrating their first Christmas, even if they are too young to know the difference.

"One day, at the very least, we'll have a good story to tell them. I put my troops to work," Samuel said, waving his hand over his children, "and here we are."

"I don't know what to say, Samuel. You've already done so much," Naomi said.

"Don't be foolish, Naomi. You don't need to say anything. It's the Lord's work that I'm doing, not my own. The fact that I'm enjoying myself immensely is an extra blessing for me.

"Besides, when I told my children about the babies, they wouldn't let up on me until I brought them here to see the babies themselves."

"Come on inside," Naomi said. "It's too cold out to have these children tarryin' here on the porch."

Abigail and the children fell into step behind Samuel and paraded through the door Karen held open for them. Abigail looked like a mother duck leading her brood.

Once inside, they placed their bags and boxes on the kitchen table. Naomi spied the legs of a turkey sticking out of one box.

"My Lord," she said "it looks like you done gone and brung enough to feed an army. But we can't take this food 'less ya'll agree to join us for Christmas dinner. You've brung enough for us all. And I got some Christmas fixings here myself."

Abigail looked at her husband and then back over at Naomi. "Are you sure, Naomi?" Samuel asked. "You've got your hands full already. We're a family of seven, and some of our younger members can be a bit rowdy, particularly on an exciting day like Christmas. Having us for Christmas would mean a lot of work, and I daresay aggravation for you."

"Nonsense. Having ya'll won't be no trouble a'tall," Naomi replied. "A couple of days ago me and Karen faced our first Christmas without Washington.

"I don't mind tellin' you, things looked pretty bleak. The two of us mopin' 'round like we done saw our last good day. We can all pitch in. Christmas is a time for fellowship. Please join us."

"Mama's right," Karen chimed in. "We want you with us. A house full of people, includin' rowdy little ones, is just what the doctor ordered."

"What do you think?" Samuel said to Abigail.

"I think that it's settled," she replied with a big grin. "We're having Christmas dinner here."

"Let's go on in by the fire," Naomi said, "and warm these youngens up."

Bessie crouched down lower into the rocker positioned next to the cradles where the babies were sleeping.

"Mrs. Whatley, how are you feeling today?" Samuel asked.

"I reckon I'm 'bout as good as can be 'spected," she replied.

"Let the Lord be your strength," Samuel said, patting her shoulder.

"Now, I don't believe that you've met my children. Allow me to introduce them." Samuel turned to face the children who were all huddled behind Abigail.

Abigail stepped aside, and Samuel placed his hands on the head of each child as he called that child's name.

"This is my oldest son, Ezekiel; my second son, Joshua; my third child, Mary; and her younger sister, Magdalene. These are their Christian names, but they answer to Zeke, Josh, Mary and Maggie.

"In fact, if you call out their Christian names, they're liable to suspect trouble because we only use those names for emphasis—when extra attention is required. Oh, and that little guy asleep in his mother's arms is our youngest, Jeremiah. We call him Jerry."

The children grinned shyly. They liked the roll call.

"Children, this is Mrs. Whatley," Samuel said, smiling over at Bessie.

"It's nice to meet ya," Bessie said awkwardly. She did not like so much attention focused on her. Naomi came to her rescue.

"If you children could be so kind as to satisfy an old lady's curiosity," she said, "how old are you youngens now. You've been growin' up so fast, I ain't been able to keep up with your ages."

The younger children had retreated back behind their mother's skirt after the introductions. Zeke stepped forward and spoke for the group.

"I'm ten, Josh is nine, Mary is eight and Maggie is four. Mama calls us oldest three her triplets." Zeke thought that the mention of triplets was appropriate because they had come to see twins.

"Jerry, will have his first birthday on January the first. He's a New Year's baby," Josh said with pride, falling back into place by his mother's side.

"Thank you, son," Samuel said. "And now there are two more people you need to meet," he added, stepping up next to the cradles, which the children had been eyeing since they came into the room. "Come on over and have a look."

The children quickly gathered around the cradles and peered in, the smaller children jostling for the front.

"These are Mrs. Whatley's grandchildren," Samuel said. "They're the twins that I told you about."

They're so tiny," Josh said.

"Babies," Maggie said, as she reached out to touch the boy's hand.

"Let's not touch them," Abigail said. "We don't want to wake them up and make them cry."

"They oughta be wakin' up soon anyways to eat," Karen said. "You kids can get a good look at 'em then."

Bessie stood up from the rocker and whispered to Naomi as the others admired the babies. "Ya'll got company. I best be gettin' on home."

"What's your rush?" Naomi asked. "If it's Ephram that you're worried 'bout, I'm sure that Samuel wouldn't mind checkin' on 'im."

"I ain't worried none 'bout Ephram Whatley," Bessie said with disdain. "Besides, he ain't even there. He left this mornin' with his cousin, Fred. I reckon he aims to spend Christmas with him."

"Then why go home? Stay with us. You don't want to miss your grandbabies' first Christmas."

"I don't aim to be no bother," Bessie said.

"I don't know why you would even think that. You're a big help with the babies. Me and Karen couldn't a got a thing done this mornin' if you hadn't been lookin' after the babies. I insist that you stay, Bessie; I won't take no for an answer."

CHAPTER SEVEN

The wind howled. It shook the windows and whistled around the corners of the Ivey house like a distant freight train. The temperature had been steadily dropping since the sun went down, and nobody was the least bit surprised when the Reverend Spears' Inspirational Hour was interrupted by a weather forecast alerting the residents of Trinity to expect another hard freeze.

"Keep those spigots on, or you're liable to spend Christmas morning fixing busted water pipes," the radio announcer warned his listeners.

The Taylors had stayed on throughout the afternoon. While Naomi and Abigail cooked, Karen and the children decorated the tree. Samuel split extra wood and stacked it into a large pile next to the front door. Bessie stayed busy by tending the babies, including Jerry.

As darkness started to creep in on them, Naomi called for everyone to gather around the fire. She had made sandwiches for supper.

She and Abigail had agreed that this light fare would do just fine, particularly in light of the fact that they had managed to prepare a genuine feast to be served the next day.

The children fanned out around the hearth, Karen and Abigail sat down on the sofa and Bessie reclaimed her favorite seat in the rocker.

Samuel placed a baby in the lap of Karen, Bessie and Abigail, and Naomi followed up with a bottle. He then dropped down amongst the fidgeting children, reclining against the ottoman, while Naomi lowered herself into the easy chair.

A peacefulness descended over the room.

Mary broke the silence.

"What are the babies' names?" she asked, speaking to no one in particular. The adults all looked at one another, surprised that they had not been the ones to broach this subject.

"That's a good question," Karen said. "I don't think their grandma has named 'em. Or if she has, she ain't told us their names yet."

Shrugging her shoulders, Bessie said, "I ain't even thought 'bout namin' 'em. My mind has been on Lily."

The children gave their father a quizzical look. There was no Lily in the room.

"Lily is the babies' mother," Samuel said to the children. "She had to leave the babies, and that's why they're here."

"Leave?" Mary asked. Abigail placed one finger over her lips and nodded her head back and forth. All of the children knew this signal to drop a subject. They were, after all, the children of a reverend.

"I reckon they oughta be named," Bessie mused. She had missed the exchange between Abigail and the children, lost in her own thoughts of Lily.

"We could help," Zeke offered with enthusiasm.

"We could give them name," Zeke said. "It would be kinda like giving them a Christmas present." He beamed, thinking that he had hit upon an extremely clever idea.

"That's a nice thought, son," Abigail said to Zeke and to the other children, whose heads had turned in unison to look at her. They liked Zeke's idea. "But Mrs. Whatley probably has names already selected. We don't want to interfere."

"The truth is," Bessie said, "that I don't got a single name in mind. Givin' 'em names as Christmas presents suits me. But my mind is blank. I'd 'preciate some help."

"In that case, let's have a go at it," Samuel said. "How about ladies first. Let's start by naming the girl."

"Any suggestions?" he asked, scanning the room. Everybody sat thinking.

After a few moments, Naomi spoke first.

"How 'bout Lily after her mama," she said. "I always liked Lily's name. For me, it conjures up thoughts of somethin' fresh and new, like spring."

"Lily's name suited her," Bessie said. "But there ain't gonna never be another Lily for me. This baby needs her own name."

"I suppose that's true," Naomi said.

"My mama's name was Mildred," Bessie said. "When I had Lily, I wanted to name her Mildred. But Ephram said no. He never took to my mama. Probably 'cause she never took to him. She said he was shiftless. Lookin' back, I'd say that she was right on the money. I had to run off to marry him."

"What does *shiftless* mean?" Mary asked.

"Never mind about that," Abigail said. "We're getting off track."

Bessie picked up the hint and moved along.

"Ephram named Lily," she said. "I don't know where he come up with the name. After I got over bein' mad, 'cause she weren't named after my mama, I liked the name."

"Why not name this baby after your mama, Bessie," Samuel suggested.

Bessie sat mulling over the idea.

"You could call her Millie," Josh said. "There's a girl in my class named Mildred Messer, but we call her Millie. She's nice and pretty, too," he added.

"Son, I didn't realize that you had taken an interest in pretty girls," Samuel said, poking Josh in the ribs. Josh blushed.

"Samuel," Abigail said, coming to Josh's rescue. "We are naming the baby. Stay focused."

"That Millie girl is real nice," Mary said.

A Watch in the Night

"She never calls us little kids names. Some of the big kids call us rats, when the teacher can't hear. But that Millie told those mean kids to leave us along." Mary heaped praise on the fourth-grade Millie.

"Leave you *alone*, not along," Abigail corrected Mary. "But thank you. I'm sure Millie Messer is a fine girl."

"What do you think, Bessie?" Samuel asked.

"I like it," she said emphatically. "I like it a heap."

The children grinned. Even Bessie smiled. Naomi squeezed her hand.

"It's settled then. I'll name her Mildred and call her Millie, for short," Bessie said. The children clapped their hands in approval.

"That just leaves you little fella," Samuel said to the baby lying draped across Karen's shoulder.

Karen, who was patting his back, turned so that the others could see his face. He gave a wide yawn and then a loud burp, which sent the children into spasms of giggles.

"Do you have any boy names that you like, Bessie?" Abigail asked. "What did you plan on naming Lily if she'd been a boy?"

"I don't rightly know," Bessie said. "That was so long ago. I can't remember now if I ever even picked out a boy's name.

"I suppose that Ephram woulda settled that, too. He woulda probably named a boy after hisself. But I don't want to saddle this child with havin' to carry the weight of Ephram Whatley's reputation on his back."

The smile faded from Bessie's face. She clenched her teeth and furrowed her brow. She was getting worked up just thinking about Ephram.

"I guess we all know what we won't name him—Ephram," Samuel said, seeing the change come over Bessie.

"That much is settled," Samuel added. "And if we unsuspectingly happen upon any other Whatley family names that you don't like, Bessie, let us know. We'll put them on the no-count pile with the name Ephram."

Abigail tried to help her husband.

"Children, do you have any ideas for naming Millie's brother?" she asked.

"It ought to sound like Millie," Josh said.

"I think what you mean to say is that the names should rhyme," Abigail said. "When names or words sound alike, then we say that they rhyme."

"I knew that," Mary said, eager to steal the stage from Josh. "Like words in a poem," she added.

"That's right," Abigail said.

Josh knew he had to counter quickly if he was going to take center stage back from his know-it-all sister.

"There are twins in my school," he said. "And their names *rhyme.*" He drew out the long "i" sound of the vowel, throwing a smirk in his sister's direction.

Mary hesitated, trying hard to think of something to say to make a comeback. Her hesitation spelled defeat.

"Jerry and Terry are their names. Their names rhyme," Josh added, emphasizing the long vowel sound a second time for the benefit of his sister, who sat struggling to come up with anything to halt his roll.

"Jerry and Terry; that's their names," Josh said one more time for good measure.

"We get your point, Josh," Abigail said firmly, trying to take some of the pressure off of Mary. She had refereed this game of sibling rivalry on countless occasions.

"Josh does have a point," Samuel said.

"Does anybody know a name that rhymes with Millie?" he asked. Nobody answered.

"I have an idea," Abigail said. "Let's go through the alphabet and stop on names that rhyme with Millie."

"Maggie, if you'd like, you could run through the alphabet to refresh everybody's memory," Abigail added. She wanted Maggie to have an opportunity to participate.

Josh rolled his eyes as his youngest sister stood up to recite the alphabet.

A stern look from Abigail settled him down. Maggie triumphantly recited the complete alphabet, and then she looked around the room for approval.

"That was an excellent job, Maggie; thank you for the help," Abigail said. Everybody nodded, agreeing that Maggie had given a stellar performance by not missing a single letter.

"I can recite the 23rd Psalm," Mary said, not wanting to be shown up by her four-year-old sister.

"I don't think the 23rd Psalm would be particularly helpful now," Abigail said. "We can save that for another time." Disappointment clouded Mary's face.

"But you might want to start us off by selecting the first name from the alphabet," Abigail said, giving Mary's head a little stroke.

Mary discarded the letter "A" immediately and settled on Billie. "Billie rhymes with Millie," she said proudly.

"Good start," Karen said. "Let's keep goin'. If anybody else has a name, sing out."

"D," Josh said, "Dilly rhymes with Millie." Everybody laughed. Josh didn't mind because they were having fun.

Mary continued on through the alphabet, and every silly name threw the children into another fit of laughter. When they were done, the only names they had come up with for Bessie's consideration were Billie and Willie.

"They're both good names," Bessie said to the children. "And I'm sorely tempted to go with Willie. But I had my heart set on somethin' a bit more special. What I'm after is somethin' different."

"Let's try a new approach," Samuel said. "Let's try names that begin with the letter 'M.' There's no written rule that twins' names must rhyme."

Using this suggestion, they called out every boy name they could think of—Mark, Matthew, Martin, Moses, Mabry, Malcom, Manchester. They went with the common and the uncommon, but Bessie kept shaking her head no. Nothing fit. They were stumped.

Mary broke the stalemate. "I know another 'M' name," she said.

"Let's hear it," Samuel said.

"Mango," Mary said. "It's from a book at school," she quickly added, before anybody could veto the name.

"The book is about a family who lives on a faraway island. The island has palm trees with coconuts. The family has a boy named Mango." Mary smiled triumphantly.

"You made that up," Josh retorted. He was the one who had first suggested Millie as short for Mildred, and Mary had cut in on that. He wanted to be the one to find the right name for the boy. For Pete's sake, they were naming a boy, he thought. What would a girl know about *that*?

"You made that up," he repeated. "There ain't no book with a boy named Mango. That's not a boy's name. There's no such word. Why don't we just name him coconut from that dumb book?" Josh was hoping to get a laugh with this last remark.

"Joshua," Samuel said. Josh sat chagrined. He had gone too far. His father had used his Christian name, and that was always a bad sign.

"We use respect when speaking to one another in this family," Samuel said, his eyes fixed firmly on Josh. "Your sister's idea was not dumb. I want you to apologize."

"I'm sorry," Josh said sincerely. He knew better than to half-step it now.

Mary accepted the apology with renewed smugness. She had landed the knockout punch. She had managed to get her name thrown into the ring and humiliate her brother at the same time. Abigail gave her the *look,* and Mary dropped the grin.

Her ego was further deflated when her father added. "While Josh forgot his manners, he might have a point. Although Mango might be a good name for a boy on an island; this name, perhaps, wouldn't fit so well on a boy in Trinity."

Mary immediately defended her choice. "And why not?" she demanded to know. "Mrs. Whatley said she wanted a different name. Mango is different. That *is* what you said, isn't it, Mrs. Whatley?"

Samuel was secretly pleased at Mary's tenacity. This one might be a lawyer, he thought.

Bessie came to Mary's defense. "That's right. I do want a different name. I've never heard that name before, but it has a nice ring."

"I've heard it before," Naomi said. "But not as a boy's name. Mango is the name of a fruit."

"A fruit?" Josh said incredulously. He might be redeemed after all, but he dared not say more. He was still stinging from being chastised by his father, and he secretly planned to even the score with Mary later.

"That's right, a fruit," Naomi answered. "It only grows where the weather stays warm year 'round. Washington brung me a basket filled with mangos on one of our anniversaries. Now there's a story."

"Mama, I never heard this before," Karen said suspiciously.

"Maybe not. But that don't mean it ain't so," Naomi retorted.

"You simply must tell us more," Samuel pleaded. "You can't just say that Washington brought you a bushel of strange fruit and stop there."

"Yes, tell us the story," Abigail said.

"Alright," Naomi said. "It's a bit long, but here I go.

"Washington always tried hard to come up with a special gift each year on our anniversary. We didn't have much of a weddin'. Or at least that's what he thought.

"Times were hard. People didn't throw big weddings like they do today. They went to the courthouse for the legal papers and to the church for its blessin'. And that's what we did. It was fine with me. But Washington always felt bad that we didn't have more."

"I'm trying to figure out what fruit has to do with weddings and anniversaries," Samuel said.

"I'm gettin' there," Naomi replied.

"Washington always tried to outdo hisself on our anniversary. One year he picked me a dozen roses from the bed planted next to the First Baptist Church. I was sure that Sheriff Tate would arrest him. But Washington didn't care none. He said it would be worth a night in jail to give me those roses."

"Tell us about the fruit, Naomi. Where does the fruit fit in?" Samuel asked again.

"I'm getting there. Be patient." Naomi stood up and warmed her hands by the fire.

"Our anniversary was in the spring. Times was harder than usual that year. Nathan had come down with the croup in the winter. We had to call Doc Adams, and he ordered some medicine from the drugstore in town.

"My own mama had a remedy for the croup passed down from the Indians. But Washington called that *mojo* medicine. He wouldn't hear of givin' Nathan that. I argued with him. That *mojo* medicine brung up all six of my mama's youngens just fine.

"Washington held firm. He wanted the medicine Doc Adams ordered. And I give in to him. The truth is I was scared slap out of my wits. Nathan's fever had shot up, and I couldn't bring it down no matter how hard I tried. Nathan needed the medicine. So, Washington made a trip to the Rexall Drugstore.

A Watch in the Night

"The man who owned the Rexall Drugstore made the coloreds go to the back door. They wasn't allowed inside back then. Washington stood next to that door for over an hour while the drugstore man helped the white folks. But he held his ground. He got the medicine. It took ever cent we had, but he got it."

"Mama, you was gonna tell us 'bout the fruit," Karen said, rolling her eyes. "While I like hearin' these family stories, the others might not."

"Nonsense," Abigail said. "Let your mama tell her story."

"I reckon that I done strayed a bit," Naomi conceded. "But here's the point. We was out of money—flat busted. And Washington told me later, he was clean out of ideas for an anniversary present. He was drivin' home when it happened."

Naomi stood up and poked at the fire.

"What happened?" Bessie asked. Everybody was caught up in the story. Even Josh and Mary had buried the hatchet and sat leaning, one on the other, hanging onto Naomi's every word.

"Patience," Naomi said with a wicked grin, taking another poke at the fire before she sat down.

"Anyways, Washington said he was feelin' lower than a snake's belly on the drive home."

"A snake's belly?" Zeke said.

"That's what he said," Naomi answered, "lower than a snake's belly."

"You've got to admit," Samuel said, joining in Naomi's fun. "You can't get much lower than a snake's belly."

"Shush, everybody," Abigail said, "and let Naomi get on with her story."

Silence fell over the room. All eyes were on Naomi. She hesitated, cleared her throat and rolled her eyes up as if she were thinking hard, trying to remember. "Karen, could I get a glass of water," she said, "I'm a little dry."

"Mama, please," Karen blurted out, "just get on with the story."

"Alright then, I will. But if my throat gets dry and gives out, don't blame me. It sure seems like . . ."

"You win," Karen said, defeated. "Zeke, honey would you fetch my mama a glass of water? The glasses are up over the sink."

Zeke jumped up, ran into the kitchen and then quickly returned with a glass full of water.

"Thank you, Zeke," Naomi said, taking the glass from him. She took a few sips, cleared her throat again, and took a couple more sips before saying, "Where was I?"

"Daddy was on the way home," Karen said, rolling her eyes again at her mother.

"Oh yeah," Naomi said, "now I remember. Washington was headed home when he spotted a truck stuck in the ditch. It was loaded down with somethin'. Its hubcaps were near 'bout to the dirt. Washington pulled over to offer help. The man in the truck turned out to be a stranger—not from 'round these parts. You don't often find a stranger in Trinity."

Naomi paused. She shifted in her seat and scratched her head as if she couldn't remember what came next. Karen started to speak, but before she could say anything, Naomi continued.

"The stranger had done run his truck off the road's steep shoulder, and he had got hisself stuck in the soft sand of the ditch. If you ain't use to drivin' these roads 'round here, runnin' off the shoulder always spells trouble."

"Mama!" Karen blurted out, exasperated. Everybody shushed her.

"I could go a lot faster if you wouldn't keep interruptin' me, Karen."

Karen threw up her hands in resignation. There was no moving her mother along. Naomi was having a ball.

"Where was I?" Naomi asked.

A Watch in the Night

"The truck was stuck in the ditch," Josh said.

"Oh, yeah. That's right. Washington said that he walked up on the man. The man was just a sweatin' and cussin'. It was a hot day for that time of year. As I recall it was a particularly hot summer that year, too."

"Mama, please," Karen pleaded. "Don't make these people think that you are some old woman who can't keep her mind goin' in one direction."

"You're right, girl," Naomi said contritely.

"Anyways, Washington offered to help the stranger. But he told 'im that first he's gonna have to stop all that cussin'. Washington was a Christian man, and he didn't abide no cussin', not 'round him."

Naomi leaned forward and lowered her voice to a conspiratorial whisper.

"Washington took a chance sayin' that. That stranger, see he was white. A colored didn't dress down a white man 'round here for any reason, much less cussin'."

Naomi reclined back into her chairs. The clock ticked, the fire crackled and the windows rattled, but nobody made a sound. All eyes were glued on her.

Samuel had a broad smile. As a preacher, he appreciated the art of being a good storyteller. Naomi had reined in the group, and she held them tightly. Nobody moved a muscle.

"The white man didn't take no offense. Or if he did, he kept it to hisself. He needed help. Washington figgered the man had been in the heat for quite some time, judgin' by the sweat stains on his shirt and the red color of his face. Then the man shocked Washington by sayin': 'I'd be indebted to you, mister, if you could help.'"

Naomi leaned forward again. "Now, you kids might not know this, but that was unheard of in this swamp back then. A white man callin' a colored man *mister*. Washington knew then and there that the white man must be feelin' pure desperate.

"'I'm stuck,' the stranger said to Washington, as if Washington couldn't see that for hisself.

"'You ought to count your blessings that it didn't flip on you,' Washington said, 'your truck looks a mite top-heavy.' The back of the truck was covered with a tarpaulin.

"Washington couldn't see what was underneath the tarpaulin, but whatever it was, the stranger had hisself a full load. Washington said as he got closer to that truck, it gave off a strong, sweet smell.

"Some sorta of a smell that he'd never run up on 'fore then. To hear Washington tell it that fragrance floated out from under the tarpaulin slow and tantalizin' like honey from a jar. He tried, but for the life of him, he couldn't place that smell."

"What was it?" Josh asked.

"Well, sir, I am glad you asked me that," Naomi said, leaning in closer to Josh, "'cause that is 'xactly what Washington wanted to know."

Naomi stopped herself and settled back into her chair. "But I'm gettin' to that. I don't wanta lose my place in the story and have Karen get her feathers all ruffled up."

"Mama, please," Karen almost shouted.

"Anyways, Washington always carried a loggin' chain in his truck. So, he hitched that chain to the man's truck, pulled that truck on up outta the ditch and waved the stranger on."

Naomi relaxed back into her chair. "But the stranger didn't leave. No sir, he didn't leave. Instead, he pulled up alongside Washington's truck, stopped, got out and stuck his head inside Washington's cab.

"'I don't know how to thank you,' he said.

"'There is one thing that you can do for me, mister,' Washington said.

"'Mister Gonzalez, my name is Gonzalez,' the man said, stickin' his hand in the truck for Washington to shake. That was another strange thing. Coloreds and whites didn't shake hands much then, 'cept maybe when Mrs. Hillman brushed hands with the colored youngens at the Hillman Christmas party. I always figgered she took pure Clorox to her hands after that."

"Mama, I don't think anybody here cares 'bout the Hillman Christmas party," Karen said.

"You're right," Naomi conceded.

"Washington took the man's hand and shook it. 'Washington Ivey, that's my name,' he said.

"'And what is it that I can do for you, Mr. Ivey? I don't have any money. I barely got enough to get back home, or I'd offered to pay already.'

"'It ain't money that I'm after,' Washington answered. 'I want my curiosity satisfied. What you haulin' in that truck? I've tried hard as I can, but I just can't seem to place that smell.'"

Naomi looked around the room. She leaned forward and lowered her voice.

"'Those are *mangos*,' that Mr. Gonzalez said.

"'Mangos?' Washington said. He never heard tell of such a thing. 'What's a mango?' he asked.

"'Step on out here and I'll show you,' Mr. Gonzalez said. Washington walked with him to the back of the truck. Mr. Gonzalez reached under the tarpaulin and pulled out a strange lookin' fruit.

"Washington said that fruit was shaped like a football, but smaller—somewheres between a small cantaloupe and a good size tomato. The skin on the fruit was thick and smooth and was colored red and green and yellow, all mixed up together. It looked strange enough, but it was the smell that captured Washington's attention.

"'I drove from Miami with this load of fruit,' Mr. Gonzalez said. 'You can't give these things away there. My neighbor told me if I brought them north, I could maybe get a good price for them.'

"'Miami! You don't say!' Washington said. 'Mr. Gonzalez you the first person I done ever met from Miami. I ain't never been outside of Trinity County myself.'

"While they's talkin' that Gonzalez fella pulled out a pocket knife, reached under the tarpaulin, got one of them mangos and peeled it. He passed a slice over to Washington. 'Try it,' he said. 'It tastes as good as it smells.'

"Washington took the piece of fruit. It was so slick that it almost slipped out of his hands. First thing that he did was to put it up to his nose. With the skin gone, the smell was even stronger.

"Then he popped it in his mouth. He said when he bit down on that piece of fruit, the juice gushed out from the pulp, fillin' up his mouth, slidin' down his throat and even drippin' out of the corners of his mouth onto his shirt. It was that juicy. He said it had a different taste—sweet and sour like—all at the same time.

"'Eat some more,' Mr. Gonzalez said, stripping back the skin and feeding the fruit to Washington piece by piece.

"'I reckon this here is pert near the best piece of fruit that I ever tasted,' Washington said in between bites. He finished off the mango and wiped his mouth on his shirt sleeve. It was a work shirt, so that part didn't matter."

"*Mama*," Karen screeched. Naomi looked at her and clucked her tongue before continuing.

"'Mr. Gonzalez, I know that I only asked for one favor,' Washington said, 'but I'm gonna ask you for one more. You can stop me if you're a mind to. But I'm gonna ask you for one more favor.'

"'You name it,' Mr. Gonzalez said.

"'I'd like to buy one of them mangos.'

"'I won't hear of it,' Mr. Gonzalez said, making Washington's smile disappear. Mr. Gonzalez saw that he had upset Washington so he quickly added: 'You can't buy one of these mangos, but I'll give you a whole bushel.'

A Watch in the Night

"'That's too much,' Washington said. He weren't never one to take no charity. He figgered that he earned one mango, but not a whole bushel. But Mr. Gonzalez wouldn't let up.

""I picked this fruit up in my yard,' Mr. Gonzalez said. 'It didn't cost me anything. I'd like to repay your kindness by giving you a whole bushel. Chances are I won't be able to sell them before they go bad anyways.'

"Washington hesitated so Mr. Gonzalez went on talking. 'Mister, it didn't go unnoticed on my part that you, a colored, stopped to help me, a white. But what may have gone unnoticed by you is that my skin is not as white as most men that you would probably call a white. I have some Latin blood in me, and in Miami, the whites treat us Latin people a little different, too. They don't treat us as bad as they treat you coloreds, but they don't treat us white neither. I appreciate your stoppin'. Just believe this: it would make me feel good if you would take this fruit off of my hands.'

"It was just gettin' dark when Washington got home that night. I was worried. He was never late for supper.

"I was watchin' for him out the window, and I went runnin' out to meet him when I saw his truck. He hopped out, bounced across the yard like a jack rabbit and swept me clean off my feet.

"He twirled me 'round like I was a rag doll. I was a little lighter back in them days. I 'bout lost my breath he squeezed me so tight. I had to beg for him to put me down. I didn't bring up the anniversary. And neither did Washington. We went on inside and had our supper.

"After we was done eatin' Washington said that he wanted to look in on Nathan. I started washin' the dishes. I was standin' at the sink, and I didn't hear him come back in.

"But I did catch a bit of this wonderful smell. I know the smells of my kitchen. That particular smell was somethin' new. I didn't have time to wipe my hands and get myself turned 'round, 'fore Washington come up behind me.

"'I got somethin' for you,' he said. 'Sit at the table and close your eyes.' I did what he asked. All the while that smell floated across the room like the sweetness of magnolias in the summer heat.

"'What's goin on?' I asked.

"'Patience woman,' was all that he said.

"He told me to open my mouth. By this time, I thought we was both crazy, but I opened my mouth. I was feelin' foolish, sittin' there with my mouth gapin' open. We was both actin' like kids, but it felt good to be so light-hearted.

"Then Washington slipped a large piece of that fruit into my mouth. When I bit into it, the juice spewed out, runnin' down my face and onto my good apron. But I didn't care.

"Like Washington, I thought it was one of the best things that I'd ever tasted. I opened my eyes. I was chewin' and laughin' and spittin' juice everywheres. He looked so prideful that it almost bordered on bein' a sin. He was kneelin' down next to me and beside him was that bushel of mangos.

"'Happy Anniversary, honey,' he said to me. 'It ain't much.'

"I put my arms 'round his neck and hugged him tight. That mango juice was all over both of us now. We laughed so hard that we cried.

"'What in the world is this fruit called, and where in the world did you get it?' I asked.

"'These are mangos, and where I got 'em is a story for another day,' he said. 'Let's just say for now that God put these mangos in my path.'

"This mango,' he said, holdin' the fruit up in his hand, 'is somethin' sweet and different and magical. I 'magine it to be somethin' that come straight from the Garden of Eden. This fruit is somethin' special sent straight from God to us to lighten up our hard way here on earth.'

"I smiled at him and then he said, 'just like you Naomi—this fruit is somethin' special in my eyes, sent straight from God to me to lighten up my way.'

"At that moment, my heart swelled up so full of love for Washington that I thought it would bust right out of my chest. And then I gave him my anniversary present.

"'I got a present for you, too,' I said. 'God's done sent us both another blessin'. We gonna have us another baby.'

"That was how your daddy learnt 'bout you, Karen.

"And it don't shame me none to say that we hugged each other and cried like babies. Both of us so grateful to God for puttin' us together on this earth and blessin' us with you and your brother, Karen."

Tears filled Naomi's eyes as she spoke. "My Washington he was somethin' else. Too good for this ole earth, I often thought."

Naomi leaned back in her chair and closed her eyes. "And I ain't never seen or tasted nothin' as special as that mango ever since."

Karen got up and put her arms around her mother. Tears ran down her cheeks. Bessie and Abigail dabbed at their eyes. Even Samuel had to clear his throat.

"Mama, that's a beautiful story. Why ain't you never told me that story before now?" Karen asked, still holding her mother.

Naomi lifted her daughter's head up and looked her in the eyes.

"I guess stories is like fruit, baby girl; they ain't good 'til they ripe," Naomi said. "Just like fruit shouldn't be eaten 'til it's ripe for eatin', a story shouldn't be told 'til it's ripe for tellin'. And that story weren't ripe for tellin' 'til now."

"That is a marvelous story, just simply marvelous," Samuel said, speaking for the whole group. The children even clapped their hands.

Your Washington was right, Naomi," Bessie said. "God does have a way of puttin' things in your path to lighten your load. My Lily sure fit that bill."

She looked over at the baby sleeping in Karen's lap. "That fruit was different but good. I like that. Maybe this boy can be just like that fruit, different but good. He won't be like the Whatley men before him. He'll be different and good. I'm gonna name him Mango."

"One thing is fairly certain," Abigail said. "I don't believe that he'll share that name with anyone."

They all laughed. After hearing Naomi's story, everybody had warmed up to the name Mango.

"Millie and Mango. I like the sound of that," Bessie said, smiling.

Mary squealed with absolute delight. She had been the one to suggest the name. Even Josh liked the name so much that he couldn't muster up any jealousy over the fact his sister had been the one to suggest it.

"Job well done, troops," Samuel said. "You did a splendid job of naming the babies. But now my own precious little children, it's high time that we headed home."

"It's Christmas Eve. We need to leave some time for Santa to come visit us," he added, with a wink. "But tomorrow we'll come back. And together, we'll show Millie and Mango how to have a rip-roaring good time on Christmas."

The Taylor clan made a hasty exit, Samuel carrying Maggie, Abigail carrying Jerry and the other three children walking behind, dragging their tails like little raccoons returning home after a busy night of mischief.

Naomi saw them out the door and then turned to Bessie and Karen.

"We need to get to bed ourselves," she said. "Bessie, you'll sleep in Karen's room in the back. Me and Karen will split our time here on the sofa."

A Watch in the Night

Bessie opened her mouth to protest, but Naomi cut her off. "You done been through a lot, Bessie. For the life of me, I don't see how you been holdin' up. Don't argue. You'll be sleepin' in the bed."

Naomi settled Bessie into Karen's room before going into her own room. As she was preparing for bed, she realized that she had not seen Bessie take a drink all day.

Naomi returned to the door of Karen's room and knocked. Bessie called for her to come in.

"I got some rum that I use to make cough syrup," Naomi said. "It's one of my *mojo* remedies. If it'll help you to sleep, I'll fetch you some."

"That's mighty thoughtful of you," Bessie said. "I know I ought not to be drinkin', 'specially not at a time like this. But I don't 'spect I'll be able to sleep a wink without somethin' to help me."

"I'll be right back," Naomi said. She left the room, and when she returned, she had a glass in one hand and a bottle of rum in the other.

"You drink what you need to sleep," Naomi said.

Naomi didn't feel any guilt for giving Bessie the rum. It felt like the Christian thing to do. She couldn't judge her. She'd never walked in Bessie's shoes. Maybe if she had, she would be the one eyein' the rum. Naomi placed the rum on the night table and turned to leave. "Good night," she said softly.

"Naomi, wait," Bessie said. Naomi stopped and turned to face Bessie.

"I don't know why you been so good to me and the babies," she said. "I never did nothin' to earn your favor. And you was always so kind to look after my Lily. I know how you and your family took care of Lily when me and her daddy was laid up drunk. I shoulda thanked you long 'fore now. I'm ashamed that I didn't. But I'm thankin' you now."

"Don't worry 'bout thankin' me. We loved Lily. We only did what any decent people would do," Naomi said.

"That's the point," Bessie said. "Your family is decent people. Mine never was, 'cept for Lily. That's why I never come to thank you. I was too ashamed."

"I don't agree that you ain't decent folks," Naomi said. "You're a good woman, Bessie. You just lost your way a bit. We all do that from time to time. Don't be so hard on yourself. Now, goodnight. We both need some sleep."

"Good night and God bless you," Naomi heard Bessie say as she closed the door.

Naomi leaned her back against the door. "He already has," she whispered.

CHAPTER EIGHT

Two days after Christmas, Trinity laid Doc Adams to rest with all the pomp and ceremony it could muster. His funeral was held at the First Baptist Church with the Reverend Samuel Spears presiding. It started promptly at 1:00 o'clock.

Although the weather remained bitter cold, by noon the church was filled. Latecomers had to stand outside. All of the businesses closed for the afternoon. Even Harry's Tavern closed, although Harry let it be known that he planned to open immediately after the graveside service.

The sky was overcast. Scant patches of snow remained in isolated areas. As people milled about on the church lawn waiting for the service to begin, they looked at the sky and speculated aloud there might be more snow, despite the weather forecast to the contrary.

School was out for the Christmas vacation, but school officials had managed to round up the members of the high school marching band and the ROTC. Their services were generally required in any civic event of this magnitude.

After much discussion, nobody could come up with a selection suitable for a funeral, which the band already knew. The band usually just played at the local sporting events, and the school fight song was the only number they had truly mastered.

Everybody agreed that selection would not be appropriate. So, the band was ruled out in favor of the ROTC.

It was finally decided, again after considerable debate, that the ROTC would line up on either side of the front entrance to the church and give the 21-gun salute as Doc Adams' casket passed by.

Sergeant Fisher, who was officially in charge of the ROTC program, vehemently objected on the grounds that this was strictly a military honor; and Doc hadn't been in the military.

But Superintendent Gray pulled rank. "There ain't no law against it," he had argued. "It's gonna be a part of the service and that's that!"

Later, most people agreed that the salute had been the highlight of the service even though they didn't have the slightest inkling of its meaning.

Walter Jr. gave the eulogy, which he concluded with the startling announcement that he would be returning to Trinity to take up his father's practice.

Eyebrows shot up and tongues wagged upon hearing that news. Several people, who were seated out of earshot of the family, remarked that it was too bad that he had waited until his father died before making this decision.

After Walter Jr.'s eulogy, the crowd marched by the open casket and paid Doc their last respects. "He sure looks good," some remarked.

When the last of the mourners took their seats, Reverend Spears wrapped it up with a closing prayer, and the pallbearers processed down the aisle carrying the casket.

They paused briefly outside for the 21-gun salute, loaded Doc into the hearse and moved on to the cemetery. Because it was so cold out, Reverend Spears mercifully cut it short at the graveside.

The crowd expressed their final condolences to the Adams' family, and then most of the men, even those who didn't drink, made a beeline for Harry's to thrash out the details of the day's events.

A Watch in the Night

The women hurried home to get themselves and their children out of the cold. Any gossiping they wanted to do would have to be done later on the telephone.

Nobody was around to see the Davis wagon return for the second time that day to the city cemetery.

Just as dark was closing in on the town, the Davis wagon, followed closely by Reverend Taylor's station wagon, pulled up to a second freshly dug grave in the far corner of the cemetery.

There were no flowers and no crowd of mourners at this gravesite—nothing to suggest that a second funeral was in the works other than the deep, pungent aroma of recently turned soil.

When the wagon stopped, two men climbed out and opened its back door. Reverend Taylor and Bessie looked on while the Davis workers lowered the casket containing Lily's body into the ground. Samuel said a few brief words, and Lily was buried.

The thermometer was already near the freezing mark as Samuel's car pulled away from the cemetery. The two men, who had sat in the Davis wagon during the brief ceremony, were out of the wagon and shoveling dirt onto the casket before Samuel's car was out of sight.

They worked feverishly to finish the job. Neither saw the truck pull up to the edge of the cemetery and stop.

As soon as the Davis wagon left, Trey Hillman got out of his truck. Daylight had faded, and he had to use a flashlight as he made his way across the grounds.

He could smell the fresh dirt even before he reached the grave. Once there, he stooped down to shine his flashlight on the temporary marker.

"Well, it is true, Lily," he said to the dark, as he picked up a handful of dirt and let it sift slowly through his fingers. "It was you."

He stood up and ground the temporary marker into the dirt with the heel of his boot before turning to leave.

The coming weeks brought a number of changes to Trinity: Walter Jr. came home to take up his father's practice; Sheriff Tate retired; and Reverend Taylor left the Shady Grove Baptist Church.

Walter Jr. arrived the first week of January and moved into his father's office on Duval Street. He wasn't there a week before he announced his plans to modernize and expand the office. He even hinted that "an associate" was soon to follow him from Raleigh but refused to give any other details.

His wife and children were to remain in Raleigh until the end of the school year. This arrangement brought its share of rumor and speculation regarding the state of Walter Jr.'s marriage and unbridled scorn from the women towards his wife.

They recognized only two legitimate reasons that a wife should spend even one night away from her home—sickness and death—certainly not something as persnickety as having your kids complete the year in some fancy, private school.

On the heels of Walter Jr.'s news, Sheriff Tate announced his retirement, effective immediately. While many had suspected that Sheriff Tate would not be running for re-election, none had suspected that his departure would take place any sooner. The Tates moved out to their place on the river.

The same week that Sheriff Tate retired Reverend Taylor flabbergasted his flock with the astounding news that he was being transferred to Miami. The Southern Baptist Conference, of which Shady Grove was a member, decided Reverend Taylor's talents would be better utilized in a larger church. The Taylors moved the third week in January.

The governor appointed "Bud" Akers to replace Sheriff Tate until the next general election. Bud's Christian name was Rudolph Alexzander Akers, but he had gone by the name Bud for so long that nobody remembered his given name or how he had come to be called Bud.

While nobody knew Bud's Christian name, they knew his reputation. Bud had distinguished himself in two very distinct ways: he was the best friend of Trey Hillman; and he was the best football player Trinity ever produced.

In Trinity, where football was king, Bud became a hero almost from the first time he took the field as Trinity High's quarterback. He was that good.

During his senior year, it looked as if Bud might get a shot at playing college ball, an accomplishment that had, thus far, eluded any Trinity High players. But that all ended the night Trinity played Roswell High.

The game was for the regional championship, an honor coveted by Trinity for years. Several times, Trinity came perilously close to taking the trophy home, but victory always evaded them. The year before Bud's fateful night Roswell High defeated Trinity by a single point, a long field goal, kicked during overtime.

Trinity was certain that this was the year. As the players waited in the wings, slapping one another's rear ends and banging their helmets together, the rumor swept through the crowd that the college scouts were in the stands to watch Bud play.

After three rousing renditions of the school fight song and some enthusiastic gyrations by the cheerleaders, the excitement of the hometown fans bordered on hysteria by kickoff.

Bud played a flawless game, and Trinity led by one touchdown at the beginning of the fourth quarter. He had thrown two touchdown passes, one a short toss and the other his specialty, the "long bomb," plus he had run one in.

Bud's star was definitely on the rise, when a 230-pound Roswell tackle knocked it out of the sky.

It was a late hit, and it was called as such by the referees. But that didn't help Bud. As Bud went down, his knee ripped out of its socket.

The referees stopped the clock, and the coach stormed the field when Bud didn't get up after the play. The Trinity players buzzed around Bud on the field like hornets around their nest.

Some of the spectators left the stands and rushed the sidelines to get a firsthand account of what had happened.

When Bud had to be carried off the field on a stretcher, tempers flared and pandemonium soon engulfed the stadium.

A pushing match quickly turned to blows among the players, and enraged fans poured out of the stands and stormed the field to join in the fracas.

Sheriff Tate had to call in the local fire department to hose down the rabble-rousers before he could bring the melee under control. Both teams were disqualified from the regional play-offs, and no trophy was awarded for that year.

After surgery and a two-week stay in the Cartersville hospital, Bud recovered. But his football career was over—a bitter pill to swallow for a poor kid who had already come to believe that he would ride the football train of glory out of Trinity.

Bud turned to his best friend, Trey Hillman, to help him get over the disappointment. Together, they terrorized the town—drinking, fighting and chasing girls.

Sheriff Tate had to be called in regularly to "settle them down." But without the support of Mr. Hillman, who took a boys-will-be-boys' attitude, there was little the sheriff could do.

Bud and Trey's debauchery continued unimpeded until the night Trey shot and killed Ronny Diaz.

Trey and Ronny had a running feud from as far back as anyone could remember, a feud that boiled over into fisticuffs on a regular basis.

A Watch in the Night

While nobody could remember how it started, they all would remember how it ended on a hot summer night at Johnny's Amoco when the heat had everyone's nerves on edge. It was only weeks after both boys had just graduated from Trinity High.

Ronny was gassing up his truck at the station when Trey and Bud pulled up along beside him. Trey later told Sheriff Tate that the shooting had been an accident. He thought the gun was unloaded, and he had only been "horsing around" when he pointed the gun at Ronny's chest and pulled the trigger.

Bud, the only eye witness, backed up Trey's story. Sheriff Tate had no choice but to rule Ronny's death an accidental shooting, although nobody in town believed for a second that was the case.

After that night, Mr. Hillman stepped in and put a screeching halt to Trey and Bud's reign of terror. He put both boys to work: Trey in the lumberyard and Bud on a shrimp boat. The town didn't hear much from Trey and Bud during the next year.

Then Trey caught the whole town off guard by announcing that he intended to marry Bud's sister, Susan. Trey was known for pulling outrageous stunts, but even by Trey's standards, this was a doozie.

"Just tryin' to get the old man's goat," everybody said. "The Hillmans ain't gonna never let this fly."

The Akers' family lived in a small house just shy of Tate's Hell and barely managed to stay ahead of the bill collectors. Although they didn't actually live in Tate's Hell, they were close enough that Susan was regarded as a highly unlikely choice for a Hillman bride.

But if the Hillmans disapproved of the marriage, they didn't give anyone the satisfaction of letting it show. At least not in public.

They even went so far as to pay for the wedding, a lavish spectacle, the likes of which the town had never seen. After the wedding, Bud was made a deputy sheriff and the elder Akers moved to a larger house in a more suitable part of town.

And Susan didn't let her humble beginnings hold her back. Under Mrs. Hillman's close tutelage, she plunged wholeheartedly into church functions, charity work (such as it was in Trinity) and social engagements. It wasn't long after the wedding that Susan began putting on more airs than Mrs. Hillman herself.

As a wedding gift, Mr. Hillman built Trey and his new bride a home out on the river. It was a monstrosity of a house built in the old southern plantation style, complete with four white pillars and a sloping green lawn adorned with the replica of a hitching post that featured a black boy dressed in riding clothes (although neither plantations nor horses figured anywhere into the history of Trinity).

The house appeared quite ostentatious to the simple people of Trinity, although ostentatious was not the word they used to describe Trey's new home.

The house was too "showy" people said, even for the Hillmans, who were known for putting on a show. Mansions didn't sit well with people who worked long hours for low wages and then came home to houses with two bedrooms and a single bathroom. Some didn't even have that.

One year later Susan and Trey had their first child, a scrawny boy who weighed in at only five pounds at birth. Mr. Hillman bought Susan a new Cadillac to mark the occasion.

People barely had time to swallow and digest the house and Cadillac, when Susan arrived for Sunday services at the First Baptist Church with a "nanny" in tow. Just the word nanny sent most of the women's nerves to the breaking point.

The woman was a *babysitter*—everybody knew that. When discussing the issue all of the women agreed that the word nanny had to come from one of those fancy magazines that Susan spent her time reading while they were busy scrubbing floors and cleaning house.

It didn't seem right for Susan Hillman to put on such airs, when most of their husbands worked daylight to dark for the Hillmans just to put food on the tables and a roof over their heads.

But they were *the Hillmans*. And what could people do other than talk about them behind their backs.

When Bud was appointed to replace Sheriff Tate, everybody said that Mr. Hillman surely had a hand in this. While they all regarded Bud as a poor choice for sheriff, considering his wilder days as Trey Hillman's sidekick, nobody voiced an objection.

It helped that Bud had married and settled down months earlier. Most people hoped, but seriously doubted, that Bud had changed. Regardless, he was now their sheriff, like it or not.

It was the last week in January and the babies were still with Naomi and Karen. The welfare people never came. Naomi wondered if Sheriff Tate had forgotten to call or had simply decided to let it be. Whatever the reason, she was glad that they hadn't come.

The day after Christmas Bessie called her sister. The sister agreed with Bessie that the babies might be the answer to her daughter's prayers. But the daughter was up North with her husband visiting his ailing grandmother. She wasn't sure how long before they planned to return home.

"If you can hold out 'til then, I'll talk it over with her," she said. Bessie agreed to wait. What else could she do?

When Bessie offered to take the babies home with her, Naomi vetoed that idea.

Bessie couldn't manage the babies without help. And the Ivey home was better suited for them. Bessie only had the kerosene heat—with its fumes. And she had no place for them to sleep other than Lily's old room, which was too cold. Then there was Ephram to contend with.

After a brief discussion, Bessie and Naomi agreed it was best to leave the twins at Naomi's.

A few days later, Naomi returned to work, leaving Karen at home to care for the twins. Karen had been laid off from her job in the office at the oyster house in November, and she hadn't been able to find more work.

Bessie came over and helped Karen until Naomi came in from work.

This arrangement worked well, and the days flew by. Karen quickly became adept, with Bessie's help, at caring for Millie and Mango. Naomi knew that losing her father had left a void in Karen's life; the babies seemed to fill that void. Naomi was glad to see Karen smiling again.

Bessie adored the babies; she turned out to be a great help in caring for them. Naomi noticed an improvement in Bessie's spirits as well. And Naomi realized that even she felt better.

The babies had breathed new life into all of them. There was no denying that fact.

And that was what worried Naomi. The longer the babies stayed, the more difficult it was going to be on everyone when they left, including the babies.

Bessie needed to make another call to her sister. Naomi resolved to talk this over with her immediately. But Ephram brought matters to a head before she could act. He took the babies.

Naomi worked until noon on Saturdays. On the last Saturday in January, she returned home and found the babies gone. As soon as she walked through the door, she knew something was wrong. The fire had burned down to coals, and the house was silent.

She hastily looked in the cradles and found them empty. She then made a cursory search of the house calling Karen's name.

When Karen didn't answer, she sensed trouble. She hoped they were all at the Whatleys, but she feared the welfare people had finally come.

Naomi set out immediately for the Whatley house. It had rained earlier in the day, making the path muddy and slippery, and she watched the ground as she walked to avoid the puddles.

As she rounded the first bend, she ran headlong into Karen. Both women jumped back, startled.

"Good grief, child, you 'bout scared me to death," Naomi said, after she caught her breath.

"I'm sorry, Mama. But thank the Lord you're home." Karen was pale and shivering, and her eyes were red and puffy. Naomi could see that she had been crying.

"What's wrong?" Naomi asked.

"It's Millie and Mango. Ephram Whatley up and took 'em," Karen said, putting her hand up to her mouth to stifle a sob.

"What do you mean he took 'em? Where?"

"Over to the Whatley house. He made Bessie bring 'em to him."

"Are they alright?"

"They was when I left 'em."

"And you and Bessie. Are ya'll alright?"

"I guess so."

"Let's go," Naomi said. It had started to drizzle rain. "You can tell me what happened at home."

The rain changed from a drizzle to a downpour just as they reached the end of the path. They made a run for it—as much of a run as Naomi could make—but both were soaked when they reached the porch.

"Take your muddy shoes off out here," Naomi said, wiping the water out of her eyes. The water ran off of their coats and puddled on the floor.

"Let's get outta these wet clothes," Naomi said. "Ain't no use in us takin' our deaths of a cold standin' 'round in wet clothes."

"But, Mama . . ."

"Don't 'but Mama' me. Shoo."

When Naomi returned to the living room, Karen sat in the rocker her knees drawn up to her chest.

Karen had put some more logs on the fire and stoked the coals before sitting down. The fire burned furiously.

Naomi wrapped a cover around Karen before sitting down on the sofa.

"Now then; tell me what happened," she said.

"Ephram Whatley took the kids; that's what happened."

"Well, I know that, but tell me how that all came 'bout."

"This mornin' Bessie come over, same as always. But today she was in high spirits. Her sister had called; her niece agreed to take the babies. And here's the kicker. She wanted Bessie to come, too—to help with the babies. Bessie had decided to go."

"Can't blame her for that," Naomi said. "I don't know how she's put up with Ephram for this long."

"After lunch Bessie went home. Said she wanted to start gettin' her things together for the move. I told her to go on. I could watch the babies.

"I had put 'em down for a nap and was outside hangin' some sheets on the line when I saw her comin' back. As she got close, I could tell somethin' was wrong. She was nearly 'bout as worked up as the night Lily died."

Naomi sat straight up. "Go on," she said.

"She was outta breath and her face was flushed. At first, I thought that she mighta been drinkin'. But then she started to tell me 'bout her run-in with Ephram.

"As soon as he got home, Ephram had set in on her 'bout the babies. He wanted them brung back over to their house right then."

"But why would he want the babies?" Naomi said. "I heard him say myself that he didn't want no part of 'em."

A Watch in the Night

"I don't know," Karen said. "Ephram told Bessie he was the grandpa, and that give him rights to 'em. He said that he's gonna fetch the welfare people if she didn't bring 'em home with her."

Blood rushed to Naomi's face when she heard this. She and Karen leaned forward putting their heads close together.

"She come for the babies," Karen said. "'I ain't got no choice,' she kept saying. I asked her 'bout the plan to take 'em to her niece. She said that was gonna have to wait. She was scared to death 'bout what Ephram might do. I tried talkin' to her, but it didn't do no good. And I was scared myself. So, I give in. We took 'em over, together."

Karen looked up at her mother.

"It broke my heart, but I didn't know what else to do. I helped her settle 'em in by the heater. Ephram, he come out from a side room, took one look at 'em and went back in the room. I stayed as long as I could, but I didn't want you to get home and find us gone. That's when I run into you on the path."

Naomi sat up and shook her head.

"I don't like the sound of this one little bit," she said. "Ephram Whatley is up to no good. He ain't the kinda man to go havin' no change of heart."

"I agree," Karen said.

"But what's he up to?"

"I don't know," Naomi said, patting Karen's hand reassuringly. "But don't fret. I aim to find out."

CHAPTER NINE

Trey Hillman stomped the accelerator of his truck. The tires spun in the mud before catching. The truck swerved and barely missed hitting the three, mongrel dogs sunning themselves in the Whatley's front yard.

Clearing the lane in record time, he turned onto Highway 27. His thoughts raced through his head like a runaway freight train. He rounded a sharp curve without touching his brakes, passing the sign announcing Trinity's city limits.

When he saw the flashing lights in his rear-view mirror, he let go of a stream of profanities and hit the brakes. The patrol car narrowly avoided a rear-end collision by veering off of the road.

Trey ground his truck to a halt, throwing up gravel from the shoulder of the road. Fuming, he rolled down his window and waited.

"Damn, boy, are you drunk?" Bud Akers asked. "You pert near killed us both. I ain't even been sheriff that long. How'd it look for me to rear-end the town's leading citizen?"

"We gotta talk," Trey said.

"What's wrong? You look like you lost your best friend. But that can't be so 'cause here I am big as life." Bud laughed. Trey didn't.

"Cut the bullshit," Trey said. "We gotta talk."

"Okay." Bud answered. "Simmer down. Let's go over to Harley's place. We can talk there."

The sun was beginning to sink below the horizon, when Trey and Bud walked into Harley's, a run-down, juke joint on the edge of town. Trey threw himself into a booth, and Bud slid into the booth opposite him.

"Two beers," Trey yelled across the bar at the waitress.

She grabbed two long-necks out of the cooler and hustled over to the booth where Trey and Bud sat. She could tell that *Mr. Hillman* was in a tizzy.

Trey snatched one of the beers out of her hand and took a long pull. She placed the other beer on the table in front of Bud where he let it sit.

"So, let's hear it," Bud said. "What's up?"

"I'm bein' blackmailed," Trey said, before draining his beer and slamming the empty bottle down on the table.

"Goddamn it. Bring me 'nother beer," he shouted at the waitress.

"You gotta be kiddin'," Bud said. "Who's blackmailin' you? And for what?"

The waitress deposited the beer on the table. Trey waited until she was out of earshot to answer.

"Do I sound like I am goddamn kiddin'," Trey barked.

Bud just shook his head.

"It's Ephram Whatley. I knocked his girl up last year. She had twins, if you can believe that. He's threatenin' to tell people they're mine, if I don't pay 'im off."

"Now I know that you gotta be kiddin'."

"Like I'd kid 'bout that," Trey snapped.

"How'd the hell did *that* happen?"

"Easy." Trey looked at Bud and rolled his eyes. "I started seein' the bitch, she got knocked up and now her daddy's threaten' to blow the whistle." Trey drained his second beer.

"And what do you need me for smart ass?" Bud snapped back, standing up to leave. He was in no mood for Trey's bullshit. He had promised his wife that he would be home for supper.

"Hey man, don't go," Trey said. "I didn't mean nothin'. It's just that I'm so pissed off right now."

Bud hesitated and then sat back down. He picked up his beer and took a drink.

"It started last winter," Trey said, more subdued. "Susan had just had the baby. Things weren't exactly great at home, if you know what I mean. I met Whatley's girl over at Harry's."

"No, I don't know what the hell you mean, Trey. Let me get this straight. Your wife has a baby so that gives you the red light to take up with some tramp from Harry's."

"Don't start with me, Bud. Don't you start with me," Trey snarled.

"You know that I ain't cut out for the family life. I woulda never married if my old man weren't harpin' on me night and day to settle down. Keep the Hillman name goin' and all that crap. I ain't cut out to be with just one woman. That's the way I am—plain and simple. I can't help that no more than I can help that my eyes are brown. Save the sermon."

"Yeah right," Bud said. "It's never your fault is it, Trey?"

"I didn't come here to get in no goddamn fight with you."

Trey stood up to leave and knocked his empty beer bottle off of the table. It landed on the cement floor and shattered.

The waitress grimaced and reached for the broom and dustpan propped up against the wall behind the bar.

"Sit down, Trey. You're right. There ain't no need for us to squabble. Go on and tell me what happened." The last thing Bud needed was for Trey to storm out of Harley's drunk and wrap his truck around some telephone pole.

Trey slumped back down in the booth and slugged his third beer while the waitress swept up the glass. When she sauntered off, he leaned across the booth and continued.

"Like I said, I met the bitch over at Harry's. She had an old beat up car. It quit on her one night. I gave her a ride home. One thing led to another, and well, you get the picture. Things went on great for a while. Then she fell all in love. I didn't give a shit. I was gettin' what I wanted."

"So, what happened?"

"Your sister happened. That's what. Susan got suspicious. She hired that damn *nanny* for the baby. That gave her more time to worry 'bout what I was doin'. She started raisin' so much hell that I decided to break it off with Lily."

Trey drained his beer before continuing. "That was the girl's name. I was startin' to get bored anyways. We were back in that clearin' behind her daddy's place—that's where I'd take her—when I told her."

Trey stopped talking long enough for the waitress to deposit two fresh long-necks in front of them. Bud picked up his second beer.

"Go on" Bud said, as the waitress swished away.

"She went batshit crazy when I told her that it was over. Said that she loved me. I said tough shit; that I sure the hell didn't love her. Then she dropped the bomb—told me that she's knocked up."

"It figgers," Bud said. "Damn! What did you do?"

"What do you think I did? I didn't even know if she was tellin' the truth. But I told her to get rid of it. That I knew a doctor in Cartersville."

"Go on," Bud said. He really didn't want to know what happened next. It was like looking at a car wreck. You looked even when you knew that you were going to see something awful.

"At first she begged and cried. Kept sayin' how much she loved me. She actually thought that I was gonna leave my wife and take up with her. I laughed in that bitch's face. That pissed her off—but good. She started screamin' that she's gonna ruin me. That she's gonna tell the whole damn town that I was her baby's daddy. I lost it."

"What do you mean *you lost it!*" Bud was no longer looking at a car wreck as he passed by. He was stopping, walking up and opening the door.

"Just what I said. I lost it. That bitch went nuts. Slapped my face. Clawed at my neck. Screamin' at the top of her lungs the whole time. She raked her nails down my neck so hard that she drew blood."

Bud mentally opened the door to the wrecked car. He knew that he would find carnage inside, but he felt compelled to open the door.

"Then what?" he asked.

"I ain't never been hit by no woman. Somethin' came over me then."

Bud held his breath. Here it comes, he thought.

"I dragged that little slut out of the truck and threw her on the ground. I reached in the back of my truck. All I could lay my hands own was a dog leash. I snatched her up by the hair, and I started to beat her with that leash. Once I started, I couldn't quit. She was screamin' and hollerin' and tryin' to crawl away. But I held onto her. I beat her 'til my arm was so tired out that I couldn't lift it no more. When I was done, I dropped her on the ground. She laid there all balled up whimperin' like a dog. She didn't want no more of me. That was for damn sure."

"Goddamn it, Trey. You coulda killed her."

"She's damn lucky that I didn't. After I caught my breath, I pulled her up by the hair to my face and told her that she *was* gonna get out of my life. If there was a baby, then she was gonna get rid of it. And if she caused me any trouble that I'd kill her. She knew that I meant it."

Trey took another long pull on his beer. His face was splotchy and beet red from anger and alcohol.

"I made her crawl back to my truck. Then I threw her over into the back. When I got to the edge of her daddy's yard, I rolled her out. I left her layin' there in the yard.

A Watch in the Night

"I didn't hear no more from her. She musta quit Harry's 'cause I didn't see no more of her in there. I figgered if there ever was a baby that it didn't survive that beatin'. I didn't give it no more thought 'til Doc Adams' funeral."

"You've lost me," Bud said. "What's Doc's funeral got to do with all of this shit?"

"I was a pallbearer," Trey said. "Didn't wanta be, but my old man made me do it. Right before the funeral started, I slipped over to Johnny's for a shot of Wiley's shine. While I was there, I heard somethin' that didn't sit quite right with me."

"Which was?"

"Bo Thompkins, who was one of Davis' gravediggers that day, was drinkin' at Johnny's. He was bitchin' 'cause Davis was makin' him work late."

"Yeah."

"I asked him what the hell he was so fired up about. Doc was supposed to go in the ground at 3:00. That ain't late."

"Get to the point, Trey." Trey was drunk now. Bud would have to keep him on track, or they'd be in here all night.

"The goddamn point is this. Bo weren't pissed off 'bout Doc. It was a second funeral that had 'im mad. One scheduled for 5:00—a charity case. Bo said Doc had been in Tate's Hell the night he died—deliverin' a baby. Bo was cussin' up a storm 'cause he had to work 'til dark in the cold buryin' Ephram Whatley's girl while Ephram stayed inside by the heater drinkin'."

"No shit."

"No shit," Trey snorted.

"So, what's your problem. The girl is dead."

"She's dead alright. I checked that out for myself. What Bo said stayed with me durin' Doc's funeral. I was thinkin' on it so hard that I stumbled and near 'bout dropped Doc comin' outta the church. If Ben Russell weren't strong as an ox, we mighta all ended up sprawled out on the church lawn."

"You got that right. He 'bout bust a gut tryin' to hold up Doc for that gun shootin' sideshow with the ROTC."

"Anyways, after Doc's funeral, I went over to Harry's for a spell. About dark, I decided to ride out to the cemetery and see for myself.

"The Davis wagon was just leavin'. I waited 'til I was sure the wagon was gone, and then I took my flashlight and walked towards the back of the cemetery where I'd seen the wagon parked. I smelled the dirt before I found the grave. It was spooky as hell out there, but I found the grave. It was Lily Whatley alright. I read the marker myself."

The waitress brought two more beers. Trey was slurring, but he picked up the beer. He took a long pull and wiped his mouth with the back of his hand.

"So? That's my point," Bud said. "The girl is dead. What's your problem?"

"That's what I thought. Then the call came."

"*The call?*"

"The call from Ephram Whatley. Didn't I start off by tellin' you that Whatley was blackmailin' me?"

"Oh yeah, right."

"It was last Sunday. Whatley called my house. Can you believe that? I don't even know how the old bastard got my number. But he did.

"When he said it was Ephram Whatley, I 'bout croaked. I woulda cussed him out right then and there, but Susan was standin' next to the phone. I waved her off, but she wouldn't budge. Whatley said that we needed to talk. Told me to come out to his place the next day and hung up the phone in my ear."

"Let me guess. That's where you were comin' from when I stopped you," Bud said.

"That's right, Sherlock," Trey said. "I thought 'bout not even goin' out there. But my gut told me I'd better hear him out."

Bud leaned in closer to Trey.

A Watch in the Night

"Trey, please tell me that you didn't kill Whatley," he said, afraid to hear the answer.

"Relax. I ain't killed 'im. Not yet, anyways."

"What exactly happened out there?" Bud asked.

"The old man was waitin' on me. I'd no sooner pulled up in the front yard than he's out on the porch. I didn't wanta get out, but he kept wavin' me in.

"The old bastard can barely walk. He's only got one good leg—uses a crutch. Against my better judgment, I followed 'im inside. The place was hotter than hell. And stunk like kerosene."

"Get to the goddamn point, Trey."

Bud felt like his brain was going to detonate and blow into a million pieces. Now that Trey was completely drunk, he was rambling.

"Lily had twins. That's the goddamn point. And they lived. Both of 'em. Can you believe that shit?"

"Right now, I'd believe 'bout anything."

"Whatley accuses me of bein' the father," Trey snarled, slamming his fist on the table.

"Of course, I said that I weren't. And that I'd kill 'im if he told anybody that I was. But he's either too damn drunk or too damn stupid to be scared."

"What happened?" Bud asked Trey. Bud did not like the way this story was going.

"That heat and kerosene was makin' me wanna puke. That and I drunk a six-pack on the way out there. I had to get outta that house. I headed back to the porch with him trailin' behind me, yappin' at my heels. I was out on the porch when I heard it."

"*It?*"

"Yeah. *It* was a goddamn squallin' baby. 'Hear that,' the old bastard hissed at me. I was sicker than a damn dog by then. Couldn't think straight. I cleared that porch and headed on out to my truck with Whatley hobblin' 'long behind me.

"'That's your flesh and blood,' he hollered at my back. 'I might be old and crippled, but I ain't blind. I seen you slippin' back off to that clearin' with my girl. Them youngens are yours and *you gonna pay.*'

"When I heard that I stopped dead in my tracks. *That* pissed me off. If I'd had my gun on me, I'd shot him. But like a damn fool, I'd left it in the truck."

"So, what did you do?"

"I turned and snatched that scrawny bastard up by the throat. I was pissed off enough to choke 'im to death with my bare hands. I squeezed down so hard that his damn eyes near 'bout popped outta his head.

"'What if I did bed down your girl?' I said to 'im. 'Everbody knows the whores from out here in Tate's Hell would screw anybody.' That shut him up.

"'You tell anybody—I mean any goddamn body—that I fathered any bastards by your girl, and I'll kill you deader than a goddamn doornail, old man. You got that.'"

The waitress headed towards the booth with fresh beer, but Bud motioned her to stay away.

"Alright. What happened then?" Bud asked.

"I dropped 'im on the ground and started back to the truck. He choked and gagged and flopped 'round on the ground, but he weren't done. He grabbed holt of my leg. He got his wind back while I was tryin' to kick 'im off. Feisty old bastard. I'll give 'im that. 'The boy looks just like ya,' he said. 'Bring the youngens out here,' he hollered back towards the house.

"I was still tryin' to kick 'im off, but I's gettin' sicker all the time. Them damn fumes, that heat inside, the beer. It was all gettin' to me. You ain't gonna even believe what he said next."

"Try me," Bud said.

"'*I want fifty thousand dollars to keep my mouth shut!*' That's what he said. Can you believe that shit?"

"Fifty thousand damn dollars!" Bud said, locking eyes with Trey. He said *that*. Hell, that old coot can't even count that high."

"Well, you know me. I did go slap damn crazy then. "Say what?" I said to 'im. Now I know that you're outta your mind old man.

"I's gonna choke 'im to death right then and there. I figgered if he was crazy enough to say that, he was crazy enough to do anything. I reached down to grab holt of 'im again, but the blood rushed to my head or some shit. I was still sick. You ain't gonna believe what happened next,"

"Try me."

"I puked all over 'im."

"He let go of my leg then and started scramblin' 'cross the dirt back towards the house. That's what saved 'im. While I's standin' there puking my guts out, he managed to get his crutch and get back up on the porch.

"Once he's on the porch and outta of my reach, he hollered over to me, 'one week. If I don't get the money in one week, I'm gonna give them brats to the welfare people. Tell 'im you the daddy. See how that sits with your highfalutin wife and ma.'

"I was still doubled up, pukin'. He went on back in the house then, and I stumbled back to my truck. I swear to God, I thought for a second there that I was gonna pass out or somethin'."

"Fifty thousand dollars," Bud said, letting go of a low whistle under his breath. "You got to be kiddin' me."

"Do I look like I'm goddamn kiddin'?" Trey growled.

"You already told me that you didn't kill 'im. What did you do?"

"I hauled ass back to town. I thought 'bout takin' my gun and killin' 'im. But I didn't know who else he had in that shack with 'im. He hollered to somebody to bring out the kids, remember?

"And I was still sick; couldn't shake it. All that heat. And them fumes so thick that you coulda cut 'em with a knife. Kerosene always did make me sick. That on top of a six-pack. I weren't exactly up to no showdown, if he did have somebody to back 'im up. So, I just went on and got the hell outta there."

Bud sat back in the booth. "Damn Trey, you got to hand it to the old bastard. He's either dumb as hell, or he's got balls the size of watermelons to try and pull this shit on you. This is hard to believe."

"Well, you better believe it," Trey said, "'cause ever goddamn word I just said is true."

Bud whistled under his breath again, long and low. "I'd say your ass is in one helluva big crack old buddy."

"You think so," Trey said. "Well, listen up, *old buddy*, 'cause I saved the best for last."

"There's more?"

"Yep. You know that my old man's been funnelin' money to the damn Republicans for years. Me, I never give no rat's ass 'bout politics. But not the old man. That shit's real important to 'im. A couple weeks back, it finally paid off for 'im. Seems like them Republicans got some big plans for the old man. Want to run him for state senator. My old man—a goddamn senator. Can you believe it?"

"Not really. That's some heavy shit, Trey."

"It's gone straight to the old man's head. Hell, he's been primin' the pump for years. He called me into his office last week and told me. The plan was for me to take over the business. All these years, I've had to take orders and fetch and tote like some slave for 'im. Now, when there's finally some light at the end of the tunnel, Whatley calls."

"Bad break, old buddy," Bud said.

"Bad break my ass. You don't think for a second do you that I'm gonna sit back and let Whatley screw this up for me.

"If I screw this senator shit up for my father, I'm done. I'll be beggin' 'im for pocket change for the rest of my goddamn life. And that, *old buddy,* ain't gonna happen. Now I don't know for sure if Whatley would follow through on his threat or not. Or if anybody would even listen to 'im if he did. But I ain't takin' no chances. I'll just have to go back out there and finish the job."

Bud studied Trey's face. He was serious. He intended to go back out there and kill Whatley. Bud leaned across the booth.

"Hold on," Bud said.

"We need to think this shit through, man. From what you've told me so far, you can't be sure that this is somethin' that Whatley cooked up on his own. Sounds like he might be gettin' some help. Has your old man told anybody 'bout this senator shit?"

"I doubt it. He told me to keep a lid on it. That there would be an official announcement later. Hell, the election ain't 'til next year. He was just givin' me a heads up 'bout 'im expectin' me to take on the business. We's gonna make the shift to me runnin' the business gradual like."

"Trey, we need to take some time and think 'bout this."

"I ain't got time."

"He gave you a week. Didn't he? Let me think on it. There might be some way other than killin' Whatley. Hell, we don't even know who else knows 'bout the babies. Whatley comes up dead. News leaks out 'bout the babies. You do the math."

"So what? If I kill Whatley that oughta scare anybody else who knows into keepin' their mouths shut."

Bud put his hands onto Trey shoulders and pulled his face in close.

"Now, you listen to me, *old buddy,* and you listen good. I need to think this through. So, you don't go tearin' out on your own and do somethin' crazy. I got your ass off once for murder when you killed Ronny. But that don't mean that I can do it again. You stay away from Whatley 'til I figger a way out of this shit. Do you understand me?"

Trey flexed his forearms and threw off Bud's grip. "Get your goddamn hands off me," he growled. "Nobody puts their goddamn hands on me, not even you, Bud."

"Alright, alright," Bud said. "We ain't got no problem between us, Trey. Remember, I'm on your side. My ass is on the line, too. Now, come on. I'm gonna drive you home. Let's sleep on this. Let me think."

Trey settled back down. "Alright. It ain't like he's gonna go spreadin' the news tonight."

"Right," Bud said. "Let's get outta here."

Trey stood up and fished around in his pocket. He staggered over to the bar and slapped a fifty-dollar bill on the counter with the palm of his hand.

"Keep the change, sugar pants," he said to the waitress, who was wiping down the bar.

Trey leaned into the bar to get his balance. He didn't resist when Bud came over and wrapped his arm around his shoulders.

"Let's go, old buddy," he said, winking at the waitress. Bud led Trey outside and loaded him up into the front seat of the patrol car. Trey was passed out before they got out of the parking lot.

Bud rolled down the window, hoping the cold air would help to sober him up. He hadn't intended to drink so much beer. He needed to think straight.

If Trey hauled off and killed Whatley, this whole mess might come down on his head. Trey could turn off bad in a second. Bud knew this. And when he did, there was no controlling him.

The last thing he needed was for Trey to commit murder on his watch. When old man Hillman got him appointed as the sheriff, Bud had wondered why. Now it all made sense. With him running for the Senate, he needed some lackey to keep an eye on his wayward son.

Bud saw the curtain drop closed in the front window as he pulled up to Trey's front door. Just what he needed. Susan must be waiting up on Trey.

He was right.

Susan flung open the door before Bud even had a chance to ring the fancy chimes.

"Where you two been?" she demanded to know. "I see that you're drivin' 'im. What did he do? Wreck another truck?"

"Shut the hell up, Susie-cue, and help me get 'im inside," Bud said.

Susan could see that Trey was too drunk to care what she said and that Bud was too pissed off. She held the door while Bud practically carried Trey inside.

"You might as well put 'im in there," she said, pointing to an open door.

Trey could sleep it off in the guest bedroom, Susan thought, and then she would have it out with him in the morning.

Bud struggled to get Trey into the room where he dumped him on the bed.

Susan stood in the doorway, looking on, sulking. "Don't put his nasty boots on that spread," she ordered Bud.

Trey weighed over two-hundred pounds. Solid muscle. Bud's shirt was soaked through under his armpits with sweat from carrying him inside.

Pissed, Bud spun around, took three long strides across the room and snatched Susan up by her forearm, pulling her face up next to his. He was sick of this shit.

"Listen up, little sister," he said. "I don't know what your goddamn problem is, but you need to get your head screwed on straight. Look around you. This marriage has been good for you. It's been good for all of us."

Susan glared back at him, but she didn't say a word.

"You thinkin' that you're some big-shot, high-society lady from up on the hill? You startin' to believe your own bullshit? Is that it, Susie-cue? You startin' to forget what it was like livin' one paycheck away from Tate's Hell?

"Well, let me tell you one thing, sister, I sure the hell ain't forgot it. And I sure the hell don't want to go back. You need to get off your high horse and start appreciatin' what you've got here. You need to start tryin' to make that husband of yours over there happy so that he'll want to come home."

Susan snorted, her nostrils flaring out like an angry bull. She tried to wrench herself free from Bud's grasp, but he held firm.

"Don't you make the mistake of thinkin' that you're gonna change Trey Hillman; 'cause you ain't. And you best be rememberin' that, Susie-cue. Blood runs thick in the Hillman family. You might be old lady Hillman's darlin' now, but she'll never side with you over Trey.

"And don't try to fool yourself into thinkin' that kid you had by Trey gives you any bargainin' chips. He don't. You better straighten up and fly right, little sister, or you're goin' down. We all are."

Bud let go of her arm and turned away in disgust. Susan stroked her arm and fire flashed in her eyes, but she didn't say a word. She didn't dare. She hadn't seen Bud this pissed off in a really long time.

"Come on and help me put your husband to bed," he said. "And when he wakes up, don't start some shit with 'im. Make 'im glad that he come home."

Susan walked over to the bed. She yanked off one of Trey's boots and flung it against the wall. It made a dent and a black smudge on the pink floral wallpaper. Wallpaper that she had ordered all the way from Atlanta. She tugged at the other boot.

Bud turned to leave, but then he stopped at the bedroom door.

"Oh, and sis, fix yourself up. You look like a goddamn cow since you had that baby."

The other boot went skimming past Bud's head and then landed with a loud thud on the thick, plush carpet that covered the living room floor.

CHAPTER TEN

Bud opened his eyes and rolled up next to his wife's warm back. She pulled her knees towards her chest and pushed her buttocks into his stomach. He hadn't slept well, worried about Trey's latest fiasco.

He was tired of being burdened with Trey's problems. As a boy, he had been willing to go along with Trey. But they were grown men now. The time to live on the wild side of life had come and gone.

And Bud liked being the sheriff. Growing up still haunted him. For a short while in high school, football had caused people to respect him. But that all ended the night his knee went out. Now he was the sheriff, and people respected him again. He didn't want to lose that.

He buried his face in the sweet smell of his wife's hair and kissed her neck before rolling out of bed. Despite all of his tough talk around Trey and the boys, Bud loved his wife.

Pulling on his pants and shirt, he tiptoed out of the bedroom and went into the kitchen to call Trey.

The phone rang once before Susan answered.

"Put Trey on the phone," Bud snapped.

"What the hell," Susan muttered, before Bud cut her off.

"Shut up and put Trey on."

"It's Bud," Susan said, shaking Trey's shoulder and thrusting him the receiver.

"What's he want?" Trey asked, still half asleep. He had forgotten last night.

"You," Susan shouted, throwing the phone at Trey. She remembered last night even if Trey did not.

She wondered how and when Trey had managed to get himself up and out of the guest bedroom into their bed.

"Yeah," Trey said into the receiver. His head pounded and his mouth was so dry that he found it almost impossible to speak.

"Meet me at Harry's in thirty minutes."

Bud hung up the phone before Trey could answer.

Trey opened his eyes just enough to see the clock. It was only 5:30.

Slowly, the fog started to lift from his brain, and the events of the day before came flooding back into his consciousness.

He tried to hold his thoughts at bay, but they spewed forward, filling his mind like vomit that needed to be wiped up off of the floor.

His feet hit the plush carpet, and he made a run for the bathroom. He was going to be sick.

When Bud pulled into Harry's, the front lot was empty with the exception of a few cars pulled up next to the back door. The lights were on inside.

Bud could see the breakfast crew setting up. He tried the front door. It was still locked so he rattled the doorknob and pounded loudly with his fist.

"Open up. This here's Sheriff Akers," he hollered.

He heard the clunk of a retracting deadbolt, and then the door swung open. Harry stared down at him. Although Bud was a big man, he paled in comparison to Harry.

Harry was Greek, which everybody said must account for the weird salad full of olives and hot peppers that Harry included on his menu, although nobody ever ordered it.

Maybe his Greek ancestry also accounted for his size. Bud didn't know for sure nor did he care—Harry was the only Greek person he had ever met. But he did know that at six feet, six inches and close to 300 pounds, Harry was the largest man that he had ever seen.

Harry's gargantuan head was bald on the top. But Harry had grown the hair on the side of his head into a long strand, which he parted just above his ear and then looped over the bald spot. It was plastered into place by Alberto VO5.

Bud recognized the smell; it was the same hairspray that his mother had used for years. Harry was married to a local beautician, half his age. Bud gave her the credit for Harry's innovative hairstyle.

"You're early," Harry said. "We ain't set up."

"Coffee'll do," Bud said.

Harry grunted for him to come inside. If it were anybody but the sheriff, they would have had to wait.

Bud dropped into a booth by the front window, and Harry poured him a cup of dark, strong coffee. He was on his second cup when Trey's truck swung into the parking lot.

Harry opened the door for Trey, and Trey sauntered over to where Bud sat. His eyes were puffy and bloodshot, and his brow was knit tightly together into a painful grimace.

"What the hell we doin' up at this hour?" Trey snarled.

"This's when most men go to work," Bud replied. "If you weren't some coddled pantywaist, you'd know that."

"Don't start with me, Bud. I'm nursin' one helluva of a hangover."

"I was with you, remember, Trey? I'm surprised that you're able to move at all this morning."

Harry came and poured Trey a cup of coffee.

"Leave the pot," Trey said.

Harry placed the pot in the middle of the table and went back to his chores.

Trey drained his cup and reached for the pot. He refilled his cup and then rubbed his temples with the tips of his fingers.

"This Whatley business has got me worried," he said. "And just when things was goin' so good for me." He slid down into the booth in a sulk.

"Things been goin' pretty goddamn good for you your whole life, Trey. You're just too damned spoiled by your old man to see it."

"Seriously, Bud?" Trey shot back.

"Yeah seriously, Trey. No matter what you got, it ain't ever enough—you're always wantin' more, wantin' quicker, wantin' better. You ain't the first man that's ever had the wolf come howlin' at his door. So stop whinin'."

"Cut the crap. I'm knee-deep in shit. And it's your job to get me out, *Sheriff*."

"Yeah, right." Bud would have liked to have said more—a lot more. But arguing with Trey was a waste of time. And Trey was right. His job depended on his cleaning up after the bastard.

Trey fidgeted with impatience.

"So, you musta come up with somethin' to get me up this early?" he said.

"Yeah well, while you was sleepin' off your hangover, I was layin' awake most of the night tryin' to put together a plan," Bud snarled.

"And?"

"And you gotta pay the old man somethin', at least for now."

"To hell you say," Trey said, slamming his cup down so hard that the coffee sloshed out onto the table.

"Trey, be reasonable. There's a good chance, a real good chance, them babies are yours. Just the mention of your name in connection with 'em could set off a scandal."

Trey stirred his coffee without looking up so Bud continued, hoping that he was getting through to Trey.

"If Whatley calls the welfare, whinin' and cryin', there's no tellin' what'll happen. Could be enough to throw your old man's chances at senator right off track."

A Watch in the Night

Still no response from Trey.

"Now nobody around here would give a good goddamn," Bud said. "But Trinity County ain't the same as that tight-assed Republican committee, full of *Bible*-thumping Baptists. Hell, maybe they wouldn't care neither. Hard to say. But one thing for certain is your daddy will care. Do you wanta face that?"

"Then I'll kill Whatley and be done with it," Trey retorted. "Who'd ever miss the old coot anyway?"

"Think this thing through," Bud said. "Whatley's dumb as a fence post. His brain has been pickled for years. Maybe somebody else cooked up this scheme for him. You said yourself there was another person out at his place yesterday."

"So what?" Trey said.

"Just this," Bud responded. "We don't know who he's told. You kill 'im, and you could be blackmailed for fatherin' bastard youngens and murder. If you're even accused of murder, that'll be enough to blow your old man's plans sky high. We got us a tickin' bomb here. We gotta shut Whatley up, leastways for now. And that'll take money. The question is how much."

"It sure the hell ain't gonna be fifty grand. I can't put my hands on that kinda money."

"My guess is he'll take a lot less. But you'll have to talk him down. I got a plan."

Trey smashed his cup onto the table again, this time sending the coffee flying. He pushed out of the booth and collided with a table, which sent a chair skidding across the room before it crashed into the counter where Harry stood setting up the cash register.

"Oh hell!" Bud said.

Trey slammed the door shut on his way out of the restaurant with a loud bang. Before Bud could get out of the booth and shove past a startled Harry, Trey was in his truck.

The wheels of Trey's truck squalled as he rounded the corner out of Harry's parking lot. Bud made it outside just in time to see Trey swerve into the path of Ralph Jeeters' Merita Bread truck.

Ralph barely missed plowing right into Trey's truck by pulling his wheel hard to the left. The bread truck left the road, rocked from side to side and then smashed into Harry's sign, causing the top of the sign to break away from the pole and come crashing down on the hood of Jeeters' truck.

"Damn," Bud said, under his breath. "What'll he do next?"

Bud yelled over to Harry and the two waitresses, who stood staring out of the front window.

"Trey had a fight with his wife. You know how it is. I'll be back later to straighten this out. Ya'll keep your mouths shut 'bout this. You hear me?"

Harry and the waitresses nodded to Bud. None of them knew *how it is*," but they could hear in the sheriff's voice that he meant business. They understood when to hold their tongues.

"You alright?" Bud called over to Ralph, who had climbed out of his truck and stood surveying the damage.

"Yeah, I think so," Ralph shouted back. "But the fool messed up my truck."

"I'll be back to settle up with you later," Bud yelled over to Ralph, as he slid behind the wheel of his patrol car.

"Damn," Bud said to himself. "What a damn mess."

Bud knew that he couldn't catch Trey. No need to make matters worse by having everybody heading out for work seeing him chasing after Trey before it even got daylight. He had a good idea where Trey would go.

About ten minutes later, Bud turned onto a dusty country road known to the locals as simply River Road. The ruts of the road were so washed out that Bud wondered if the car could make it through.

The patrol car bumped along, occasionally bottoming out. Suddenly, the road ended abruptly. Bud parked the car behind

A Watch in the Night

Trey's truck, climbed out and walked over to a steep bank overlooking the river.

Below him the river made a sharp turn, causing the current to deposit enough sand to form a long, sloping sandbar. When the river was low, like it was today, the sandbar stretched for almost thirty yards.

During those times, the water was so shallow that a person could walk to the other side. Bud looked across the river where a limestone wall formed the opposite bank. Perched on the top of the wall was a rock platform, six feet long.

The sandbar sat in the middle of a stretch of right-of-way, cleared by the electric company. Huge metal towers, strung with electrical lines, were stationed every one hundred yards in both directions.

Bud always thought that these towers looked like giant soldiers standing in perfect formation. The brush grew up under the wires, but the power company kept the trees cut back and the road passable. That's how Trey and Bud found the sandbar when they were still boys.

At one time this had been one of Bud's favorite places. But not anymore—not since Tommy Long had drowned here.

The day that Tommy drowned the river was high, only a foot below the rock platform. The current was swift and powerful, creating treacherous perils for even the best of swimmers. Tommy was not the best of swimmers.

The boys had crossed the river before when it ran high; but never when the river was as high as it was on that day.

They all knew that pulling against a strong current was an exhausting task. And they knew that the key to swimming the river when the current was strong was to pull up onto the rock platform on the opposite side and rest before attempting the return.

Five boys met at the river that day. Bud and Trey, riding in Trey's truck, followed Larry Sanders. Larry drove his father's pick-up with Larry's brother, Carl, and Tommy Long riding in the back to catch the wind.

Football practice had been long, tedious and hot. Bud thought a swim would cool them off. It had been his idea to go to the sandbar.

When they arrived at the sandbar, Bud knew almost immediately, his idea to come out to the river was a mistake.

The river was almost over its banks. Tree limbs and other debris floated swiftly down the river caught up in an extraordinarily strong current. Bud suggested they leave; come back another day.

Trey, on the other hand, had taken one look at the river and set in for them to swim to the other side. That idea was crazy.

And Bud had emphatically told them so. Still Trey wouldn't let it go. Bud was certain that had it not been for Trey, the others would have agreed with him and gone home.

But Trey always had the last word. Fueled by Trey's taunts, all five stripped down and hit the water. Trey went first, daring the others to follow.

They did.

Trey was by far the best swimmer in the group, and as always, he reached the opposite bank first. Bud was close behind him. He remembered seeing Trey reach for the platform.

"Snake," Trey shouted, flipping away from the platform. Instinctively, Bud flipped, too.

"Goddamn moccasin on the platform," Trey called out, swimming up next to Bud.

Trey and Bud both fought against the current. If it pulled them too far off course, there would be no getting back to the other side.

"Cottonmouth," Trey cried out to the others, before dropping his face into the water and starting the long haul back.

A Watch in the Night

As Bud stood looking out at the river, he still didn't know how he had managed to make it back to the other side that day.

He remembered his arms and legs were numb with exhaustion and the current had dragged him twenty yards upstream. He recalled flailing about in the water, fighting to stay afloat, when his hand hit something solid.

The root of a tree saved him.

The root had grown down the bank and stretched out into the water. Bud grabbed onto the root, and pulled himself up onto a limb, where he collapsed, sucking air, until he was recovered enough to crawl through the bushes back to the sandbar.

There he found Trey sprawled out face down in the sand. Trey's back was heaving up and down as he tried to force air into his lungs.

Bud remembered scanning the sandbar for the others. He saw Carl about five feet downriver, gasping for breath, his eyes crazy with fear, as he clung desperately onto a root that was gradually starting to pull away from the bank.

Somehow, he managed to find the energy to wade into the water after Carl. He was knee-deep and fighting to keep his footing when Carl latched onto his outstretched hand.

Both he and Carl were being dragged down into the water when he heard Larry call out to him from the shore. With Larry's help, he had pulled Carl from the water. All three then collapsed on the sand, scared and exhausted.

Bud was the first to miss Tommy.

"Where's Tommy?" he said to Larry and Carl.

"Don't know," they both said back, sitting up to look around.

"You seen Tommy?" Bud yelled over to Trey, who was still lying face down in the sand.

"Nope," Trey called back.

"Get up," Bud screamed at the others. "We gotta find Tommy."

They all forced themselves up, scouring the banks of the river for Tommy. But he was nowhere in sight.

"Fan out and search," Bud yelled.

Frantically, they had searched the banks, calling Tommy's name. There was no trace of him.

The others kept searching while Bud ran up the bank to Trey's truck. On the main road, he flagged down the driver of a logging truck who radioed into the sheriff.

Sheriff Tate was at the sandbar twenty minutes after the call. Within the hour, a search party of twenty, including Tommy's father, had formed, all hoping to beat the odds and find Tommy alive.

Sheriff Tate called the search off when it got dark. Even Tommy's father had to admit there was no way to search the banks of the river after dark.

The next morning at daybreak the search started again. It continued for another day and a half until the body washed up down at the Tallapeeca Bridge.

A couple of old men, fishing from the edge of the bridge, were the first to see it, lodged between the cement pillar, which supported the bridge, and a tree branch.

Tommy was buried two days later. The pallbearers were the first string of the football squad, which included Bud and Trey.

They were preparing to carry the casket out of the church when Trey leaned over to Bud and said rather nonchalantly. "There never was no snake. It was all a joke."

Bud couldn't say anything back. It was time to pick up the casket and go. But as soon as the funeral ended, Bud had taken Trey aside.

"What do you mean, there weren't no snake?" he demanded to know.

"Just what I said," Trey said, a smirk curling the corners of his mouth. "There never was no snake. It was all a joke."

A Watch in the Night

Bud pushed Trey backwards with the palms of his hands. "You goddamn piece of shit," he screamed at Trey. "You killed Tommy. You knew he didn't have a prayer of makin' it back without restin'. He wouldn't even been in the river if you hadn't egged him on. We coulda all drowned, you stupid bastard."

Trey shoved back at Bud. "I didn't kill the little sissy," he growled. "He wanted to swim the river. I didn't put no goddamn gun to his head, now did I?"

Bud stood glowering at Trey. "And what's the big deal?" Trey added, his voice now calm. "It's not like he was your goddamn brother or somethin'."

Trey had sauntered off, leaving Bud standing at the edge of the cemetery.

Bud didn't speak to Trey for a month after the funeral. And when they did talk, neither of them ever mentioned Tommy's death again.

While Trey didn't seem to be the least bit bothered by what had happened, Bud had spent many sleepless nights imagining how Tommy must have felt being swallowed up by that black water. He knew that if he hadn't been lucky enough to latch onto that root, he would have drowned along with Tommy.

Neither Bud nor any of the other boys, except for Trey, had ever wanted to go back out to the sandbar. But Trey seemed to like the sandbar better than ever. Bud guessed that he would find Trey at the sandbar today.

He was right.

Bud could hear Trey firing off rounds from his pistol. But he couldn't see Trey—the bank was too steep. Patiently, Bud waited for Trey to reload, before he called out to him.

"Trey, I'm comin' down."

The shots started up again. Judging from the echo, Bud could tell that Trey was shooting across the river. He walked down the sandbar to where Trey stood at the water's edge firing another round.

"Get a holt of yourself, man," Bud shouted.

Trey stopped firing, but he didn't look at Bud.

"For Pete's sake, Trey, I'm not the enemy here," Bud said. "I'm tryin' to help. You almost killed Ralph Jeeters in that bread truck. Your hot head's gonna take us both down."

Trey turned and looked at Bud.

"I'm just so goddamned mad," he said. "I can't believe that some old drunk from Tate's Hell's got the best of me."

"He ain't got the best of you. Not yet. All we gonna do is buy a little time to figger things out. There's a way 'round this, Trey, but you gotta keep your head. Killin' the old man ain't the answer."

Trey didn't say anything back, but Bud knew that he was listening.

"Here's the plan. Call 'im on the phone. Tell 'im to be in Harley's parkin' lot at 4:00 this afternoon. You'll approach him. It'll looks like you just ran into him thataways."

Trey listened so Bud continued.

"You can't take a chance on bein' seen back out at his place. Nobody'll think much of it even if somebody should see you talkin' to 'im at Harley's. I'll be sittin' in Sheila's car watchin' the two of you, in case you was to need me. Tell 'im that you can't come up with a lump sum. Not yet. That it'll take some time. Offer 'im $500 a month in the meanwhile. Promise him that you'll get more later. See if he'll take it."

Trey fired off a couple more rounds before answering Bud.

"As much as it sits in my craw to give that son-of-a-bitch a nickel, you're right. I can't take the chance of him doin' somethin' crazy right now."

Trey fired off another round while Bud waited.

"If the old geezer will go away for $500 a month," Trey finally said, "that'll be money well spent. I won't miss it. I can run it out of the company books. I can't get my hands on a large sum of money; the old man watches me too close for that. But $500 a month; that I can cover. At least, for now."

"Alright then, it's settled," Bud said, relieved. "I'm goin' back to town and try to smooth things over with old man Jeeters and Harry."

"What the hell?" Trey asked, letting his pistol drop to his side.

"Jeeters hit Harry's sign. You'll have to pay for that. Call Whatley. Tell 'im Harley's at four o'clock. And stay out of any more trouble. We can talk there. In the meanwhile, go to work. And, for the love of the Lord, stay cool."

"Sure thing," Trey said. He raised up his pistol and started to reload.

Bud called Trey at noon. "Meet me over at Harry's for lunch?" he said. "I straightened things out with Jeeters and Harry. But it wouldn't hurt none for you to smooth things over with Harry yourself."

When Bud walked into Harry's, Trey was standing with his arm wrapped around Harry's shoulders. Harry was all smiles.

"I's just tellin' old Harry here that maybe I got a little too over-heated this mornin'," Trey said to Bud. "You know how much I love your sister, Bud, but even the best of women can get on your nerves at times."

"I promised 'im that you'd get his sign put back up," Bud said.

"I'll do better than that," Trey said, squeezing Harry's shoulder. "It's high time that our buddy here had a new sign. Order yourself a new sign, Harry. Somethin' fancy like that new fish house in Cartersville put up. You know, the one with the shrimp dancin' 'cross the top wearin' top hats and carryin' canes."

Harry's grin grew broader. He wasn't sure what Trey meant about dancing shrimp; he'd never seen the fish house in Cartersville. But he understood what it meant to get a new sign—for free. Harry was notorious for squeezing a dollar. The prospect of a free sign had his face lit up like a new moon.

Trey and Bud slid into the same booth where they had sat earlier.

"Bring us two of your specials, sugar," Trey said to the waitress, who had bustled over to wipe down the top of the booth.

"I got Whatley on the phone," Trey said, as soon as the waitress left. "I told 'im to meet me at Harley's just like you said."

"Did he agree?" Bud asked.

"Sorta."

"What do you mean sorta?"

"He said that he can't drive. That he'd have to find his cousin Fred and have him drive 'im to Harley's, so he weren't sure 'bout the time."

"And?"

"I didn't like that. First off, I don't want his cousin involved; and second off, I don't particularly wanta be stuck waitin' 'round Harley's and then him maybe not even show up at all. So, I changed the plan."

"No, Trey."

"Yeah, Bud. I told 'im to be standin' by that big oak in his front yard at four o'clock sharp. I'm gonna take him back to the clearin' for our little chat. What do you think?"

Bud didn't answer right away. He had thought of the clearing himself as a possible meeting spot, but he had discarded the idea because of Trey's temper.

He had chosen Harley's, hoping to maintain some control over the situation. Trey wasn't as apt to do something stupid out in public—Bud hoped—and he could have been only seconds away if things got out of hand. He didn't think much of Trey's new plan."

"I don't know," Bud said. "That sounds a little too risky to me."

"Well, it don't sound too damn risky to me," Trey snapped back.

"Besides, it's already set up. I can't call Whatley back now. So that's that." Trey's voice grew louder, and his eyes narrowed as an angry scowl crept over his face.

Bud realized that Trey was starting to get riled up again. He didn't want a repeat of Trey's earlier outburst, so he gave in to him.

"Don't go gettin' your undershorts all in a wad. I's just thinkin' it through. That'll work."

The waitress brought the food to the table.

"Thank you, darling," Trey said.

Bud could see him staring down her blouse as she leaned over to set Trey's plate on the table.

Some things never changed, Bud thought.

Ephram was waiting for Trey under the oak when he heard the roar of Trey's approaching truck. He stood propped against its broad trunk, steadying himself by leaning on his crutch, as he watched Trey's oversized pick-up clear the lane and then roll across his front yard, stopping a few yards shy of where he stood.

He was surprised to see the passenger door swing open. Ephram hadn't planned on getting into the truck. He would have preferred to talk in the yard.

But, when Trey pulled out his pistol and motioned with the barrel for him to get in, he didn't see that he had much choice.

He hobbled over to the truck, pulled up onto the running board and dropped into the seat next to Trey. Anchoring his good leg against the floorboard, he lifted his bad leg into place and slammed the door.

Trey stared straight ahead. At the sound of the slamming door, he floored the accelerator.

Ephram lurched forward, thrown off balance. He flattened both his palms against the dashboard just in time to keep his head from striking the windshield.

It had rained off and on for the past few days, and the road was full of potholes and mud slicks. Trey dropped the truck into four-wheel drive, and it ground its way back towards the clearing.

The pines cast long, ominous shadows across the road. Already the daylight was starting to fade, and without the sun, the air was turning cold.

Trey wedged his pistol against his leg on the seat next to him and gripped the steering wheel with both hands. He glanced over at the old man out of the corner of his eyes and was pleased to see that he was bouncing him around.

But the place was creeping him out. He wanted to be done with Ephram and out of these woods before it got dark.

Trey stopped the truck at the edge of the clearing and shut off the engine. He swiveled around in his seat to face the old man, but Ephram stared out of the windshield.

The odor of alcohol and kerosene fumes made the cab of the truck smell rank. Despite the frigid air, Trey lowered his window.

"You thought over my offer?" Ephram asked.

Trey didn't answer. He was watching a buck with a handsome spread of antlers, step out into the clearing, raise its head and sniff the air.

"Either you brung me out here to make a deal or to kill me. Which is it?" Ephram asked.

The deer cocked its head in their direction, caught their scent and then bolted back into the cover of the woods.

A Watch in the Night

When Trey didn't answer him right away, Ephram cut his eyes over to have a quick peek at him. He cringed at what he saw. Trey's face was flushed red, and his jaw muscles were taut.

Ephram hadn't really thought that Trey brung him back to the clearin' to kill 'im, but now he wasn't so sure. He squished up closer to his door and pressed its handle. The door was locked.

Ephram was instantly sorry that he hadn't agreed to meet Trey at Harley's.

Hoping to catch another glimpse of the buck, Trey scanned the woods. It had been a beauty. He let Ephram sweat.

"I ain't here to kill ya," he finally said. "I'm here to deal. Now I'm gonna tell you exactly what I plan to do, and you're gonna listen. Don't interrupt me."

Ephram cowered down lower in his seat, somewhat relieved, but still wishing that they were at Harley's.

"I ain't admittin' to havin' fathered them bastards you got holed up back at your place," Trey said.

"But I won't deny here between you and me that I messed with your girl. As to who else messed with her, I don't rightly know and don't care. I just don't want to be linked up with them kids. For that reason, I'm willin' to pay you off. But it sure the hell ain't gonna be fifty thousand dollars. There ain't no way that I can put my hands on that kinda money."

Ephram sat up straighter, slightly encouraged, but he didn't dare speak.

"I'll pay you five hundred dollars a month," Trey said. "That oughta buy plenty of bottles for you and the babies."

Ephram had been looking for one big payoff. He hadn't ever really expected fifty thousand, but he had planned on a lump sum.

His plan was to get out of town with his cousin Fred and leave Bessie with the problem of the babies. He hadn't even considered a monthly payoff. This changed everything.

"I don't know," he whined. "I thought that you'd just pay me once. You do that, and you won't hear no more from me. You Hillmans got the money."

"What sort of a damned fool do you take me for?" Trey said. His voice was loud and angry as he spun around in his seat.

Ephram hugged the door.

"It'll be a cold day in hell 'fore I pay you front money. I'll pay you along each month, and thataways, you'll know that if you run off at the mouth, there won't be no more payday. A little extra insurance for me."

Ephram dared to look up from the spot on the floorboard where he had been intently staring. He locked eyes with Trey and immediately surmised that he had lost on the one payment.

But he still hoped that there might be some room left for negotiating—five hundred a month wasn't much. It didn't appear as if Hillman intended to kill him, so he bucked up and decided to give it one more try.

"Make it fifteen hundred a month, and you got yourself a deal," Ephram said. "That ain't much."

Ephram squeezed up closer to his door. "I bet if the courts got holt of this, a rich man like you'd be made to paid more 'n that in child support. Remember, we're talkin' 'bout two youngens."

"The courts! What the hell do you know 'bout the courts?" Trey sneered over at Ephram, enunciating his every word, his voice growing steadily louder.

"The courts ain't gonna never get a holt of this. Us Hillmans own the courts 'round here. We got that old fool of a circuit judge in our pocket, and he wouldn't cross us, not on his life."

Trey let that sink in before he continued.

"And it's for damn sure that he ain't gonna go against us Hillmans, not for the likes of you, old man. You'd best be puttin' any thoughts you got 'bout goin' to the law outta your head."

A Watch in the Night

When Ephram didn't answer him immediately, Trey snapped.

In one swift motion, he leaned across the seat, throttled Ephram by the throat and choked down on his windpipe.

Ephram floundered around on the seat, his arms flailing helplessly in the air as he tried to break Trey's hold.

But he was no match for Trey. When the old man's eyes started to protrude out of their sockets, Trey applied more pressure.

Ephram's neck was as brittle as a dry twig, Trey thought. He could break it with one quick snap. He squeezed harder, and the veins in Ephram's forehead popped out, thick and purple.

As suddenly as Trey had grabbed Ephram, he released him, recoiling away from him in disgust. A stench emanated up from where Ephram sat and filled the cab of the truck.

A stain formed, at first a spot and then an advancing circle, on the front of Ephram's trousers. Trey flung open his door and hung his head outside to get some fresh air while Ephram sat gagging and spitting and gasping for breath.

"I'll give you one thousand a month, take it or leave it," Trey said. He pulled his door closed.

"Right now, I don't much care," Trey added. " I'm thinkin' it'd be better to kill you right here and now and be done with this bullshit."

Ephram couldn't force enough air into his windpipe to speak. He shook his head to indicate that he would take the money. At that moment, he would have agreed to anything just to get away from Trey.

"But know this old man," Trey growled. "Don't even consider crossin' me; 'cause if you do, I'll come back and kill you. If I hear so much as a rumor that I'm connected with them babies, you're one dead son-of-a-bitch. Do you understand me?"

Still unable to get enough air into this lungs to speak, Ephram nodded his head that he understood.

"You better," said Trey.

"And don't go paradin' them brats all over town. You keep 'em out in Tate's Hell. Twins will be noticed. No need to give folks somethin' to raise their curiosity. Don't let them brats leave Tate's Hell."

Ephram nodded again.

"Ever month on the first, check your mailbox 'round noon. There'll be an envelope in the box with one thousand cash inside. You keep your mouth shut, and the money'll be there. But if you screw up, there won't be no place that you can hide. You'll pay then, not me. Do you understand?"

Ephram shook his head that he understood.

"Say it, old man. *Say, yes sir, Mr. Hillman, I understand.*"

"Yes sir," Ephram muttered to the windshield, gasping for air.

"Not good enough you no-count bastard. Look me in the eyes and say it."

Ephram turned to look at Trey.

"Yes sir, Mr. Hillman, I understand," Ephram croaked, struggling to get out each word. His throat burned as if he had swallowed gasoline.

"Again," Trey demanded. "Louder this time. Say it like you mean it." Trey was enjoying seeing the old worm squirm.

"Yes sir, Mr. Hillman, I understand."

"I think that you do," Trey said. He placed one hand around Ephram's throat and used the other to pat him on the cheek. Sweat poured out of every pore on Ephram's body, and his eyes were ablaze with fear.

Releasing Ephram's throat, Trey drew back his hand and slapped him so forcefully that the old man's head spun up and then back towards the windshield.

"Looks like, we got us a deal," Trey said, laughing.

He cranked the truck and jammed the accelerator, catching Ephram, who was still dazed from Trey's blow, off guard.

A Watch in the Night

Ephram's head smashed into the windshield with a loud pop. Blood spurted from his nose and gushed down his face in a thick, jagged stream.

Trey drove as fast as he could without losing control.

Ephram flopped and flounced in his seat doing the best that he could to hold on. Blood poured from his nose spilling onto the dashboard, before dripping down in little rivulets onto the seat and floorboard.

Trey glanced over and saw the blood, but he didn't care.

The truck approached the Whatley's yard, and Trey slowed down. When he was even with the oak, he pumped the brakes and the truck skidded to a stop, sinking up to its hubcaps in the mud.

Trey stretched his arm behind Ephram, who now was slumped low into the seat, opened the passenger door and shoved him out.

Ephram tumbled out onto the ground, and Trey smashed the accelerator, slinging mud on Ephram as the tires spun before catching.

The truck had only gone about fifty yards when Trey stopped, jammed the gearshift into reverse and came careening back towards Ephram.

Ephram panicked. Without his crutch, which was still in the truck, he couldn't get up. He frantically tried to crawl towards the oak, but he couldn't keep his balance even using his bad leg for leverage.

At the last possible moment, Trey pulled the wheel hard to the left to avoid hitting him.

When the driver's door was even with Ephram, Trey rolled down his window. First, he threw out Ephram's crutch.

"Here, you might need this," he said, laughing, when the crutch smacked Ephram on the side of the head.

"And here's your first payment." Trey dropped an envelope into the mud. "It ain't but five hundred. You'll get the full amount next month."

Ephram waited until Trey's truck disappeared before creeping over to retrieve the envelope. Bessie, who had been watching from the living room window, hurried outside as soon as the truck was gone.

"What's going on?" she demanded to know.

"Don't ask me no questions, old lady, just help me inside," Ephram croaked.

Bessie helped Ephram to his feet and handed him his crutch, which she had retrieved from the ground. He was a mess—covered with blood and piss and mud. As he huffed off inside, she noticed that he clutched a muddy envelope in his hand.

The babies were asleep on the sofa. Bessie held the door and let Ephram pass. He collapsed into the chair, and flung his crutch across the room where it struck the wall with a loud bang and then clattered to the floor.

This ruckus woke the babies, and they immediately started to cry.

"Shut them bastards up; shut 'em up," Ephram shouted at Bessie.

"And get me a goddamn drink of whiskey. Do it now," he bellowed, the sound of his voice reverberating off the walls of the small room.

Ephram's outburst petrified Karen. She had come in through the back door just moments earlier, and she stood watching the commotion from the kitchen, although neither Bessie nor Ephram realized that she was there.

Bessie scurried frantically into the kitchen to find the whiskey. She saw Karen and quickly raised one finger up over her lips, cutting her eyes back towards the living room.

Trembling, Karen tiptoed over to her where Bessie stood rummaging through the cabinets.

A Watch in the Night

Grabbing a full bottle of whiskey from a cabinet, Bessie hurriedly returned to the living room where Ephram sat cussing under his breath while the babies continued to scream.

"Damn son-of-a-bitch. Who the hell does he think that he is?"

"Here," she said, thrusting the bottle at him. Ephram took the bottle and turned it up, chugging the whiskey while he ignored her.

Bessie plucked the babies up from the couch, sticking one under each arm, before she hastily retreated back into the kitchen.

"Take 'em home with ya," Bessie pleaded, as the babies squirmed and screamed. "Their cryin' will only make things worse. He'll pass out soon enough, and then I'll come for 'em."

Karen quickly took the babies, fearing that Bessie would drop them. She wrapped them in her arms and swayed back and forth to try and calm them down.

"I don't wanna leave you," Karen said. "Come with us."

"No. I can handle myself. You go. I'll be over quick as I can."

Trey saw Bud's car parked on the side of the road as he made the turn onto Highway 27. He pulled up beside him and rolled down his window.

"Everything went off without a hitch," he said. "Meet me at Harley's. I'll give you the skinny."

Trey's truck squalled off, leaving a trail of rubber on the road.

When Bud arrived at Harley's, he pulled into the space next to Trey's truck. Trey sat behind its wheel, drinking from a flask.

Bud got out of his car and opened Trey's passenger door.

"Good god almighty! What happened?" Bud said. His heart jumped up into his throat at the sight of all the blood in the truck. The odor made him pull back.

"You killed 'im, didn't you, Trey?" Bud asked, afraid to hear the answer.

"I ain't killed nobody, so relax" Trey said. "I just roughed the old bastard up to get my point across. He pissed all over hisself. Can you believe it? The blood is where he hit his head on the windshield. Smell is awful, ain't it?"

Trey got out of the truck and came around to where Bud stood.

"He took the money," Trey said, taking another pull from his flask. "I had to up it to a grand a month. But it didn't take much persuasion to get 'im to take it."

"Yeah, right," Bud said.

"I' was thinkin' on my way back into town that with any luck Whatley will drink hisself to death or have an accident with that kinda of money. That accident part started to make sense."

"Forget 'bout it," Bud replied." For now, anyways. Pay the damn money, and let it be."

Trey offered Bud a pull from his flask.

"I'm not in a drinkin' mood," Bud said, refusing the flask. "I'm headed home to bed. You oughta do the same."

"Yeah, sure."

Trey followed Bud back into town. At the edge of town, Trey turned off onto the road that led out to his house. He made it a point to wave to Bud.

When Bud was outta sight, Trey looped back and turned into Langley Motors, a small used car dealership. Langley's only salesman came out to greet him.

"What can I do for you, Mr. Hillman?" he asked.

"My dog got hit," Trey said. "I took 'im to the vet, but lost him anyways. He messed this cab up somethin' awful. How 'bout you give me the keys to that truck over yonder. I'll be back in on

Monday. Langley can order me somethin' new from Cartersville Ford then."

"Sure, Mr. Hillman," the salesman said. "I'll get you a truck. That one you pointed to belongs to me. But I'll find you somethin' else to drive."

"Correction. That truck *belonged* to you," Trey said.

"I don't think Langley wants to lose my business. So just hand over the keys and I'll be goin'."

"Sure, Mr. Hillman," the salesman said, flipping Trey the keys. "No problem."

CHAPTER ELEVEN

Naomi was surprised to see Millie and Mango asleep in their cradles when she got home from work. She smiled down at them. The Reverend Samuel Spears' Inspirational Hour played softly in the background, and a fire blazed in the hearth. She was glad to be home.

She followed the smell of baking chicken into the kitchen where Karen was stooped over, lifting a tray from the oven.

"I didn't hear you come in," Karen said, as she stood up and placed a pan of chicken on the top of the stove.

"I saw the twins," Naomi said. "What are they doin' back?"

"Sit down. I'll tell you what I know over supper, which ain't much. They just went to sleep. It's so good to have 'em back. It ain't so lonely here when they're 'round."

"I know you been lonely, Karen. You've hardly left the place since them babies was born. But they ain't yours. I don't know what Bessie'll do, but she can't saddle you with 'em."

"Oh, Mama, please don't start in on me. I wanta help."

"Don't you 'oh Mama' me," Naomi said. "You know that I'm right. If Bessie don't take 'em to her niece's soon, we gonna have to make some other 'rangements for 'em."

"Now, Mama, don't you go talkin' like that. I can't bear the thought of Millie and Mango bein' turned over to perfect strangers no more than Bessie can. Leave it be. Bessie'll work things out soon enough."

"Now, tell me how you gotta 'em back over here?"

"There ain't much to tell," Karen said. "I walked over to the Whatleys late in the afternoon to help Bessie bathe the babies, feed them and put them down for the night. Then all she's got to do is feed 'em durin' the night."

"When I got there, I heard a terrible ruckus inside the house. The babies was cryin', and Ephram was hollerin' at Bessie.

"I went on in. Ephram didn't see me, so I hung back in the kitchen and waited. When Bessie came into the kitchen to get somethin', I could tell right off that she was relieved to see me.

"She was all flustered, and she pert near begged me to take the babies. I didn't take the time to find out what was goin' on. Not with Ephram carryin' on like somethin' crazy. I picked up Millie and Mango and fled outta there. Bessie said she'd come for the babies later."

"You see that's what I'm talkin' bout," Naomi said all flustered. "This whole set up worries me. Bessie ain't able to care for two babies. And then you throw in Ephram's drinkin' and his temper. That place ain't fit for the babies."

"Calm down, Mama," Karen begged. She had not seen her mother this upset for some time.

"No, I won't calm down," Naomi retorted. "I don't even like you goin' over there at all even durin' the day. It ain't safe. And them youngens alone with Bessie over there at night. Ain't no tellin' what could happen. It's gotta stop. I'm callin' for help."

Before Karen could answer, there was a knock at the back door.

Karen rushed to open the door, hoping the distraction would give Naomi time to calm down.

Bessie stood shivering in the cold. She didn't even have on a sweater.

"Come on in," Karen said.

Bessie stepped inside. "How are the babies?" she asked, out of breath. "I come as fast as I could. I hope they ain't been a bother."

"Of course, they ain't been a bother," Karen answered. "Mama was just sayin' how glad she was to see 'em."

"I can take 'em now," Bessie said. "Ephram's passed out. He won't bother us no more tonight."

"They're sound asleep," Karen said. "Eat some supper with us. They'll wake up soon, and I'll help with the feedin'. That'll give Mama a little time to spend with 'em."

Karen tried to make her voice calm and cheerful as she fussed with setting a place for Bessie at the table. Out of the corner of her eye, she watched her mother for a reaction.

"Yes, eat with us," Naomi said. "We need to talk."

Karen gave her mother a pleading look, but Naomi's face was firm; her jaw set, her stare back at Karen unwavering.

Bessie timidly pulled out a chair and sat down. Naomi passed her the chicken, and she forked a small piece.

"Go on, Bessie, take more than that. You gotta eat," Naomi said, her voice softening.

Karen heaped some potatoes onto Bessie's plate. "Mama's right, you gotta eat," she said.

"How was work today, Mama?" Karen asked, trying to skirt the issue of the earlier episode at the Whatley house.

"Work was just fine," Naomi said. The women ate in silence. The tension hung in the air like a stale odor. Finally, Karen pushed back her plate. She had lost her appetite.

When a cry came from the living room, Karen jumped up from the table.

"That's Mango," she said. She rushed over to retrieve the bottles, which sat warming in a pot of water on the stove. "I can tell the difference in their cryin'. Millie squeals, but Mango bellows like an old milk cow."

"Ya'll go on and feed the babies," Naomi said. "I'll put the dishes in the sink. Then we'll talk."

Naomi took longer in the kitchen than she had planned. She worked slowly washing each dish, wiping it dry and returning it to the cabinet. She needed time to think. Her last chore was to take the scraps out to Duke.

"Come on, boy," she called over to Duke, who was lying in a pile hugging the warmth of the chimney bricks.

Duke limped over to his plate, favoring his left hip. Naomi scratched behind his ears.

"We both gettin' old and stove-up, boy," she said, rubbing the small of her back.

Looks like another a freeze tonight, she thought. Naomi took a few more moments and carefully covered some of her plants.

"I didn't mean to take so long," she said, finally strolling into the living room.

Nobody heard her but Millie.

Mango lay sleeping in his cradle, Karen sat nodding in the rocking chair and Bessie sat slumped against the back of the sofa snoring.

Naomi walked over to Millie whose eyes were bright and twinkling from the light of the fire as she followed the flickering shadows on the wall.

"You got it all to yourself, my little night owl," Naomi said. She stooped and lifted Millie from the cradle.

Naomi slowly lowered herself into the easy chair and relaxed, while softly crooning to Millie. It felt good to have a baby in her arms. It was not just Karen who had been lonely.

She pressed Millie against her chest, and Millie's head nuzzled Naomi's neck; the soft blonde hair felt like silk against her skin. The baby smelled sweet and fresh.

The room felt peaceful as Naomi rocked Millie in her arms. After a few minutes, the rising and falling of Millie's chest and the little warm, wet wisps of breath on her neck, signaled Naomi that Millie had fallen asleep.

After a brief respite, Naomi pushed herself up from the chair and placed Millie back into her cradle.

She shook Karen awake. "Go on and get in your bed. We'll leave the babies here tonight."

She lifted Bessie's feet onto the sofa and lowered her head onto a cushion. She placed a quilt over her and stoked the fire one last time before she went to her own bed. There's nothin' that can't wait 'til mornin', she thought.

The next morning everybody in the Ivey household was up before the sun—Millie and Mango made sure of that.

"I'm gonna make us a pot of strong coffee," Naomi said, "and then we gonna talk 'bout the babies."

When the pot stopped perking, Naomi poured three cups. She handed a cup to Karen and Bessie, and they all sat down at the table.

Karen was glum; she anticipated the worst. Bessie was jittery, distracted. Naomi was determined. She had slept fitfully for the first part of the night, but in the wee morning hours, she had made up her mind what to do.

"Millie and Mango are over a month old," Naomi said. "We can't put off decidin' what to do 'bout 'em no longer. Not after what happened at your place yesterday, Bessie."

"It weren't nothin'. Ephram got worked up, that's all."

"It was bad enough that you sent the babies here. So, don't say that it weren't nothin'," Naomi snapped back.

Bessie shifted uneasily in her seat. Naomi pushed on.

"First of all, you ain't up to carin' for two babies on your own, Bessie. You and me both done got too old for that. And even if you could, we all know the real problem is Ephram Whatley."

Karen swirled the cream around in her coffee with a spoon. She didn't look up or speak. She knew her mother well enough to hold her tongue. Bessie squirmed some more in her seat.

Naomi pressed on. "With his drinkin', we can't tell what he'll do next. That's what worries me. The plain truth is that place ain't fit for the babies with Ephram there. I ain't said nothin' yet,

A Watch in the Night

but I don't like Karen bein' 'round Ephram neither. It ain't no secret how Ephram Whatley feels 'bout us black folks."

Bessie jumped to Ephram's defense. She knew where the conversation was going. Naomi wanted the babies out of the Whatley house.

"He's harmless; he really is," Bessie said. "He gets drunk and he cusses and hollers. But that's all. He wouldn't hurt nobody, Naomi. He never laid a hand on Lily, not even once. He's passed out drunk or gone with his cousin most of the time. He ain't no threat."

Naomi wasn't backing down.

"That ain't the point, Bessie," Naomi said. "Even if he never hit Lily that don't mean he won't get drunk and hurt one of these babies."

Bessie and Karen didn't respond so Naomi continued on.

"And they can't live 'round all that racket—the cussin' and hollerin'. It ain't right."

"If that ain't enough," Naomi continued, "there's more. The only heat you got, Bessie, is that old kerosene heater, and it the coldest winter on record. You know it, I know it—we all know it. Time has done run out. Somethin' has got to be done 'bout Millie and Mango."

Bessie suddenly sat up defiantly in her chair. This surprised both Naomi and Karen. Bessie was always so meek.

"Naomi, I don't mean you no disrespect, but them are my grandbabies. I 'preciate all that you and Karen done to help me. Lord knows that I do. And if Karen can't help me no more, I understand. But I'm keepin' the babies with me. It ain't for you to decide, Naomi."

"Bessie, Mama didn't mean that we ain't gonna help you no more," Karen said, looking pleadingly at her mother. "You don't mean that do you, Mama?"

Naomi softened. She had never seen Bessie so riled up before.

Bessie's head shook slightly as she sat with her lips pursed tightly together, her fingers grasping the cup.

"No, of course, I don't mean to say that we won't help," Naomi replied gently. "But we need a better plan. What 'bout your niece? Why don't ya'll go there?"

"I ain't give up on that notion," Bessie answered, the edge gone from her voice, too. "But Ephram says the babies gotta stay in Tate's Hell."

"But why?" Naomi said, boring down on Bessie. "He don't care 'bout 'em. He's up to somethin'. And I got a good notion of what it might be."

Bessie avoided looking directly at Naomi.

"I don't know what you mean," she said. "Ephram's always been peculiar. He was the same way with Lily."

"It's more than Ephram bein' peculiar, and you know that, Bessie," Naomi said, sternly this time. She was not going to let Bessie wiggle off of the hook.

"Ya'll lost me," Karen said.

Sensing a chance to leave, Bessie grabbed it. "It's time me and the babies got on home. Ephram will be up soon. I don't want 'im to find us gone."

Bessie stood up to go.

"Mama," Karen said, looking first at Bessie and then at Naomi. "Do somethin'."

"Wait, Bessie," Naomi pleaded. "Hear me out."

Naomi reached up and took Bessie by the hand.

"Don't leave like this," Naomi said. "We all want the same thing. We all want what's best for Millie and Mango."

"Yes, wait," Karen implored Bessie, grabbing her hand.

"I think that I figgered this out," Naomi said, "provided that we can get Ephram to go along with us. We'll help out if the babies stay here at our house 'til you go to your niece."

"I don't know if Ephram will agree to that," Bessie said.

"Well, if he don't, I'm callin' the welfare people today. They can take the babies or leave 'em with you, but leastways I tried to do what's right."

It was obvious to Bessie that Naomi meant business. She might be the grandmother, but she couldn't stop Naomi from placing the call. And she knew that it was anybody's guess what the state would choose to do with babies.

"I'll go talk to 'im," Bessie said.

"I'm goin' with you," Naomi replied, rising from her chair. "And the babies stay here."

Bessie stiffened at this suggestion.

"I don't know 'bout you goin' over, Naomi. Ephram had hisself a lot to drink yesterday. He'll wake up in a foul humor. And if the babies ain't with me, I don't know what he'll do."

"I'm goin' with you, and the babies are stayin' here. Otherwise, I'm placing the call right now."

Naomi wasn't budging. She had made up her mind.

"Let's go then," Bessie said, with a sigh of defeat.

Ephram was still asleep when Naomi and Bessie arrived. The house was freezing.

"What's wrong with your heat, Bessie? This house is like an icebox."

"I 'spect the kerosene run out durin' the night. I been meanin' to call over to Hodges Oil and get some brung out, but it slipped my mind."

"You won't get none today. Not on a Saturday. Not with the freeze last night."

"I reckon not."

"Go on, wake up Ephram. I'll put on some coffee."

Naomi busied herself makin' bottles and coffee while Bessie went to get Ephram.

The coffee had just finished perking when Bessie came back with Ephram lumbering behind her. He dropped down into a chair sullenly.

"What the hell is she doin' here?" he growled at Bessie.

Naomi ignored his remark and poured him a cup of coffee. She noticed that his neck and face were badly bruised.

"Why's it so goddamned cold in here?" he said, picking up the coffee.

"I musta forgot to call 'bout the kerosene," Bessie answered.

"Then we ain't gonna get no heat 'til Monday. Hodges can't get them no-count drivers to work when it's cold like this. Everbody knows that. Fetch me a quilt. I'm liable to freeze my balls off sittin' here at my own table."

"Hush up old man," Bessie said, her face flushing a bright red. "Hush up talkin' like that."

Bessie left the room and returned with a quilt, which she thrust at Ephram.

"Drink your coffee," Bessie said. "I got somethin' to talk over with you. It's 'bout the babies."

At the mention of the babies, Ephram snapped to attention.

"Where're the little bastards?" he said.

"Ephram, don't call 'em that," Bessie said. "It ain't right. They got names."

"Don't tell me how to talk in my own home. Answer me. Where the hell is them *bastards?*"

"I took 'em over to Naomi's when the heat gave out," Bessie lied. "They can't go without heat."

Ephram seemed satisfied with that answer and went back to his coffee.

"We need to talk 'bout 'em," Bessie said. "I can't hold out to tend to two youngens by myself."

"Ain't her girl been helpin' you," Ephram remarked, nodding his head at Naomi. "So, what's the goddamn problem?"

A Watch in the Night

"The problem is this," Naomi said sternly. "My girl ain't comin' in this house no more what with all your drinkin' and carryin' on. The only way we gonna help out anymore is for them babies to stay at our house. Otherwise, I'll call the welfare."

Naomi wasn't afraid of Ephram. His hands shook so badly that he could barely pick up his cup.

Ephram pushed back from the table. "Ain't no old woman comin' in this house and tellin' me what to do. Go on; get up out of here."

Bessie snatched up Ephram's cane. He couldn't get up without that.

"She's right, Ephram. Either the babies stay over there, or I'm leavin' with 'em."

As Ephram glared up at the two women, his face pulsed with outrage. His cheeks flushed red, and the bruises stood out in ugly purple patches as the veins swelled in his neck and forehead.

"My own wife and some old bitch talkin' to me like that in my own house. If I could get up from this chair, I'd wring the necks on both you old worn-out hens."

"Well, you can't get up," Bessie shot back, waving his cane from across the room. "You ain't got no choice but to simmer down and listen. What do you care where the babies live anyways, so long as they stay in Tate's Hell? Answer me that old man."

Slumping lower in his chair, Ephram slurped his coffee loudly as he pondered the situation. Bessie had a point, he conceded in his mind.

Them damn youngens was drivin' him crazy, squallin' all night and day. He couldn't get a minute's peace in his own house. He hadn't figgered on *that* when him and Fred hatched their plan.

Bessie was right he decided. All he really cared 'bout was that them youngens stayed in Tate's Hell. Better them bitches' house than here.

Ephram looked up from his coffee, and he confronted the women head-on.

"Them babies ain't leavin' Tate's Hell. You old women better know that. As far as who takes care of 'em, I don't give a good goddamn. Ya'll work that out. Hell, if the truth be told, I'd rather them little bastards stay over with *them bitches*."

If looks could kill, Bessie's eyes would have dropped Ephram dead. In return, Ephram reared up and shot Bessie a menacing glare of his own as he shook his fist at both her and Naomi.

"Now hear me both of you. Them babies best not leave Tate's Hell. And I will be checkin'. When I tell you to bring 'em over here for me to see, then you'd best be bringin' 'em. Otherwise, there's gonna be hell to pay. Do you two old biddies understand that?"

"Alright then, it's settled," Bessie snarled back at Ephram. "The babies'll stay at the Iveys' place."

"I said they could, didn't I, old woman? Just so I can see 'em when I say."

"Then I'm goin' on home where it's warm," Naomi said, turning to leave.

"Call Fred," Ephram said to Bessie, ignoring Naomi who bustled out of the room. "I can't stay here without heat."

Naomi was alone in the kitchen when Bessie knocked at the back door. She opened the door and let Bessie in. They sat down at the table.

"Bessie, what's goin' on with Ephram? First, he demands the twins be brung back to 'im, now he says they can stay here, so long as they don't leave Tate's Hell. I got my own thoughts 'bout what's goin' on, but you tell me what you know."

"I don't know much more than you, Naomi. Just that Ephram is actin' peculiar."

A Watch in the Night

Ephram had sternly warned Bessie not to breathe a word to anyone about the visit from Trey Hillman. While Bessie hated to deceive Naomi, her fear of Ephram warned her to keep the secret.

"Bessie," Naomi said. Her voice was soft and kind. "There's more. We both know that. You can trust me."

"I can't say no more, Naomi. Please, don't ask me to."

"You know that we don't mind helpin' with the youngens. Lord knows that we love them," Naomi said.

"But, for the life of me, Bessie, I just don't see how this can go on much longer. I'm back at work. And Karen is lookin' for work. With Washington gone we need the money."

"That's what I come to talk 'bout. I got a plan. Will you hear me out?" Bessie asked.

"Alright," Naomi said, sighing.

"Your Karen needs work," Bessie said. "You just said that. Jobs are hard to come by this time of year 'specially for you black folks. I was thinkin' that I could pay Karen for watchin' the babies. Not much. But I'd pay. Whata you think?"

"And where you gonna get the money?" Naomi asked. "We can't take what little bit you got. But we got bills to pay same as you."

"Ephram said he'd pay," Bessie said.

"Ephram! Now where's he gettin' money. That's what I was talkin' 'bout earlier, Bessie."

"Ephram gets a check," Bessie retorted.

Bessie didn't have any intention of letting the conversation go any further. She wouldn't tell Naomi about the visit from Trey Hillman, and the money she found in the muddy envelope after Ephram passed out.

"After you left, we had us a fight," she quickly added. "I told 'im that we couldn't just dump these youngens on ya'll. That ya'll done enough already. That you worked and Karen was lookin' for work. Then he said somethin' that almost made me pass out."

"What's that?"

"He offered to pay Karen to tend the babies."

"Ephram offered to pay! Now I know somethin' is up. Bessie, this all sounds wrong."

"I'm beggin' you, Naomi. There ain't no other way. I could help out. It'd just be for a short while, Naomi—'til I can figger a way to get to my niece's. Just think 'bout it. Please."

"It ain't even for me to decide, Bessie. It'd be up to Karen. I can't speak for her."

"I'll do it," Karen said. Naomi and Bessie had not seen Karen standing in the doorway.

"Karen, you ain't thought this through," Naomi said, giving Karen a stern look.

"There ain't nothing to think about. I want to do this," Karen retorted.

"Alright," Naomi said, throwing her hands up in exasperation. "We'll try it for a while. But you got to lay plans to go to your niece, Bessie, quick as you can."

Bessie and Karen exchanged a brief smile.

"You two stop it. You mighta won this battle, but you two ain't won the war."

Naomi tried to sound stern, but she couldn't.

"You don't got no heat at your place, Bessie. Why don't you stay here with us the rest of the day. You two can mind the babies. I'm gonna make us a pot of stew. Now shoo, both of you. I feel like I need to cook."

After the discussion in the Whatley kitchen that cold January morning, life settled into a routine for the Ivey and Whatley households.

The twins lived with Naomi and Karen, except for a visit to the Whatley house on the first day of each month. Ephram

A Watch in the Night

insisted that the children be brought over on that day so that he could be absolutely certain that they remained in Tate's Hell.

No babies, no money. It was that simple. And he sure wasn't about to trust those two bitches, or even his own wife.

"After all, who'd thought that she'd take up with them bitches or even carry on so 'bout them two brats like she does," he said to Fred after one of the monthly visits.

But the monthly visit was all the reassurance that he required regarding the whereabouts of the babies.

It had been Fred's idea to blackmail Hillman, although after the plan had worked out so well, Ephram later took full credit.

Fred had a tad more business savvy than Ephram, which wasn't saying much since Ephram had an I.Q. not much higher than that of his dog, Clover. It was Fred who had recognized opportunity when it came knocking at Ephram's door.

The plot had been hatched over a bottle of Wiley's moonshine on Christmas Eve. Fred had stopped over at Ephram's for a drink of whiskey, a family tradition that he and Ephram had established years before.

When he arrived, he was surprised to find Ephram already drunk and carrying on like a crazy man—something about a visit from Sheriff Tate.

A visit from the Sheriff couldn't be good news. But Ephram was so distraught, that it was impossible for Fred to flesh out any of the details of what had happened.

Ephram begged Fred to take him home with him—immediately. So, he did. He hadn't planned on having Ephram for the holidays; he hadn't planned on anything other than getting drunk.

But Fred lived alone, and he couldn't just go off and leave Ephram, not in his present condition. When Ephram sweetened the deal with the offer of bringing along two bottles of Wiley's shine, pity overcame Fred, and he loaded Ephram up into his car.

So, he and Ephram spent Christmas Eve at Fred's house drinking shine. They would have preferred Jim Beam, but times were tough. The shine had to do, and it worked fine in a pinch.

They were about halfway through the second bottle when Ephram told Fred about the babies, and they started discussing the plan to go after Hillman for the money.

Ephram was in a bad way; that much was clear as day to Fred. He had lost Lily, the only person who was willing to look after him.

"My old lady ain't good for nothing' no more," he told Fred. "And if that ain't bad enough, she's done gone and dumped two screamin' brats on us in a shack that's so flimsy you can hear a dog fart from the back porch anywhere in the place."

Fred had to agree that the future did look rather bleak for Ephram.

"It ain't right that Hillman gets off scot-free, while I'm left holdin' the bag. He oughta be made to pay."

Those were the words that fired up what few brain cells Fred Whatley still possessed after thirty years of steady drinking (Fred was younger than Ephram) and enabled him to come up with the idea of going after Hillman.

It had taken a lot of convincing by Fred to persuade Ephram to call Hillman. Ephram had been willing enough to go along with the plan when he had a full bottle of shine under his belt.

But once he had sobered up the next day, Ephram wasn't as enthusiastic about the plot, especially when he realized that he was the one who would have to do the dirty work and confront Hillman.

Only after a week of steady drinking, did Ephram see the light again and agree to go make the call.

"For God's sake man wake up and smell the coffee," Fred said, in an effort to bolster Ephram's courage. "A chance like this don't come by ever damn day."

It was this logic that brought Ephram around.

And then it was Fred who had managed to get the Hillman's private number from an old girlfriend. That had taken a couple of weeks.

The girlfriend had been Susan Hillman's housekeeper until she got caught stealing. The woman didn't have any use for Fred anymore; hell, she practically despised the man. And she knew full well that Fred had to be up to no good. But she was carrying quite a grudge against her former employer.

Susan had treated her practically like a slave when she had worked for the Hillmans, and that was after they had gone to high school together. Of course, they hadn't been friends in school, or anything like that. But still, there was no call to go treating her like the colored help and then to up and fire her.

Fred's offer to throw in a ten-dollar bill made the decision a no-brainer for Fred's ex-girlfriend. She even offered to give him the Hillmans' post office box number, but Fred didn't think that would be necessary.

Once Fred got the private number it was a done deal. Fred, with the help of Wiley's shine, had to prop Ephram up during the call. And it was Fred who came up with setting the meeting in Tate's Hell, instead of in town.

"Gives you the home field advantage," Fred explained to Ephram. "Lets 'em know who is callin' the shots."

At the time, Fred hadn't figured on Hillman beating Ephram nearly to death. But later, much later, after Ephram had healed up some from the beating, and after they had polished off a bottle of good whiskey, not the shine, they agreed that the plan was "a pure stroke of genius."

After the money started to flow in from Hillman, Fred and Ephram became inseparable.

They spent most of their time drinking at the Dew Drop Inn, a seedy little juke, located just over the Trinity county line. Ephram and Fred had always been loyal patrons of Harley's, funds permitting, but they had judiciously decided that it was best to take their business elsewhere.

Neither of them wanted to risk running into Trey Hillman, who was known to occasionally drink at Harley's.

It was while at the Dew Drop that Ephram and Fred renewed their acquaintance with two of their old drinking buddies, the Seever brothers, J.H. and Toppy. In fact, it was the Seever brothers who had championed Ephram's cause when he campaigned against the Hillman Lumber Company selling the land next to his house to the Ivey family.

At the time, both Seevers profusely proclaimed that they wouldn't live next to "no pack of coloreds" a statement, which was just a tad bit hypocritical on their part, given the fact that they lived in a dilapidated one-room house on the edge of Tate's Hell, no more than a stone's throw from the beginning of the "colored quarters" in Trinity. A rental at that.

One rainy afternoon, when foul weather had ruled out fishing, some of the locals, including Sheriff Askers, saw Fred Whatley cruise slowly past Harry's picture window in a new car, with the Seever brothers encamped in the back seat, and Fred's cousin, Ephram, riding shotgun.

"Ain't that Fred Whatley in a new car?" Bo Thompkins remarked to nobody in particular, pointing out the window at a passing car.

"I wouldn't exactly call that *new*," Ralph Jeeters threw in.

"Well, it is damn sure new for Fred Whatley," Bo shot back. "It's a used car, for sure, but it is a far sight better than anything else I ever seen Fred Whatley drive; he usually ain't got nothin' more than a pair of boots to travel in." Some of the men chuckled at this last remark.

"Wonder where he got the money for that car?" Ralph said what everybody else was thinking. "Fred Whatley ain't never worked a job that I know of."

Bud, who sat listening to the exchange, found this last comment a bit unsettling; he hoped that the interest in Fred's new car was just idle bar talk.

"That's Fred," Shorty Bailey said. "And it looks like the Seever brothers in the back. I ain't seen them 'round here for a spell."

"That's the Seevers in the back alright," Dwight Green threw in. "I'd know them two bastards anywheres. I remember them from when I was a kid livin' with my grandma and grandpa out in Tate's Hell. They lived close by." Dwight took a swig of his beer.

"Of course, that was a good while back," he added. Dwight had worked himself up to be a foreman at the Hillman Lumber Company, and he wanted to be certain that everybody took note of the fact that he no longer lived anywhere close to Tate's Hell.

"Some things never change," Dwight said, staring at Fred's car, which sat idling at a crossroad just past Harry's. "Them Seevers always was one for a handout. When I was a boy, they come 'round our place real regular like lookin' for a free meal."

Dwight hesitated and then went on with his story.

"We's dirt poor 'bout like everbody else durin' them days. My grandma kept a yard full of chickens. Ever Sunday she fixed us a big fried chicken dinner—it was the only decent meal we got the whole week.

"Anyways, on Sunday mornin', me and my brother hung round the back porch like those stray cats down to the fish house. Our mouths plumb watered when we smelt that chicken fryin'.

"Somewheres 'bout time for that chicken to all be fried up, me and my brother would start watchin' down the road, just prayin' that them Seever brothers weren't gonna come walkin' up. We'd rather seen a ten-foot rattlesnake crawlin' up that path straight at us than to see those two Seevers turn the corner.

"The story played out the same way every time. The Seevers would show up 'bout the time that my grandma took up the last of the chicken. My grandfolks was a hospitable lot. Them Seevers knowed if they hung 'round long enough that my grandpa was bound to ask 'em to stay and eat.

"Sure enough, as soon as my grandma called us to the table, my grandpa would look at 'em and ask if they wanted to stay and eat.

"Now polite folks woulda never come visitin' at dinner time, or they'd gone on 'bout their way when they seen a family fixin' to sit down to eat. But not them Seevers.

"'Well, if you're sure you got enough,' Toppy would say, knowin' damn well there weren't enough. We was like everybody else in them days, always fallin' just shy of enough. Still, my grandpa's pride would get the better of 'im, and he'd say 'sure there's enough'.

"Them Seevers would walk right in, bold as you please, and take the places set at the table for me and my brother. We only had enough room at the table for the family.

"The blessing was no sooner over than they'd light into that chicken while me and my brother would have to sit on the back porch waitin' for the grown-ups to finish up so we could eat. By the time them Seevers was done with that chicken, we'd be lucky to get the back and the neck.

"As soon as dinner was over, they'd leave, 'til a couple of more Sundays went by and then they'd be back. If cussin' can send a man to hell, then me and my brother are bound to burn, 'cause we cussed them Seevers with ever swear word we knowed. They're a bad lot them Seevers."

"Nothin' good will come of them sons-of-bitches hookin' up with the Whatleys," Ralph Jeeters added, shaking his head in agreement.

"I just wonder where Fred got the money for that car." With this remark, Bo Thompkins turned the conversation away from the Seevers and back to the car.

"It's for sure that he didn't get it from workin'. Fred takes after the rest of the Whatleys when it comes to that. There never was a Whatley who didn't abhor (Bo had picked that word up in church and had been waiting for a chance to use it) an honest day's work."

Bud listened carefully. But the men soon lost interest in Fred's new car, and when the conversation moved back to the weather, he relaxed.

Fred's car was a red Ford Galaxy 500, and although it wasn't a new car, it was by everyone's account a much better car than any of the Whatleys had ever been seen driving in before.

"My wife told me that she heard over at the beauty parlor that Fred bought the car over at Langley's," Harry said. "Langley's bookkeeper, Sally Deas, told my wife that Langley took Fred's old cars as a trade-in."

"But here's the kicker," Harry added. "Langley let Fred pay the rest of the money on time. And if that ain't strange enough, according to Sally, Fred comes in on the second day of the month with two $100 bills to make his payment. Whata you think of that?" Harry threw the question out for discussion.

"Well, I don't make it my business to bother 'bout where other folks get their money," Wiley Grantham said, pushing off of his bar stool.

Even Wiley was known to come into Harry's on a rainy day to get out of the house even though he had plenty of his own moonshine at home to drink.

"People's money is their own business," Wiley added emphatically, before strolling out the door.

"Hey, ya'll heard that Susan Hillman is 'spectin' another baby?" Harry asked. He knew that it was time to get the topic off of other people's money.

"That's true," Bud said. "Oh, happy day."

Once the Seevers took up with Ephram and Fred as regulars, the foursome moved their drinking back to Harley's.

The Dew Drop was no more than a hole in the wall with only two tables and one brand of beer. At the first mention of going back to Harley's, Ephram refused. But when the others insisted, he relinquished.

He found a small degree of comfort from the thought that there was safety in numbers, although he wasn't at all certain that this would be true in the event of any trouble with Trey Hillman. But Hillman had nothing to gain by starting up with him in a public place, or so Ephram hoped.

The trips to Harley's were sporadic in the beginning, when it was too much trouble to make it as far as the Dew Drop. Ephram quickly took courage when he didn't see Hillman on any of the first few visits.

Besides, drinking should not be inconvenient, and going to the Dew Drop was inconvenient. It wasn't long before the Whatleys and Seevers were regulars again at Harley's.

Beginning in early February, the foursome hit their hot spot almost every night, drinking until the place closed down, or they were too drunk to sit up on a stool, whichever came first.

On several occasions, Sheriff Akers found all four of them passed out dead-ass drunk in the parking lot, sprawled in various contorted positions in the Ford Galaxy 500.

Some of the regulars in Harley's couldn't help but notice that Ephram's pocketbook appeared to have grown in size, judging by the way he was throwing around money. And they said so.

"He's spendin' money like it's done gone out of style," one of the regulars said.

"Ephram, you rob a bank, or what?" another asked.

Eventually, Fred felt compelled to satisfy everyone's curiosity by announcing, while Ephram was in the back relieving himself, that poor old Ephram had lost his only child around Christmas time and that he had come into some insurance money. But, out of respect for Ephram, it was just best not to talk about it.

That explanation was good enough for the regulars. Everybody knew that folks in Tate's Hell bought life insurance when they couldn't buy food.

Life expectancy in Tate's Hell was short, so life insurance was akin to gambling. Questions about Ephram's money dried up.

CHAPTER TWELVE

Naomi drove along the winding beach road on her way to the island. The water in the bay was calm, a flat, gray sheet under a dreary, cloudless sky. It was the first week in February, and the weather had remained mostly wet and cold since Christmas.

A few small flat boats sat anchored offshore, trying to make the most of what had, thus far, been a lackluster season for the oyster houses. Men dressed in heavy slickers, with woolen caps stretched tightly over their heads, stood hunched over the sides of their boats working wooden tongs.

These men lifted the cumbersome tongs chest high, and then with a powerful thrust, sent them plunging to the bottom of the bay. Forearms flexed and backs strained as the men clamped the tongs shut. With another burst of effort, the men lifted the tongs up and over the sides of their boats, releasing their catch of oysters to drop in a thick, gray pile in the hull of the boats.

The women in the boats, dressed in the same heavy slickers, with woolen scarves instead of caps protecting their heads, sat perched on wooden benches stooping low to cull through the pile. Large oysters were tossed into a wooden trough in the back of the boat with small ones pitched back into the bay.

Rhythmically they worked, the men their arms like the wings of gulls, flapping slowly, methodically; the women their arms like the constant rapid flittering of a humming bird.

This drive to and from work had always been cherished time for Naomi. It was the only time that she had completely to herself. The only time that she did not spend taking care of others. Her time to contemplate the comings and goings in her own life.

Now that the twins were settled, Naomi realized, she was able to relax for the first time in weeks. She found peace in the hum of her tires against the wet pavement.

Naomi took her first job away from home the year that Karen started to school. At first, Washington resisted. But with both children in school and money tight, as usual, she had argued with him that it just made good sense.

"Money ain't gonna never get tight enough for my wife to sit round them drafty fish houses shuckin' oysters," he announced to Naomi, when she brought up the idea of going to work. "I'll work nights 'fore it comes to *that*," he said, with finality.

It never came to *that;* Naomi, with the help of Doc Adams, stumbled upon a good job.

Each child enrolled in Trinity County public schools was required to provide proof of proper vaccinations. Doc provided these vaccinations free of charge the week before school started.

So, the week before Karen's first day of school, Naomi loaded her into the family car and made the trip in to visit Doc. During this visit, Naomi mentioned to Doc that she was looking for work.

"Well, I'll be dogged," Doc said. "I had a call not more than a week back from some folks who live at the Plantation. They are in dire need of a housekeeper. Would that interest you, Naomi?" he asked, as he presented Karen with a lollypop for a job well done in sitting still for her injection.

"I reckon so," she answered, taking Karen's hand as Doc lifted her down from the examination table. "I ain't never been out to the Plantation. Ain't that a pretty far piece from town?"

"It's a good thirty miles," Doc said. "But the people looking for help are fine people. And the pay is good. You think about it Naomi, talk it over with Washington, and if you are interested, I'll place a call for you."

"Thank you, Doc; I 'preciate that," Naomi said, preparing to leave.

On the ride home, Naomi considered Doc's offer.

The idea of going anywhere near *the island*, much less *the Plantation*, she found to be extremely intimidating. All she knew about that island was the fact that only rich, white folks lived there.

And she had never spent any time in the company of white people, other than a few visits to Doc Adams and the occasional encounters she had with the next-door neighbors, Bessie and her surly husband, Ephram.

Come to think of it, Naomi mused, she had never spent much time with anybody, white or black, other than her family. She and Washington kept to themselves except for attending church.

But black folks could only make money working for whites. And Doc had said the pay was good. She resolved to at least talk it over with Washington.

Later that evening, when she broached the topic with Washington after supper, he immediately vetoed the idea.

"I know some black folks work *the island*, but I don't like the notion of you bein' that far from home. Let them rich, white folks clean up their own messes," Washington harrumphed.

But when Doc called up and said that he had arranged an interview, Naomi bridled her courage and decided to go.

"What can it hurt?" she insisted to Washington, when he balked at the idea of her going. "Doc ain't steered us wrong yet. If it weren't for Doc talkin' these folks up so, I woulda never give it no second thought."

"I reckon you right on that count," Washington conceded.

He scratched his head and paced the floor.

"Go on then," he finally said. "You won't be happy 'til you do. Lord knows you one strong-willed woman, Naomi. But you are my strong-willed woman, and I love you like a weary man loves a soft place to lay his head." Washington patted her rump as she scurried out of the room to place the call to Doc.

On the day of the interview, Naomi was tempted to turn back when she reached the bridge over to the island. It was the prospect of the salary that Doc had hinted at that bolstered her courage and allowed her to continue.

Times were hard. Washington worked as hard as any man could work, but two growing youngens put a strain on the pocketbook.

Following Doc's instructions, she made a right turn at the base of the bridge and drove along about a mile before she saw the sign announcing the entrance to *the Plantation.*

Behind the sign was a private entrance blocked by a gate staffed with guards.

Naomi slowed her car to a crawl and inched up to the gate. All of her senses were on full alert. When a uniformed guard stepped out of a small building, she lowered her window and put a tremendous effort into trying to give him a smile.

"Can I help ya?" the guard asked. He picked his teeth with a blade of grass as he gave Naomi and her little car the once over.

"I'm here to see the Brodies," Naomi stammered, too afraid now to be concerned with a smile.

"Security will take you in," the guard said. He nodded towards a red pick-up truck equipped with a siren on top. The red truck rolled out in front of her, and when the bar blocking the road lifted, she fell in behind the truck.

As Naomi followed the truck, she was surprised to discover that the Plantation looked almost deserted. The only sign that she detected of human habitation was the intricate pattern of well-manicured roads that she traveled on.

As far as she could tell, it appeared that the main road cut straight through the middle of the island. Occasionally, a smaller road would veer off towards the beach on the left or the bay on the right. There wasn't another soul in sight other than the anonymous head at the wheel of the security truck. There were no houses visible from the main road.

An odd feeling of familiarity descended over Naomi as she trailed closely behind the truck. At first, this feeling came as a mystery to her.

She had never been to the island before. Then it came to her. The Plantation bore a startling similarity to Tate's Hell—at least in one respect. The houses and people were hidden from view, tucked away into secret, private havens far back in the woods—the same as Tate's Hell.

The similarity stopped there.

In Tate's Hell, people yielded to nature, eking out small sanctuaries in the swamp, which nature could reclaim on a whim.

At the Plantation, nature yielded to people. Here the land had been permanently altered with bulldozers and saws. Nature could never fully reclaim this land, Naomi thought.

The truck turned onto a smaller paved road, and Naomi threw off her stray musings as she realized that she was getting perilously close to her first job interview.

The road curved around and then she saw it—the Brodie estate. Her jaw dropped open, and her eyes blinked several times as if she had been startled by the sudden, unexpected flash of a camera.

Doc had tried to prepare her. He had told her that, "the Brodie estate was a rather awesome establishment, even by the Plantation standards."

But Doc's words had been meaningless to her—in one ear and out the other as Washington was fond of saying. Nothing in her frame of reference, not even in the magazines that Doc kept in his office, prepared her for the grandiosity of the Brodie estate.

"It's probably 'bout like Hillman's place out on the river," Washington said, when she recounted Doc's description of the Brodie estate to him.

She and Washington had taken a Sunday drive by the Hillman home soon after its completion. And they had gawked and marveled, like all of the other people in Trinity, at the sheer size of the Hillman home.

But the Hillman home was simple compared to what she saw sitting right in front of her own two eyes. This house was bigger than the First Baptist Church, and that was the largest building Naomi had ever seen.

The security truck rolled to a stop, and an arm appeared out the driver's window pointing to the front door of the house before the driver continued on around the circular drive and then disappeared back down the entrance road.

Naomi felt small and insignificant as she hunched over the steering wheel of her car, mouth open, staring in total disbelief at the enormity of the Brodie estate.

She didn't make the slightest move to exit her car and go up to the door. Such a bold move was inconceivable to her at the moment. Instead, she sat frozen like a small animal caught in the headlights of an oncoming vehicle: afraid to get out; afraid to leave.

Later, Naomi thought that she might have sat there indefinitely had it not been for her encounter with Mrs. Brodie.

Mrs. Brodie lived on the estate with her ailing husband. On this particular morning, she had been working in her garden when she saw the strange, little car pull into her driveway.

Upon seeing the car, she stood upright, shielding the sun from her eyes with the tip of her hat, to get a better look at the car. But nobody got out.

Visitors were unheard of at the estate. Curiosity finally got the better of her, and dropping her pruning shears, Mrs. Brodie set out to investigate.

A few quick, spry steps and Mrs. Brodie traversed the short distance to the driveway. Parting the palm fronds of the trees lining the driveway, she stepped out onto the pavement and rapped on the passenger's window to Naomi's car.

Naomi had not seen Mrs. Brodie approach the car. Startled, she lurched forward in her seat hitting the horn, which responded with a loud blast.

Mrs. Brodie reacted to the sound of the horn by instinctively jumping backwards. Her hair, which was twisted into a tight bun on the top of head, caught in the fronds of the pygmy palms.

When Naomi looked over, the first thing that she saw was an indignant Mrs. Brodie struggling desperately to untangle her hair from the mass of vines and palm fronds, which bordered the driveway. This sight brought Naomi to her senses. She quickly exited the car and rushed to assist Mrs. Brodie.

Mr. Brodie watched the scene out of the front window of his study. The guards had called to inform him that security was escorting his prospective employee to the house. He intended to meet the woman at the end of the driveway, but he had been distracted by a long-distance call.

The blast of the horn made him remember that he was expecting a visitor. That's one way to announce your arrival, he thought.

He looked out of the window in time to see a rather rotund black woman emerge from a very small car and rush towards his wife, who appeared to be somehow caught in the pygmy palms.

"I'll have to call you back," he said, before dropping the receiver.

The sound of Mr. Brodie's laughter caused both women to abandon their efforts to disengage Mrs. Brodie's hair from the vines and fronds and to look up. There stood Mr. Brodie, his arms folded across his chest, a devilish gleam in his sky-blue eyes, a wicked grin plucking at the corners of his mouth.

"If you aren't a sight for sore eyes, Rebecca," he said.

Mrs. Brodie had lost the hairpiece holding her bun in place, and her hair was caught tightly in the vines, which grew up and around the palm fronds.

"You look like Medusa herself, trapped in that tree." He broke into a hearty chuckle.

"Horace, please, I fail to see the humor here," Mrs. Brodie said, piqued at what she considered to be her husband's total disregard for her current dilemma.

"I am so sorry, my dear. Of course, there is nothing funny here. Stand perfectly still now, and I'll release you from the clutches of these wretched vines and fronds. Now do be still, dear. I fear that if you thrash about anymore, I'll be forced to use your gardening shears to complete the rescue."

"Horace, please," Mrs. Brodie said, an obvious edge in her voice now.

Naomi stood mortified. This had to be her fault. She wasn't sure how, but this had to be her fault.

"Step aside, please, madam," Mr. Brodie said to Naomi.

Naomi gladly did as she was told and stepped over next to her car. She wanted badly to leave, to forget about the job, but she was trapped. Mrs. Brodie, who was less than a foot from her car, blocked her exit.

Strand by strand, Mr. Brodie patiently untangled his wife's hair. It was all over in a matter of minutes.

"There you are. Freed, darling," he said, giving Mrs. Brodie a kiss on the cheek.

"Horace, really," she snorted, stamping her foot.

"If you'll excuse me," she said curtly to Naomi, before spinning on her heels and walking briskly towards the back of the house.

When she rounded the corner and dropped out of sight, Mr. Brodie turned to Naomi and broke into a belly laugh. In spite of her discomfort, Mr. Brodie's infectious laugher seized Naomi, and she could not suppress a chuckle.

"Horace Brodie," Mr. Brodie said, regaining his composure as he dabbed at the corner of his mouth with a white handkerchief that he had retrieved from his pants pocket. He extended his hand to Naomi with a warm smile.

Over Mr. Brodie's shoulder, Naomi could see several long strands of the woman's hair still caught in the vines and flapping about in the wind. This was a sobering sight for Naomi, and her facial muscles constricted into a tight grimace.

She still believed Mrs. Brodie's ordeal to be her fault. If that wasn't enough to rattle her nerves, there was the hand, still reaching out to her.

No white man had ever offered her a hand to shake. But there it was, poised in front of her, demanding a response.

Naomi took the hand lightly, as if it might be scalding hot, and hurriedly gave it a quick pump.

"I'm Naomi, Naomi Ivey," she stuttered. "I'm here 'bout the job."

"I've been expecting you," Mr. Brodie replied, his smile broadening. "You come highly recommended by my dear friend Doctor Adams," he continued.

Naomi did not know until this moment that Doc Adams actually was friends with these people or that he had been so kind as to put in a good word for her. Naomi let down her guard, but only a bit.

"Please come inside, where we can talk," Mr. Brodie said. He swiped at his mouth again with the handkerchief. Naomi detected a slight slur in his speech.

Mr. Brodie didn't wait for an answer. He turned and started down the same path his wife had taken moments earlier. Naomi dutifully followed.

A Watch in the Night

When Mr. Brodie turned the corner of the house and crossed a patio to a humongous back door, Naomi was right on his footsteps. Although Mr. Brodie attempted to carry himself erect, Naomi noticed a stoop in his shoulders and a slight drag to his right foot.

He pushed open the door. "After you," he said, extending his arm out and sweeping his up-turned palm towards the door.

Naomi crossed over the threshold, and her hand flew up to her chest. Her next breath caught in her throat, the air trapped on the back of her tongue.

The room she entered was a kitchen. But it was not like any kitchen that Naomi had ever seen, not even in those picture books in Doc's office. This kitchen was larger than her entire house.

Mr. Brodie waited patiently in the doorway as Naomi's eyes perused the room.

Pots and pans hung from the ceiling above an island in the middle of the room. One wall consisted of two large sinks and long stretches of cabinets.

The adjoining wall had a double oven, a monstrosity of a stove and a refrigerator large enough to store food sufficient to feed her entire church.

A large brick hearth filled one corner before jutting out into a sunny alcove, with waist-high brick walls. Above the walls, plate glass ran up to the ceiling, which let the sun bathe the alcove in warmth and light. A round table sat in the center of the alcove surrounded by plants, hanging from the ceiling and stationed on the floor.

"Please, sit," Mr. Brodie said, motioning for Naomi to have a seat at the kitchen table.

Surprised that she was actually able to make her feet move, Naomi crossed the room and sat down on the edge of the chair that Mr. Brodie had pulled out for her.

There she sat, perched like a bird about to fly away, as Mr. Brodie poured two cups of coffee from a silver urn before sitting down next to her. He placed one cup in front of Naomi and pushed a silver tray, containing a sugar bowl and creamer, towards her.

"I like my coffee black," she managed to say, waving off the tray.

"As do I," Mr. Brodie said, looking up to meet Naomi's fixed stare.

He liked her immediately. Perhaps, it was the sheer warmth that radiated from her, he thought later. Or her gentle smile. Perhaps, it was the way she sat at his table, shy, overwhelmed by her surroundings, but erect and proud. Or that she looked him straight in the eye when she talked, even though she obviously found him intimidating. He couldn't quite put his finger on it, but he knew she was the one for the job.

And the feeling was mutual. Although Naomi didn't even come close to relaxing on that first visit, not in the presence of this white man who lived in such a magnificent house, she did find Mr. Brodie to be kind and considerate.

When he offered her the job, Naomi accepted, agreeing to start the following Monday.

Monday arrived, and Naomi found herself jittery as she prepared her family's breakfast. "You don't got to go to work, Naomi," Washington said, sensing her anxiety.

"I wanta go," she said. She dropped an egg, which splattered on the floor. Naomi gave Washington a bewildered look. "I'm just a little nervous bein' it's my first day and all."

Washington took the dishrag from her hand and stooped to wipe the egg up for her.

"Then go," he said, as he stood up and rinsed the cloth. "But if them people don't treat you right, you get on in that little car of yours and hightail it right back home. We'll make ends meet. We always do."

"Really, I'm fine," Naomi said, as she handed him his breakfast plate.

When she arrived at the guard shack, the same white guard, the one who had barely spoken to her on her first visit, slapped a sticker on her windshield, which read "Plantation."

"Welcome aboard," he said, with what almost amounted to a smile.

"Thank you," she replied.

Mr. Brodie answered the door. "Good morning," he said. "Come on in. I suppose that I'll have to show you the ropes myself because our last housekeeper quit without notice, and my wife is a late sleeper. But there's no rush. We could have a cup of coffee before getting started. Maybe get to know one another a little better. The cups are in that cupboard over the sink."

Naomi couldn't imagine what could possibly be in all those cupboards. She opened the one next to the sink and removed two cups from the dozens available to her.

The cups were light and dainty, decorated with flowers. Not at all like the heavy white mugs she and Washington used to drink their coffee.

If the truth be told, Naomi would have much preferred to skip the coffee and go straight to work. But she didn't see any getting around the talk, so she poured the coffee and then sat down in a chair that Mr. Brodie had pulled out for her at the table.

Mr. Brodie took a seat next to her. Naomi stared into her cup and only looked up when he asked her a question. Thirty minutes later, when Mr. Brodie rose to leave, Naomi was shocked to realize that she had done most of the talking.

She knew almost nothing about him, but he knew almost her whole life story.

While Naomi and Mr. Brodie bonded immediately, the same was not true for Naomi and Mrs. Brodie. Naomi found Mrs.

Brodie to be aloof and withdrawn, although these were not the words that she used to describe her.

"She's a loner," Naomi said, when describing her to Washington later. "Sometimes I wouldn't even know that she's on the place 'cept I hear her playin' that piano."

At times, Mrs. Brodie's aloofness bordered on rudeness to Naomi. But Mr. Brodie explained away his wife's behavior by saying that she meant no harm; that she was a bit eccentric, a word that Naomi had to look up in Nathan's dictionary when she got home.

Mr. Brodie died almost two years to the day after Naomi started to work for him. It came as a blow to her. She and Mr. Brodie had grown close. Naomi was his only contact with the outside world other than his telephone calls to friends back in Boston.

The same was not true for Naomi and Mrs. Brodie. She had barely formed any relationship at all with her. Naomi even feared that she might lose her job, although that didn't happen.

After her husband's death, Mrs. Brodie became even more withdrawn than before. She spent most of her days working in the garden, playing her piano or just walking through the grounds. She rarely spoke a word to Naomi.

Several times Naomi tried to reach out to her, but Mrs. Brodie made it clear that she wanted nothing more from Naomi other than a clean home and food.

This task was relatively easy for Naomi. Mrs. Brodie moved through the place like a ghost never disturbing anything, and she barely touched the food Naomi prepared for her.

The Brodie home was by any standards a grandiose construction, but the true magnificence of the estate was defined by its grounds.

Mr. Brodie, after moving to the island, became somewhat of a horticulturist to occupy his time and satisfy his creative urges. He hired and then directed a legion of landscape specialists to design, plant and maintain a lush, tropical paradise on the grounds.

"I ain't never seen nothin' like it," Naomi said to Washington. "That man has done gone and hauled in enough plants, trees, bushes and flowers that I declare it looks like the Garden of Eden over there."

"Well, if a snake comes offerin' you an apple, you hightail it outta there, woman," Washington said, slapping her playfully on the rump.

"You beat all, you know that," Naomi said indignantly. "I try to tell you 'bout the place and all you do is cut the fool."

After her husband's death, Mrs. Brodie spared no expense in maintaining the grounds, nurturing them as if the plants and trees were a living monument to her husband.

Blooming flowers, vast seas of them, were Mrs. Brodie's passion. The grounds, during all but the winter months, were ablaze with color: tall gladiolas in a vast array of colors, tiny golden marigolds, blue heather, purple petunias, pink daisies, beds of white impatiens, watermelon red azaleas and sweet-smelling gardenias.

"Color, vibrant color, that's what makes you feel alive," Mrs. Brodie once said to Naomi, flinging out her arms and holding them high in the air like a maestro preparing to conduct his orchestra.

Naomi had simply nodded her head as she took the basket of cut flowers from Mrs. Brodie to take inside where Mrs. Brodie would use them to fill an assortment of crystal vases.

When Mr. Brodie was alive, every room of the house was adorned with flowers. But after he died, much of the house was no longer used.

Although Naomi kept the wooden shelves dusted, the doorknobs polished, the floors waxed and the windows washed, the abundance of fresh-cut flowers were no longer needed.

Mrs. Brodie confined herself to her favorite rooms downstairs. These were the only rooms filled with the flowers.

After Mr. Brodie's death, Naomi struggled to find enough to keep her busy. Even with the dusting, polishing, waxing, and washing, "there's just so much that a body can do," she told Washington.

"Mrs. Brodie, she never messes up a thing," Naomi explained to Washington "And she eats like a bird. I can't just sit 'round with my hands folded."

"I wouldn't mind havin' a go at that garden at Mrs. Brodie's place. I might even grow us some vegetables," she remarked to Washington one evening as they picked the peas in their own garden.

"So, offer to help outside," Washington suggested, as he stood up and wiped his brow. "What's the worst thing that can happen? The woman will just say no."

But Mrs. Brodie didn't refuse Naomi when she finally garnered the nerve to offer her services outside. Mrs. Brodie wasn't enthusiastic, but she didn't reject the offer.

Each morning, weather permitting, when Naomi arrived for work, she joined Mrs. Brodie who was already up and in the garden. When Mr. Brodie was alive, his wife would sleep until the sun crawled up the horizon and started its path across the sky. After his death, Naomi never found her asleep.

"It don't make no never mind what time I get there, Mrs. Brodie is up," Naomi told Washington. "I declare I don't think that poor thing sleeps a wink no more."

Side by side, the women started to work together in the garden. Silently at first, but then occasionally a word was exchanged here and there. And like the seeds they planted, a relationship, fragile as a bud, formed and from it a friendship blossomed and grew.

It was on one of these mornings, as they toiled together under a warm, morning sun, that Mrs. Brodie struck up her first real conversation with Naomi.

The women had worked up a sweat pruning the roses. At Naomi's suggestion, Mrs. Brodie sat down on a bench in the shade to rest while Naomi went inside to fetch a pitcher of iced tea.

As the two women sat sipping tea from tall frosty glasses, a cool morning breeze drying the sweat on their faces, Mrs. Brodie started to talk. And Naomi listened.

"Did you know these roses came from Europe?" Mrs. Brodie asked, pointing to a basket of cut roses, which sat at their feet.

"No ma'am," Naomi replied. She had no earthly idea where Europe was, but if they had roses as beautiful as those at her feet, it must be a nice place.

"Mr. Brodie and I went to Europe on our honeymoon. He had the rose bushes shipped to Boston. Later, he transplanted them here."

"That's nice," Naomi said.

"Before we married, I was a concert pianist in Boston, and Mr. Brodie owned a shipping company. Did you know that, Naomi?"

"Yes ma'am, Mr. Brodie told me that," she replied. "Me and Mr. Brodie talked a lot."

While she and Mr. Brodie had conversed quite freely, Naomi felt at a loss for words with his wife.

Naomi was as clueless about the concert pianist business as she was about Europe. The only piano playing that she knew anything about was that which was done in the Shady Grove Baptist Church or on the radio when she listened to the Reverend Samuel Spears' Inspirational Hour.

"Mr. Brodie was a patron of the arts, and he was particularly fond of classical piano," Mrs. Brodie said.

Naomi nodded as she thought that it would help if she had that dictionary Nathan used for school. The phrase "patron of the arts" was completely lost on her, but she did guess that classical music was the piano playing that she often heard coming from Mrs. Brodie's music room.

"I like piano playin' a right smart," was all that Naomi could think of to say.

"He always said that it was love at first sight when he came to hear me play for the first time."

"Now, I know something 'bout love at first sight," Naomi said, heartened. "That's how I felt 'bout my Washington."

Mrs. Brodie smiled over at her.

"Naomi, you never told me your husband's name was Washington."

"No ma'am; you never asked," Naomi said.

"Horace and I were married in less than a year. How about you and your Washington, Naomi? Did you have a lengthy courtship?"

"No ma'am, we met in the winter and married in the spring. It was a day just 'bout like today," Naomi said.

"How lovely," Mrs. Brodie replied, staring out across the bay.

Naomi looked up at the sun advancing in the sky. If they intended to get any more gardening done, the time for doing it was slipping away, Naomi thought.

Still, Mrs. Brodie made no move to go back to work, so Naomi sat resting, enjoying the cool breeze that continued to blow up from the ocean.

"Horace insisted that I give up my career on the stage. Until I met Horace, I could never have imagined leaving the stage, but he was that important to me."

"Yes, ma'am," Naomi replied.

"I missed the stage, but I loved Horace more than music. I continued to practice each day, but the only concerts I performed after my marriage were for my husband. I have no regrets about that decision." Mrs. Brodie leaned back on the bench and stared wistfully out into the garden.

"We led a full life in Boston," she added.

Naomi had no idea what *a full life in Boston* entailed. But it couldn't have been any better than the life she had lived in Tate's Hell with Washington.

She didn't say this to Mrs. Brodie. It still felt awkward to be having this conversation with Mrs. Brodie at all.

"Then Horace had his first stroke. It left him partially paralyzed on his right side, causing his speech to slur and a steady stream of drool to trickle from his mouth, which he wiped incessantly with a handkerchief."

Naomi knew this already; after all, she had spent two years with him. But she let Mrs. Brodie talk on.

"Of course, that didn't bother me. I loved Horace. I was so grateful that he had survived. But Horace was a proud man, and after the stroke, he refused to go out in public. He sold the shipping company, and we moved to this island."

Naomi looked up at the sun, which was now high overhead, and decided that they wouldn't do any more gardening today.

She leaned forward to freshen up Mrs. Brodie's glass of tea, but it sat untouched.

Mrs. Brodie sat quietly, and Naomi thought to herself that she ought to go on into the house and start lunch.

Before Naomi made the move to go inside, Mrs. Brodie picked back up with the conversation.

"We vacationed on this island every year after our marriage. After Horace had his stroke, it quite naturally seemed the place to go to retreat from the public eye. I would have preferred to stay in Boston, but I never considered leaving Horace's side. As a concession to me, he shipped my grand piano here, knowing that I took solace and comfort from my music."

Naomi relaxed, sipping her tea. Lunch could wait. She understood that what Mrs. Brodie needed more than lunch was a patient ear and that no comment was required from her other than an occasional acknowledgement that she was still listening.

"I did briefly consider leaving this island after Horace died. But then where would I go: back to Boston? I wouldn't fit in there, not without Horace. I don't have any family, and I never acquired any real friends over the years. Horace was always enough for me. Do you have many friends, Naomi?"

"Not really," Naomi answered. "My family's been my life. I know some of the folks at church, but that's mostly to say hello on Sunday."

"Well, Naomi, it seems as if we have something in common other than just this garden. Horace was my family, and he was my life. I buried Horace right here in his garden," Mrs. Brodie added.

Naomi knew this; she had been at the estate the day Mr. Brodie was laid to rest. And often she had seen Mrs. Brodie sitting on the cement bench next to his headstone.

Mrs. Brodie stared out towards the bay, towards the part of the garden where Mr. Brodie was buried. She spoke to herself now more than to Naomi.

"When I married Horace, I said 'to death do us part.' But even death can't part us. I have never left him. I haven't set foot off of this estate since the day he died; and I never will. And when I die, I'm going to be put in the ground right next to my Horace. "

Mrs. Brodie sat silently for a few moments. Naomi knew that she was lost in her thoughts. Finally, she spoke.

"I suppose that it's time to go inside," Mrs. Brodie said, rising from her seat.

"Yes ma'am. I need to see 'bout our lunch," Naomi replied.

A Watch in the Night

"You go on ahead," Mrs. Brodie said. "I'll be in shortly. And, Naomi, thanks for listening to an old woman's ramblings."

Naomi stood up to go inside.

"Naomi, one more thing," Mrs. Brodie said, turning to face Naomi.

"Yes, ma'am," Naomi said.

"Could we drop the use of the word 'ma'am'. I daresay we're about the same age. I don't recall you being so formal with my husband."

"If that's what you want," Naomi answered.

"It's what I want," Mrs. Brodie said, reaching over to give Naomi's hand a little squeeze.

After Naomi left to go inside, Mrs. Brodie put away her gardening tools and walked down the garden path towards the water.

The estate had its own private beach on the bay. She had spent countless hours there with Horace. It was their favorite spot other than the garden. After he had died, she often found herself, as if by chance, walking this beach.

Today she meandered along the water's edge, looking across the bay towards the bridge. She and Horace had discovered the island quite by chance while on a fishing trip in the Gulf of Mexico.

Their boat developed engine trouble, which required them to drop anchor for repairs. During the wait, they decided to overcome the boredom of sitting on the deck of a boat, stranded in the middle of what seemed to be nowhere, by paddling ashore in the dinghy.

"The island" was located ten miles out on the northern most portion of the Florida Panhandle. She had never heard it referred to by any other name, although Horace told her it was listed as *Palm Island* on the map.

The island was ten miles long, and for many years, it could only be reached by boat or ferry. In the late 1940's, the federal government designated the eastern tip of the island a federal wildlife preserve and took over active management of the property.

Eventually a bridge was built, and the entire acreage on the western end of the island was purchased by a development corporation, rumored to be owned by a rich industrialist.

A guard gate was installed blocking access to this portion of the island by the public. An airport for private planes was built, and an exclusive development began to take shape for those with sufficient resources and the inclination to build in such a beautiful, but remote place.

Over the years, a number of magnificent homes were built, but all paled in comparison to the Brodie estate. The island was mostly a summer retreat, a second home for most. In the winter, it was all but deserted.

Trinity was the closest town, located thirty miles north of the island's bridge. Although the middle of the island, a small strip between the wildlife preserve and the development, remained open to the public, few people ever ventured over.

The dense vegetation made it impossible to reach the sand beaches by land. A few fished off of its shores, but there were better places to fish closer to home.

Once the government and the developers took over, everybody except those who worked for the developers and then the residents of the island stayed away. Most people in Trinity did not trust the government or *outsiders*, particularly very rich outsiders.

Other than an occasional encounter, the locals had little contact with or interest in the people who lived on the island.

These outsiders came and went from their lives elsewhere, while locals went about the business of making a living, each group, for the most part, oblivious to the other. Mrs. Brodie had never met anyone from Trinity except for the gardeners and the housekeepers.

Mrs. Brodie realized with shame that until today she had never even known the name of Naomi's husband. A woman who had served her faithfully for going on three years, and she had never taken the time to learn the name of her husband.

CHAPTER THIRTEEN

When Millie and Mango first came to live with Naomi and Karen, Naomi worried that the living arrangement was not one that could be workable for long.

But as time passed, everbody adjusted and her concerns subsided. She constantly reassured herself that she was making the right decision. And then there was no decision to be made at all.

The twins and Bessie became such a part of her life, and Karen's too, that she couldn't imagine life without them. The word "welfare" fell out of their vocabulary and talk of Bessie and the twins going to live with Bessie's niece dried up. Bessie and the twins became *family.*

The only fly in the ointment was Ephram. Naomi remained on high alert where he was concerned.

But he seemed content enough to leave them be so long as Bessie complied with his orders to produce the twins for *a monthly viewing.*

Naomi thought that she had pieced together Ephram's interest in the children. It didn't take a genius to figure out that he had some personal stake in their staying in Tate's Hell, although she didn't know the exact details.

She suspected that Bessie knew the truth. But after several aborted attempts to bring up the topic with her, Naomi gave up, although she kept her guard up where Ephram was concerned.

She always accompanied Bessie over to the Whatley house for the viewing. Her excuse was that Bessie wasn't strong enough to carry both children without some help. And that was true after the twins were a couple of months old.

On the walk over, she would carry one of the twins and Bessie would carry the other. At the back door, Naomi passed her baby over to Bessie.

She remained in the kitchen while Bessie took the children into the front where Ephram sat, usually with a man Bessie told her was Ephram's cousin, Fred, waiting. Naomi surmised that he too must have some stake in the twins remaining in Tate's Hell.

After one quick look, Ephram, with a wave of his hand and the same stern warning, banished the twins from his presence until the next visit.

"Go on now get," he would say, handing Bessie the two hundred dollars a month that he paid Karen—always two one-hundred-dollar bills.

"Take them little bastards back over to them bitches place. But remember this: ya'll damn well better not take 'em out of Tate's Hell—not for any goddamned reason. There'll be hell to pay if ya'll double cross me."

Naomi seethed as she waited and watched. There'll be hell to pay old man, she thought, and you and that half-wit cousin of yours is gonna be the ones settlin' up that debt with Satan.

She certainly didn't like being called *a bitch*—even if it was Ephram Whatley doing the talking. But it was him referring to the twins as *the little bastards* that made her blood boil. It took Naomi a week of praying before she could get over the visit.

"The Lord says you gotta forgive seven times a hundred and I do believe that Ephram Whatley is gonna put me to that test," she would tell Karen later.

By spring both twins were sitting up, by summer they were crawling and by fall they were pulling up and teetering around.

A month before her first birthday Millie surprised everyone by taking her first steps. Mango followed soon after.

Millie, who was tiny and incessantly chattering and chirping and flitting from one place to another, Naomi affectionately dubbed "the baby bird."

"What's the baby bird been up to today?" she would ask over supper.

"Flittering," Karen would answer. "It takes both me and Bessie to keep an eye on that one."

"And our old fat cat?" That was Naomi's nickname for Mango. He was more complacent and relaxed than Millie, content to languish in anyone's lap who would take the time to rock and sing to him.

"Same as always," Karen answered. "I'm lookin' for him and Bessie to rock the rockers off our rockin' chair any day now. But he ain't a bit of trouble 'til he gets hungry. That little fella loves to eat."

"Puts me in mind of Nathan," Naomi said, smiling

"And the toy wars? Who is winning these days?" Naomi asked.

"Still Millie," Karen said. "She's so much quicker than Mango. But if he can catch her still long enough, he ain't got no trouble takin' his toy back. He's that much stronger than her."

When Naomi laughed, Karen talked on.

"And when that happens, here comes one of her little hissy fits. She plops right down on that little bottom of hers, that little mouth flies open and she lets go like a screech owl."

"Now that sounds like you. You did 'bout the same thing to poor little Nathan," Naomi said.

"He'd be down by the fire with his colorin' book, mindin' his own business when you go after one of his crayons. He didn't have but three or four. He'd grab it back from you, and you'd scream so loud that it would set the dog off barkin'. After you started to crawl, I didn't get many peaceful days 'til he started school."

"Mama, do you realize that them babies gonna be one-year-old here soon," Karen said.

"Time sure flies when you get old," Naomi said. "I can't believe that we've had them youngens for *that* long."

"Well, we have," Karen said. "But if it makes you feel any better, the time flew by for me, too. I don't think you can blame that on old age. I was thinkin' 'bout tryin' to put together some kind of little party for them. Whata you think?"

"Sounds fine," Naomi said.

"I even thought of invitin' Samuel and Abigail and their kids if that's alright with you. I gotta a letter from them yesterday. I put it on the table in the hall for you to read. They plan on comin' back to Trinity for Christmas. The party will give 'em a chance to see the twins. Bessie has already said that she would help me."

"That's fine, honey. Ya'll do what you want. I gotta work, but I'll do what I can to help."

"What 'bout this, Mama? Let's have the party on Christmas Eve. The youngens are too little to know the difference. And you only work a half day on Christmas Eve."

"That sounds good," Naomi said, not realizing at the time that with these words she set a tradition in motion—the twins' birthday was changed to Christmas Eve.

It was the morning of the twins' first birthday.

Naomi left for work early, before the twins woke up, so she could arrive home early for the party. The sun was not yet up as Karen stood on the porch, a heavy woolen sweater pulled up around her neck, waving good-bye to her mother.

We are in for a beautiful day, Karen thought. For the past few days, it had been unseasonably warm. As soon as the sun comes up, it might climb as high as the fifties, she mused, loosening the sweater. A perfect day to be outside. A perfect day to go to the clearing.

Duke limped past Karen on his way to go and meet Bessie. He met her every morning. Bessie always took the time to scratch his ears and give him a kind word. Karen followed after Duke.

"Good mornin'," she called to Bessie as she strolled into the yard. Bessie wore her same faded housedress, but draped over one arm was a blue-flowered dress and a pale blue sweater. A paper grocery bag was tucked under her other arm.

"Good mornin' to you," Bessie called back, as she approached Karen. "It's gonna be a beautiful day."

"I was thinkin' the same thing myself," Karen said. "In fact, if you don't mind watchin' the twins for an hour or so alone, I thought that I might go chop the Christmas tree a day early. It would be nice to have it for the party."

"I don't mind a'tall. I got a plan of my own," she said, holding up the paper grocery bag.

"And what would that be?" Karen asked.

"You'll see," Bessie said, looping her arm through the crook of Karen's elbow for the walk across the yard. "Go on and get your tree. I'll get the babies up and dressed."

"Okay," Karen said. "I'll see you in an hour or so."

When Karen burst through the kitchen door a couple of hours later, she had her sweater tied around her waist and her long braid pinned up in a knot on her head. She was sweating and out of breath.

"It's so warm in here," she said, fanning her face. "Outside it feels almost like spring."

"I've had the oven on," Bessie said.

The twins sat in their highchairs. Each had a beater, which they were licking so intently that neither paid attention to Karen's arrival. They were still dressed in their pajamas, and their faces, hands, clothes and highchair trays were smeared with cake batter and chocolate icing.

Millie's blonde hair was plastered down with brown streaks. Mango's hair was stuck to his forehead, although Karen couldn't see the chocolate that was concealed in his black curls. The usually spotless kitchen floor beneath their chairs was splattered with yellow and brown spots.

"Well, whatever it is that you're bakin', it smells wonderful," Karen said. She walked over to where Bessie stood at the counter.

There were flecks of flour in Bessie's hair, and her apron was dotted with chocolate splatters. Karen peeked over Bessie's shoulder. Two cakes sat on the counter, and Bessie was using a wooden spatula to spread the thick, dark mounds of chocolate heaped on the top of each cake.

"Cakes. So that was your secret," Karen said.

"Yep. I baked two birthday cakes."

"How'd you manage that with the kids?" Karen asked.

"Easy. I put 'em in their highchairs and let 'em lick the spoons and beaters."

"If they ain't a sight for sore eyes," Karen said. "It looks like they got more chocolate on them than you got on them cakes."

Bessie shrugged her shoulders. "They've had 'em a big time. And I finished these here cakes."

Bessie turned to the sink, wrung the water out of a washcloth and handed it over to Karen.

"If you don't mind takin' a stab at cleanin' 'em up, all I've got left to do is the decoratin'."

Karen untied the sweater from around her waist, pulled an apron over her head and took the washcloth.

"I ain't gonna let you two ruin one of my good sweaters with all that goo," she said, turning to the twins.

Neither twin noticed Karen until she tried to take the beater from Mango so she could wipe his face and hands. Mango was having no part of that and clutched the beater tightly in his small fist.

As Karen pried his fingers loose, he started to scream, loud and angry; red splotches popped out on his face under the chocolate. Karen dropped his beater in the sink and then took Millie's. Millie screamed even louder than her brother, kicking her hands and feet.

"Lord, where does she come by the hissy fits?" Karen exclaimed to Bessie, who because of the ruckus, stopped what she was doing in order to give Karen an assist.

"Her mama," Bessie said, as she struggled with Millie. "When Lily was this age, she would scream and then hold her breath 'til she was blue. It 'bout scared me to death the first time she done it."

"Well, I hope she outgrows it," Karen half-shouted to Bessie.

"I think the best thing to do is to put 'em in the tub," Bessie shouted back to Karen over the twins' caterwauling. "It's time for them to go down for a nap."

With considerable effort, Bessie lifted Mango from his highchair and stuck him under Karen's outstretched arm. Once they had Mango corralled, Bessie wrestled Millie from her highchair, depositing her under Karen's other arm.

Karen clamped down, pinning both babies to her sides, before she made a beeline out of the kitchen, a red-faced, squirming, screaming baby dangling under each arm.

Karen didn't stop until she deposited the twins in the big, porcelain, claw-footed tub in the Ivey's small bathroom. The tub dominated the room.

This tub was Naomi's pride and joy, an anniversary gift from Washington. The only time that Naomi was totally off limits to her family was when she allowed herself one precious half-hour each night to soak in that tub.

A Watch in the Night

When Karen returned to the kitchen thirty minutes later, the only sign of the chocolate fiasco was the cakes stationed in the middle of the table.

Each cake had *Happy Birthday* spelled out in colored sprinkles with a single candle adorning the center. Bessie sat in a chair at the table, sipping a cup of coffee, staring proudly at the cakes.

"So that's what you had in your bag this mornin'," Karen said, running her finger around the rim of one cake and then licking the chocolate off.

She retreated to the coffee pot when Bessie swatted at her hand. Karen poured herself a cup of coffee and sat down next to Bessie.

"I had to pure beg Fred, Ephram's cousin, to get me the fixins' in town," Bessie said.

"Mama coulda picked that up for you. We probably had most of what you needed right here in the cabinets," Karen said.

"I know. But I wanted the cakes to be my present to the twins. I was actually surprised that Fred helped. Sometimes, 'bout once in a blue moon, he gets a soft spot.

"I found the bag, the top all rolled down, out on the back porch when I come in last night. I reckon he was hidin' it from Ephram. I don't know, and I don't care. I got what I wanted: cakes for my grandbabies. He even got the sprinkles and the candles like I asked. That goes to show—most people, ain't all bad."

"I suppose," Karen said halfheartedly. She would never have any use for Ephram or his cousin Fred.

"The babies are asleep—for now, at least," she added. "This was a real nice thing that you did, Bessie."

"Lily always liked chocolate cake the best," Bessie said sadly, still gazing at the cakes. "I wish now that I could say that I made her a chocolate cake on ever one of her birthdays, but I can't. But so long as I'm able, I'll see to it that her babies get a cake each and ever birthday. I just wish I had done that for Lily."

"Don't be so hard on yourself," Karen said softly, patting Bessie's hands. "Lily knew that you loved her, and that's really all that matters. Put those thoughts aside. The babies won't sleep for long, and we got a lot left to do to get ready for tonight."

While Karen cooked, Bessie decorated. Even with her shortness of breath, Bessie managed to blow up enough balloons to fill the living room, although a few managed to float past the wire screen over the fireplace and land with a loud pop in the fire, which sent the twins squealing into the kitchen.

As a finishing touch, she taped a banner that Naomi had purchased at the local five-and-dime, which spelled out *Happy Birthday* in glittery, neon letters over the fireplace.

Late in the afternoon, when the cooking was done and the twins were down for their afternoon nap, Karen brought in the tree, which she placed in the same corner of the room where all of the Ivey Christmas trees had stood.

When this was done, she and Bessie collapsed on the couch, propped up their feet on the ottoman and admired their handiwork.

"Nice job decoratin'," Karen said.

"Beautiful tree," Bessie responded.

They shook hands and laughed. Karen and Bessie dozed by the fire until Millie's high-pitched cry woke them.

Shortly before her mother was to arrive home, Karen dressed the twins in new clothes handstitched by Naomi.

Millie wore a red, velour jumper-dress, with a crisply starched white blouse underneath, which had green Christmas stars embroidered on the collar. She pinned Millie's wispy strands of blonde hair away from her face with red ribbons.

A Watch in the Night

Mango wore green, velour overalls over a starched white shirt. His collar had red embroidered stars. She slicked his dark curls back with some hair oil left by her father, thinking that after Christmas he really did need to have his first haircut.

"Perfect," she said, as she kissed each of them on the top of the head. "Let's go watch for Mama."

As they stood waiting at the window, watching for Naomi's car, Bessie emerged from the back in the blue-flowered dress and matching sweater. Her gray hair was brushed smooth and clamped tightly back with a pair of tortoise shell combs. She had on pink lipstick.

"Bessie, you look beautiful," Karen exclaimed.

Bessie blushed.

"These here tortoise shell combs belonged to my mama," Bessie said. "She said they come all the way from a big store in Memphis, Tennessee, but I reckon that don't matter none now. Still, I wouldn't take nothin' for 'em. My mama she weren't from Westberry. Her people was from Memphis and fine folks. She even went to college for a year or two. Studied to be a teacher."

"You don't say," Karen said. Bessie had never mentioned her family other than the remark that her mother had not wanted her to marry Ephram.

"And the lipstick, it was Lily's," Bessie said. "You don't think that it's too much do you, an old lady like me puttin' on pink lipstick?"

"Not at all. With them combs and that lipstick, you look real nice. You'd make your mama proud."

"I don't know 'bout that," Bessie said, hanging her head.

Just then a set of headlights came rolling down the lane and stopped in the yard. A hundred yards behind was a second set of headlights.

"That's Mama. And that must be the Taylors bringing up the rear. Let's go outside and meet 'em."

"You go," Bessie said. "I'll wait in here." She retreated to her seat in the rocker.

Karen hurried excitedly out onto the porch, a baby in each arm. She hadn't seen the Taylors since they moved to Miami the past January.

She watched as the Taylor children come spilling out of their station wagon and gathered in a cluster around Naomi like drones buzzing around their queen.

"Ya'll come on in," Karen called to the swarming hive.

"Lord, do have mercy!" Abigail exclaimed, as she stepped up on the porch next to Karen. "*This can't be Millie and Mango!*"

Abigail threw her hands on her hips and shook her head in astonishment. The twins took one look at her and tried to burrow their heads into Karen's neck.

"It's them alright," Karen said. "I'm afraid they're gonna act shy. They ain't use to company."

Karen adjusted the babies on her hips. They were heavy, and if they had not been clinging to her like baby monkeys, they would have surely slid down to her side by now.

At the sight of Naomi, Millie lunged forward and locked her arms around Naomi's neck. Naomi scooped her up and pecked her cheek before Millie buried her head into Naomi's ample bosom.

Karen wrapped her free arm around Mango and hoisted him over her shoulder. From this vantage point, he took an occasional peek around, still ducking his head down when anybody came to close.

"Let's all go on in where it's warm," Naomi said, stroking Millie's hair to reassure her. Millie had yet to come up for air.

Karen noticed that Millie's ribbons had disappeared and that her hair, which was full of static electricity, floated around her head like a halo.

She held Mango out at arm's length and looked him over. The hair oil had ceased working in the humidity of the night air, and black curls cascaded around his face and down onto his shoulders. His shirttail was out, and he had lost one shoe, which Abigail held in her hand.

Once inside, the kissing and hugging began in earnest. Even Bessie, who tended to shy away from such outward displays of affection, found herself enjoying being passed around from one set of arms to the next.

When she and Karen found themselves hugging, they burst out laughing and hugged one another even harder. After all, they had made this party happen.

Next came the admiring of the children. Samuel and Abigail catalogued their children's accomplishments for the past year, while Bessie, Karen and Naomi gushed out comments like "you don't say; Lord have mercy; and if that don't beat all."

As each child came up for review, the women put up a fuss over how much that particular child had grown and set off on another round of kissing, hugging, hair tousling and cheek pinching.

The children, especially the older boys, screwed up their faces in a tight grimace as they were squeezed and hugged for the umpteenth time, even as they basked in the praise heaped upon them by their proud parents.

But it was Millie and Mango who stole the show. By now they had lifted their heads and sat perched in Karen and Naomi's arms, necks craned out like baby birds, sizing up all of the strangers.

Karen thought that her mother was half right—little Millie with her long, thin neck and tuft of blonde fuzz on the top of head did look like a baby bird. But Mango, with his thick black curls, looked more like a cocker spaniel than the fat cat, Naomi had affectionately nicknamed him.

"I just can't believe how much these babies have grown," Samuel said. Bessie beamed from her spot behind the rocker.

"You must be so proud," Abigail said, trying to draw her out. Bessie blushed and then dropped her head, nodding that she was indeed proud of her grandchildren.

It wasn't long before the twins warmed up to the crowd, wiggling and squirming to the point that Karen and Naomi had to put them down on the floor. When they took their first few steps, the Taylors applauded.

"For heaven's sake, they're walking!" Abigail exclaimed, as if that fact wasn't already perfectly obvious to everyone in the room. "And not but a year old. Our Jerry, he's just now pulling up."

This new development enthralled the Taylor children. They had come expecting to find the two tiny babies, who they had not been allowed to touch the year before; instead, here were two squirming, giggling live toys.

Abigail helped her children shuck their coats, and then she joined Karen, who had already taken a seat on the sofa. Bessie sat in the rocker, Naomi the easy chair and Samuel stood with his back to the fire, keeping an eye on his children, who were chasing a squealing, but delighted Millie and Mango around the room. Jerry crawled behind them in hot pursuit. The adults chatted while the children romped.

Samuel and Abigail reported they liked their new church but missed living in a small town.

"I still get lost going to the grocery store," Abigail said, "and once inside I can't find anything because I'm too busy chasing my crew down the umpteen aisles they got. They must have ten brands of dish detergent. Now I ask you. Who needs ten brands of dish detergent to choose from?"

The women shook their heads agreeing with her that ten brands of dish detergent bordered on being ridiculous. The talk from the Ivey and Whatley side of the conversation focused entirely on the twins.

A Watch in the Night

After a good half hour of *catching up*, Naomi, Bessie and Abigail retreated to the kitchen to set out the food. Samuel and Karen stayed by the fire to supervise the children.

When the horseplay bordered on getting out of hand, Karen settled the children down by suggesting that they help her decorate the tree. "After all, ya'll did such a good job last year," she reminded them.

The tree was almost finished—only the top portion remained untrimmed and that required Samuel's assistance because he was the only one who was tall enough up to reach up that high without a ladder—when Naomi called supper.

The group gathered around the kitchen table, whose four wooden chairs had been augmented for this occasion by folding seats borrowed from the church social hall.

It was a tight fit, but everyone managed to squeeze in, with little Jerry sitting in Abigail's lap, Maggie sitting on a booster seat created by placing an old, tattered catalogue in the seat of a chair and the twins sitting off to the side in their highchairs.

Nathan and Karen's favorite pastime as children had been trolling the catalogue for toys. Naomi never had the heart to throw it away. Samuel said grace, and Naomi started the bowls flowing around the table.

When the meal was over, and the adults sat vowing that they, "couldn't possibly eat another bite," while the children's eyes pleaded with their parents to be set free, Bessie brought out the birthday cakes and lit the one candle in the center of each.

After two rousing rounds of *Happy Birthday*—one for Millie and another for Mango—during which the twins joined in by clattering their spoons against their trays, Bessie suggested that the Taylor children collectively blow out the candles for the twins. She did not want to run the risk of another chocolate debacle by placing the cakes directly in front of the already over-excited birthday boy and girl.

Both cakes were eaten; barely a crumb was left. The group heaped accolades on Bessie's baking skills until she blushed a bright red.

"Ya'll go on and hush up now," she said. "It weren't nothin' but two pound cakes and some plain old chocolate icin'." But clearly, she was pleased to be the center of attention.

This time when the plates were pushed back, the adults meant it when they said, "I *really* couldn't eat another bite," and the children *really* couldn't sit still a minute longer.

Naomi, Bessie and Abigail remained in the kitchen and tackled the dishes, while Karen took the twins to the back to clean them up and change them into their pajamas.

It was well past their bedtime, and she knew they were certain to fall asleep as soon as they got in front of the fire. Samuel ushered his crew into the living room to finish off the top of the tree.

When the kitchen detail finished up, they came in to join the others by the fire. Millie and Mango were lying on the couch with their heads in Karen's lap, asleep. Jerry dozed in his father's arms. The rest of the children languished in front of the fire admiring the now completed tree.

Naomi surprised everyone when she went out for wood and returned with a large bag, which she had stashed in Washington's shed.

"Merry Christmas," she said, dropping the bag in front of the fire.

"What's this?" Samuel asked, raising one eyebrow.

"If I didn't know better, I'd think that Santa might have stopped by here a little early." The Taylor children perked up, staring at the large bag.

"I reckon maybe he heard that ya'll would be in Miami for Christmas day, eating mangos instead of pecan pies, so he dropped a few things off a little early." Naomi's remark brought a chuckle from the group.

"Go on," she said, dumping the contents of the bag on the floor. "Samuel, would you pass out the presents?"

"I'd be honored," he said.

For the girls, Naomi had made ragdolls dressed in outfits to match Millie and Mango's Christmas clothes. For the boys, she had used canvas to make small backpacks. When deciding what gift to make for the boys, she remembered how Nathan had carried his treasures in a backpack until he was in junior high school.

When Naomi finally found the strength to go through Nathan's things the year after he died, she found the pack, still filled with his most prized possessions: a pocketknife, which had been a gift from his father, an arrowhead, a tiger's eye marble and a faded school picture of the girl he had adored in third grade.

She gave all of his belongings to the church rummage sale, except for the pack. That she kept in the bottom drawer of her dresser.

Shortly before Millie and Mango's second birthday, Trinity was hit with three pieces of big news. The more superstitious people in Trinity—which accounted for about the whole town—believed that good news, as well as bad, came in threes, and so at the first sign of either, they braced themselves for what was next.

During the Thanksgiving service that year, Reverend Spears regretfully announced that Susan Hillman had miscarried her second child. He asked that prayers and condolences be extended to the Hillman family.

Susan, it was reported by the Saturday morning clique at Annie's Beauty Parlor, was so distraught that she stayed in bed for the better part of a month and only roused herself when there was talk that she would be hospitalized for emotional problems.

Trey, for his part, politely accepted condolences with the same response each time: *it was God's will.* Although Trey knew little and cared less about God's will, he understood that this was what people expected him to say.

And he was right. Upon hearing this remark, most people shook their heads in agreement and moved on.

But folks quickly forgot about the Hillman's baby when the news hit town that the "red tide" was back and that the state environmentalists planned to close the bay to harvesting oysters.

"Red tide" was the state's way of saying that algae blooms had become so numerous as to discolor the water as well as to release toxins into the gulf significant enough to cause illness in people. Red tide made oysters unsafe to eat.

With no oysters to harvest, many people were left without a way to make a living, and their lives, which under ordinary circumstances were hard, grew harder.

"Ain't' gonna be much of a Christmas for nobody this year, 'cept maybe Wiley Grantham," one fisherman remarked when he heard the news.

"That's two pieces of bad news, and it's a full moon to boot," somebody else said, as he hauled in his boat. They all waited for the final blow to strike.

So, nobody was the least bit surprised when Bud Akers came into Harry's the week before Christmas and announced that Sheriff Tate had died.

Although some said that it was a crying shame that he hadn't been able to enjoy his retirement out on the river with his wife, most people were secretly relieved that the third disaster had struck the Tate family and not their own.

"What happened?" Harry asked, speaking for the bar.

"Who knows?" Bud said. "Probably heart attack or stroke. His wife called sayin' he'd gone out deer huntin'. Didn't come back in for lunch. I found 'im not a quarter mile from his house, keeled over. He's dead."

"That's a shame," somebody remarked. Most nodded their heads in agreement that it was indeed a shame.

"I called the preacher's wife to come see 'bout Mrs. Tate, called James to send out the wagon and I come on in," Bud said. "That's all I could do."

"At least he died doin' what he loved. There's somethin' to be said for that," a sad voice said from a darkened corner of the bar.

"I reckon," Bud said.

"Didn't Doc Adams die 'bout this same time of year?" Harry asked Bud.

"That's right. It was Christmas two years ago," he answered. "It was Sheriff Tate who found Doc's body. I reckon James Davis will try to put on the dog again like he did for Doc."

Naomi heard about Sheriff Tate when she stopped off for gas on her drive home from work. Nobody at Johnny's Amoco would, of course, tell her the news. She overheard it, when she went inside to pay, from a group of men gathered inside the station to socialize.

They were leaning against the wall or stretched out in a few folding chairs hovering around the warmth of a gas heater pushed back into one corner. Some were smoking, and others were spitting tobacco into paper cups.

Without the oysters to harvest, there wasn't much else for them to do other than gather in clusters to drink, talk and wait out the "red tide."

No work meant there was no money to spend at Harry's. It was Wiley's shine or nothing. Nothing was not an option.

So the men gathered at Johnny's—the local distributor for Wiley's shine—hashing and rehashing the least bit of news.

When Naomi entered the station, the room was abuzz with the news of Sheriff Tate's passing.

"I forgot to tell you 'bout Sheriff Tate," Naomi said. She was seated with Karen at breakfast the next morning.

"Tell me what?" Karen asked.

"He died. I heard it at the gas station on my way in last night. Heart attack or somethin' like that."

"That's a shame," Karen said. "I only met 'im that one time. The day after the twins was born."

"I never had no dealings with him to speak of neither until that day," Naomi replied.

"You know, Mama, I always wondered why them people from the welfare never came. You reckon he just never told 'im 'bout the babies. Forgot. Maybe he felt sorry for Bessie. Or maybe the welfare people just didn't bother to come out to Tate's Hell."

"I wondered the same thing myself. My guess is that he got so caught up in Doc's death that it slipped his mind. The law ain't never cared much 'bout what goes on out here in Tate's Hell."

"We'll never know now," Karen said. "I'm just glad that he didn't tell, no matter the reason."

"We've had them youngens two years! Time sure gets away from you when you're old."

"That's what you said last year, Mama. It ain't got nothin' to do with bein' old. Life just moves quicker when you got two babies to keep up with."

"Come on in, it's open," Karen yelled at the door, when she heard Bessie's knock.

Bessie pushed through the back door, stomping the frost off of her boots. "We had a hard freeze last night. The pipes froze up at my place. How 'bout ya'll. You got water this mornin'?"

"I left the faucets drippin' and the pumps covered. We got water," Naomi said.

"I oughta done the same. But I didn't. There ain't no use to go cryin' over spilt milk now," she said, sighing. She poured herself a cup of coffee and sat down at the table.

"We was just discussin' the twins' birthday," Karen said. She slid Bessie the cream and sugar.

"It's hard to believe they're two already," Bessie said, stirring two spoons of sugar and a dollop of cream into her coffee. "Time sure flies when you get old."

Karen and Naomi laughed.

"Did I say somethin' funny?" Bessie asked, looking up.

"Nope. It's just that was exactly what I said, but Karen here tells me that it has nothin' to do with old age."

"I wanted to have 'em a party again this year," Karen said. "But the Taylor youngens got the measles. They won't be comin' up for Christmas."

"That don't mean we can't throw a party. What's wrong with havin' just us?" Bessie asked.

"Nothin'," Karen said. She stood up and went to rinse her cup in the sink. "We'll have a party."

Millie and Mango were only weeks from turning three when the Hillmans made it back into the news. Susan gave birth to a robust nine-pound girl she named Misti Michelle.

"Now what kind of name is that," one of the women said at the monthly meeting of the First Baptist Ladies Auxiliary, as she fluttered around the room setting up the refreshments. The meeting fell on the day after Susan delivered her daughter.

"I'll tell you what kind of name it is," Rita Jeeters said. Rita sliced up her pound cake and laid it daintily in a circle on a large platter.

"It's somethin' from one of them magazines that Susan Hillman spends all her time readin'. I'm first cousins with Julie May. You know she's been hired on as Susan's *housekeeper*. She tells me that Susan Hillman don't hit a lick at a snake. Sits 'round readin' magazines all day while somebody waits on her, and that little boy of hers, hand and foot. One of them magazines is where she got that name."

"Humph!" Fannie Leggett snorted, as she laid the prayer books on the seats. "If that just don't beat all. I can remember the time that Susan *Akers* couldn't afford the postage it takes to get all them magazines."

"I don't know why she even bothered to have another youngen," Rita quipped. "According to Julie May, she don't pay no never mind to the first one she had. He stays with old man Hillman most of the time. The old man's slap crazy 'bout that grandbaby of his."

"Money," Carlene Lee threw in. "That new baby is about money."

"Well, if old man Hillman takes to this new baby like he took to that first one, he's liable to up and leave them grandbabies all his money when he dies," Edith said. "Now that would serve Mrs. Trey Hillman right."

Edith felt sorry for her cousin who was stuck working for that sassy hussy just so she could feed her own two youngens. Julie May's husband had drowned after falling off a shrimp boat in rough weather two years back.

"Ladies, please," the Reverend Samuel Spears' wife said, clapping her hands to call the meeting to order.

"Do I need to remind you that it ain't Christian for us to go talkin' down our sister, Susan. Take your seats and let's start by liftin' Susan and Misti Michelle up to the Lord in prayer."

"Humph!" Fannie Leggett snorted, loud enough for all to hear, before she took her seat and closed her eyes.

But Carlene Lee had been right. The birth of Misti Michelle was all about money. The elder Hillmans practically worshiped their first grandbaby, especially the old man who took the boy everywhere he went with him in his truck.

Trey didn't care much about having more children, but he aimed to please his father so he could dig his hand even deeper into the family till. If turning out grandchildren was what it took to keep the old man happy, then so be it.

As for Susan, she was more than willing to stay pregnant. Each new baby solidified her claim to the Hillman fortune, or so she thought.

Susan, however, missed the mark on that account. What neither Trey nor Susan knew was that Mr. Hillman had altered his will to have his grandchildren share equally in his estate with Missy and Trey.

If Trey and Susan had known that each new Hillman grandchild diminished their share of the pie, they might have looked upon birth control with a little more fervor.

But ignorance is bliss. Susan celebrated the birth of Mistie Michelle by throwing a lavish affair at her and Trey's home on the river.

It was the Christmas season, and the place was decorated up to the hilt. Susan had spent months ordering decorations from the stack of catalogs that sat in the den piled knee high next to her magazines.

"She had so many baubles, do-dads and Christmas fixins stuck 'round that place that you could hardly turn 'round without knockin' over some Santa or wise man," Annie reported at the beauty shop.

She had not been invited to the party but had gone out to style Susan's hair the day of the celebration. Annie did not as a rule talk down one of her clients, but she was harboring a grudge over the slight of not being invited to the party, and she let go with full force when Susan's name came up.

"If you think that's somethin', you ought to seen it at night," the mayor's wife, LuEllen Paulk, said. She sat perched in Annie's chair having her hair teased, smoothed and sprayed until it stood at least six inches off of the top of her head.

She wanted everyone to know that she and the Mayor had made the cut. "It was lit up brighter than the Big Dipper. Lights strung up everwheres. The electric bill for them lights alone is probably more than most of their help down to the lumberyard make in a month."

"She'll get her comeuppance one day. You mark my words on that," Annie said, as she vigorously worked the comb up and down to tease LuEllen's hair.

If she was good enough to do Susan's hair, Annie reasoned, then she ought to have been good enough to go to her party. Her face flushed red at the thought that Susan hadn't seen it that way.

Millie and Mango celebrated their third birthday on the same night of the Hillman bash. Naomi and Karen knew this because Susan had sent her cook over to the Shady Grove Baptist Church to hire some of the women to cook and serve at the party.

Naomi declined the offer of working for Susan Hillman. She had no intention of going anywhere near the Hillman house, and besides that, she had to prepare for her own party.

The Taylors were in town for Christmas, and Karen had planned another gathering for the twins' birthday.

When they arrived, the Taylor children were delighted to discover that the twins were not only talking, but singing as well.

"If that don't beat all," Samuel said, when the twins took the opportunity to show off by singing a shortened version of their favorite Christmas song, *Jingle Bells*.

Karen and the twins had rehearsed the song for weeks, and she started them off when it came time to trim the tree. After one verse, she signaled for the Taylor children to join in.

Samuel gave them a round of applause when the song was over and persuaded them to repeat the number later, when everybody was gathered around the fire after supper.

"They want that radio on if they're up," Karen said. "We was all surprised that they could sing so good."

"It is amazing," Abigail said.

"And the doggonest thing is that they just love the Reverend Samuel Spears' Inspirational Hour," Naomi said. "They sing along with that radio like they's two cooing turtledoves."

"Well, I be," Samuel said. "These children can't go to church, so God brings the Church to them. God sure does work in mysterious ways."

"You spoke the truth there," Naomi said, gazing fondly over at the twins.

CHAPTER FOURTEEN

On the twins' fourth birthday, Karen rose earlier than usual. She had decided that the twins were old enough to go along with her to chop the Christmas tree. And she wanted to go at daybreak, the same as she had done with her father.

She told Naomi about her plans the night before, and Naomi had offered to rise early and help her get the children dressed.

"You don't gotta do that, Mama," Karen said. "Daddy never got you up to get me and Nathan dressed. We'll manage."

Naomi understood that Karen wanted to re-create the experience she had with her father as much as possible for the twins.

"A little extra sleep would be nice," she said to Karen.

Karen woke up before daylight and stoked up the fire before tiptoeing into the twins' room to wake them.

"Shush," she whispered, putting her finger over her lips. "We don't want to wake up Mama."

Wasted effort.

Naomi had been awake from the minute Karen's feet hit the floor. Naomi had slept with one eye open since the day Nathan was born. Nothing escaped her attention in this house.

She snuggled down under the covers and listened to the twins' excited whispers as they scurried in by the fire where Karen had already laid out their clothes.

When she heard the door open and close, she rolled over for a few more minutes of sleep.

The darkness faded to a gray, shadowy light as Karen and the children stepped out onto the porch. Frost covered the ground.

Clover, Ephram's dog, who had followed Bessie over to the Ivey house and then never gone back home, sauntered over to join them.

Grabbing the sled she had brought out of the shed and left by the back doorsteps the day before, Karen took a calming breath before heading out. Clover and the twins fell into step beside her, and together they crossed the back yard.

"Good boy," Mango said, scratching Clover's head. The children adored Clover.

For days, Karen and the children had talked about little, other than the search for the tree. This was a monumental moment for the twins; they had never been farther from the Ivey yard than their monthly walk to the Whatley house.

As they approached the entrance to the path, Millie and Mango moved closer to Karen. She remembered how foreboding the dark tunnel of trees had looked to her when she was their age and how she had slid under the protective arm of her father at this juncture. She gave Millie's hand a reassuring squeeze when she felt it slip into her own.

Mango, who was a little more adventurous than Millie, scurried slightly ahead of Karen and Millie, although he stayed close to Clover's side and constantly glanced back to be certain that he didn't get too far ahead.

The first rays of the morning sun brightened the sky and bathed the path and the surrounding swamp in a warm glow as they left the forest behind. Millie dropped Karen's hand and skipped ahead to join Mango and Clover. Karen quickened her pace to keep up with them.

"Where are the gators?" Millie asked, as the path wound in close to the swamp. Karen had taught them all about the swamp.

"Hibernating," Mango proudly announced. They sleep all winter, right, Karen?"

"Almost," Karen answered. "Actually, the word is brumation, not hibernation." Karen smiled as she recalled this lesson from her high school science class.

"But don't worry little man; it's too cold out to see gators today."

"And snakes, too?" Millie asked.

"Snakes, too," Karen said. "There's nothin' to fear today. But in the summer now that's a different story. We couldn't walk back here in the summer without bein' on the lookout for snakes and gators."

"We ain't never 'pose to leave the yard without you, anytime," Millie said. "Don't matter if it's summer or winter."

"That's right, sugar plum," Karen said. "Never. But look up ahead. We're almost to the clearin', and that's where we'll find our tree."

As they approached the clearing, Karen and the children began to scope the landscape for a suitable tree, which was easy because the evergreens stood out against a bleak backdrop of plants and trees turned brown by winter.

"How 'bout this one," Mango called out. He pointed to a seven-foot juniper.

"Too tall," Karen said, "but that smaller tree next to it looks good to me. Whata ya'll think?"

"Looks good," the twins answered in a single voice. The sun was up and shining down warmly on their faces. They were so delighted to be out in this mysterious place on a bright winter's morning that any tree would have suited them.

They watched as Karen started to chop the tree, but soon lost interest and went chasing after Clover across the clearing, dodging saplings and small palmetto bushes.

Karen was tying the tree to the sled when she heard Millie's squeal. Immediately, she dropped the tree, stood up and blocked the sun from her eyes with her hand as she scanned the clearing for the children. She saw them in the distance running towards her with Clover in the lead.

"What's wrong?" she called, running to meet them.

"Look," Millie shouted. She ran up to Karen and stopped to catch her breath.

"I found a treasure," she said. Panting, she proudly thrust her hand up for Karen to see. Dangling from her fist was a silver necklace, tarnished from the weather and covered with dirt. A pendant dangled on the chain.

Karen brushed off the dirt, and her heart skipped a beat when she read the name "Lily" etched in block letters.

"Me too, me too," Mango chimed in. He tugged at Karen's coat to get her attention. "I found a treasure, too."

Karen was still shaken by seeing Lily's name on the pendant when she looked down at Mango's treasure. He held up a dog leash. The leather was weathered—cracked and caked with dirt—and the buckle was rusted; but Mango proudly held up his prize for inspection.

A chill ran up Karen's spine, and a shiver convulsed throughout her body. She felt engulfed, almost suffocated, by some unknown fear.

"Put it down, Mango," she shouted at him, "it's dirty." Karen snatched the leash from his hand and flung it to the ground.

Mango looked at the leash and then at Karen before he burst into tears and took off running towards the woods.

"Mango, stop," she shouted after him, but either he didn't hear or he didn't obey. When he kept running, Karen took off after him. Clover loped along next to her, and a bewildered Millie stumbled behind them.

Karen caught up to Mango at the edge of the woods. She almost had to tackle him to get him to stop. When Mango stumbled, she grabbed him up and pulled him into her chest.

He had lost his hat. Karen placed her face in the softness of his curls and rocked him back and forth in her arms as he sobbed.

Karen was stricken with remorse. She hadn't meant to be harsh. She wasn't even sure what had come over her.

"It's alright, Mango," she whispered into his ear. "I'm sorry, little man. I didn't mean to scare you. Please, don't cry," she begged him.

Millie caught up to them. When she heard Mango crying, she started to cry, too.

"Don't cry, don't cry," Millie said. She stroked Mango's head.

Karen reached out and pulled Millie into her arms. "It's alright, babies," she kept repeating. "Everthing is alright."

Mango continued to cry for a few more minutes, and then he went limp in her arms, his sobs becoming an occasional sniffle. Millie stopped crying, too, but she continued to rub Mango's head.

Karen pulled them gently away from her and held them at arm's length. When they were calm enough, she pulled a handkerchief from her pocket and wiped Mango's eyes and then Millie's.

"Blow," she told Mango, wiping his nose. She folded the handkerchief. "Now you Millie, blow."

Gently brushing the hair back out of their faces, she looked them in the eyes.

"It's alright," she said. "I'm so sorry. I love you. I would never ever scare you on purpose. Do you understand?"

The children nodded that they did. When Clover licked the salt off of Mango's face, a little smile started to form at the corners of his mouth.

"No Clover," Millie said, giggling. "You ain't 'pose to lick our faces. You got germs. Granny said that you did."

A Watch in the Night

"Silly Clover," Karen said, standing up and pulling the twins in close to her side. "I'll tell you two a secret if you won't tell Granny."

"What?" they both asked.

"Dog germs won't really hurt you. Buck, that was our dog before Duke, he licked me and Nathan the whole time that we was kids, and it didn't hurt us not one little bit."

Karen took Millie by one hand and Mango by the other. She could see that Millie was still clutching her necklace, but she didn't say a word about that. Swinging their hands, she walked the children back to where she had left the sled.

This clearing felt all wrong to her now, and she trembled inside. If she had not brought the children with her, she would have left the tree and sprinted for home.

Once they were back at the tree, she didn't waste any time. She tied the tree on the sled with one quick loop of the rope. Together, she and the children trudged down the path, dragging the tree behind them. Clover brought up the rear, as if on guard for danger.

The twins relaxed once they were out of the clearing, and she was glad. They let go of her hands on the sled and skipped along beside her.

Karen, however, remained shaken. To quieten her own nerves and to reassure the twins, she began to sing *Jingle Bells*.

"Dashing through the snow . . . ," she sang.

"We was born on a night that it snowed. Ain't that right, Karen?" Mango asked.

He always asked her this same question when they sang *Jingle Bells*. As soon as he heard the word snow he asked this question.

"That's right, little man. You and your sister was born on a night that it snowed right here in Tate's Hell."

"That makes us special, don't it?" he asked, knowing the answer.

"That makes you very special," Karen said.

They entered the forest trail. She wanted desperately to get home, but she didn't want to frighten the children by hurrying them.

"And one day, it'll snow again, won't it?" Mango continued with his questions. Millie was silent, sticking close to Karen's side.

"That's right," she said, trying to keep the tremor out of her voice. "And when it does, we'll build snowmen and angels just like in our books. Now hurry 'long 'cause I'm gettin' cold."

Bessie met them at the back door. "I was startin' to get worried," she said. "Ya'll was gone a long time."

Bessie held open the door, and a gush of warm air, filled with the smell of fresh-baked cakes, poured out of the kitchen.

"Go on, Clover. You ain't gettin' inside." Bessie nudged Clover away from the door with her foot. He ambled off of the porch and dropped down next to Duke by the chimney.

The twins forgot about the tree and rushed inside to inspect the two chocolate cakes sitting on the counter.

"Now who loves you?' Bessie asked. She held up a bowl with two beater handles sticking out of the top.

"You do," they shouted.

"That's right," she said. She handed them each a beater covered with chocolate. "That's why I saved you the beaters."

All during that day Millie hung onto the necklace, although Karen made several attempts to lure it away from her. She feared that Millie might show it to Bessie and upset her.

Eventually, Millie put the necklace down, and Karen placed it on the kitchen window sill out of her reach. But the necklace and the episode in the clearing weighed on her mind, and on more than one occasion, the twins had to prod a distracted Karen back to reality.

The Taylors came for the birthday party, and in all of the excitement, Karen forgot about the necklace and the clearing. It did cross her mind once when the children were going through their repertoire of Christmas songs and got to *Jingle Bells*. But she pushed the incident out of her mind.

It was Christmas morning when Naomi noticed the necklace lying on the window sill. She picked it up and examined it carefully.

"What's this?" she asked, holding the necklace out for Karen to see when she came into the kitchen. The twins were still sleeping. Karen and Naomi were alone in the kitchen.

"Ugh, I forgot all 'bout that thing," Karen said. She refused to touch the necklace.

"Millie found it back in the clearin' the day we went to chop our tree. I meant to throw it away."

Karen poured her coffee and sat down next to her mother. "And of all things, Mango found an old dog leash.

"It all gave me the *willies*."

"Not the *willies*," Naomi said, mocking her. I ain't heard you use that word since you was a little girl." The *willies* was Karen and Nathan's word for anything scary.

"Well, it did give me the *willies*. And I don't know why." Karen told her mother what had happened and how she had shouted at poor little Mango. "I felt just awful," she said.

"He seems to have weathered the storm," Naomi replied, still teasing her.

"I can't believe that I forgot to tell you. It really was upsettin'. What do you make of it, Mama?"

"I don't make nothin' of it. Really, I don't, Karen. I'm sure it's nothin'."

"I can understand the dog leash," Karen said. She wasn't as eager as her mother to drop the subject. "A hunter coulda dropped that. But how do you figger that necklace got back there in that clearin'? And it did give me the *willies*. I don't care what you say, Mama; it was spooky."

"Don't talk foolish girl. I do declare you and Nathan could find a bogeyman anywheres. I don't know where my youngens got their spooky ways. It musta come from somewhere back on your daddy's side of the family." Naomi dropped the necklace in the pocket to her dress.

"Merry Christmas, Merry Christmas," the children shouted, as they came skidding around the corner in their pajamas.

"I know now why they put rubber pads on the bottom of youngens' sleepers," Naomi said, shaking her finger at the giggling twins. "It's to keep 'em from knockin' over old ladies like me."

"Come over here and give me some Christmas kisses this minute." Naomi pulled the children down on her lap and nuzzled their necks, causing another spat of uncontrollable giggling. They squirmed out of her arms onto the floor.

"I do declare I don't know what's come over you youngens this mornin'. I bet this ain't got nothin' to do with Christmas now does it?"

Just then, a knock sounded at the door. The twins jumped up and looked at each other. "Granny," they squealed in unison.

"That's right it's Granny," Karen said. "And now that we're all here, you can go see what Santa left you under the tree. Shake a leg and open the door. Don't leave Granny out in the cold."

That night as Naomi undressed for bed she pulled the necklace out of her pocket. She sat down on the edge of her bed and looked it over again. The chain slipped slowly through her fingers until she was staring at the tarnished pendant bearing Lily's name.

She stared at the pendant and remembered the headlights moving down the lane to the clearing. Poor Lily, she thought.

But as far as she could tell, Karen didn't suspect the truth, and Naomi felt it best to keep her in the dark. Although she and Bessie had never discussed it, Naomi was certain that Bessie knew more about the children's father than she let on.

She stood up, slipped her dress over her head and pulled on a flannel nightgown. She walked to the window and looked through the thin rim of frost that had formed on her windowpane.

In the light of the full moon, she could just barely see the outline of Washington and Nathan's headstones. Better to let sleeping dogs lie, she thought.

She lay down on the bed and stared at the shadows the moonlight cast on the ceiling.

"It won't do no good to go meddlin' in other people's business, 'specially when them people is the richest white folks in the county."

Naomi heard Washington's words as clearly as if he were lying in the bed next to her. She pulled the cover up, fluffed her pillow and closed her eyes. He might be four years in his grave, she thought, but he's still my partner.

The year after the twins turned four more changes came to Trinity. Walter Jr. announced that he would be adding another physician to his practice. A young man would be coming down from Atlanta to join him.

This fact immediately made the town suspicious of the new doctor's qualifications—nobody ever merely up and moved to Trinity. A person had to be born in Trinity, or at the very least have some family ties to want to live there. Something had to be up with this doctor.

Walter Jr. took over his father's medical practice and the official title of "Doc Adams" almost immediately after his father's funeral. Leona did not join her husband in Trinity with their children until the following summer.

Once she arrived, she did not readily adjust to rural living. After making the move, she frequently traveled back to Raleigh, without her husband, which by Trinity's standards wasn't a natural thing for a married woman to do.

These trips fueled the speculation that Walter Jr.'s marriage might be on the ropes, barely held together by two thin threads—his children.

"She's up in Raleigh with her mama and daddy more than she's at home," Rita Jeeters said, while sitting in Annie's chair during her regular Saturday morning visit.

"Well, that's her business now ain't it," Annie said, in a feeble attempt to defend Leona. As the proprietor of a beauty shop, she knew that gossip was bound to happen when you put more than two women in one room. But she saw it as her job to keep the comments from getting too one-sided.

"And she don't even take the kids with her half the time. Leaves them with Mildred. I don't care what you say, *that* ain't right," Rosie Jenkins said, fanning herself with a magazine.

Rosie owned the local diner so the women credited her with being in the know. Tongues clucked and eyebrows shot up when Rosie made this announcement.

"If that don't take the cake," Mary Grace Dorsett said. She closed her *Ladies' Home Journal* to join in the conversation.

Annie circled Rita's head a couple of times with a can of Alberto VO5 hairspray and then twisted her "hussy curl" into place on her forehead. This curl was Rita's signature look.

"See ya'll in church tomorrow," Rita said. As she stood up to leave, she gave the women a dainty little flip of her wrist to wave good-bye.

"Bye-bye now," several of the women called after her.

As soon as she was out the door Miss Janie Tompkins turned to the others and said, "I do not for the life of me understand why she won't get rid of that hussy curl."

Janie was the spinster in the group, still living with her father at the age of forty. As a young girl she had dated Ralph Jeeters, but he had all but jilted her at the church alter for Rita. That was over twenty years back, but Janie still held an ever-simmering grudge.

A Watch in the Night

"There ain't a thing wrong with her wearin' that curl," Annie shot back. "Now get on up here in this chair, 'cause I'm runnin' late."

"The curl was fine when she was twenty years old," Janie said, unwilling to go down without a fight. "But she's a grandma now. It makes her look *cheap*."

"It don't do no such thing," Annie quickly snapped back just as the door opened and everybody turned to see who was coming inside.

It was Mildred Adams, which was a bit of surprise. Mildred was not a regular. She wore her hair pulled back in a tightly-wound, grey bun at the nape of her neck. This had been her hairstyle as far back as anyone could remember. A style that did not require Annie's services other than a trim on rare occasions.

"Mildred, honey, it's so good to see you," Rosie crooned in a voice smooth as fresh butter. She stopped to embrace Mildred on her way over to Annie's chair.

"Your Walter Jr. was in the diner a few days back with his family. I do declare them youngens of his are growin' like weeds. And Leona looks good. How are they doin'?"

"They're fine. All just fine," Mildred said. "Thank you for asking."

Turning her attention to Annie," Mildred said, "I stopped by to see if you got something that might help me get the tangles out of Lizzie's hair."

Lizzie was Walter Jr.'s daughter. Her given name was Elizabeth, but much to Leona's consternation, her grandmother had taken to calling her Lizzie. And no matter how many times Leona corrected her—much to Elizabeth's unbridled delight—Mildred persisted in calling her Lizzie.

"You got the grandchildren this weekend, do you Mildred?" Rosie asked.

"I do," Mildred said. "Their mama's in Raleigh. Her mother has been awfully sick since Leona and the children got here."

"You don't say," Rosie said. She rolled her eyes at the others when Mildred turned away. Annie shot Rosie a scalding glare.

"Here you are, Mildred. Take this," Annie said. She handed Mildred a bottle of pink liquid. "This oughta take care of Lizzie's tangles."

"How much do I owe you?" Mildred asked.

"Your money ain't no good in here," Annie said, smiling. "Lord knows your husband, God rest his sweet soul, took care of me and my family through enough hard times. He took care of all of us."

"Well, thank you," Mildred said.

"See ya in church tomorrow," Rosie called out to Mildred as she went out the door.

As soon as the door slammed shut, Annie turned on Rosie and her cronies.

"Ya'll oughta be ashamed of yourselves," Annie scolded them. "Why Doc Adams looked after you and all your families; and he didn't do it for the money neither."

"What? We didn't do nothin'," Rosie said defensively. "I just asked about her son. Is that a crime?"

She looked over at the others for support, but everybody had their heads back in their magazines. Annie had struck a raw nerve. Doc Adams had seen them all through hard times at one time or another. Annie was right. It weren't fittin' to go talkin' down his family.

If Leona failed to thrive while living in Trinity, the same was not true for Walter Jr., who enthusiastically took up his father's work.

And as Walter Jr. promised, a new doctor arrived in the fall. The new doctor came all the way from Atlanta, too. But the most astounding fact about Dr. Lucas Lowry was not that he hailed from Atlanta.

A Watch in the Night

It was this: Dr. Lucas Lowry was black. Walter Jr. had neglected to add this detail to his announcement regarding Dr. Lowry's pending arrival.

Once Dr. Lowry settled in and the town settled down, Walter Jr. sprang a new surprise: he remodeled and expanded Doc's old office. Nobody could even recall the last time Doc had given his office a fresh coat of paint.

But here was his son, not only painting the old wooden building a white so bright that it out sparkled the First Baptist Church, but putting on a new shingled roof and adding on some more space.

The clincher, however, was the sign, which hung suspended between two white posts on the small patch of green lawn between the building and the road. It read in big block letters: THE TRINITY MEDICAL CLINIC.

"Now, if that don't beat all," folks said. "Doc never even had a sign. It ain't like everbody in town don't know where the doctor's office is."

When *the Clinic* officially opened for business both Walter Jr. and Lucas expected that Lucas, as a black doctor, would meet with some resistance, if not outright hostility. They both understood that his presence in the Clinic would take some getting used to by the town.

But folks came around soon enough. In Trinity a person would go to the doctor only if the situation were dire. Under these circumstances, few could afford to be choosy. It was either the Clinic or a drive to Cartersville, which wasn't an option for most.

Even if they could get to Cartersville, which most couldn't, the Clinic extended credit; the doctors in Cartersville didn't. While the blacks mostly asked for "Dr. Luke" and the whites for Doc Adams, the barrier gradually eroded.

Karen and Naomi first met Dr. Luke at the Shady Grove Baptist Church where he became a member the week that he arrived in town.

Lucas Lowry was an imposing figure, and all heads turned and stared the first time he strode down the aisle of the church, smartly dressed in a blue-striped shirt, a blue suit, a red tie and fancy leather shoes polished to a high gloss.

Everybody had heard about the new doctor; however, few had met or even seen him. And he was a sight to behold.

He was tall—well over six feet—with broad, powerful shoulders that tapered down to a narrow waist and hips. His black curly hair was cropped close to his scalp, and his skin, the color of a moonless midnight, was stretched tautly over the finely chiseled features of his angular face.

Dr. Lucas Lowrey was, in fact, a sight to behold. On that fact everybody agreed.

The color of the doctor's skin was a pleasant surprise for the parishioners. Because he was a doctor, most of them had half expected him to look white.

In Trinity, educated blacks were as rare a breed as liberal-minded whites. The opportunity simply wasn't there for either to flourish. As Dr. Lowry took a seat near the front of the church, the flock was pleased to see that he was clearly *one of them.*

Most people observed that he looked very young to be a doctor. "He don't even look to be outta his twenties," Bertha Jones said. She directed her remark to a group of women who had gathered on the front lawn of the church after services to chat.

"Actually, I left my twenties behind me several years back; I'm thirty-three," Dr. Lowry said, walking up behind Bertha.

She turned and stared up into a penetrating pair of black eyes. His lips parted in a broad smile revealing perfectly even and dazzling white teeth.

Bertha looked away chagrined, unable to hold his gaze. The other ladies chuckled softly. They were of the opinion that Bertha was a smidge *too talkative.* It didn't hurt one bit for her to be taken down a notch or two.

"Dr. Lucas Lowry," he said, extending his hand to Bertha in a conciliatory move. He had not intended to embarrass her.

"I'm Bertha Jones," she stammered, grasping his hand. "I surely didn't mean no harm by talkin' 'bout your age like that Dr. Lowry."

"There's no harm in discussing a man's age that I know of," he replied, covering Bertha's hand with his own. Bertha's pudgy little paw was trapped, held firmly by large hands with long, slender fingers.

"But if it's all the same to you, you can just call me Dr. Luke." He released Bertha's hand and flashed the ladies a quick grin and a playful wink.

"That's fine," Bertha said. "Dr. Luke why don't you come on over to my house for Sunday dinner."

She had regained her composure somewhat. "I got the preacher comin'. He's a bachelor like you. You are a bachelor, ain't you Dr. Luke?"

Bertha and the other women had discussed Dr. Luke's marital status at length when he had shown up in town with no sign of a wife in tow. The consensus was that he must be a bachelor.

All conceded, however, they could be wrong. After all, that white doctor's wife had not joined him in town for months after his arrival.

"I am," he replied. "And if you're sure that it wouldn't be any trouble, I would be delighted to join your family for Sunday dinner."

"No trouble a'tall," Bertha gushed. She had a girl who was twenty-six and not yet married off. Having an eligible, young doctor over for Sunday dinner would not trouble her in the least.

That Sunday, Dr. Luke was the talk over every black family's dinner table, at least the ones who went to church. Naomi's table was no exception.

"You got to admit that he's handsome," Naomi said to Karen. Bessie had prepared Sunday dinner while Karen and Naomi were at church, and they all sat gathered around the table.

"I didn't notice," Karen said.

"Well, I sure nuff did, and I'm an old woman. I ain't seen a man with that kinda good looks 'round these parts since your daddy was a young man," Naomi remarked, as she pulled her chair up to the table.

"In fact, he puts me in mind of your daddy some—the way that he's tall and dark-skinned. Some women prefer a light-colored man, but not me. Your daddy was black as coal and that suited me just fine."

"Mama, really I wish that you'd listen to yourself. This ain't decent talk in front of the children."

Millie and Mango looked at each other perplexed. They hadn't noticed a thing wrong with what Naomi had said.

"Nonsense, girl; there ain't nothin' wrong with talkin' 'bout a man and a woman. God meant for them to be together. It says so in the *Bible*."

"I ain't got no earthly idea what ya'll talkin' 'bout," Bessie said. She heaped some more potatoes onto Mango's plate.

"We're talkin' 'bout that new colored doctor that come to work with Doc Adams. He showed up at church today."

"Mama, please," Karen said, in an exasperated tone, "the word is *black*, not colored. No black person uses the word colored no more."

"I beg your pardon, but I do, Missy. And so do a lot of the other old-timers. I do declare, gal, I can't say a thing that you ain't findin' fault with me today."

"I ain't even heard that a new doctor come to town," Bessie interjected.

A Watch in the Night

"Well, one did. And he's *black*, young and single. I'm thinkin' 'bout invitin' him to Sunday dinner next week."

"You ain't gonna do no such thing," Karen said. She got up and huffed over to the sink with her empty plate.

"Do not," she hissed, turning and pointing her finger at Naomi, "give that thought any more attention; and I mean that, Mama!"

The following Sunday at church Naomi and Karen were formally introduced to Dr. Luke. On the ride home, Karen had to admit to her mother that he was indeed handsome. "Seems to be real nice, too," she added.

"Nice. He's downright charmin'; that's what he is," Naomi responded.

"I heard that he is lookin' for somebody to work in his office two or three days a week," Karen said.

"It was Tilly Sparks who told me. She plans on goin' after the job herself. She didn't even finish high school, and the only job that she's ever had is shuckin' oysters. She and her mama are makin' plumb fools out of theirselves, the way they're fallin' all over him."

"Now girl, it ain't like you to talk down other people thataways. Them Spark youngens had 'em a hard row to hoe. Tilly had to go to work to help feed all of the youngens under her."

"I suppose," Karen conceded.

"Bertha and her husband musta had 'em ten head 'fore Tilly's daddy drunk hisself to death," Naomi added.

"It ain't Tilly's fault that she didn't finish school. And there ain't nothin' wrong with shuckin' oysters—it's an honest day's work. You can't blame Tilly for wantin' to better herself. You need to mind your mouth. And us on the way home from church, at that."

"Me?" Karen fired back. "You the one who said Tilly's daddy drunk hisself to death."

"Well, he did. Bertha is a God-fearing woman, but that man of hers, he loved the bottle a lot more than he loved Jesus. That's just the truth—plain and simple."

"I reckon you're right 'bout Tilly. She deserves a chance at betterin' herself just like everbody else," Karen said. She turned her head to look out of her window. They drove along in silence for a few minutes.

"Why don't you go after that job with Dr. Luke?" Naomi asked nonchalantly, as she turned the car onto the lane leading up to the house. She knew that she would need to sneak up on this subject with Karen.

Karen turned and gave her mother a wide-eyed stare.

"What on earth are you talkin' 'bout, Mama? I got a job. I take care of two small children seven days a week. Remember? That's a sure nuff job!"

"I ain't sayin' that you don't work, child. But Millie and Mango ain't babies no more. Bessie could watch 'em by herself a couple of days a week. It might do you some good to get out of Tate's Hell a little. That job with Dr. Luke ain't but a couple days a week. You said that yourself."

"Mama, you know good and doggoned well that Bessie can't look after the twins without me! That is pure nonsense."

"Yes, she can," Naomi fired back. "And you know it, too,"

Trying to calm herself, Naomi took in a deep breath.

"Them ain't your youngens, Karen. You need to start facin' up to that fact. You need to think 'bout makin' some life for yourself other than lookin' after them youngens."

"I may not have given birth to 'em," Karen retaliated, "but I've looked after 'em since the day they's born. I'm the only mama they know. And I ain't gonna leave 'em. They are too young."

A Watch in the Night

Naomi stopped the car in the front yard. Immediately, Karen got out and slammed the door, pushing past Bessie and the twins who were waiting for them on the porch. She stormed straight to her room, closing the door with a clamorous thud.

"What's wrong with her?" Bessie asked.

"It's nothin'. Go ahead and put dinner on the table. We'll be in directly."

"Come on," Bessie said, herding the twins towards the kitchen. "Ya'll can set the table and put the ice in the glasses."

Naomi went into the back of the house and knocked softly on Karen's door. When Karen didn't answer, Naomi went in. Karen sat on the bed, hunched over, her head in her hands, crying.

"Honey, I didn't mean to hurt your feelings none," Naomi said. She sat down on the bed next to Karen.

"But what I said is true. Them ain't your babies. The fact is they ain't even babies no more. They are growin' up. Right or wrong, them youngens belong to Bessie and Ephram."

"Ephram! He ain't never done nothin' but cuss 'em and call 'em names since the day they's born. How's he got any claim to 'em."

"Cause they his blood kin. And you know that. Now I ain't sayin' that things is gonna change; not right now anyways. But in a couple of years them kids gotta go to school. You need to make your own life, Karen. You can't keep holdin' on to them youngens, like they's yours."

"But they feel like mine. They really do, Mama." Karen looked up and out the window with sad eyes, the tears rolling down her cheeks.

"And they feel like my grandchildren, but they ain't. I had the same feelings for Lily. But then I had to give her up when she growed up some. It ain't wrong to love 'em. But you got to always bear in mind that them babies are white, Karen. They ain't gonna never be yours."

Naomi sat quietly for a few minutes letting Karen have her cry.

"I weren't gonna say nothin' 'bout this 'til later," Naomi finally said, "but I guess this here's as good a time as any. I spoke with Dr. Luke 'bout that job after church. It ain't took yet. He says that you can come in and give it a try if you're a mind to."

"Mama! You didn't have no right to do that," Karen said indignantly. Stiffening her back, she whipped her head around to face her mother.

"I know. I know," Naomi said. Her voice was soft as she tried to smooth Karen's ruffled feathers. "I overstepped my bounds, and for that I'm sorry. I truly am. But right or wrong, I did it 'cause I want what's best for you. I see a whole lotta heartache headin' your way, if you try and hang on too tight to them children in there."

"I know you meant to do what's right, but you can't go decidin' what's best for me." Karen's voice softened as well.

"You right, girl. I won't go meddlin' no more."

"I doubt that," Karen said. She wiped her eyes with the hem of her dress.

Naomi pulled a handkerchief out of her pocket and held it up to Karen's nose. "Blow," she said. Karen blew, rolling her eyes at her mother.

"You beat all, Mama," she said. "You know that!"

"A mama don't stop worryin' 'bout her youngens just 'cause they grow up. Sometimes I think they worry more. It ain't as easy to fix your youngen's hurt when they growed up. I want you to think 'bout that job. Will you do that for your old mama?"

"I'll think 'bout it," Karen said. "But you've got to promise me that you'll let it be. It's my choice."

"I promise," Naomi said, rising from the bed. "Now go wash your face and come on in to dinner. Little Mango must be starvin' by now."

A Watch in the Night

The next Sunday Dr. Luke cornered Karen after church. She was sure that her mother had put him up to it.

"I had hoped to see you at the Clinic last week," he said. "Your mother told me you might be looking for a job."

"I did mean to come by, but . . . ," Karen stuttered, looking for an excuse.

"I'm desperate for help. There's so much that needs to be done. I'm told that Abigail Taylor used to deliver most of the black babies and do some of the other doctoring. But now that she's gone, I'm all they've got. You'd be doing God's work, Karen."

"My mama put you up to this, didn't she?" Karen demanded to know.

"Well, she might have broached the subject with me. But, Karen, I really do need the help."

"Alright," she said, throwing her hands up in defeat. "I'll help out. But just for a couple of days a week. I can't work no more than that. And just until you can find somebody on a more permanent basis."

"Thank you," Dr. Luke said, flashing her that brilliant smile. "I'll see you tomorrow then."

"No, Tuesday. I got some 'rangements to make. But I'll be there on Tuesday."

On Monday, Karen spent all day coaching Bessie and the twins on how to get along without her.

"Don't let them outside," she said to Bessie, as she squashed a meatloaf through her fingers in a large mixing bowl. She was making one large enough that there would be enough for the next day.

"Lord only knows what they could get into. If you don't watch Mango like a hawk, he'll be outside before you know it."

"We'll do just fine," Bessie said. She stooped down to search in the cabinet for the large baking pan.

"And ya'll mind Granny," Karen said, turning her attention to the twins, who stood in two chairs pulled up to the sink washing potatoes.

"Don't let me come home and hear that ya'll been bickerin' and fussin' and not mindin' Granny. Do you hear me?" she said sternly.

"Yes ma'am," they responded in unison.

On Tuesday, Karen reluctantly prepared to go with her mother. Naomi was going to drop Karen at the Clinic on her way over to the island. Before they could leave, Naomi had to wait for Karen to lay out the twins' clothes and put breakfast on the table.

"Call me if you need help," she said to Bessie, who had walked outside to see them off. "I left the number to the Clinic by the phone. And just warm up that meatloaf for lunch."

"We already plowed this ground," Bessie said, winking at Naomi. "We'll manage. Don't fret 'bout us. Put your mind on your work at the Clinic."

Naomi dropped Karen at the Clinic promptly at 7:00 o'clock. She waved good-bye and then watched in her rear-view mirror as Karen disappeared inside.

Dr. Luke was waiting for Karen behind the receptionist desk. As soon as she walked through the door, he put her to work. The morning flew by as a steady stream of patients flowed through the Clinic.

Karen's plan to call every hour to check in on Bessie and the twins quickly went awry. The steady stream of patients at the Clinic left no time for phone calls.

Lunch consisted of stolen bites from her meatloaf sandwich as she answered the phone, signed people in, or ushered them to the examination room.

When Dr. Luke announced that it was time to go home, she wouldn't have believed him, except that the clock on the wall told her that what he said was true.

"Do you need a ride home?" Dr. Luke asked.

"No. Mama will be along directly," she said. A car horn sounded outside. One short beep.

"That must be her now," Karen said, gathering up her things.

"See you on Thursday?" Dr. Luke asked.

"I suppose," she said, hurrying out the door.

"You did a fine job," Dr. Luke called after her.

When Karen decided to keep the job, Naomi called a family meeting, which included Bessie.

"The only thing that's gonna change is that Karen will be gone two, sometimes three days a week," Naomi said to Bessie.

"That's fine," Bessie replied. "I'm proud that Karen took herself a job. Me and the youngens will get on just fine."

"But I think they ought to keep livin' here with us," Naomi quickly added. "It's the only home they know. And I don't mean to hurt you none by sayin' this, Bessie, but so long as Ephram stays over to your place, I think the kids are better off here."

"That don't hurt me none," Bessie replied. "I ain't got no love for Ephram Whatley. And what you say is true. Them youngens don't need to be 'round him."

"So, you'll keep comin' over here ever mornin' like you've always done?" Naomi asked.

"You can stay right here with 'em. I ain't sayin' that you shouldn't take 'em to your place some. I know you got things to do at your own house. Just come back here when Ephram comes 'round."

"Don't you worry none 'bout that," Bessie said. "I ain't got no intentions of puttin' the youngens in Ephram Whatley's path."

The following Saturday, Bessie watched the children while Naomi and Karen went into town. Naomi had been dropping Karen off and picking her up at work. That arrangement meant Karen arrived at the Clinic long before it opened, and on some days, she had to wait on Naomi after it had closed.

Karen needed a car.

Sally Deas sat behind a small desk in the front office of Langley Motors when Karen and Naomi walked inside. When the bell tinkled over the door, signaling that someone had come inside, she looked up from the desk where she had been intently applying fire-engine red polish to her nails.

Usually, Sally would have been at Annie's having this done for her, but Langley's wife, who covered for her on most Saturdays, was out sick.

Naomi and Karen stood awkwardly, barely inside the door, waiting for her to acknowledge them. Finally, Sally held up her hands, blew on her nails and said in a curt tone, "Can I help ya'll?"

"We're here 'bout buyin' a car," Naomi said.

"Well, ya'll gonna need to talk to Mr. Langley hisself 'bout that. He's in with another customer. If ya'll wait outside, I'll tell 'em that ya'll are here."

Naomi and Karen went back out the door.

"Mama, let's go on home," Karen whispered to her mother. "This weren't such a good idea. I don't mind spendin' a little extra time at the Clinic. I can get some of my paperwork done."

"Swallow your pride, girl. We come here 'bout a car, and I ain't leavin' 'til I talk to this Langley fella. Your daddy always traded here."

The conversation ended when Mr. Langley came huffing through the door. He was the son of the original owner. The old man had passed away years back leaving the business to his only son.

The younger Langley was as round as he was tall. Took after his mama, who was always stout, folks said. His plaid sans-a-belt trousers hung down below a humongous belly, covered so tightly by a Banlon shirt that Naomi thought the fabric resembled gauze.

White shoes, scuffed and worn down on the sides, finished off his outfit. When he lifted the clipboard in his hand, an inch of white, flabby belly slipped out from under the shirt.

"What can I do for ya'll?" he asked, looking them over.

"I'm Naomi Ivey and this here is my girl, Karen. I'm the widow of Washington Ivey. He traded here with you."

"I remember Washington. But what can I do for ya'll?"

"My girl here needs a car. We brung in my husband's truck for a trade," Naomi said. She pointed towards Washington's truck, which sat parked off to the side of the lot.

Naomi hated to see it go, but Karen needed a car.

"The truck's old but it still runs good," Naomi said. "Washington, he took good care of it. Karen here works over at the Clinic. We gotta make payments on what the truck won't cover."

Langley looked them over again, more carefully this time, and then looked over at the truck.

"That truck don't look like it's worth much, and as a rule, I don't extend credit."

Naomi's cheeks burned with sudden anger. That was an outright lie. The truck was in good condition, and Washington had bought it on credit.

Just about everthing Langley sold was on credit, Naomi thought. Everbody knew that. People livin' in Trinity didn't have the money to pay cash. That's how Langley made the bulk of his profit by charging poor folks high interest.

Langley ambled over to the truck and kicked the tires. Karen took this opportunity to whisper to her mother once again that she wanted to leave.

Naomi ignored her. They had come here to get a car, and she wasn't leaving without one.

Circling the truck slowly, Langley assessed the situation.

The truck was old, but immaculate. Washington Ivey always kept his trucks up; he knew that from experience. And he had a little Ford in the back that he had got for almost nothing—repo'ed it from one of the oystermen when the red tide hit. It had been sitting on the back of the lot ever since.

He had been hoping to unload it, and he saw a chance to make a good profit on these two.

"I got a little red Ford in the back that might work for ya. But I'm gonna have to check with Doc Adams 'bout your job."

"It's Dr. Luke, Lucas Lowry, that I work for. He's the new doctor at the Clinic," Karen muttered.

"Like I said, I gotta check with Doc Adams. Ya'll wait here." He turned and puffed back inside, his trousers making a swishing noise as his thighs rubbed together.

Sally was finishing her second coat of polish.

"Get Doc Adams on the phone," Langley barked. He wasn't takin' no colored doctor's word for nothin'.

Sally gingerly stuck one finger in the rotary phone and started to dial. "Damn," she said, under her breath when the polish smeared.

It was noon before Karen and Naomi, driving the red Ford, exited the car lot. Huddled next to window in the front office, Langley and Sally watched them go. "If them women are one day late on a payment, you be sure to let me know," Langley instructed Sally.

Karen drove proudly down Main Street. This was her first car. Naomi sat beside her. They had paid too much for the car—Naomi knew that for a fact. Not to mention the 18% interest.

She would have liked to pay for the car out of her savings. But that had gone down to almost nothing when she paid the Davis Funeral Parlor for Washington's funeral.

Davis operated a second funeral home on the edge of the quarters for blacks. It had taken several years for her and Washington to pay off Nathan's funeral. That's how she had learned about interest payments.

When Washington died, she didn't go that route again. Instead, she paid cash for his funeral even though it wiped out most of her savings.

Mrs. Brodie paid her a good wage, but there wasn't much left over these days to save. The money that Bessie gave Karen didn't pay for the added expense of having two children in the house to feed and clothe.

Not that she begrudged the twins a penny. She didn't—not for a second. But her savings had suffered.

When Karen arrived at work the following Monday, Doc Adams was there to meet her. He handed to her the title to the red Ford.

"I stopped over to see Mr. Langley on Saturday afternoon. It seems as though he made an error when pricing your car."

Karen looked at the car title and then up at Doc Adams.

"I can't take this," she said.

"Doctor Luke and I discussed this matter earlier. You will need a car to run errands for the Clinic. We have allocated you a car allowance. If we set off that allowance against what you owe us for the car, we ought to be even at the end of the year."

He turned and left before Karen could compose herself enough to respond.

"Thank you," she called out after him, as he pushed out the front door.

What Doc Adams didn't tell Karen was that Langley had insisted that he come over to co-sign Karen's loan. When Doc saw the deal that Langley had cut with the Iveys, he and Langley had gone at it.

Doc won.

Langley knew that Doc wielded a good deal of clout in town, and he had enough business savvy to know when to throw in the towel.

When he dropped the price to what he had paid the oysterman for the car and upped the trade-in value of the truck, Doc added insult to injury by writing him a check for the balance. There went his only chance for a profit: the interest.

"I didn't make one red cent on the deal," he fumed to his wife later.

"That Adams' bunch always did take up for the *coloreds*. If he weren't the only white doctor in town, he wouldn't get away with *that,*" his wife said, sympathetic to her husband's plight.

The breezy falls days passed quickly away as Karen continued to work at the Clinic. Thanksgiving came and went and before she realized it, they were only a couple of weeks away from the twins' fifth birthday.

"Ya'll do remember that we're closing in on the twins' fifth birthday," Karen said to Bessie and Naomi. They sat drinking their morning cup of coffee together.

This had become a ritual for the women over the years; one last cup of coffee when Bessie arrived before Naomi and now Karen headed out for work.

"Time sure flies," Naomi said, shaking her head. "Washington in the grave five years now, the twins shooting up like bean sprouts and me dryin' up like an old prune."

"It's old age," Bessie said. "My arthritis is worse, my hearin' is goin' and I can't seem to remember a thing."

"We have this same conversation ever year, and it still ain't got a thing to do with old age," Karen said. "This year I feel it more than ever. Sometimes I look at the twins, and I can almost see them changin' before my very eyes."

A Watch in the Night

"Lily looks more like her mama ever day, and Mango he . . . ," Bessie murmured. She looked down at her coffee without completing her sentence.

"Let's throw another big party for them, Bessie," Karen said She wanted to lift Bessie's spirits. She knew that Bessie was missing Lily.

"Reckon we can manage with you workin'?" Bessie asked.

"Of course, we can," Karen said. "The Taylors will be back in town. At least that's what they said in their latest letter."

"How 'bout let's invite Dr. Luke," Naomi suggested. "He ain't got none of his people in these parts, and here it is Christmas time with him all alone." She winked at Bessie behind Karen's back, as Karen stood up to rinse her cup.

"It would be a neighborly thing to do. We always got plenty," Bessie added.

"You two can stop right there," Karen said, without looking up from the sink.

"I know what ya'll are up to. But I don't mind if he comes. I heard him tell Doc Adams that he would be here for Christmas. Just don't you two go makin' old fools out of yourselves in front of everbody."

"I don't know what you're talkin' 'bout," Naomi said. She gave Bessie a second wink. "And callin' us two old fools. I don't know what this world's comin' to when a gal sasses her own mama like that."

"Oh, you don't know what I'm talkin' 'bout," Karen said. She turned and looked at her mother who stood with a straight face.

"I thought you and Bertha Sparks was gonna break a leg last Sunday after services the way ya'll was racin' each other out of the church and down the steps to see who could invite him to dinner first. You was packin' up to go even 'fore the alter call. And I weren't the only one who seen it. The whole church knows what's goin' on, includin' Dr. Luke. It is embarassin', Mama."

"I only invited him 'cause I wanted him to take a look at Mango's sore throat. That and to give him a decent meal. I'm sure he's tired of eatin' Bessie Sparks old stringy fried chicken. I swear that woman makes awful chicken."

"I wish you would listen to yourself, Mama. Who's the one that always says it ain't right to go talkin' down other people?" Karen snapped the dishcloth and folded it over the sink.

"Well, her chicken ain't no good," Naomi muttered.

"Is he your boyfriend, Karen?" All heads turned to look at Millie, who stood in the doorway rubbing the sleep out of her eyes.

"And what would make you think that, Millie?" Karen asked.

Millie shrugged her shoulders and looked over at Naomi and Bessie.

"You two beat all; you know that," she said to Naomi and Bessie. "And you better behave yourself at that party. Do you hear me?"

"Yes ma'am, Missy," Naomi said.

When Karen stomped out of the room, Bessie and Naomi laughed so hard that Bessie had to sit down to catch her breath. Naomi leaned against the sink wiping sweat off of her forehead and tears out of the corners of her eyes with the skirt of her apron.

"What's so funny?" Millie asked.

"It's nothin' sweetheart," Naomi said, "you'll understand when you're older."

On Christmas Eve, Karen took the whole day off to prepare for the twins' birthday. She and the children left before daylight to go and chop the tree.

Bessie baked two large chocolate sheet cakes. The Taylor children, like Millie and Mango, were growing. And Dr. Luke had accepted their invitation. Two small, round cakes would no longer fit the bill.

When Karen heard the knock on the door later that evening, she sighed. She wasn't quite ready; she was still fussing with her hair.

When the knock came again, louder this time, she took one last look in the mirror and went to answer it. Her mother and Bessie had either disappeared or gone deaf, she thought, annoyed with them.

She knew that it had to be Dr. Luke—the Taylor clan would make much more of a racket than a simple knock—and she didn't want to keep him waiting in the cold.

"Come on in," she said, opening the door wide for Dr. Luke. He brushed his polished shoes on the doormat and stepped inside.

"Let me take your coat," she said. He took off his overcoat and handed it to her.

Karen took one look at him and her breathing reflex went on hold. He was dressed in a white pull-over cotton shirt which fit snugly over his broad shoulders and then tapered down to his thin waist. The shirt was stuffed into a pair of blue jeans, which had a sharp crease running down the middle of each leg.

She had never seen him dressed in anything other than his Sunday suit or his work clothes, which consisted of a long white coat over khaki slacks.

He held out two wrapped gifts to her and smiled. "Is something wrong?" he asked, when Karen stood staring at him, not taking the gifts or uttering a word.

"Oh, no, no," she said. She dabbed at the tiny beads of sweat that had popped out on her forehead with a handkerchief that she plucked out of the front of her dress. As the guardian of two five-year-old runny noses, she always kept a handkerchief handy.

"I'm just a little warm. The kitchen. I've been in the kitchen cookin'," she stammered.

"You look lovely this evening, Karen," he said, his deep voice calm and relaxed. He was not in the least bit flustered, which made Karen even more nervous. She took a full-fledged swipe at her forehead this time.

"Red is a good color for you," he added.

"She does look real nice in red. Her daddy always told me to dress her in red," Naomi said. She walked into the room and gave Dr. Luke a hug.

Naomi was a hugger. She didn't waste time with a flimsy handshake or a peck on the cheek for people she liked. She gave Dr. Luke an especially hard squeeze.

It had taken Naomi two weeks of sewing every evening to finish Karen's dress in time for the party. Earlier, when Karen had modeled the dress for her, she knew that the dress was worth every second.

As Karen twirled around to show off the dress, Naomi stooped and opened her dresser drawer. When she draped a pearl necklace around Karen's neck, the world for one brief moment stopped spinning for Naomi.

The necklace was Naomi's only piece of jewelry, other than the thin gold band she wore on her finger. Washington had presented Naomi with the single strand of cultured pearls as an anniversary gift the year that Nathan was born.

He had worked overtime four weeks in a row to pay for those pearls. Naomi kept them in a velvet bag with a little drawstring in the bottom drawer of her dresser, next to Nathan's backpack.

Naomi brought herself back to the moment.

"I believe that's the Taylors' headlights comin' up the lane," she said. "You two young folks go in by the fire, and I'll welcome the Taylors. Go on now. Scat! I'm quite sure that Dr. Luke would like to warm up."

All during the meal, Naomi and Bessie took every opportunity to sing Karen's praises.

"Karen cooked the whole meal by herself," Bessie said. "I didn't do nothin' but bake the cakes."

Naomi followed up with, "She is one of the best cooks in Trinity County." They pretended to ignore Karen's scalding stare.

Karen was convinced of the plot, when after supper, Naomi, Bessie and even Abigail shooed her into the living room where Dr. Luke and Samuel stood by the fire. Later, as everyone gathered by the fire and the twins stood up to recite *Twas the Night Before Christmas,* Naomi scooched over on the couch and patted the seat between her and Karen.

"Dr. Luke why don't you sit here," Naomi suggested. Karen punched her mother on the arm when Dr. Luke wasn't looking before making room on the sofa for him.

As soon as the good-byes were said and the cars pulled out of the drive, Karen turned on her mother and Bessie.

"Well, if you two don't beat all," she said to them. "Ya'll made Bertha Sparks look like an amateur the way you carried on tonight. *Karen cooked the meal; Karen chopped the tree; Karen has such a way with children; sit next to Karen, Dr. Luke.* Really! And both of you promised to behave. I'm going to bed. You two can put the twins to bed. I'm sure ya'll got a lot to talk about."

As soon as Karen was out of the room, Bessie and Naomi covered their mouths to stifle their laughter.

CHAPTER FIFTEEN

The catastrophe struck in the spring after the twins' fifth birthday; after Bessie had proved herself to be quite capable of caring for the children alone; after Karen had accepted the job for three days a week at the Clinic; after everyone had weathered the necessary adjustments.

It happened as trouble is apt to do when all seems to be going so well. And it set all their lives on a different course, although, as is so often the case, nobody realized that change was in the making until much later.

It happened late on a Thursday afternoon when the sweetness of the first warm day of spring had lured Karen and the twins outside like bumble bees drawn to fresh pollen.

Karen was hanging sheets on the line, methodically stabbing the wooden clothes pens on the nylon cord. A light wind whipped the sheets and cooled her face, which was flushed with the heat of the late afternoon sun.

She could hear Millie and Mango playing in the back yard, their squeals and Clover's occasional yap blending peacefully with the flapping of the sheets.

She finished hanging the sheets and lifted the straw laundry basket, lodging it against her hip as she looked up at the sky. She hoped there was enough sunlight and wind left to dry the sheets before nightfall.

She thought of how crisp the sheets would feel, how fresh they would smell at bedtime. She lingered, sucking the fragrance of the first blooms of spring deep into her lungs, surprised to discover when she perused the woods that the brown of winter had been swallowed up by the green of spring.

She swallowed one last gulp of the day's sweetness and then reluctantly turned to go inside. When Millie and Mango came sprinting around the corner of the house, almost bumping into her, she thought they were playing a game.

"Hey, watch where you're goin'," she said, stepping aside to avoid a collision.

"Granny's hurt," they both shouted at once.

The basket fell from hands as she took off running after them. She rounded the back of the house and saw Bessie lying sprawled out at the bottom of the porch steps.

"Bessie," she called, sprinting the last few yards and dropping down beside her.

"It's my back," Bessie groaned, trying to force herself up off the ground. She fell back, her head sinking into the soft dirt of the flower bed, her face contorting into a painful grimace.

"Don't try to move again," Karen said. She jumped up and cleared the back steps two at a time.

"I'm gonna call Dr. Luke," she called over her shoulder to the twins. "Ya'll stay with her." The twins hovered over Bessie, their faces anxious and afraid.

Mango appointed himself as the lookout for Dr. Luke, stationing himself at the top of the front steps where he could get a good view of the lane.

Karen and Millie stayed with Bessie comforting her as best they could. Karen wiped Bessie's head with a cool cloth while Millie stroked her hand.

In less than half an hour, Karen heard the faint sound of a car engine, which quickly escalated as Dr. Luke raced down the lane, his truck rocking and bucking with each pothole he struck.

Seconds later, Mango came skidding into the back yard and announced in a high-pitched, hysterical voice. "He's here."

"Well, go meet him! Karen exclaimed. "Show him where we are."

Mango spun on his heels like a whirling top. Within seconds he was back, tugging Dr. Luke along by the hand.

Dr. Luke dropped Mango's hand when he saw Bessie on the ground with Karen and Millie kneeling over her. His medical bag banged against his thigh as he trotted swiftly across the back yard.

"Let me get to her," Dr. Luke said to Karen and Millie as he drew closer. They moved aside, and he squatted on his haunches next to Bessie.

Her breath came out in a low, guttural moan, her brow was knit tightly into one deep furrow and her eyes were squinted shut from the pain.

Dr. Luke manipulated her arms, legs and neck, speaking to her in a low, reassuring voice. Karen wrapped an arm around Millie and Mango's shoulders as they stood, one on either side of her, anxiously awaiting the verdict.

After several minutes, Dr. Luke rose up, rubbed his thighs and turned his attention to Karen and the twins.

"Nothing is broken; thank God for that. She'll be fine with some rest. But for now we need to move her inside. Karen you help me lift her. And you kids hold the doors."

When Naomi turned off the lane into her yard, she spied Dr. Luke's car parked in the driveway. Then she spotted the twins, their hands covering their eyes to block the glare of the setting sun, as they paced around the yard with their gaze clearly focused on the lane.

A Watch in the Night

As she rolled to a stop, the twins stormed her car. "Granny's hurt," they shouted, before Naomi could even turn off the engine.

"What? What's that?" She couldn't hear over the sound of the car's motor and Clover's barking. She flipped off the ignition and climbed laboriously out of the car.

"Get Clover. Go on get," she said, nudging Clover with the toe of her shoe. "And you two, calm down and tell me what's got ya'll in such a dither."

"Granny's hurt; she fell down and Dr. Luke is here and everthing," Millie said. The words bubbled out of her mouth like water from a mountain spring.

"How bad is she?" Naomi shouted over Clover's incessant barking.

"Hush up, Clover," she commanded him sternly. Clover retreated to his spot by the chimney where he thumped his tail on the ground, reducing his barking to an occasional yelp.

"How bad is she?" Naomi asked.

"Don't know," Mango said, while skipping around Naomi. "Dr. Luke put her in the bed. And it ain't even dark. Him and Karen told us to come wait for you."

Naomi quickened her pace. The twins ran ahead of her. When she and the twins burst through the front door, Naomi was shocked to see Karen and Dr. Luke sitting calmly on the couch. She stopped dead in her tracks, and her jaw went slack.

"The kids said Bessie was hurt," she said, puffing to catch her breath.

"Calm down," Dr. Luke said. "She took a bad fall, but she'll get over it. There's no need to get yourself all worked up into a *tizzy*.

Dr. Luke loved this word. He had laughed for days the first time he heard Karen use it; that and *hissy fit*.

"She give me and the youngens a scare. But it turned out to be nothin' more than a bad sprain," Karen added.

"Praise God for that," Naomi said. She plopped down on the sofa next to Karen, gasping for breath.

The startling news and the rush inside had left her completely winded. Millie and Mango dropped to the floor by her feet, panting like puppies.

"I gave her something for pain," Dr. Luke said. "She should sleep through the night. I've given Karen some extra pills in case she needs them. But she'll need complete bedrest for at least the next week. I'll re-evaluate her then."

Supper was an assortment of leftovers. By the time Dr. Luke left it was late, and nobody felt up to a meal. When the twins merely picked at their food, Karen hustled them off to bed.

She read them a book, as she did every night. Usually when the book was done, she left them to talk to one another until they fell asleep. But tonight they were whiny and fretful.

"Granny will be just fine. You'll see," she said to them for the hundredth time. "Now close your eyes, and I'll sing you a song."

Their lids fluttered like butterfly wings as they fought sleep, but the soothing sound of Karen's voice lulled them to sleep. When Karen was sure they were asleep, she tiptoed out of the room.

She found her mother sitting at the kitchen table staring out the back door. The wooden door was propped open, with the screen door latched shut.

The faint smell of gardenia blossoms floated across the room. Night sounds drifted in on a light breeze—Clover snoring on the porch; the raspy chirp of crickets; the hoot of a lone owl from far off in the distance.

"A penny for your thoughts," Karen said, sitting down next to her mother.

Naomi turned and smiled at her. "They asleep?"

"Finally. And I looked in on Bessie. She's still out. It must be the pill that Dr. Luke gave her."

"Poor old thing," Naomi said. "Lord knows that woman has had her share of trouble."

"It coulda been worse," Karen said. "Let's count our blessings. I'll have to take off from work. I don't see no way around that. She sure can't be chasin' after two five-year-old youngens with a sprained back, and they can't look after theirselves. But it's only for a week—I hope—the Clinic should be able to get by without me for that long."

Naomi got up and walked over to the screened door, gazing out into the darkness. She swatted at a mosquito that buzzed around her head. A bolt of lightning blazed across the night sky in the distance, followed by the low rumble of distant thunder.

"Probably gonna rain tonight," she said.

"Maybe," Karen replied absent-mindedly, as she crossed the kitchen to the sink. She needed to wash the supper dishes.

Naomi stood at the door for several more minutes before joining Karen at the sink. The dishes were a nightly ritual the women had shared for years. Karen washed; Naomi dried. Karen was already up to washing the pots when Naomi picked up her drying cloth.

"There might be another way to skin this cat," Naomi said. She dried a plate and placed it in the cupboard over the counter.

"What?" Karen said distractedly. She was thinking about the Clinic. Dr. Luke depended on her. She hated to let him down.

"I said there might be another way to skin this cat," Naomi said. Karen put the pot that she was scrubbing back in the soapy water and looked over at her mother.

"What in the world are you talkin' 'bout?"

"Your job. I know that's troublin' you."

"And how would you know that?" Karen picked up the pot and started to scrub it vigorously.

"A mama senses her youngens' troubles. Tell me you weren't studyin' on your job."

"I was. But the twins come first. Dr. Luke will understand."

"Maybe he won't have to," Naomi said.

"And what does that mean?"

"It means that I aim to figger somethin' out. Tomorrow is Friday. Dr. Luke ought to be able to get by without you for one day. I'll see what I can do for next week."

"Dr. Luke already knows that I can't work next week so forget 'bout it. It ain't like it's the end of the world."

She pulled the plug out of the sink, swished the suds down the drain and wrung out her dishcloth, draping it over the facet to dry. "I'm goin' on to bed now."

"Good night, baby girl," Naomi said, pecking her daughter on the cheek. "And don't fret none 'bout your job."

"It's been a long day. I'm too tired to fret 'bout anything."

Naomi saw Mrs. Brodie's straw hat bobbing up and down in the rose garden when she arrived for work the next morning.

"Good mornin'," Naomi called to her.

Mrs. Brodie stood up, mopped her brow and waved. "It's going to be a scorcher," she called back to Naomi.

"Early summer," Naomi said, walking up next to Mrs. Brodie. "I'll get my things and be right out."

Mrs. Brodie stooped back over the rose bushes while Naomi went inside to fetch her gardening gear: a pull-over smock to keep her dress clean, some rubber boots, a wide-brimmed hat and a pair of gloves.

When Mrs. Brodie had first suggested that Naomi wear gloves, she had balked at the idea. She and Washington never wore gloves when workin' the soil. She liked the feel of fresh-turned dirt in her hand.

A Watch in the Night

When Mrs. Brodie insisted, she relented. Later, when the rose thorns poked at the gloves and caught on her sleeves, she understood Mrs. Brodie's wisdom.

Naomi outfitted herself up and then fell in beside Mrs. Brodie, who was pruning the rosebushes; the fancy ones from that place far away.

"How are you this morning, Naomi?" Mrs. Brodie asked.

"Fine, just fine," Naomi answered, over the click-clack of her pruning shears.

Naomi and Mrs. Brodie worked silently for the next half hour. When the sweat started to roll into her eyes, Naomi tied a cloth that she kept in the pocket of her smock around her head. She looked up at the sky. It was clear and blue; not a cloud.

Naomi put down her shears and picked up the hose. There weren't gonna be no rain today. And she didn't fancy that sprinkler contraception that Mrs. Brodie turned on at night. It didn't work half the time. Needed fixin'.

Some of the more fragile plants were already starting to wilt. Naomi liked to water her plants. That was all part of growing things. Digging and weeding and watering. She and Washington had carried water to their garden more than once when the rain didn't come, lugging it from the pump in five-gallon buckets.

"Naomi! Naomi! For heaven's sake what is on your mind this morning."

Naomi looked up to see Mrs. Brodie standing next to her.

"Did you say somethin'?" Naomi asked.

"I most certainly did. But your mind is a million miles away this morning. I said that it's too hot to work out here any longer. At our age, we could have a heat stroke in this sun."

Naomi followed Mrs. Brodie up the path towards the kitchen. Mrs. Brodie carried a straw basket brimming over with fresh-cut flowers. Naomi carried the gardening tools.

Once inside, Mrs. Brodie went straight to the sink and put the flowers in a vase of water. Naomi stashed their tools in a closet by the door.

"I'm going to catch my breath before I arrange those flowers," Mrs. Brodie said. She sat down at the kitchen table and wiped the sweat from her face with the tail of her smock.

Naomi filled two glasses with ice and then tea. She brought the glasses to the table and sat next to Mrs. Brodie.

"Go on. Tell me what's bothering you," Mrs. Brodie said. Naomi gave her a furtive look.

"Naomi, we've been together long enough now for me to know when something is troubling you. You watered that same bed of new blossoms three times. You can't tell me that something is not on your mind."

Naomi smiled sheepishly. "Three times?"

"Three times," Mrs. Brodie said, holding up three of her fingers as she smiled over at Naomi.

"Well, I do suppose that I been studyin' on a spot of trouble that I got at home."

"Go on," Mrs. Brodie said, taking off her hat and fanning her face. "I'm listening."

"The truth is that I need a favor from you. And I don't rightly know how to ask."

Mrs. Brodie looked up at Naomi utterly astonished. In all of the years that Naomi had worked at the estate, she had only asked for two things: a week off from work when her son died and then another week when her husband passed on. And she would not even accept her pay for those weeks, although Mrs. Brodie had insisted that she do so.

"Naomi, is something wrong with your daughter?" Mrs. Brodie asked, afraid to hear the answer. Naomi would never ask for something for herself. This favor had to involve her daughter, which was the only family that Naomi had left as far as Mrs. Brodie knew.

"Sorta. I mean she ain't sick or nothin' but she needs some help."

"So what does she need? I'll do anything for you so long as it does not involve me leaving this estate. That I couldn't do for anyone, not even you, Naomi."

While Mrs. Brodie readily agreed to let Naomi bring the twins with her to work the following week, Karen and Bessie were not quite so keen on the idea. It took a little more convincing on Naomi's part to bring them around to her way of thinking.

"Absolutely not," Bessie said. She crossed her arms in front of her and pursed her lips tightly together when Naomi mentioned the subject.

Karen didn't act much better. "I got to go with Bessie on this one," she said, sidling up next to Bessie, who sat propped up on the Ivey's sofa. Together, they dug in their heels. Naomi knew then and there that she had a tough row to hoe to make her plan work.

The problem was, as always, Ephram. Nobody spoke his name. But his orders that the twins were not to leave Tate's Hell hung in the air like a bad odor that days of scrubbing had failed to dispel.

"Ya'll worried 'bout Ephram. You ain't gonna say it, but I know that's what's troublin' the both of you. Well, he don't have to ever know," Naomi said to the obstinate pair.

"I ain't takin' that chance," Bessie retorted, now that the culprit was out in the open.

"You won't be takin' no chance," Naomi said, standing up and squaring her shoulders. She didn't intend to go down without a fight.

"For heaven's sake. In all of the years that the twins been here in Tate's Hell, he ain't never once asked to see them other than on the first of the month. Not once."

"And why is that?" Karen asked. "I ain't never quite understood Ephram's interest in the twins. It don't make one iota of sense to me."

"Nothin' a stone-cold drunk like Ephram does makes sense," Bessie snapped back. She didn't have any intentions of drifting off into the subject of Ephram's interest in the twins. Naomi didn't want to go there either.

"Ya'll are actin' like two old mama hens. I'm tellin' you that takin' the twins to the island is a good idea. Bessie, you can't do no more than sit up. How you gonna chase after them two scalawags? Answer me that!"

Bessie didn't answer.

"And Karen, are you gonna up and leave Dr. Luke in the lurch?" Naomi asked. "Folks ain't gonna stop gettin' sick 'cause we got a problem here. Think about that!"

Naomi snorted her contempt at the two and then huffed off into the kitchen.

"And neither one of you has give the slightest thought to what the twins might like," Naomi said, sticking her head back around the kitchen door to make her closing argument.

"They been cooped up out here in Tate's Hell for five years. Don't you think that it's time they saw *somethin'* other than their own front yard?"

Naomi disappeared back into the kitchen. She would let them stew over that one.

Bessie looked up at Karen.

"She's got a point," Bessie said.

"I suppose," Karen eventually conceded, sighing. "And it is only for three days. What could go wrong in three days?"

"Plenty," Bessie said.

A Watch in the Night

Naomi couldn't sleep that night. She had convinced Karen and Bessie that the plan would work without being entirely convinced herself.

She worried about Ephram. And she worried about Mrs. Brodie adjusting to having two children on the place. It was a big house, but not so large that two small children wouldn't be noticed. For years now, it had been just the two of them, except for Rodrigo. But Rodrigo had become like family.

Rodrigo first came to the Brodie estate the year that the twins turned two. Naomi remembered it well. The weather forecast predicted that a hurricane would come ashore on Palm Island, and all residents of the island were ordered to evacuate. Mrs. Brodie refused to go.

"I won't leave and that is final," she said, stomping her heel when the Plantation security came knocking at her door. "Now scat and don't bother me anymore," she snapped at the guard, before retreating to the back of the house.

"She ain't gonna go," Naomi said to the deputy sheriff, who was sent to evacuate Mrs. Brodie when the Plantation security failed.

"I been with her for a long time now, and if she says she ain't goin', then she ain't goin'," Naomi told him.

It looked like a showdown was coming when the Plantation security came up with an idea. He was acquainted with another islander defying the order to evacuate. A bit of a loner, but a decent man. A fella who went by the name Rodrigo.

Rodrigo lived on a boat; he couldn't ride the storm out on that. But like Mrs. Brodie, he also refused to leave the island.

"Put 'em together in that house of hers," the security guard had said to the deputy sheriff. "If that damn place blows away, the whole Panhandle is a goner."

"I don't know," the deputy said. He was new to the job and unsure of his authority under these circumstances.

"Hell man," the security guard countered, "you can't drag 'em outta here kickin' and screamin'. If they wanta ride the storm out on this island, it's their asses, not yours."

The deputy sheriff wasn't at all sure that it wouldn't be his ass if he let two island residents perish in the storm. But the guard did have a point. He couldn't make them leave short of using force.

At first, Mrs. Brodie had resisted security's suggestion that she allow Rodrigo to stay with her. He was a perfect stranger, and she allowed nobody into her home except Naomi.

Finally, after much persuasion, and out of concern for Rodrigo and not herself, she relented. Eventually, the hurricane was downgraded to a tropical storm before it ever hit land, but not before Mrs. Brodie and Rodrigo had spent three days together and forged the beginning of a deep friendship.

After that episode, Rodrigo stopped in to visit Mrs. Brodie almost every day, except when the shrimp were running.

From what Naomi could gather, which wasn't much, he lived on a fishing boat and fishing was how he made his living. And like Mrs. Brodie, he seemed to be an "outsider" to the island and a bit of a loner.

Still, he was a kind and compassionate young man, and Naomi welcomed his company for Mrs. Brodie. For years now, it had been just the three of them. Naomi wondered if Mrs. Brodie was up to a visit from the twins.

CHAPTER SIXTEEN

Early Monday morning the twins pattered into Karen's room and shook her awake. She bolted straight up in bed. "What's wrong?" she asked.

"We gotta get dressed," Mango said.

Karen glanced over at the clock. It read 4:00 o'clock.

"Mango, honey, it's too early to get up; it's not time to get dressed." She pulled back the covers.

"Climb in here with me. I'll wake you up when it's time to go. Mama ain't gonna leave ya'll."

"You promise," Millie said, snuggling up next to Karen.

"I promise. Now go back to sleep."

Naomi was on her second cup of coffee when Bessie hobbled into the kitchen using a cane that Washington had carved years ago. Naomi found it in the shed.

"And what are you doin' outta bed?" Naomi asked, clucking her tongue. She got up and helped Bessie lower herself into a chair.

"You know what Dr. Luke said. Bedrest for one week. Three days don't make a week."

"I wanted to talk to you. I didn't sleep a wink last night worried 'bout the twins. What if Ephram finds out we took 'em out of Tate's Hell? There'll be hell to pay. I changed my mind. I ain't gonna let 'em go. I'm feelin' a right smart better today. I can keep 'em inside here with me."

"Nonsense. You ain't *that* much better. And I done told you and Karen a hundred times, Ephram ain't gonna ever know."

Naomi got up and poured Bessie a cup of coffee and placed it on the table before sitting back down.

"Besides that, are you gonna break them youngens' hearts? They set on goin'. And what 'bout Karen? She ain't goin' to work and leave you alone with them youngens."

Before Bessie could reply, Karen hustled the twins into the kitchen. She had them dressed in their best clothes.

"Granny, you 'pose to be in bed," Millie said, wagging her finger at Bessie.

"That's right, Granny, you 'pose to be in bed," Karen said, mimicking Millie.

"You can both save your breath," Bessie said. "Naomi has done give me the *talkin' to*."

Karen sat the twins at the table and scooped out two bowls of oatmeal from a pot on the stove. She placed a bowl in front of each of the twins.

"Don't you spill that oatmeal on your good clothes," she admonished the twins.

Millie picked at her oatmeal while Mango gobbled his down.

"We're still goin' with you in the car, ain't we Naomi?" Mango asked suspiciously, between bites. He sensed that somethin' might be different from last night when they had the talk 'bout him and Millie goin' with Naomi.

"Yes sirree, you goin'. And you can slow down on that oatmeal; I ain't gonna leave you."

"We still gonna see that water, ain't we, Naomi? Millie asked. She had her doubts, too. "A puddle so big that you can't see the other side?"

"No ma'am. Not if you don't eat your breakfast. I can't have you tuckerin' out on me 'fore we even get started."

"I ate mine," Mango said. He held up his empty bowl for inspection.

Millie worked her spoon like a piston moving it rapidly from her mouth to her bowl. She had no intention of being left behind.

"That's my girl," Naomi said, when Millie displayed her empty bowl. "Now, I'm gonna get me a sweater out of the back, and then we'll go. It's a mite chilly to me this mornin'."

When Naomi came out of the back of the house pulling on her sweater, she found the twins staked out at the front door, fidgeting.

Karen stood fussing over them; smoothing Mango's hair, wiping a speck of oatmeal off of Millie's chin. Bessie looked on pensively from the sofa, where she reclined propped up on pillows to support her back.

"Ya'll ready?" Naomi asked the twins.

"Yes ma'am," the twins answered together.

"Then let's go." Naomi picked up her purse and keys from the table by the door.

Karen bent down and gave each of the twins a kiss. "Now you two be good for Mama today," she said, swiping a tear from her eye. "She's ain't a spring chicken no more. Ya'll can't be runnin' her ragged."

"I do wish you would stop with that spring chicken nonsense," Naomi huffed. "You been sayin' that for years, and I'm still here doin' everthing I always did."

Karen ignored her mother's last remark. "And be good for Mrs. Brodie. We don't want her to think that we've raised up two little heathens."

"What's *heathens*?" Mango asked.

"Never mind 'bout that," Karen said. "Just mind your manners." She squeezed them tightly.

"We gotta go or we gonna be late. You know I don't like to be late for work. A day's work for a day's pay. Give a man his due. That's what your daddy always said. You youngens give Granny a kiss good-bye, so we can get on our way."

The twins skipped over to the sofa and wrapped their arms around Bessie's neck.

"Granny won't know what to do without ya'll to keep her company all day. I'll miss you," she said, kissing first Millie and then Mango.

"We'll miss you, too, Granny," Millie said. Tears welled up in her eyes. She had never spent one day without her Granny. Unlike Mango, who was chomping at the bit to go, Millie wasn't quite so sure now that it was time to fly out of the nest.

"Go on now," Bessie said, patting their bottoms. "Shoo! Granny'll be right here when you come home."

She blew them a kiss as they went out the door; the same as she had always done for Lily as the school bus pulled away.

Karen stood at the door waving good-bye until the car was out of sight. The house was still and quiet when she went back inside.

She got Bessie one of the pain pills Dr. Luke had left and then went to her room to dress for work. When she came out, Bessie was asleep.

Karen shivered from the chill in the room. Bessie was snoring lightly. As she leaned down to tuck a cover around her, Karen suddenly saw Bessie in a different light.

She noticed how deeply the lines were etched into her face; that her hair was now completely white; that she looked frail and tired—much older, more vulnerable—these days.

Karen sighed. Her mother was right. Bessie had seen more than her share of trouble.

Millie and Mango sat in the back seat of Naomi's car, propped up on their knees to see out of the window.

They had spent countless hours in the cab of a rusty old truck Washington stored behind the shed for spare parts—with Clover between them—pretending to drive.

A Watch in the Night

Naomi realized with astonishment and regret that this was their first time ever to actually ride in a car.

Perhaps, they had been wrong, Naomi thought, to guard them so furiously; to shut them off from the world. But the threat of Ephram had always hung over their heads like the executioner's ax.

Naomi stole a peek back at the twins as she steered the car down the lane, trying to avoid the deepest of the potholes. It had been a wet winter. And the county didn't waste any money grading the roads into Tate's Hell.

While Mango sat with his eyes glued out the side window, Millie gazed out the back window, her eyes turned towards home.

"Millie honey, Granny will get by without you today," Naomi said.

She took one hand off the steering wheel and stretched her arm over the seat to give Millie a reassuring pat.

"Sit over there next to your brother and look out the window." Millie scrunched up next to Mango.

The car inched down the lane. Naomi couldn't afford to get a flat tire. As they passed under the canopy of the oaks a disappointed Mango wailed, "I can't see no water, Naomi. There ain't nothin' here but trees the same as we got 'round our house."

Naomi realized that Mango must think that the bay was just beyond the edge of their yard.

"Hang on, little man. We still got us a ways to go 'fore we reach the water. Don't you remember that I told you last night that we'll go through the town first?"

"There'll be lots of houses and stores and a church with a steeple like in the books that Karen reads to us," Millie piped in. "Ain't that right, Naomi?"

"That's right, sweet pea," Naomi said. "So ya'll settle down and enjoy the ride."

Naomi turned onto Highway 27 and directed her attention to the road. Mango and Millie sat propped up on their knees, peering out the back window on the passenger side of the car, chattering like two magpies as the miles slipped by.

As the car approached the outskirts of town, Naomi momentarily contemplated taking the road that bypassed Trinity and ran straight out to the beach road to Palm Island.

A nagging fear hung in her thoughts. It would be dangerous for her to be seen traveling with the twins. While Karen might be in the dark when it came to Ephram's interest in the twins, Naomi had a pretty good idea of what was going on.

She also knew that an old, black women hauling two white kids through town in a beat-up old car might trigger someone's curiosity.

Tongues would wag, gossip would travel and their secret could leak out. Naomi had almost made up her mind to avoid Trinity altogether when Millie called up to her.

"Where's the houses, Naomi? Where's the stores? Where's the church with the steeple?"

Naomi wavered. While she didn't want to buy trouble, the road that bypassed the town was no different than the road they had been traveling thus far.

Her eyes darted from the main road to the bypass as she approached the turn-off. She slowed down, indecision flickering in her mind.

She glanced over her shoulder at the twins. She had promised them that they would see the town. And she had never, not even once, broken a promise to them. Stepping on the gas, she whizzed by the turn-off. The twins would have their thrill.

"Look at all them houses," Mango said. "Whew doggies, them are sure a lot of houses." He whistled under his breath, the same as Karen did when anything amazed her.

"Do people live in all them houses, Naomi?"

"They sure do," Naomi said.

"Boys and girls like us?"

"Boys and girls like you," Naomi said, feeling guilty that the twins had never known the joy of having friends their own age. Thank God that he saw fit to give them each other, she thought.

Naomi slowed the car below the speed limit as they approached Main Street. She didn't want any sort of a run-in with the law.

"Look at them stores," Millie squealed. "What you reckon they got in all them stores, Naomi?"

"Stuff. Lots of stuff," Naomi answered. Her nerves were on edge now that they were actually in town.

"What kind of stuff?" Millie asked.

"Oh, I don't know, darlin'. Groceries and store-bought clothes. Tools and toys. Stuff like that. But look sharp 'cause the church I told you 'bout is comin' up."

The twins turned away from the side window and leaned over the front seat to get a better look at what was up ahead. When the First Baptist Church came into sight, they bounced up and down on the seat with excitement.

"I wish you would *look* at *that!*" Mango exclaimed in the high-pitched voice that only came out when he was excited. He gave his whistle again.

"That there thing is almost as tall as the biggest pine tree in our back yard," he said. Mango pointed to the church steeple.

"Not quite," Naomi said, chuckling. "But it's tall alright."

"And that there is the biggest house ever," Millie sang out gleefully. "There ain't no houses big as that in the books that Karen reads. Who lives there, Naomi?"

"That's God's house. That's the white folks' church," Naomi answered.

Naomi hoped they understood. She and Karen had tried to teach the children about God. They couldn't take them to church, a fact that both she and Karen sorely bemoaned.

Karen tried to close the gap in their religious training by reading to them almost nightly from her childhood Sunday school book. They knew the stories by heart. And she taught them their prayers. Then, of course, there was the Reverend Spears' Inspirational Hour, still a family favorite.

And Naomi did her part. Each Sunday evening, the twins nestled into Naomi's big, soft bed with her, where she read to them from *A Children's Bible* that had "This Book Belongs to Nathan Ivey" inscribed in bold block letters on its first page by Nathan's own meticulous hand.

It had been a gift to him from his father. Nathan's *Bible* was one of her most cherished treasures. The day that Nathan had left for his military service, she had wrapped his *Bible* in tissue paper and stored it in her bottom drawer, intending to give it to his children one day.

She had buried that dream along with her son. The reading from Nathan's *Bible* had become a sacred ritual between Naomi and the twins.

The next stretch of road was the same as the ride into town, and so the children hunkered down in the back seat and chatted.

Now that she could see the outskirts of Trinity fading in her rear-view mirror and the children had let up on the questions, Naomi relaxed and enjoyed the ride, relieved that nothing bad had happened and happy that she had taken the chance to show them the town.

"Heads up," she said, after they had traveled several more miles. "Here comes the water. Look out that other window, and ya'll gonna see the bay."

The twins scooted across the back seat and pressed their noses against the window.

"I see it," Mango yelled, when the first gray sliver of the bay appeared on the edge of the road.

"You don't gotta yell," Naomi said. "I'm old, but I ain't deaf. Not yet anyways. I may not be a spring chicken, but I ain't a wore-out, old bird neither. I ain't but inches from ya'll, not across the yard, so there ain't no need for ya'll to holler."

"I see it! I see it, too," Millie squealed into Naomi's ear.

"Lord, do have mercy! Didn't I just tell you youngens to pipe down. I can hear you."

"Where does the water stop? Mango asked. "Does it ever stop or does it go on forever?"

"Well, pumpkin, it stops sommers. But I ain't rightly sure where."

Naomi had no clear concept of the size of the bay. And even if she did, she had no words to explain it to the children.

"That would be a good question for Karen," she said. "She studied 'bout things like that at school. Me, I never learnt to do more than read and write and figger numbers. But Karen, she'd be a good one to put that question to."

"But is that *sommers* far away like the clearin' or far away like that town?" Mango asked.

"It's far, far away. That's all I know to tell you," Naomi said. "It's farther away than I've ever been."

Naomi took another quick peek in the rear-view mirror and smiled to see the twins so delighted with the bay.

"Maybe one day, when you and your sister are all growed up, ya'll will travel away from Trinity and find that place where the water ends. My Nathan did just that. He traveled far over the water, and he saw things that me and his daddy couldn't even imagine."

"What's them things on the top of the water yonder?" Mango asked.

"Boats," Naomi said, sighing. There was no peace when Mango's curiosity was aroused.

"Them little ones are what the oystermen use to gather up oysters. Now ya'll don't like fried oysters but lots of other folks do. Folks pay good money for them oysters."

"And them big ones?" Mango asked. "They look like Noah's Ark from that *Bible* book. Do they got all kind of animals in them?"

"I do declare you two youngens are more worrisome than gnats on a summer's day with all of your questions," Naomi said.

Still, she answered his question.

"No, them boats ain't got animals on 'em like Noah's Ark. They got men on 'em who throw out big nets to gather up shrimp. Shrimp, like the ones I fry up in the pan and you gobble down, Mango, fast as I can cook 'em."

"Naomi, do . . .? Mango tried to launch another question, but Naomi cut him short.

"No more questions for the time being. Save them for Karen, and let me put my mind back on this here road else we liable to wind up over there in the ditch."

The twins huddled together and started chatting with one another again. They knew that Naomi didn't mean any harm by what she said. Karen had told 'em that old people get bothered when you ask 'em too many questions. Granny did it, too.

The twins were content talking to one another and watching the bay pass by until they felt the car slow down for the turn onto the bridge.

Naomi was not surprised to see their heads pop up and over the front seat like two jack-in-the-boxes, when she applied the brakes. They craned their necks into the front seat and started to chirp like two baby birds.

"What is . . .?" Mango tried another question.

"That there's a bridge," Naomi said, anticipating his next line of inquiry. "A bridge is a road that runs across the water."

As the car started its ascent onto the bridge, Naomi rolled down her window, letting the salt air cascade into the car.

"Ya'll sit back and roll down your windows with that crank on the side of the door," she yelled, over the roar of the wind.

"We're flyin' like birds," Mango yelled up to Naomi, his voice brimming with excitement.

"Ya'll two birds alright; but you ain't flyin'," Naomi called back to them.

"This here bridge that we're ridin' on is planted down in the ground under the water by big old cement pilings. Them pilings is as thick and as strong as the trunks of the giant oaks in our front yard. You might feel like you're flyin'; but you still fastened down to the earth."

Naomi sucked the salt air deeply into her lungs. The morning sun—a huge, undulating orange orb—hung slightly above the horizon, transforming the sky into a brilliant palate splashed with a myriad of hues of red, orange and pink. The water glittered below like a million bits of colored glass.

Birds—snowy plovers, skimmers and laughing gulls—glided gracefully along the side the car. Still others sat perched on the guardrails or skittered across the small mounds of grass on the sides of the bridge—a cacophony of chirping and squawking rose up and drifted along on the wind.

"Stick out your tongues," Naomi called back to the twins. "The air taste like salt."

Naomi ventured another quick peek into the back seat.

She saw two small heads, with their eyes closed and their necks stretched up and out to capture the warmth of the first rays of the morning sun. Swirling masses of hair whipped above their heads and flicked at their faces, as they poked out their tongues, licking the salt from the air.

Naomi slowed down the car as she approached the end of the bridge to make the turn onto the Plantation road.

"I like that bridge," Mango said, disappointed that the wind no longer tickled his face and tossed his hair.

"Me, too," Millie said. There was no longer any need to shout. The wind now blew lightly in through the windows and the squawk of the birds was somewhere off in the distance.

"That's good 'cause we gotta cross back over it to get home tonight."

Naomi turned onto the road leading into the Plantation. As she approached the guard gate, she instructed Millie and Mango to duck down into the back seat.

She didn't want the guard see the two white children in her back seat. The guard might be from Trinity; he might in idle conversation mention the children. No need to tempt fate a second time in one day.

"Why?" Mango implored, not wanting to miss anything.

"Do what I say," Naomi said firmly. She adjusted her rear-view mirror to the back seat and watched as Millie and Mango slumped down in their seats.

"Go lower," Naomi instructed them. "Scoot on down to the floorboard. She slowed the car, but she didn't stop to exchange pleasantries with the guard as she did on some mornings. The guard threw up his hand and waved her through.

"Heads up," Naomi said lightly to the twins, trying to make the hiding part of a game. She stopped the car in the Brodie driveway and turned off the engine.

"Look at all of them flowers," Millie squealed. She loved flowers.

"Is that a *house?*" Mango asked. He stared wide-eyed, his mouth gaping open at the Brodie mansion. "*It's bigger than God's house!*"

The way that Naomi and Karen carried on about God Mango figured him to be a pretty important person—like a king. Weren't that *Bible* story book always talking about "the kingdom of God." So the size of the First Baptist Church, even with its tall steeple, made sense to him.

But this—this house which sat in front of him—it was something altogether different.

Naomi twisted around in her seat to face the children. In a serious voice she said to them, "This here is Mrs. Brodie's house."

The twins perked up. They had overhead a lot of conversations about this Mrs. Brodie.

"It's my job to clean and cook and help Mrs. Brodie every day. She's a very nice lady, but she's not use to havin' youngens in her home. So I want you two to be on your best behavior and do what I say. Without asking me why."

She directed her last comment to Mango. "Can you do that?" she asked the twins.

"Yes ma'am," they said back to Naomi, in voices which emulated her own serious tone.

Mrs. Brodie was in the garden when she recognized the puttering sound of Naomi's small car. She stood up and watched as Naomi and the children exited the car.

"I'm over here," she called, giving them a wave.

At the sound of her voice, the children slid behind Naomi's skirts.

Naomi tried to walk towards the garden, but the twins remained rooted to the ground refusing, like two stubborn mules, to budge.

Mrs. Brodie was the first stranger that they had ever met other than Dr. Luke. And that meeting had occurred on their home turf with Naomi, Karen and Bessie standing by. This was different.

Mrs. Brodie understood how intimidating her house must look to two small children so she went to greet them. After giving Naomi a warm smile and a cheery "good morning," she turned her attention to the children.

"Good morning," she said to the twins. "I'm Mrs. Brodie." The twins cowered behind Naomi and didn't reply.

"Shame on you," Naomi said to the twins. "Ya'll talked my head off all the way here, and now the cat's got both your tongues. Mrs. Brodie spoke to you. The polite thing to do is speak back."

"It's quite alright," Mrs. Brodie said, winking at Naomi. "I understand that a boy and girl who are new to the island might be a tad shy. I'll go back to the garden and not bother you. The children can go inside with you."

She turned to walk away and then paused.

"But I was so hoping that someone could help me find my cat, Lucy. She seems to be lost. And that's odd because she is so big and fluffy. I don't often lose track of her. Oh, I suppose she could be down by the bay chasing fiddler crabs."

The twins peeked around from behind Naomi's ample hips, a smattering of curiosity pushing back their fear.

Mrs. Brodie smiled at the two pair of sparkling eyes—one pair as blue-green as the ocean, the other pair as dark as a moonless night.

Naomi stood perplexed. Short of forcefully dragging the children out from behind her, there wasn't much that she could do. She had not anticipated this problem.

"We ain't got no cat but we got us a dog named Clover," Mango said. He took a baby step forward. "One time he got lost in the swamp for one whole day. But he come home at supper time. And what is them things you call fiddler crabs?"

"A dog you say; named Clover," Mrs. Brodie replied, feigning great curiosity. "Now that's an interesting name."

"Yes Ma'am, his name is Clover," Mango said.

"And do you have a name?" she asked Mango. "Or should I just call you a-boy-with-a-dog-named-Clover?"

Mango giggled and ventured out a little more.

"No ma'am. My name ain't a-boy-with-a-dog-named-Clover. It's Mango. And my sister's name is Millie."

"We're twins," he said, puffing out his chest proudly "And we's born on a night when it snowed right in Tate's Hell. Naomi says that makes us special."

"Oh, my," Mrs. Brodie said, arching her eyebrows up and cocking her head to one side as if she was giving serious consideration to Mango's words.

"A boy and a girl born on a night when it snowed in Florida. I daresay that Naomi is right; that would make you pretty special."

"I am pleased to meet you, Mango," Mrs. Brodie said. She smiled at the small boy with olive skin tanned brown by the sun.

"And I'm pleased to meet you, too, Millie," she said. She smiled at the fair-skinned, tow-headed little girl, whose head now poked out from behind Naomi's skirt.

Millie's head snapped back behind Naomi like a frightened turtle who returns to its shell when Mrs. Brodie called her name.

Mrs. Brodie remained undaunted. "Snow you say. Right here in Florida. When I was a girl no bigger than you two, I lived in a city where it snowed almost every day in the wintertime."

"Really?" Mango asked.

"Yes, really," Mrs. Brodie answered. "But the Florida Panhandle is quite different. I don't believe that I have seen snow here but one time and that was five years back or so."

Mrs. Brodie scrunched up her face as if she was concentrating intently. "I wonder if that was the same night that you two were born," she said. "How old are you?"

Millie's head popped back out, and Mango took another tentative step closer to Mrs. Brodie.

"Five going on six," Mango said, trying to stand taller.

"I do declare. It must have been the same night. As I recall it was almost Christmas."

"That's right," Mango said, skipping up closer. "We's born just two days before Christmas. Sometimes Karen teases us and says that Santa Claus put us under her Christmas tree."

"I need a rest from the garden," Mrs. Brodie said, turning her attention to Naomi.

"Let's go sit in the shade. I'd like to hear some more about this night that it snowed in Florida."

Naomi took the children by their hands, and together they trailed behind Mrs. Brodie as she made her way back to the patio off of the garden.

After they sat quietly for a few minutes on the garden patio, Mrs. Brodie gave Naomi another wink and said, "It's so hot out. Perhaps, you could get us something cool to drink. I'm sure Millie and Mango wouldn't mind keeping me company while you're gone. I'm wondering if Lucy might show up and stretch out here in this morning sun for a nap. She really is a naughty cat to hide and not come when I call her."

"If Clover don't come when I call him, I whistle like this," Mango said. Mango stuck two fingers in his mouth and let out a long, shrill whistle.

"Oh, my word! That might work," Mrs. Brodie said, laughing.

Naomi took this opportunity to slip away. She took her time in the kitchen.

When she returned to the patio, carrying a tray of drinks in her hands, she was not the least bit surprised to discover both twins chattering away with Mrs. Brodie.

Mrs. Brodie, the lady who lived in a house as big as a castle, who as a girl had spent days in the snow and who now had a fat cat named Lucy and fiddler crabs by her bay had managed to hook the children. But it was her soft Boston accent that had reeled them in.

Naomi sat the tray on the table.

"The children have agreed to be my helpers in the garden," Mrs. Brodie announced to Naomi.

"You don't say," Naomi said, feigning surprise.

"I do say," Mrs. Brodie replied.

"They're both good helpers," Naomi said. "I can vouch for that. I don't reckon ya'll will be needin' me. I got plenty enough to do inside to keep me busy."

"I *reckon* that will be fine," Mrs. Brodie said. "First, we're going to have ourselves a tea party, and then we're going to work."

Mrs. Brodie let the children water the flowers, while she pruned and pulled weeds.

Next, they followed behind her while she snipped fresh flowers and dropped them into a straw basket, which she had given them to carry. The sun was a quarter of the way across the sky when Mrs. Brodie announced that it was time to go inside.

It was Mango who spied the swimming pool on the way into the kitchen. The pool sat to the left of the patio behind a hedge.

"What's that?" he asked, pointing over to the pool.

"That's a swimming pool," Mrs. Brodie said.

Millie and Mango exchanged a puzzled look.

"Haven't you children ever seen a swimming pool?"

"No, ma'am. There ain't nothin' like that in Tate's Hell," Mango said.

"Well surely, you've been swimming; perhaps, in the ocean?"

"No ma'am, *surely* we ain't," Mango replied. "There ain't no ocean in Tate's Hell neither. There ain't no water bigger than a mud puddle at our house 'cept the swamp on the way to the clearing. But that's got snakes and gators."

The twins skirted around the hedge to get a closer look at the pool.

"So you children have never been swimming?" Mrs. Brodie asked, joining them at the side of the pool.

Mango looked at Millie, who shrugged her shoulders. They weren't sure how to answer.

"Sometimes, Karen lets us play in the washtubs that she fills up with water. We splash 'round a lot. But we call that bathin', not *swimmin'*."

"Well, I suppose the pool is nothing more than a big washtub. But the water is deeper in the pool. It's deeper than you are tall, so you must take care not to fall into the pool."

"Yes ma'am," the twins said together, as they stood admiring their reflections in the pool.

"Come along now, and I'll show you the inside of my home. We need to put these flowers into some water, or they'll wilt."

Mrs. Brodie led the children into the kitchen where Naomi stood over the stove stirring a large pot.

She put the spoon in a cradle on the back of the burner when she heard Mrs. Brodie, flanked by the twins, coming through the door. The twins were still pelting her with questions about the pool.

"You two little birds never stop your chirpin'," Naomi said. She turned to face the twins and Mrs. Brodie.

"I do hope they ain't been too much of a bother."

Naomi took the flowers from Mrs. Brodie and placed them in a pail of water by the sink.

"Quite to the contrary. They've been an absolute joy."

Naomi smiled over at the twins, delighted that they had made such a positive impression on Mrs. Brodie.

Up until this moment, she had continued to worry about the possibility that two restless children might be too much for Mrs. Brodie's nerves. But Mrs. Brodie appeared quite calm and happy; not the least bit frayed.

"Is this all your house?" Mango asked Mrs. Brodie. His eyes slowly traveled around the room, taking in every detail.

"This looks as big as God's house," Millie said.

Mrs. Brodie gave Naomi a bewildered look.

"They seen the Baptist Church in town this mornin' for the first time," Naomi said, by way of explanation.

"Oh," Mrs. Brodie replied.

"Is this all your house?" Mango asked again.

"Mango, don't trouble Mrs. Brodie with so many questions," Naomi said, smoothing his hair.

Karen had tried to slick his hair down with hair oil and give it a part, but the wind on the bridge had freed the unruly curls.

"Nonsense," Mrs. Brodie said. "A child is supposed to be curious. It is the nature of being a child to be inquisitive."

"If that means a youngen is suppose to ask questions daylight 'til dark, then this one fits the bill," Naomi said, having another go at Mango's hair.

"Yes, this is all part of my house," Mrs. Brodie said to Mango wistfully. "I once had a husband but now he is gone."

"Where did he go?" Mango asked.

"Mango, no more questions," Naomi said.

"Never mind about my husband," Mrs. Brodie said.

"You and your sister haven't seen the best part of the house yet. I have a music room with a piano. And don't ask me, Mango. What's a piano? You'll simply have to follow me and see for yourself."

Mrs. Brodie turned and marched out of the room. The twins looked up at Naomi unsure of what to do.

"Go on, scat," she said. The twins took off after Mrs. Brodie, who was rapidly disappearing down a long, cavernous hallway.

The piano sat in the center of a room that Mrs. Brodie had named the "music room." The twins knew about bedrooms, living rooms, bathroom and kitchens. This *music room* was a new one on them. But it was a fine room, they quickly agreed.

The front of the piano faced a large glass window, which opened out on a panoramic view of the bay.

Through the window, the outdoors appeared as tranquil as an oil painting, the wooden sills of the window forming its frame. Palm fronds crisscrossed against a blue sky dotted with little fluffs of white clouds. The green lawn sloped down to the white sand of the bay and then bled into the shimmering blue-green water.

The piano was a baby grand, the same piano that Mr. Brodie had shipped to the island many years ago. Naomi polished it daily until she could see her reflection in the sheen of the wood.

Sunlight filtered in through the window and splashed across the top of the piano, where it sparkled and danced in the luminous gloss of the wood, giving the piano an almost animate quality.

Mrs. Brodie led the children to the piano stool and sat down. She offered a seat on either side of her to the twins by patting the stool with her hands. The twins slid in beside her, and she began to play.

The acoustics in the room were flawless. Mr. Brodie had made certain of that.

As Mrs. Brodie's fingers pranced across the keys, the music swirled up and out of the piano, reverberated throughout the room and then returned to her ears so perfectly that Mrs. Brodie often felt as if she could breathe in the notes and then exhale them back out into the room.

Millie and Mango sat enthralled by the swift, precise movement of Mrs. Brodie's fingers and the magical quality of the sound that she extracted from the piano with them.

This was not at all like the music they heard coming from the radio. This music was alive, something that you could almost see and touch.

As Mrs. Brodie played the twins sat at rapt attention, not moving a muscle, hardly daring to breath, fearing that any noise or movement would shatter the moment into tinkling bits of glass all around them.

Mrs. Brodie finished her piece, and still the twins sat captive, enmeshed in the web that the music had spun around them.

"Now, I'm an old lady," Mrs. Brodie said, "and I can't play as well as I did years ago. I was quite the pianist in my day, but my fingers can't hold out to play like I once played."

She sighed and flexed her fingers. Then her face lit up.

"But I can teach your young, nimble fingers to strut across these keys," Mrs., Brodie said. A big smile swept over her face.

"You go first, Millie."

Mrs. Brodie placed Millie's fingers on the keys. The keys felt cool and smooth to Millie. She plucked at them timidly, her eyes lighting up with a child's wonderment when the piano responded to her touch.

"Now you try," Mrs. Brodie said to Mango. As cautiously as had Millie, he placed his fingers upon the keys and pressed.

And in that moment, Mrs. Brodie was quite certain she had witnessed a love take root—a love that would flourish and grow into what would one day be a mighty tree.

She felt an inexplicable, overwhelming passion emanating outward from the twins. She knew this passion. This passion was her friend. It was the same passion that had engulfed her own soul the first time she felt the keys dance under her fingers.

Naomi found Mrs. Brodie and the twins still sitting at the piano when she came looking for them to announce that lunch was ready. She waited patiently for a break in the lesson, and then she clapped her hands with delight.

"If that don't beat all," she said, "you two youngens playin' the piano. Don't a day go by that you two don't surprise me."

"My goodness," Mrs. Brodie said to Naomi "is it time for lunch already?"

"We always eat at noon; and it is twelve o'clock sharp," Naomi said.

"So it is," Mrs. Brodie replied, glancing down at the dainty watch wrapped around her wrist. "We have been at the piano for over two hours. My goodness."

Mrs. Brodie rose from the piano stool and stretched her back. "I think we might very well have two musical prodigies here," she said, looking down at the twins.

Naomi had no idea what a *musical prodigy* might be, but judging from the look on Mrs. Brodie's face, it must be something good. She smiled over at the twins who sat grinning up at Mrs. Brodie.

"Shake a leg, all of you," Naomi said, laughing. "Lunch is getting cold. I like to serve a hot meal. Always have."

As Naomi and the twins followed Mrs. Brodie into the kitchen, Mango circled Naomi's waist with his arm and squeezed her tightly.

"This is the best day ever," he whispered up to her.

"There'll be more happy days for both of you," she said. "I promise."

The twins wrapped their fingers around Naomi's calloused palms.

"And one thing 'bout old Naomi—she don't go makin' no promises that she can't keep. You're special. I said it the night that you two was born, and I'm sayin' it again now. You're special. There'll be a lot of life for you to live."

She gently squeezed their small fingers.

"God has a lot of life in store for the two of you."

CHAPTER SEVENTEEN

Naomi was a firm believer in the power of an afternoon nap. She even indulged herself on occasion, although she referred to it as "putting up her feet."

The children laughed when she said this. She often instructed them to "put up" their toys or Karen to "put up" the supper dishes. So to them, Naomi's "putting up her feet" implied that she put her feet away in a box or a cupboard.

"I put 'em right here on this pillow," she would say to them, when they snickered at this remark.

"Thataways I know where to find 'em when I wake up. And if you two would do the same with your toys, we wouldn't spend nearly as much time as we do searchin' for things that just up and get lost all on their own."

So when she said "time to put up our feet," after placing the last of the lunch dishes in the sink, the children knew what was coming.

"Naomi, pleassse, not today," Mango implored her. He wanted to go back outside, not waste time on a nap.

"Don't you 'Naomi pleassse' me, mister," she said, tweaking his nose. "Today ain't no different, just 'cause we at Mrs. Brodie's house."

The children received this edict with long faces.

"I'll *put up my feet* with you," Mrs. Brodie said to soften the blow a bit. "I can do with a bit of a rest."

Mrs. Brodie led the children back out to the patio where they stretched out on several chaise lounges. When Naomi peeked in a little later, all three were napping.

When Mango woke up, Mrs. Brodie sat reading a book in her lounge. She placed a finger over her lips, cocked her head over at Millie and beckoned to him with her other hand to follow.

They found Naomi in the kitchen baking.

"Mrs. Brodie, I reckon that I'd like to have a look at them things you called *fiddlin' crabs,*" Mango said, as he shoved the last of his cookie into his mouth.

"Mango, Mrs. Brodie has entertained you two all morning. She might like some time to herself," Naomi said. She slid another batch of cookies off of the baking sheet onto a platter.

"You can help me with these cookies until your sister wakes up."

"Nonsense," Mrs. Brodie said, winking at Mango. "It's been far too long since I checked on my *fiddling crabs.* For all I know, they could have just up and fiddled on over to the house next door."

"I suppose we should investigate," she said, taking Mango by the hand.

"I'll wait here for Millie to wake up. And then we'll walk down to join you," Naomi said.

"Scoot," she said, patting Mango on the behind. "But you mind Mrs. Brodie by the water."

Millie slept another half hour. Naomi didn't hear her come in the room. She was rinsing the last of the cookie dough from her hands at the sink when Millie came up behind her and tugged at her apron.

"If it ain't my sleepin' beauty come back to life," Naomi said, cradling Millie up next to her leg.

She turned and looked down at Millie.

"What's the matter, pumpkin?" Naomi asked, staring into the eyes of a sad face. "Have you been crying, or is that just sleep in your eyes?"

"I miss Granny," Millie said, with a little sniffle. "Do you think that Granny's alright without us?"

"Honey, I'm sure of it, Naomi said.

"But why don't you climb up here in my lap, and let me hold you for a few minutes. You're still my baby, and I like to hold you."

Millie crawled up into Naomi's lap and sat snuggled up in her arms. She closed her eyes and yawned.

Naomi looked down into the tiny face and saw Lily. Lily who worried about Bessie: Lily who had the same eyes, the same blonde hair, the same full lips as this child. She pulled Millie in closer and rocked her.

"I baked them chocolate cookies that you and that brother of yours like so much," Naomi said. Millie wiggled to get down.

"If you'll help me, we'll make a picnic basket and take some down to Mango and Mrs. Brodie. They're down at the bay looking for fiddler crabs."

As Naomi and Millie approached the bay they could see Mango and Mrs. Brodie cavorting in the water.

Naomi spread a blanket under the shade of a live oak while Millie ran down to the bay, calling to Mrs. Brodie and Mango to come and join them.

Mango had stripped down to his shorts and was splashing and prancing about in the shallow water. Mrs. Brodie, who held the bottom of her dress bunched up in one hand, stood in water up to her knees. When they heard Millie's shout, they waded out towards her.

Mango was the first to reach the blanket.

He was dripping wet. His shorts clung to his shivering body. He tried to slick back his hair by pushing through it with his fingers, but the sopping wet ringlets spiraled around his face.

"I declare if you don't look like Clover after he's had a dip in the swamp," Naomi said.

"And you need a haircut," Naomi added. "I done told Karen 'bout lettin' your hair get too long. Stand over there and let the sun dry you out."

Mrs. Brodie trudged up to the blanket. Her shoes dangled from one hand, and she held Millie with the other hand.

"And if you ain't a sight for sore eyes," Naomi said, laughing up at Mrs. Brodie. "Out here actin' like a schoolgirl, prancin' 'bout in the water, your skirt hiked up over your knees. I do declare that I don't know what this day will bring next."

"It will bring you a visitor," a deep voice said. A tall, dark-skinned man stepped out from the shadow of the trees. Startled, Naomi spun around.

"For heaven's sake. You 'bout scared an old lady to death. You surely knocked a good year off what little bit of time I got left on this earth with that jolt."

"I'm sorry, Naomi," the man said. "I thought that you saw me coming, but of course, you didn't. You were distracted by the two wood nymphs who seem to have taken a shine to the Brodie estate."

"Rodrigo, I'm so glad to see you," Mrs. Brodie said. "And I have quite the surprise for you. These are not wood nymphs at all, but rather, they're my guests." Mrs. Brodie pulled the twins up next to her as she spoke.

"Guests? I thought that I was your only guest. Now this is quite a surprise."

The twins dropped back behind Mrs. Brodie. They found two strangers in one day extremely overwhelming.

From the safety of Mrs. Brodie's skirts, the twins peeked out and saw that the man now stood only a couple of feet in front of them.

Millie wanted to make a break for Naomi. She was larger than Mrs. Brodie, and her skirts had more room for concealing a small girl. But Naomi was too far away, so Millie took a step back until she was directly behind Mrs. Brodie.

"Allow me to introduce you to my guests," Mrs. Brodie said to Rodrigo.

"This young fellow," she said, placing her arm around Mango's shoulders and drawing him forward, "is Master Mango."

Mrs. Brodie attempted to draw Millie out in the same manner, but she remained firmly planted behind Mrs. Brodie.

"And the young lady standing behind me is his sister, Miss Millie."

"What an unexpected pleasure. I'm so very pleased to meet you, Master Mango," Rodrigo said. He extended his hand for Mango to shake, while giving him a broad smile that flashed sparkling white teeth against a dark tan. Rodrigo's black eyes danced in the sunlight.

Mango looked over at Naomi. He wasn't sure what he was supposed to do in response to the man's outstretched hand. Naomi recognized his dilemma and came to his aid.

"I'm 'fraid that I ain't brung up these youngens' proper like. I ain't never had the right time 'til now to teach 'im 'bout shakin' hands."

As Naomi said this, she walked over to Mango. Bending down, she whispered into his ear. "The proper thing to do here, honey, is to give this man's hand a little squeeze with your hand. That shows 'im respect. Now go on. Don't be scared. Rodrigo's a good man. Step up and shake his hand."

Mango stepped forward and reached up to clasp Rodrigo's outstretched hand. He gave it a quick squeeze before pulling his hand back.

"I'm pleased to meet you too, sir," Naomi whispered in Mango's ear.

"I'm pleased to meet you too, sir." Mango parroted Naomi's words as he looked up into Rodrigo's face, which seemed a long distance away. He was a very large man—big like Dr. Luke.

When Rodrigo smiled down at him, Mango smiled back.

Millie was not so eager to meet another stranger. When Naomi came over to whisper into Mango's ear, Millie seized the opportunity to slide behind Naomi's broad girth.

Millie had already decided that Mrs. Brodie was much too thin to hide behind.

Even when she saw Mango shake the stranger's hand, which she viewed as a very brave move on her brother's part, she was not convinced that she wanted to do the same.

She wrapped Naomi's skirt around her face as the man stepped over to greet her. Naomi urged her forward, but Millie held her ground.

Rodrigo kneeled in the sand until he was eye level with Millie. Millie lowered Naomi's skirt until only her eyes were visible.

The man held out his hand to her. "It's a pleasure, indeed, to meet such a lovely young lady as you are, Miss Millie."

Millie sized him up. He had the darkest eyes that she had ever seen, darker than Mango's, darker than Dr. Luke's. His face was kind like Reverend Samuel and Dr. Luke's, not mean-looking like her grandpa's face.

She leaned forward, still safely ensconced behind the shield of Naomi's skirt, and placed her fingers into Rodrigo's huge hand. He gave her hand a soft squeeze and ever so slightly pulled her forward.

"Any friend of Naomi and Mrs. Brodie I would certainly like to call a friend of mine," this dark man said to her.

"How about it, Miss Millie? Is there a chance that we could be friends?"

Millie looked first at Naomi, who nodded her head, and then over to Mrs. Brodie, who gave her a wink.

A Watch in the Night

Mrs. Brodie stooped down and whispered into Millie's ear. When Mrs. Brodie stood up, Millie said, "It is a pleasure to make your acquaintance, Mr. Rodrigo."

"Wonderful. But one small thing my little wildflower," Rodrigo said to her. "There's no *Mr.* here. You can call me Rodrigo."

"And that goes for you too, sport model," he said to Mango. "If you'll call me Rodrigo, I'll drop the Master and Miss and call you Mango and Millie. Do we have us a deal?"

"It's a deal, Lucille," Mango said. He and Millie started to giggle. Karen had taught him to say this.

"Now, if I don't miss my guess, I would say that you're twins," Rodrigo said. "Am I right about that?"

"We're twins alright," Mango sang out. "And we's born on a night that it snowed in Florida. That makes us special 'cordin' to what Naomi says."

"Well, I'll be," Rodrigo said, scratching his head in consternation.

"Twins. And girl and boy twins at that. Born on a snowy night in Florida. I'd say that makes you both pretty special. It's not every day that you run into those qualifications."

Both Mango and Millie giggled with delight.

"And I would like very much to get to know you better," Rodrigo said.

"But for now, I want you to sit on that blanket and eat those cookies from Naomi's basket. When you finish, we'll see if either of you can catch one of those crabs scurrying about in the water."

The twins listened intently, never taking their eyes off of Rodrigo.

"And while you eat your cookies," Rodrigo said, smiling down at them, "I'll sit over there in the shade with Mrs. Brodie and have a chat. Mrs. Brodie is my best friend, and we have some catching up to do. Go on. Or all the ice will melt in that lemon-aide Naomi made for you."

The twins scurried over and plopped down on the blanket. They wanted to discuss this strange man and the day's adventures.

Rodrigo escorted Mrs. Brodie to one of several lawn chairs, which were set up in the shade. This had been one of her favorite spots when Horace was alive. They had spent almost every evening in these chairs watching the sun go down.

But now, Mrs. Brodie rarely sat in the chairs at all, and she was surprised to see that they were not covered in dirt. She didn't know that Naomi wiped them regularly, hoping that one day Mrs. Brodie would return to the comfort of this spot.

"Where in the name of Sam Hill did you find those two little twins?"

"I didn't exactly find them. They found me. Much like you found me."

"Bad weather is coming?"

"No. Other exigent circumstances. Naomi's daughter takes care of them three days a week at Naomi's home. Their grandmother, who is Naomi's neighbor, cares for them otherwise. The grandmother suffered a back injury, leaving nobody to look after them on the days that Naomi's daughter is working. Today is one of those days."

"I see," Rodrigo said, "well maybe."

"Naomi asked if they could come over. She has never asked me for a favor. How could I say no? So here they are. They really are quite delightful. Don't you think so?"

"They do have a certain charm," Rodrigo said.

"And when you take into consideration their ages and circumstances, they really are quite extraordinary."

"My guess is they're about six-years-old."

"Five *going on six*," Mrs. Brodie replied.

"That was one of the first things Mango told me this morning. He is the more talkative of the two. The little girl is much shyer and more reticent than he."

"And what *circumstances* are you referring to?" Rodrigo asked.

"Only what I told you; that they live in Tate's Hell with their grandmother. I got bits and pieces about their life from talking with them. Naomi has not told me much about them."

"A bit odd, don't you think?" Rodrigo said.

"Well, yes. Naomi is usually so forthcoming in our conversations. But she seems to be very guarded on the subject of these children. In fact, she has never mentioned them until she asked if she might bring them to work."

"Odd, indeed!" Rodrigo mused.

"I assumed they were neighbor children, and she was doing a good deed. Naomi is prone to good deeds, as you well know."

"She is," Rodrigo replied.

"Still, I am convinced there are missing parts to this story."

"Go on," Rodrigo said.

"Naomi and the children are quite close to one another. If I didn't know better, I would think that she was the grandmother."

"I, too, detected a strong bond," Rodrigo added.

"Obviously, that's not the case. Don't take this the wrong way, but I was taken a little aback when she arrived with two white children this morning. I assumed they would be black, living next door to Naomi. From what I've heard of Trinity, blacks and whites do not often mingle in our little rustic fishing village."

"You're right on that account," Rodrigo said. "And you are not alone in being surprised. I don't know how well I hid my shock, but I was caught a bit off guard by the whole situation myself."

"You were marvelous," Mrs. Brodie said, with a grin. "I must admit that I took a secret delight in watching you try to hide your astonishment. But I had no opportunity to apprise you of the situation."

"What else do you know about them?" Rodrigo asked.

"Not much. Oh, they did tell me they have never been away from Tate's Hell. What a dreadful name. It conjures up all kinds of sordid imagery in my mind of demons and devils. I can't imagine what sort of a place would be named Tate's Hell."

"You mean they have never been outside of Trinity. There is a big difference you know."

"I don't know. It sounds as if they have never been much farther than their own home. Astounding, isn't it? Two five-year-old children who have never been outside the boundaries of their own home—a clearing in some wooded swampland."

"It's odd, alright," Rodrigo said. "But the people living in Tate's Hell value their privacy. Like somebody else I know."

Mrs. Brodie ignored his last comment.

"Oh, and I almost forgot the most amazing thing of all about these children. They are musically gifted; and I do mean gifted. I had them at the piano with me for a couple of hours this morning. In that amount of time, both were beginning to play quite well by ear. With lessons and practice, who knows? I know natural talent when I hear it."

"For someone who said she knew very little, you've told me a lot. And something you haven't told me, but I've gathered from your attitude is that you like them, a lot."

"They have won me over. They surely own Naomi's heart. There's more to this story. I'm certain. But I'm not going to pry. Naomi will tell me what she wants me to know."

"She will," Rodrigo said.

"It's been a joy having them here," Mrs. Brodie said. "They are a sheer delight to be around. I didn't realize how lonely I've become since Horace died."

"For that I apologize," said Rodrigo. "I know that I should have spent more time with you lately, but the shrimp are running. I've got to keep the boat out to make a living."

"Oh, no no, I'm not complaining about you, Rodrigo. Nobody could ask for a better friend than you."

"The feeling is quite mutual," Rodrigo said, smiling over at his friend.

"It's just that having the children here today made me realize that I lost something years ago. Something I have never even attempted to reclaim."

"And what's that?" Rodrigo asked.

"It's hard to explain," Mrs. Brodie said wistfully. "These children have a zest for living; something that I once had. And today they breathed fresh life into a tired, jaded old lady."

Mrs. Brodie paused lost in her thoughts. Rodrigo waited. He sensed she had more to say on this topic.

"It's not that I have anything to complain about—quite to the contrary. By anyone's standards, I have lived a charmed life. But seeing life through the eyes of those children, if only in brief, subtle moments, made me feel—I don't know—young again."

"That's wonderful," Rodrigo said, leaning over to affectionately pat her hand.

Mrs. Brodie flipped her wrist at him and looked out at the bay.

"For heaven's sakes. I must sound like a foolish old lady carrying on like this."

"Not at all."

"These children helped me to remember what it feels like to get excited. It has been so long since I found anything to be excited about; and then suddenly, here are two children who are excited about everything."

"You are not being silly, I assure you," Rodrigo said. "I'm glad that you've had such a thrilling, eventful day."

"Enough of this," Mrs. Brodie said, turning to face him.

"The shrimp are running? I should have known that was what made you so scarce. I don't for the life of me understand why you will not go to work for me. Look around you, Rodrigo. Money is not an issue for me."

"Mrs. Brodie, we've been over this subject already. I come here because you're my friend. That is all I want from you. The boat is my livelihood, and that's the way it should be. Besides, I love running the boat. It clears my head and keeps me busy."

"Therein lies the truth," she replied. "It clears your head. I don't know what devils are chasing you, but I know that somehow that boat keeps them at bay."

"Why's devils chasin' you?" asked Mango.

Neither Mrs. Brodie nor Rodrigo had noticed that Mango had come up from behind them.

"Oh, that's simply a silly way of talking," Rodrigo said. "Devils aren't really chasing me."

"Me and Millie wanta go in the water. Is that alright with you, Mrs. Brodie?"

"Of course, you can go," she said. "But, perhaps, Rodrigo could be persuaded to join you."

"These children can't swim," she said to Rodrigo, "and I would feel better if someone was near the water with them. They have given me quite a run for my money today, and if you don't mind, I would prefer to rest in this chair a bit longer."

"I don't mind at all. But did I hear you correctly? These children can't swim?"

"We never had us no water to swim in 'til today," Mango said sheepishly, embarrassed by what obviously appeared to be a flaw to Mrs. Brodie and Rodrigo.

"We never even seen the bay 'til today," he said, as further explanation.

"Or a pool," Mrs. Brodie added. "These children have never seen a pool. They've been swimming in washtubs in Naomi's front yard. That's the sum total of their swimming experience."

"Well, not to worry," Rodrigo said, ruffling Mango's curly hair with his big hand.

"There's no shame in not being able to do something that you've never been taught to do. You're a boy, not a fish. Of course, you can't swim if you have never been taught to swim."

Mango breathed a sigh of relief. He did not want to be a disappointment to anyone.

"But we can remedy that situation," Rodrigo said. "I can teach both you and your sister to swim. My guess is that you're both quick learners."

"Naomi says we are quick learners," Mango quickly replied. "She says that a lot."

"I must agree with Naomi," Mrs. Brodie interjected. "You most certainly were quick learners at the piano this morning."

"Fetch your sister," Rodrigo commanded Mango. "I'll have you swimming in no time at all. We can't have a boy and girl on our island unable to swim."

By the time that Naomi loaded Millie and Mango into the car for the drive home, they were so full of stories to tell that Naomi was sure that it would take them a week of non-stop talking to tell all of what had happened to them in one short day.

Both waved good-bye to Mrs. Brodie until she was out of sight.

"She's such a nice lady," Millie said. "She's nice like you and Karen and Granny."

"And I liked Rodrigo, too," Mango said. "He promised to teach us to swim."

"How 'bout that," Naomi said. "I never did learn to swim. But Rodrigo is a man of his word. I 'spect that I'll have two fish on my hands in no time a'tall."

"When can we come back?" Millie asked.

"Mrs. Brodie said that we could come back anytime. She liked us," Mango said proudly.

"Oh, I don't know. We'll have to see. I'm hopin' that your Granny's back is better soon. We'll just have to see."

"I hope its's soon," Millie said. "I really do want to learn how to swim."

CHAPTER EIGHTEEN

The twins' second trip to the island was much sooner than anyone anticipated. Karen's regular day off at the Clinic was Tuesday and she took Wednesday off as well. On Thursday morning she went back to the Clinic for a half-day.

The plan was for the twins to play in the living room while Bessie rested on the couch. That plan turned out to be a disaster.

Karen came home to find the children grumpy from being confined to the house all morning, and Bessie was not in much better shape. She had not been able to take her pain pill, and it showed on her face and by her irritable mood.

"Call Mrs. Brodie and ask if the twins can go with you tomorrow," Karen pleaded with Naomi, when she got home. "I can't put the three of them through another mornin' like today."

"Are you sure?" Naomi asked.

"Oh my, yes. I don't want to come home to a house full of fussin' and gripin' again. It took me all afternoon to get things back to normal 'round here. They was all three *that* out of sorts."

So Naomi placed the call.

"Well, of course, they can come back," Mrs. Brodie answered effusively.

"In fact, I insist that you bring them. I haven't had as much fun in years as I had during their last visit. And I have a present for them. So, by all means, bring them; they're more than welcome."

When Naomi made the announcement that the twins would be going back to Palm Island with her for a second visit, they ran around, whooping and hollering and creating such a ruckus that Clover started to bark from the porch.

"Hush up," Naomi shouted out to Clover. "And you two settle down."

On Friday, the children were up, dressed and waiting for Naomi when she came in to have her coffee. She had heard them puttering around in Karen's room a full hour before they usually got up.

"What's this?" she said to them. "You two are all dressed up like you goin' sommers."

"We goin' with you," they said, circling around her like bees around a hive as she made her way over to the coffee pot.

"Goin' with me? Where?"

"To the island," Mango said. "You said we's gonna go to Mrs. Brodie's house today."

"I said that?" Naomi teased, scratching her head as if she were trying hard to remember.

"Naomi, you did say that," Millie insisted.

"We ain't goin'? Mango wailed, flinging his arms down to his side.

The twins faces dropped, and their smiles faded into a pout.

"You're sure I said that?" Naomi asked devilishly, screwing up her face and throwing her hands on her hips.

"We're sure," both twins assured her crossing their arms defiantly in front of them.

"Then I guess that means you're goin' so suck in those lips 'fore you trip and fall over 'em," Naomi said, tickling Millie's belly and pulling Mango's cap down over his eyes.

Mrs. Brodie was in the garden when they arrived. This time the children scrambled out of the car and bounded out across the driveway to run over and greet her.

"Hey, Mrs. Brodie," they yelled as they ran towards her waving their arms.

"Hey, yourselves," she said, throwing up her arm to return the wave.

"I'm simply delighted that you came this morning," she said as the twins drew nearer. "I am in dire need of helpers." Mrs. Brodie pointed towards two straw baskets, which sat on the ground.

"I don't reckon you'll be needin' me in the garden this mornin'," Naomi said, catching up to the twins, who had already grabbed up the baskets. "I'll go on inside and start my housework."

Within the hour, Naomi heard a racket on the patio. When she opened the door, the twins filed in behind Mrs. Brodie, each laden with a basket of flowers.

"You children help Naomi put the flowers into vases," Mrs. Brodie said, when they were all inside and the door was closed behind them.

"I have a surprise for you. I was going to wait until Rodrigo arrived, but I simply can't. I'm certain that he'll understand."

"Rodrigo's comin'?" Mango asked excitedly.

"But, of course. You don't think that he'd miss a visit by his two new friends, do you?" Mrs. Brodie asked. "When I told him that I was expecting you, he promised to bring the boat in early and stop by in the afternoon."

"You reckon he'll teach us to swim today?" Millie asked. "I sure do want to learn how to swim."

"I *reckon* he will," Mrs. Brodie said.

Naomi and the twins were arranging the flowers when Mrs. Brodie came back into the room carrying two boxes. She placed a box in front of each of the children.

"Go ahead open them," she said, "they're for you."

"But it ain't our birthday or Christmas or nothin'," Millie said confused. She looked up at Naomi.

"It's alright. Go on. Open your presents."

The children tore off the wrapping paper and pulled open the boxes. Inside were swimsuits—two for each child.

"We guessed their sizes," Mrs. Brodie said to Naomi, "so I'm hoping that the suits fit them properly."

"We?" Naomi asked.

"I had some help from Rodrigo," Mrs. Brodie replied. "He did the shopping."

"Look," both children shrieked at Naomi. They pulled the swimsuits from the boxes and thrust them up for her inspection, each trying to outdo the other and get her attention first.

"Settle down," she said. "I can't see 'less you settle down. Show me one at the time. Millie you go first."

Millie waved a pink-and-blue floral swimsuit with a ruffled skirt in one hand and a yellow polka dot one in the other hand.

"They're beautiful," Naomi said. She stretched the fabric of the floral suit to admire the stitching.

"Now, let me see yours, Mango." Mango exuberantly held up a pair of yellow-checkered shorts and a blue suit with a bright red stripe running down either side.

"That's nice, honey, real nice," she said, putting the yellow shorts up against his tawny skin. "You'll look good in this yellow one."

"I hope that I haven't overstepped my limits here," Mrs. Brodie said anxiously to Naomi. "I simply thought that if these children are going to learn to swim, they will need some swimwear."

"You ain't overstepped nothin'. It was mighty nice of you to think of 'em," Naomi said. "You got a big heart, Mrs. Brodie."

Mrs. Brodie blushed.

"Nonsense," she said, turning her attention to the twins.

"I suppose you should try on the suits to see if they are a proper fit," she said to them.

When Rodrigo arrived later in the afternoon he was surprised to find Mrs. Brodie and the twins encamped on the patio anxiously awaiting his arrival.

Mrs. Brodie was wearing a sundress, broad-brimmed hat and sandals. Millie had on the floral suit and Mango the red shorts.

"What's this?" he said, admiring the twins' swimwear. "It looks like a boy and girl all dressed up for a swimming lesson."

"Mrs. Brodie said we could get in that big pool if you go in with us," Mango said.

"You said you'd teach us to swim," Millie reminded him.

"So I did," Rodrigo said. He unfurled a pair of swim trunks that he had rolled into a ball in his hand. "I suppose that I had better suit up."

After that second day, the twins became regulars at the Brodie estate. Bessie's back failed to improve. And Dr. Luke's prognosis was bleak. There was no cure for old age.

Either Karen gave up her job, or the children had to go with Naomi to the island on the days that Karen worked. Nobody wanted Karen to quit work.

When Naomi explained the situation to Mrs. Brodie, she immediately opted for the latter option.

"Karen quit work. Oh my, no! I wouldn't hear of it. The twins are more than welcome here."

Naomi believed this to be a sincere offer. It appeared to her that it was a toss-up as to who enjoyed the visits more—Mrs. Brodie, the twins or Rodrigo.

The presence of the twins on the Brodie estate infused new life into Mrs. Brodie. She moved about the estate with renewed vigor. Her face brightened; her voice became more cheerful.

Naomi was astonished to come upon her humming in the garden one morning as she worked. She was even more surprised when she heard her playing the piano on a day when the twins didn't come. Naomi had not seen this side of Mrs. Brodie since Mr. Brodie had been alive.

And Mrs. Brodie enchanted the twins. Music was their strongest bond. Millie and Mango embraced the piano lessons she offered to them with unrelenting enthusiasm.

Mrs. Brodie was delighted to discover that both of the children had beautiful singing voices, a talent she had long coveted but never possessed. Teaching the children revived Mrs. Brodie's flagging passion for music, a passion that had dwindled to an occasional pastime after Mr. Brodie died.

The music room became their private domain. Naomi never ventured in unless she was invited to witness the twins' progress on the piano.

Cloistered in the music room, Mrs. Brodie and the children, played the piano, sang and savored her extensive recording collection.

Mrs. Brodie even gave the children a portable radio, which they listened to outside as they played. Although she might inwardly cringe at their selection of a pop or country station, she never tried to restrict them.

It was Mango, with a hint or two from Rodrigo, who discovered the radio in Naomi's car. What had once been a quiet and peaceful drive to and from the island became a raucous ramble.

In the evenings, they continued to listen to *The Reverend Samuel Spears' Inspirational Hour*. The twins' repertoire of musical selections quickly grew from gospel only to include classical, pop, country, and jazz.

And Millie and Mango absolutely adored Rodrigo. And why wouldn't they, Naomi thought?

Their only male contact, thus far, was a drunk for a grandfather, who purely despised them; Samuel Taylor, who they only got to see a couple of times a year; and Dr. Luke, who they had only met a few times.

Who could blame them for being drawn to a young, energetic man after spending the first five years of their lives with nothing but three women, and two of them old women at that?

Rodrigo seemed to relish the time that he spent with them. Almost every afternoon that the twins were at the estate, Rodrigo came to visit.

He kept his promise and taught them to swim, first in the pool and then in the bay.

Mrs. Brodie added a diving board to the pool, and after surviving a series of "belly-busters," the twins' entry into the pool progressed from a jump with their fingers clamped firmly on their noses to a graceful dive.

Rodrigo also taught the twins to fish off the end of the dock, which jutted out from the Brodie property into the bay.

As the children spent more and more time on Palm Island, their days fell into a routine.

In the early morning, they assisted Mrs. Brodie in the garden until the sun made it too hot to work outside. Then Mrs. Brodie and the twins retired to the music room while Naomi prepared lunch.

After lunch, Mrs. Brodie and the children "put up their feet," which was expanded to include a reading lesson before they fell asleep.

When they woke up from their naps, the children went back outdoors and waited for the arrival of Rodrigo, hoping to swim or fish or just play by the bay.

Summer turned to fall, and the twins became regulars at the island. When the weather got too cool for swimming, the twins wandered the grounds looking for new distractions.

On these excursions around the estate, they developed a fascination with a small clump of woods, which bordered the south side of the Brodie estate.

These woods were little more than a thicket of oaks and pines with an occasional cabbage palm or magnolia tree. Wax myrtle, ferns, briers and palmetto bushes grew interspersed among the trees.

The tiny forest was less than a half-acre in circumference, bordered on the south by the neighboring property, on the west by the bay and on the east by the main road, which intersected the island.

A footpath traversed the woods running north to south to the adjoining property; and east to west from the bay to the main road where it continued on to the ocean.

When Mr. Brodie purchased the estate, he had left the woods untouched other than to cut the footpath, which he and his wife used for their morning and afternoon walks.

After his death, Mrs. Brodie had kept the path cleared from encroaching underbrush; although she no longer walked the woods. For the children, the woods represented a whole new world of adventure.

The children's first venture into the woods was on a walk with Rodrigo and Mrs. Brodie. They had pleaded for days to take the walk before Rodrigo and Mrs. Brodie relented.

It was a blustery fall day, too cool for swimming, too windy for fishing or even sitting by the bay, but perfect for a walk.

"Come on, Mrs. Brodie," Rodrigo said, taking sides with the twins. "A brisk walk would do us all some good."

"Oh, I suppose you're right," she said, "let's go."

The sun, filtered by the lush foliage overhead, formed a lacy pattern on the path. Pine straw and fallen leaves paved the path and acorns crunched under their feet as Mrs. Brodie and Rodrigo strolled leisurely along while the twins skipped ahead urging them forward.

Birds chirped up high overhead in the trees, and an occasional squirrel darted across the path caught in the act of foraging for winter.

When the path reached a crossroads, the twins stopped and waited for directions from Rodrigo.

"The bay or the ocean?" Rodrigo asked Mrs. Brodie.

"Oh my, the bay," she replied. "I'm quite sure that the ocean would be too much of a trek for these tired old bones."

Rodrigo pointed left to the children, who resumed their sojourn, thrilled to discover that the path would dump them onto a hidden beach whose stark-white sand fanned out around the bay.

After the walk, the twins were more enchanted than ever with the woods. They even persuaded Rodrigo to walk with them the following week on the path to the ocean, although they could not cajole Mrs. Brodie to join them for this outing.

Instead, she opted to rest in the shade until they returned.

After several more of these walks, the twins started to beg Naomi unmercifully to allow them to play in the edge of the woods.

"We won't go far," they pleaded. "We promise, Naomi, please."

"I won't hear of it," she responded, "so there ain't no need for you to two to put up such a fuss. The answer is no!"

"Ah, Naomi," Mango pouted, lightly stomping his foot as he crossed his arms and dropped his head down on his chest. "Why not?"

"Don't you 'ah Naomi' me," she said. "I ain't havin' you two youngens paradin' 'round in them woods alone. You got plenty of yard here to play in, so don't go pesterin' me no more 'bout them woods.

"And you mind your manners, mister," she scolded Mango. "You been taught better than to stomp your feet. I didn't put up with that from Karen and Nathan, and I won't put up with it from you. If ya'll want somethin' to do, go on out on the porch and find Lucy. Worry her for a spell and let me be. Scat!"

"Why the long faces?" Rodrigo asked the twins, when he arrived to find the twins sitting sullenly together in the chaise lounge, Lucy nestled in their laps.

"We wanta play in them woods. We wanta build us a fort. But Naomi she says 'no no no,'" Millie said, hopping up, placing one hand on her hip and wagging her finger like Naomi had just done.

"So you two are sitting here pouting?"

"No," Mango said. "Naomi told us to get out from underfoot and to go out to play. But we ain't got nothin' to do. That's why we wanta go play in the woods."

"Shame on you two. You can't find anything to do on this lovely estate? It's not like you two to be complainers."

"We wanta build us a fort; but you can't go buildin' no fort where everbody can see you," Mango said defensively. "Robin Hood didn't put his fort in no backyard."

"I suppose that you do have a point," Rodrigo said. The twins really were quite crestfallen.

"As a boy, I built a fort myself. Perhaps, I can broker a compromise between the two of you and Naomi."

"What's a *compromise*?" Mango asked.

"It's a way of each side giving a little to get what they want," Rodrigo said, pulling Mango up by the hands. Lucy leapt to the floor and sauntered away.

"What we want is to play in them woods," Mango said emphatically.

"I understand that, sport model. But you two need to let up on Naomi. I'll have a talk with her. For now, let's go fishing."

A Watch in the Night

Later that week, on a day when the twins stayed in Tate's Hell, Rodrigo brought up the subject of the woods with Naomi.

"They're really not in harm's way so long as they stay on the estate," Rodrigo said, arguing on behalf of the twins. "They could play on the edge of the woods. You and Mrs. Brodie guard them like two mother hens. They are *going on* six. A bit of autonomy would be good for them."

"If *auto. . . whatever* means that I should turn them babies loose in the woods, the answer is still no."

"Naomi, they are not babies," Rodrigo said, sneaking a peek at Naomi to see how she responded to this comment.

She stood poised over the ironing board, her sprinkle bottle suspended in mid-air as she paused to contemplate what Rodrigo had said.

"They've got to be allowed to grow," he added softly.

Naomi dropped the bottle down and vigorously sprinkled the tablecloth on the ironing board. She pulled the edge of the cloth taut with one hand and pushed the iron firmly along the fabric with the other, the steam swooshing up to bathe her face.

Her lips pressed tightly together as she focused intently on her work, a subtle signal to Rodrigo that she wanted the topic dropped.

"Naomi, he makes a valid point," Mrs. Brodie said. She had walked into the room during the middle of the discussion. "Horace and I walked those woods for years. What harm could come of it?"

Heartened by Mrs. Brodie's reinforcement, Rodrigo decided to take another shot at convincing Naomi that the woods were safe.

"I'll draw up some boundaries for them," he said. "I'll make absolutely certain that they stay nearby. You know, Naomi, that I would never put them in harm's way."

Naomi sat her iron upright on the ironing board and looked over at Rodrigo and Mrs. Brodie. Her lips parted into a slight smile of defeat.

"Oh, I suppose that we could give it a try," she said, seeing that she was now outnumbered. "It ain't like they don't tromp 'round Tate's Hell."

"So it's settled," Rodrigo said. "The twins will have their fort."

"But you mind that they don't go far," Naomi said, resuming her ironing.

"I don't want them outta earshot. They may not be babies, but they ain't growed up enough for me not to worry. The *edge* of the woods, and I mean that!"

Naomi pointed the tip of her iron at Rodrigo when she made her final remark, the steam spitting out towards him as if to add emphasis to her warning.

When the twins returned the following week, Naomi and Rodrigo sat them down in the kitchen to give them the news.

"Do you remember our discussion about *compromise?*" Rodrigo asked them.

"Uh, huh," Mango said.

"Yes, sir," Naomi chided him. "You mind your manners, young fella."

"Yes, sir," Mango corrected himself. He sensed that something good was coming their way, and he didn't want to throw things off track. Naomi didn't leave no room for messin' up when it came to good manners.

"It means you give a little to get a little," Millie said.

"That's right, wildflower," Rodrigo said.

"And Naomi has agreed to compromise and let you two go play in the woods. But she has agreed only if you follow some strict rules."

The twins jumped up and down with excitement.

"Hold on," Rodrigo admonished them. "Naomi has agreed to give a little by letting you two go into the woods alone; but in order to gain that privilege, you must give a little by following her rules."

"We can do that," the twins sang out, clearly ecstatic at the prospect of being allowed into the woods.

"Ya'll can play there on the edge of the path," Naomi said to the children, "but don't ya'll go so far that you can't hear me callin'. When you hear me yell, ya'll best come runnin'."

"We will," the twins promised, hugging Naomi around the waist.

"Now ya'll go on and get out from underfoot. Rodrigo is gonna take ya'll out to the woods and show you where you can play. You mind what he says 'cause if I catch you strayin' one little bit, the deal is off. It's back to the yard for good."

"Yes ma'am," the twins said seriously. "We'll do *zackley* like Rodrigo tells us to do," Mango threw in.

"That's *exactly,* sport model," Rodrigo said, chuckling.

"With all of them words that Mrs. Brodie is teaching 'em from those books, I don't even get what they tryin' to say half of the time," Naomi huffed.

She was starting to regret that she had let Rodrigo and Mrs. Brodie persuade her to let the twins have the run of the place.

"Now scat, all of you. Mrs. Brodie don't pay me to stand round this kitchen jabbering. Go on now. You ain't youngens but once, so go on and have yourselves a good time."

Rodrigo walked the twins to the path, and together they set the parameters for their ventures into the woods. The twins could go as far as the intersection, which was only a very short distance into the woods.

From there they go west towards the bay so long as they stayed on the path at all times which meant that they could not cross the beach to the edge of the bay.

And he forbid them to go any farther south than the crossroads and never east to the ocean. This would have required them to cross the main road, which was strictly off limits.

The twins accepted the limits without protest. They weren't brave enough to go much farther on their own. In their minds, the designated area encompassed a vast unexplored territory. In reality, it was no more than a stone's throw and a good yell away from the Brodie backyard.

The first few weeks, Naomi called to the children every fifteen minutes after they went outside. They always came running within minutes.

Gradually, she relaxed her vigil, and the twins roamed freely on the grounds, including the woods.

It was on one of these afternoon adventures into the woods that the twins first encountered "the running lady."

A chance encounter that changed everything, for everybody—forever.

Isn't that the way of life?

One day you make a choice, choose a path, take a turn and all of your future changes.

Chance encounters could turn out well; or chance encounters could end badly.

Only time tells the story. Only time reveals the ending.

Good or bad? Only time knows!

A Watch in the Night

ABOUT THE AUTHOR

Roseanna Lee is a native Floridian. She earned a B.A. in English Literature at the University of Florida, an M.A. in English Literature at East Carolina University and a J.D. at the Florida State University College of Law. While she enjoys her career as a Florida attorney, her passion has always been reading and writing fiction.

She lives in rural North Florida, the "other" Florida of pristine rivers and springs.

When not at home on her beloved Ichetucknee River, she is an avid traveler.

A Watch in the Night

Roseanna Lee

Thank you for reading *A Watch in the Night.*

This exciting series consists of four books and may be purchased through Amazon. And, we invite you to leave a review on Amazon as well.

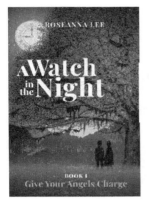

Give your Angels Charge
Book One
SBN: 978-1-945190-79-7

Shadow of Death
Book Two
ISBN: 978-1-945190-73-5

Snare of the Fowler
Book Three
ISBN: 978-1-945190-74-2

Set on High
Book Four
ISBN: 978-1-945190-75-9

Made in the USA
Columbia, SC
31 July 2023

20994287R00217